ALICE OSEMAN

HEARTSTOPPER

VOLUME 2

HODDER CHILDREN'S BOOKS

First published in 2019 by Hodder and Stoughton

9 10

Please be aware that this book contains mild violence and homophobia.

This comic is drawn digitally using a Wacom Intuos Pro small tablet directly into Photoshop CC.

A CIP catalogue record for this book is available from the British Library.

ISBN 978 1 444 95140 0

Printed and bound in Great Britain by Clays Ltd, Elcograf S.p.A.

The paper and board used in this book are made from wood from responsible sources.

FSC www.fsc.org MIX Paper from responsible sources FSC® C104740

Hodder Children's Books
An imprint of
Hachette Children's Group
Part of Hodder and Stoughton
Carmelite House
50 Victoria Embankment
London EC4Y 0DZ

An Hachette UK Company
www.hachette.co.uk

www.hachettechildrens.co.uk

www.aliceoseman.com

CONTENTS

✳ Not read chapters one and two yet?
Read the story so far in **Volume One!**

17/4

I've. Destroyed. Everything.

Me and Nick have been friends for, what, four months now? It sounds like no time at all but it feels like FOREVER. He's my best friend in the whole world. I don't

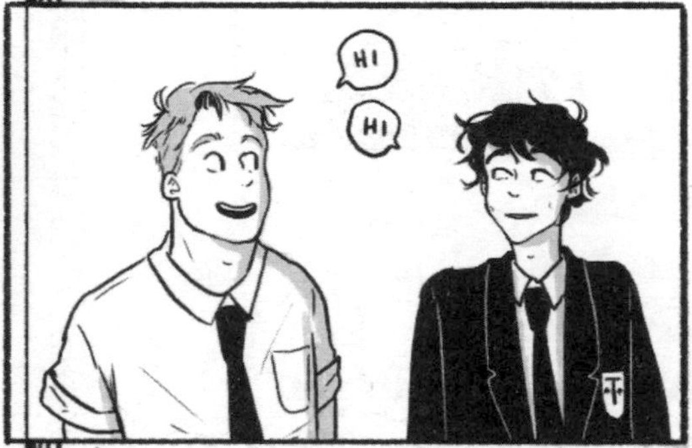
HI
HI

know how that happened. First we were just two guys who sat next to each other in form. Then he asked me to join rugby - OBVIOUSLY I said yes, just so

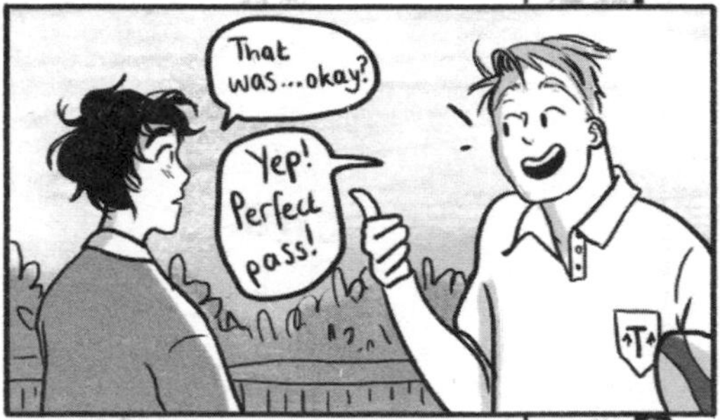
That was...okay?
Yep! Perfect pass!

I could hang out with him more. Then we were going round each other's houses. Telling each other everything.

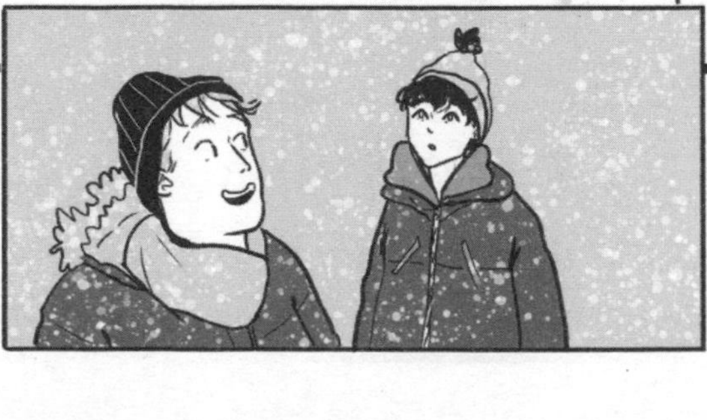

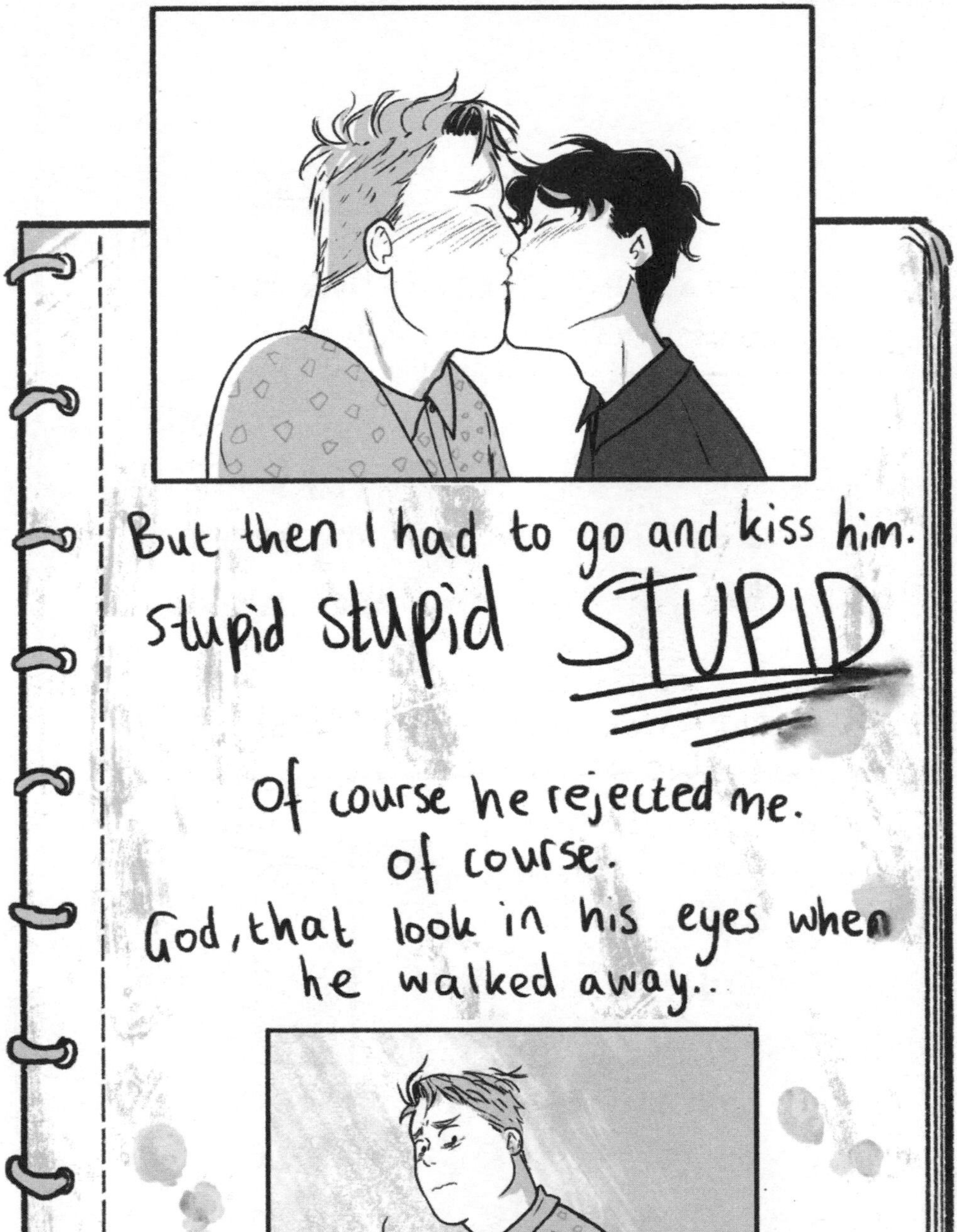
But then I had to go and kiss him.
stupid stupid STUPID
Of course he rejected me.
of course.
God, that look in his eyes when
he walked away..
I guess that's what happens when
you fall for a straight boy.

3. KISS

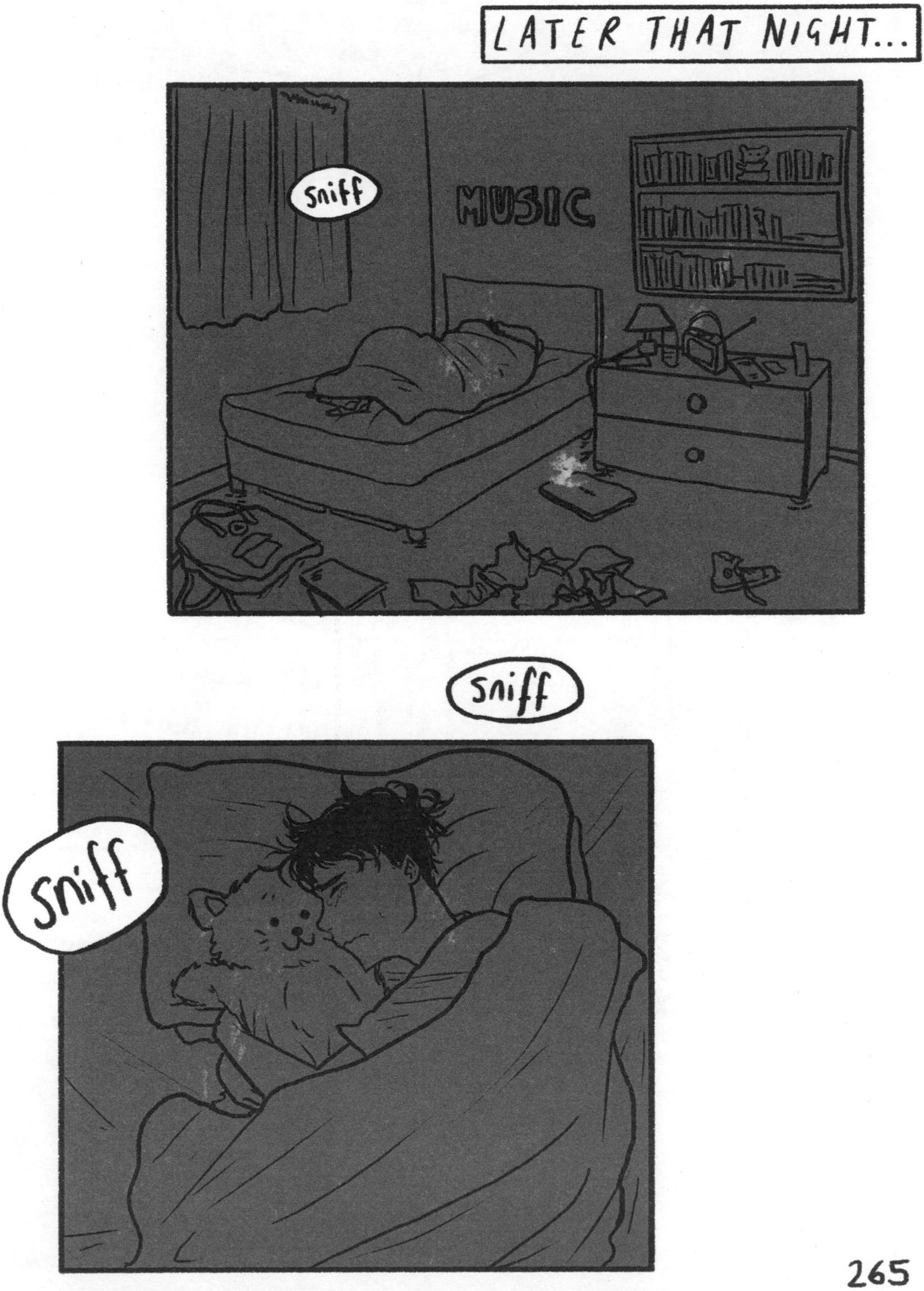
LATER THAT NIGHT...
sniff
MUSIC
sniff
sniff

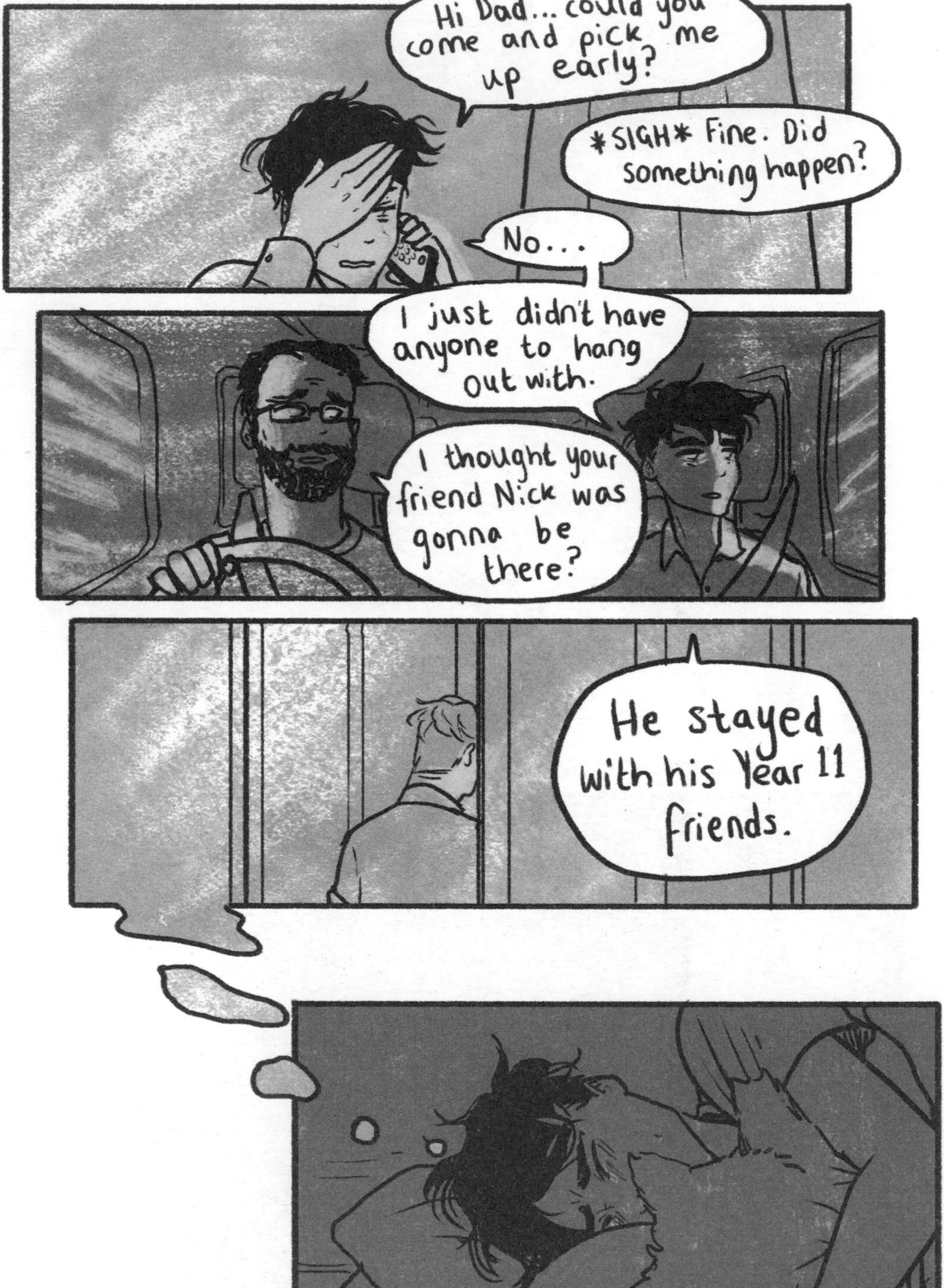
Hi Dad... could you come and pick me up early?
SIGH Fine. Did something happen?
No...
I just didn't have anyone to hang out with.
I thought your friend Nick was gonna be there?
He stayed with his Year 11 friends.

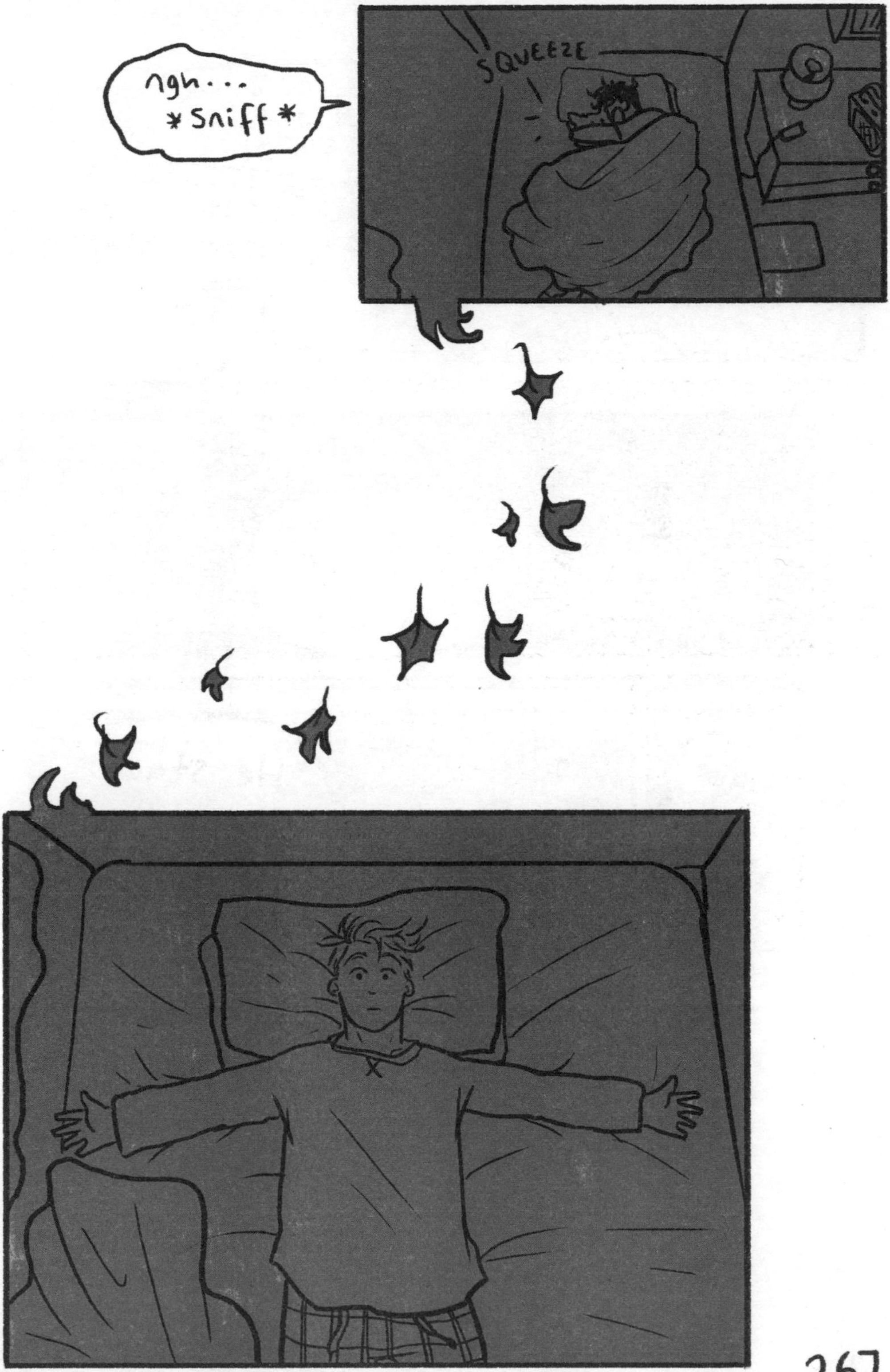
ngh...
sniff
SQUEEZE

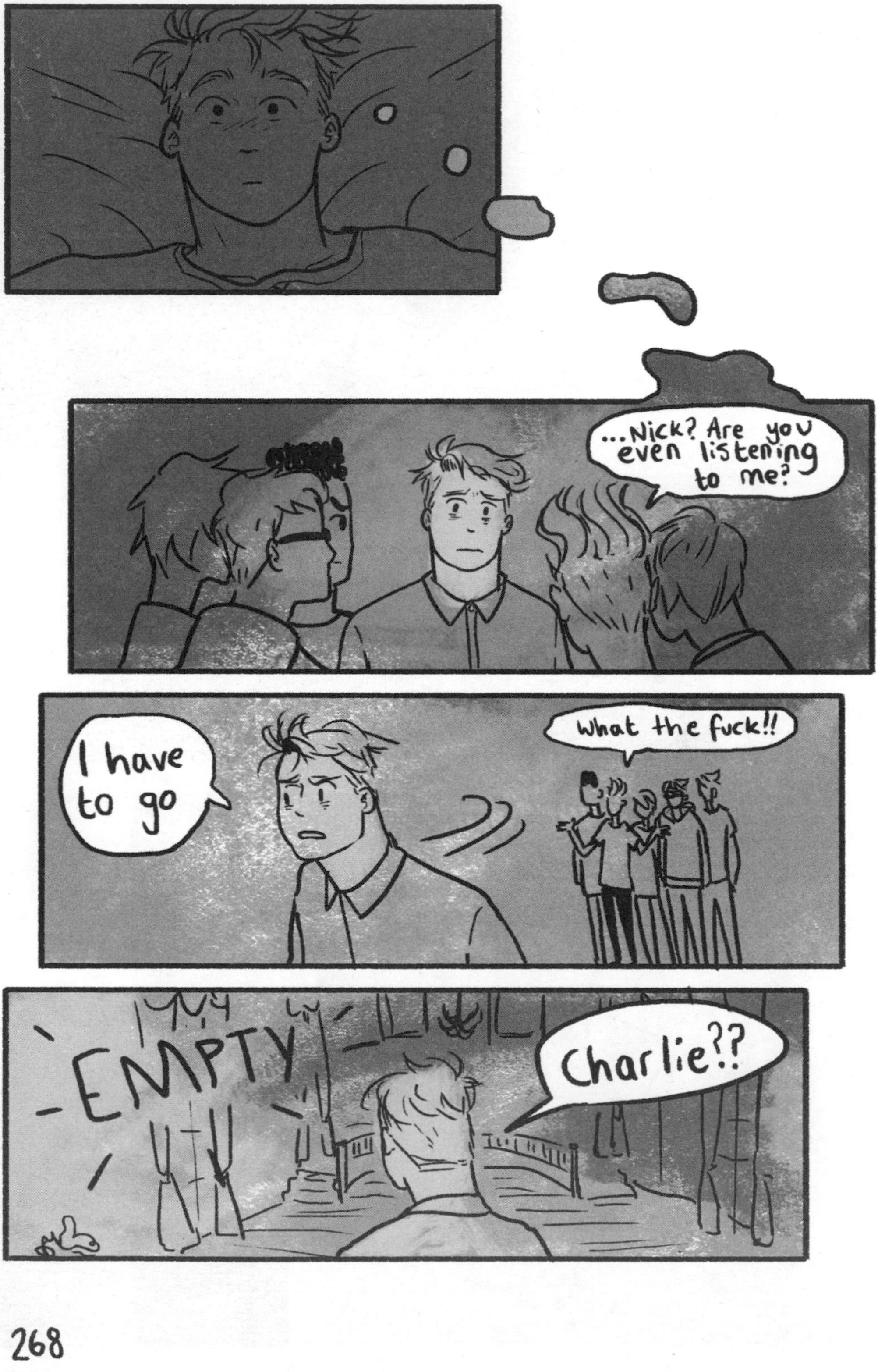
...Nick? Are you even listening to me?
I have to go
What the fuck!!
EMPTY
Charlie??

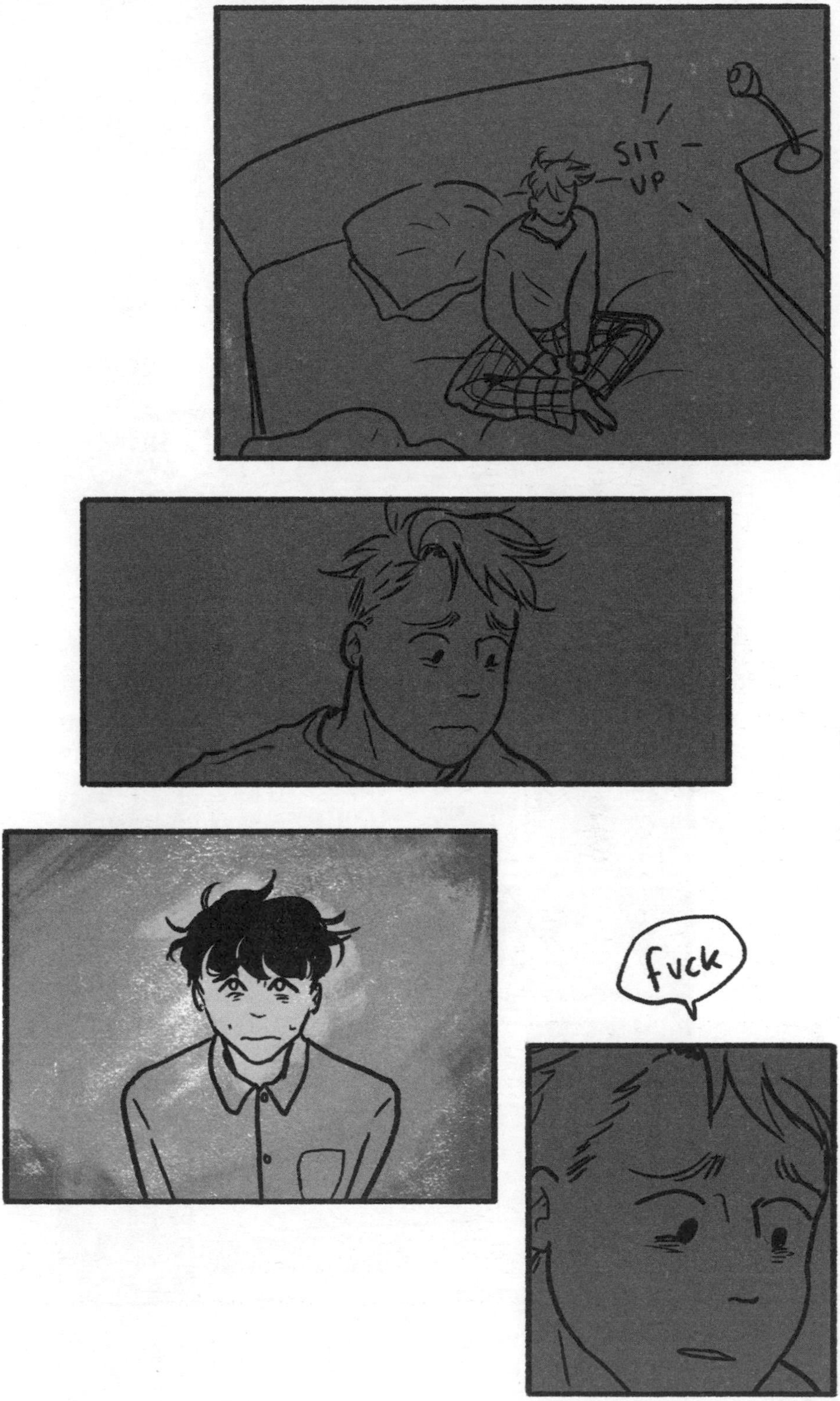
SIT UP
fuck

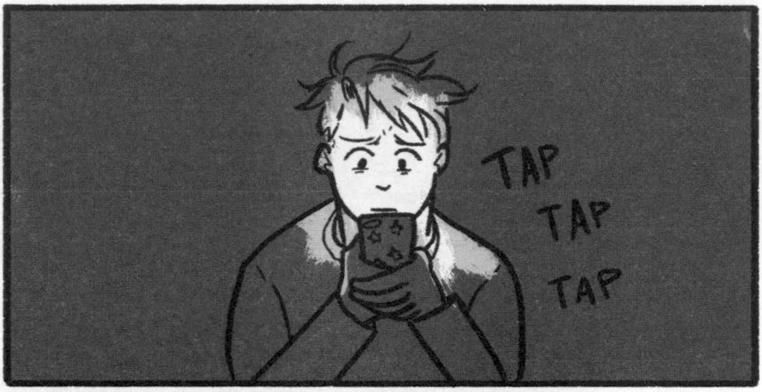
TAP
TAP
TAP

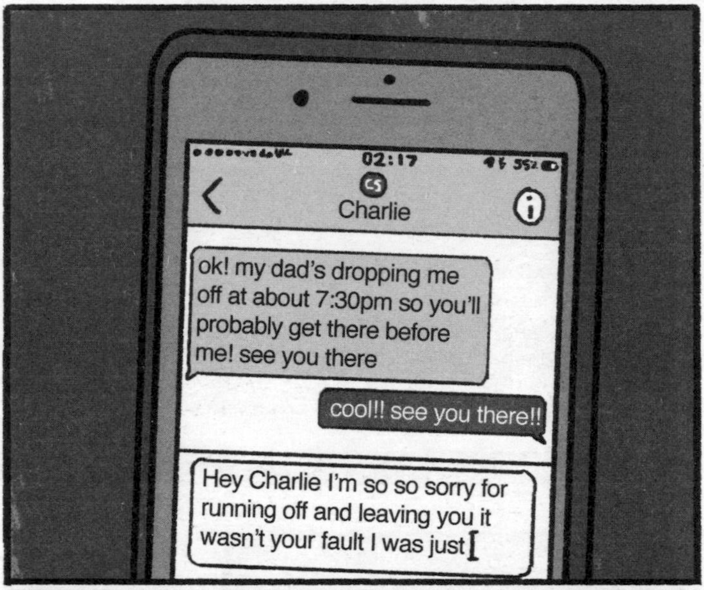
02:17
Charlie
ok! my dad's dropping me off at about 7:30pm so you'll probably get there before me! see you there
cool!! see you there!!
Hey Charlie I'm so so sorry for running off and leaving you it wasn't your fault I was just

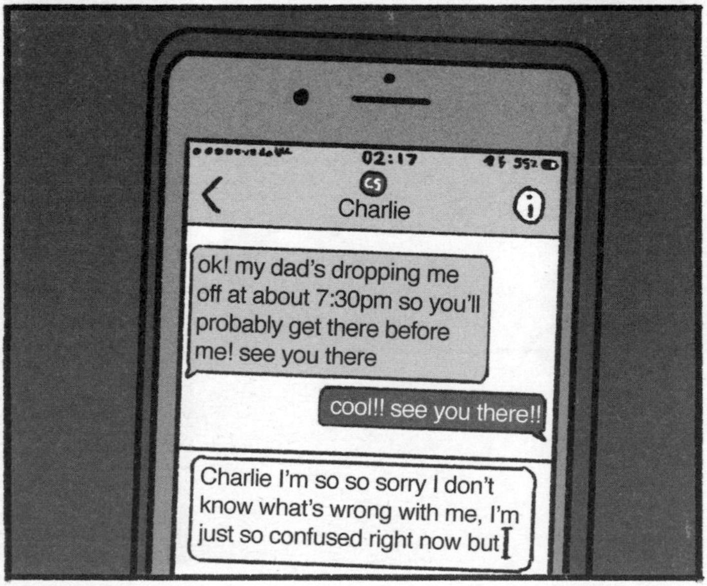
02:17
Charlie
ok! my dad's dropping me off at about 7:30pm so you'll probably get there before me! see you there
cool!! see you there!!
Charlie I'm so so sorry I don't know what's wrong with me, I'm just so confused right now but

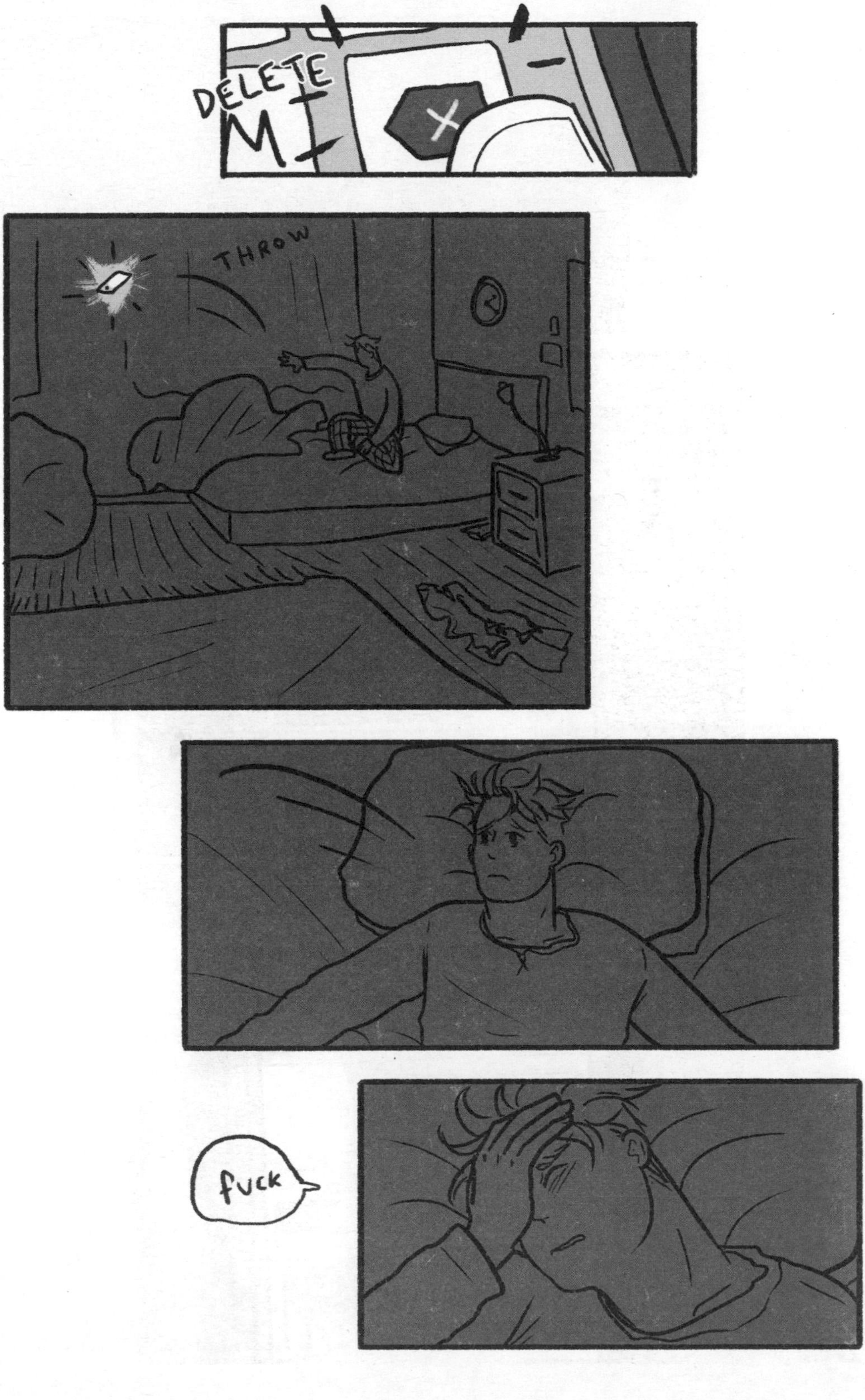
DELETE
THROW
fuck

THE NEXT MORNING

<2 HOURS OF SLEEP

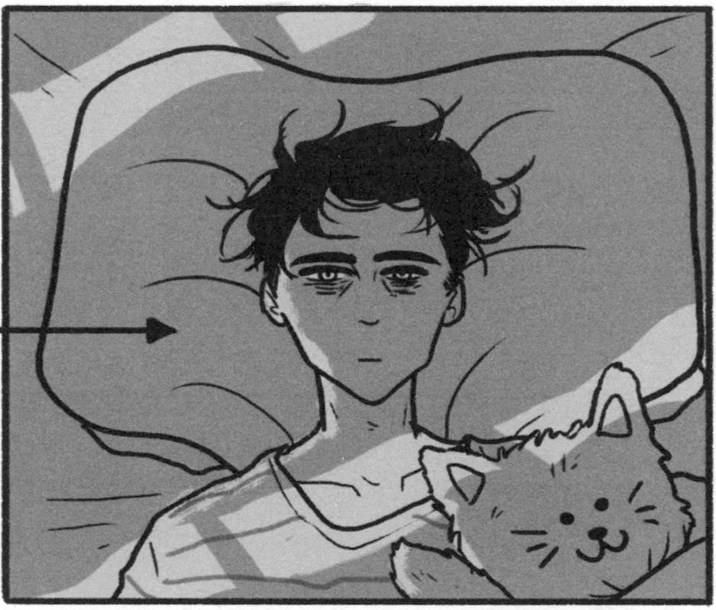

NO NEW MESSAGES

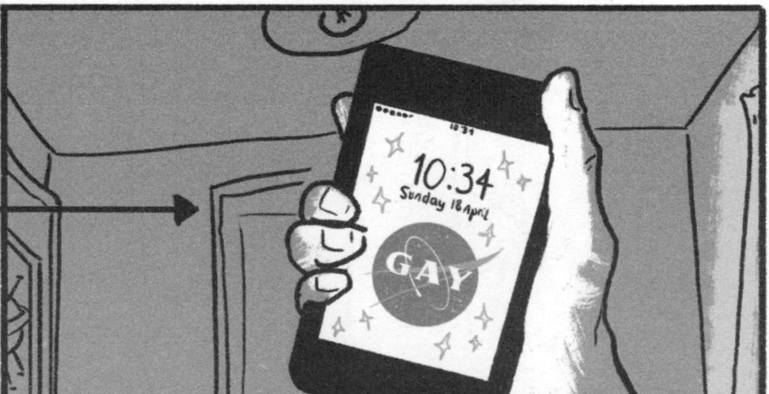
10:34
Sunday 18 April
GAY

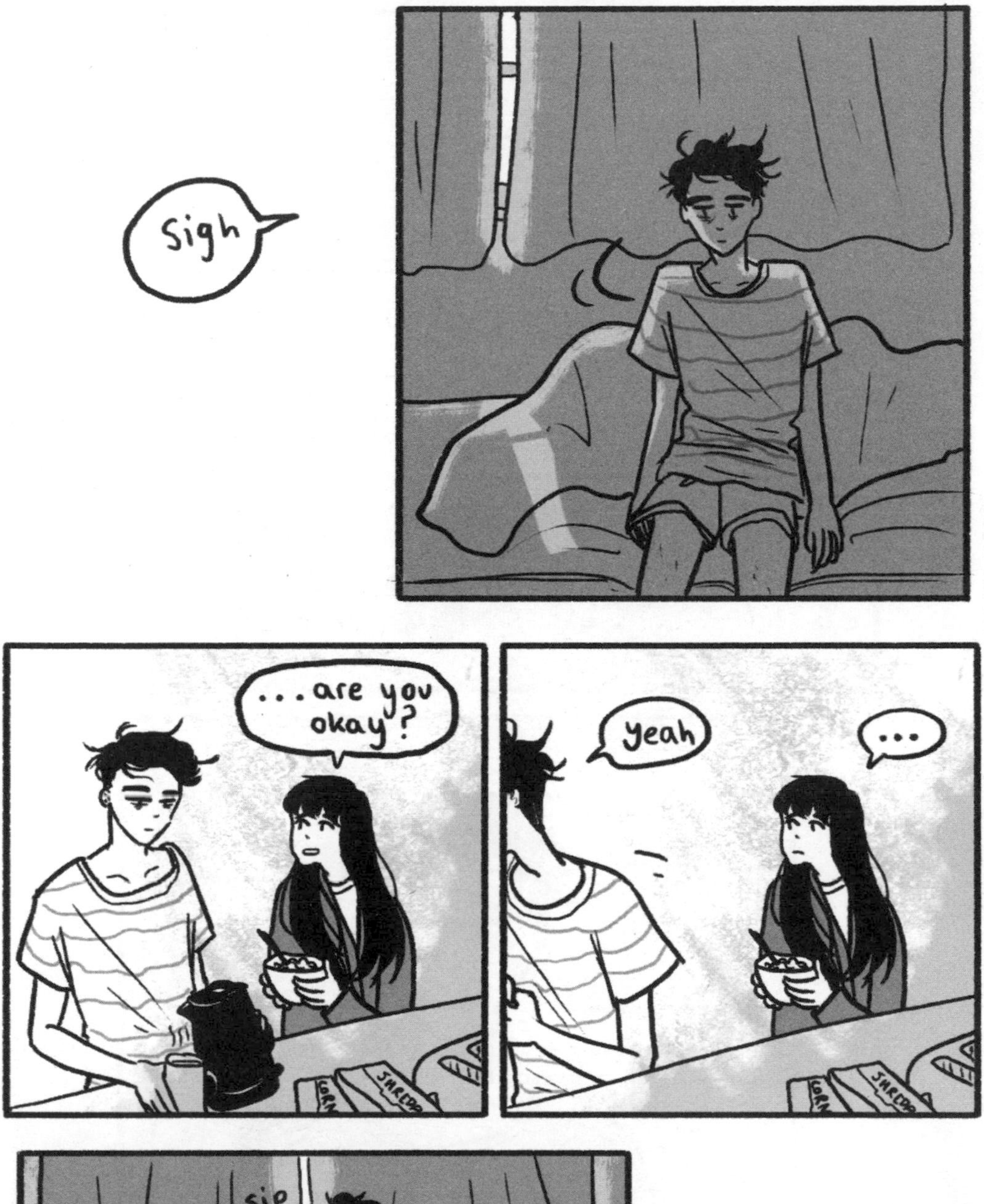
Sigh
...are you okay?
Yeah
...
sip

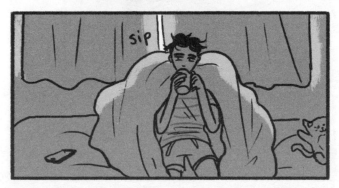

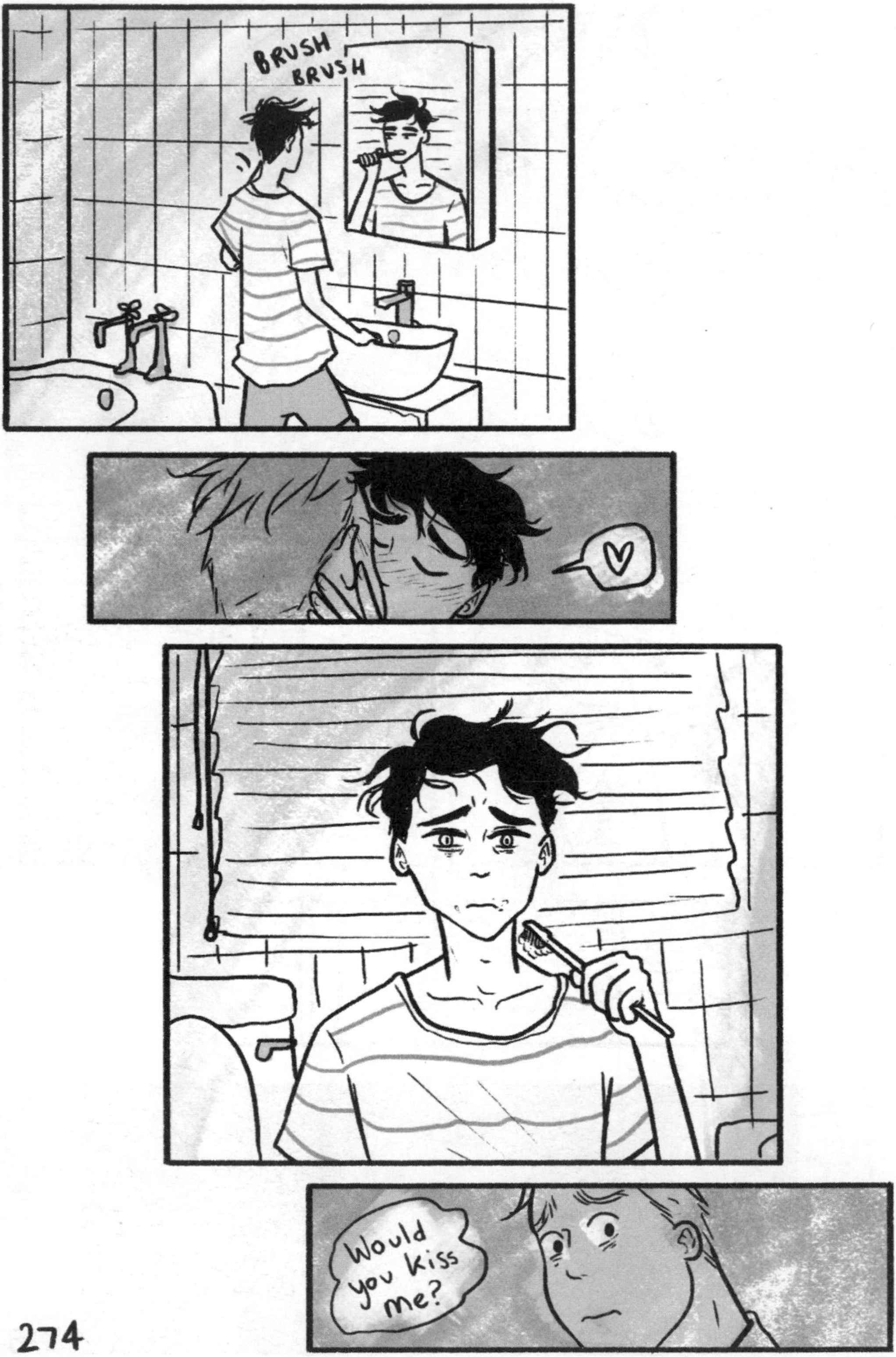
BRUSH
BRUSH
♥
Would you kiss me?

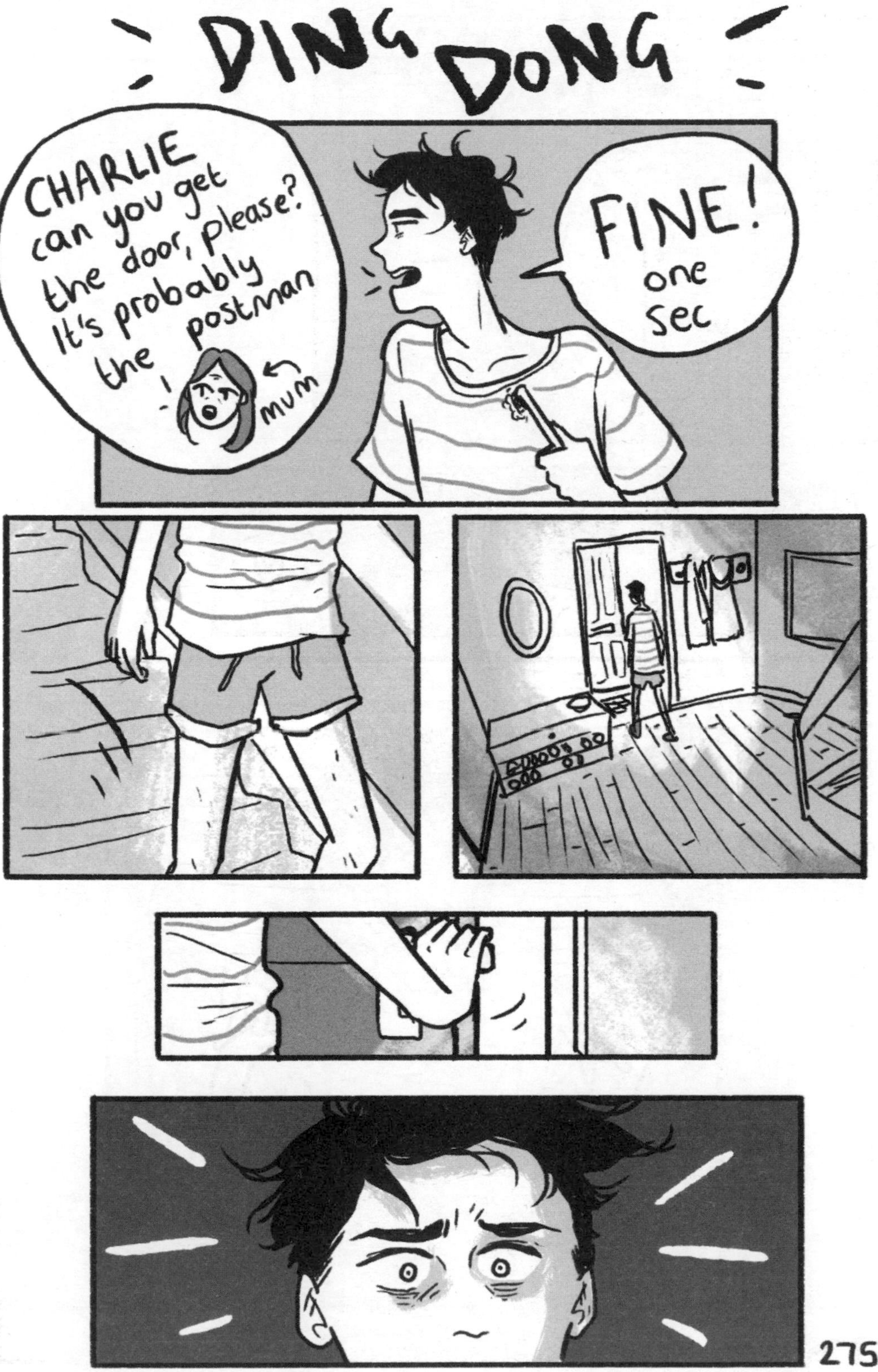
DING DONG
CHARLIE can you get the door, please? It's probably the postman
mum
FINE! one sec

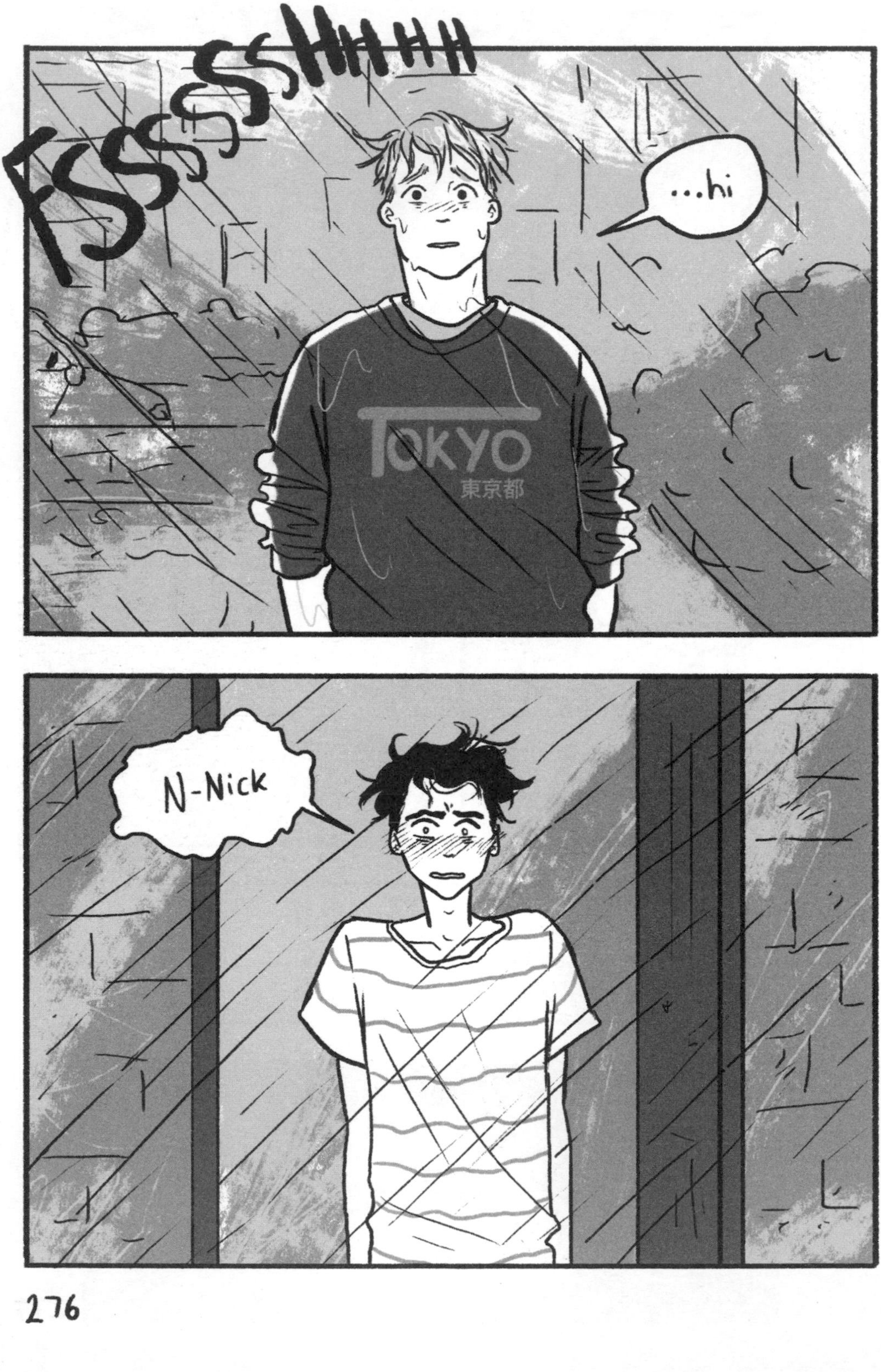
FSSSSSHHHHH
...hi
N-Nick
TOKYO
東京都

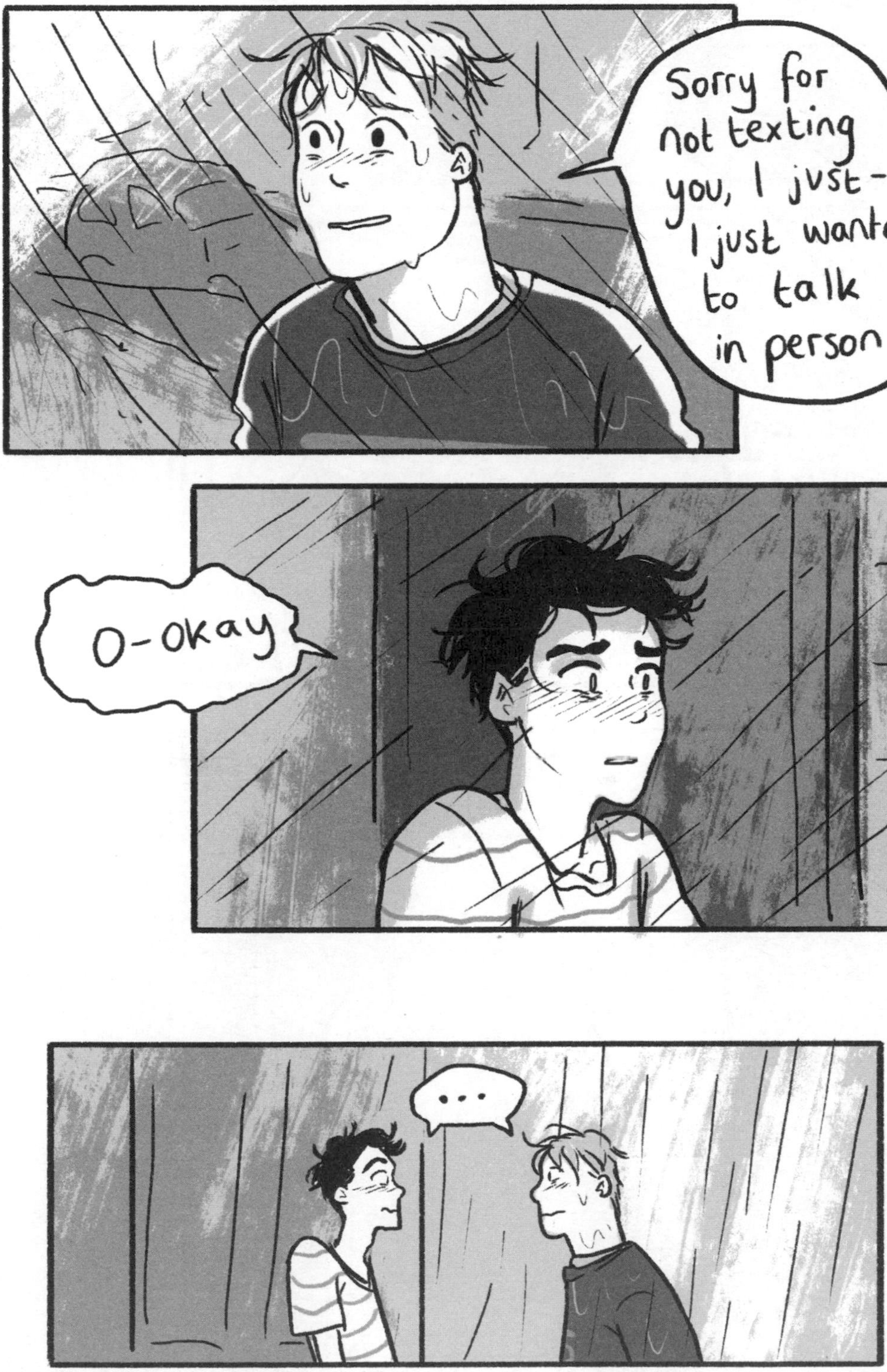
Sorry for not texting you, I just - I just wanted to talk in person
O-okay
...

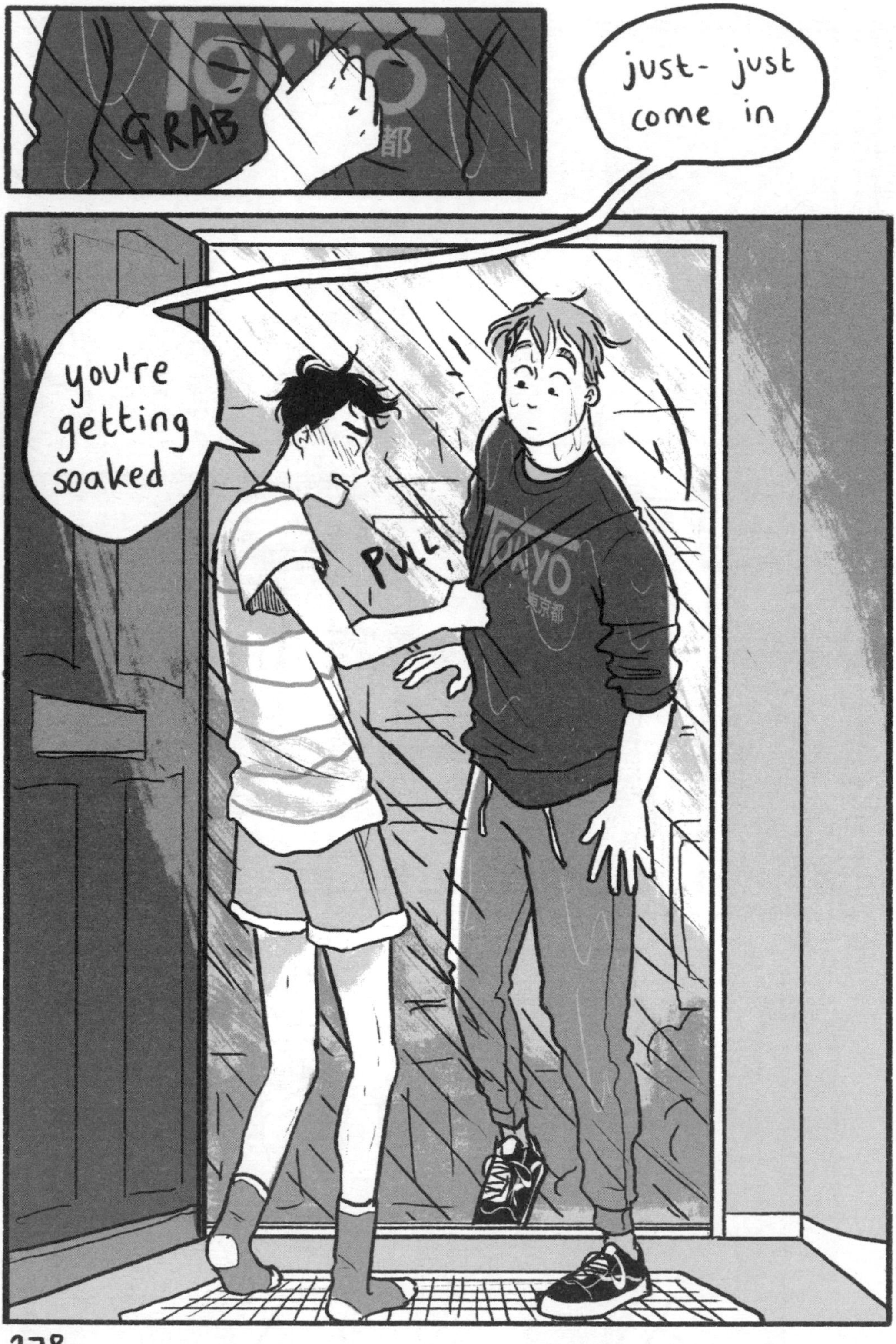
GRAB
just- just
come in
you're
getting
soaked
PULL

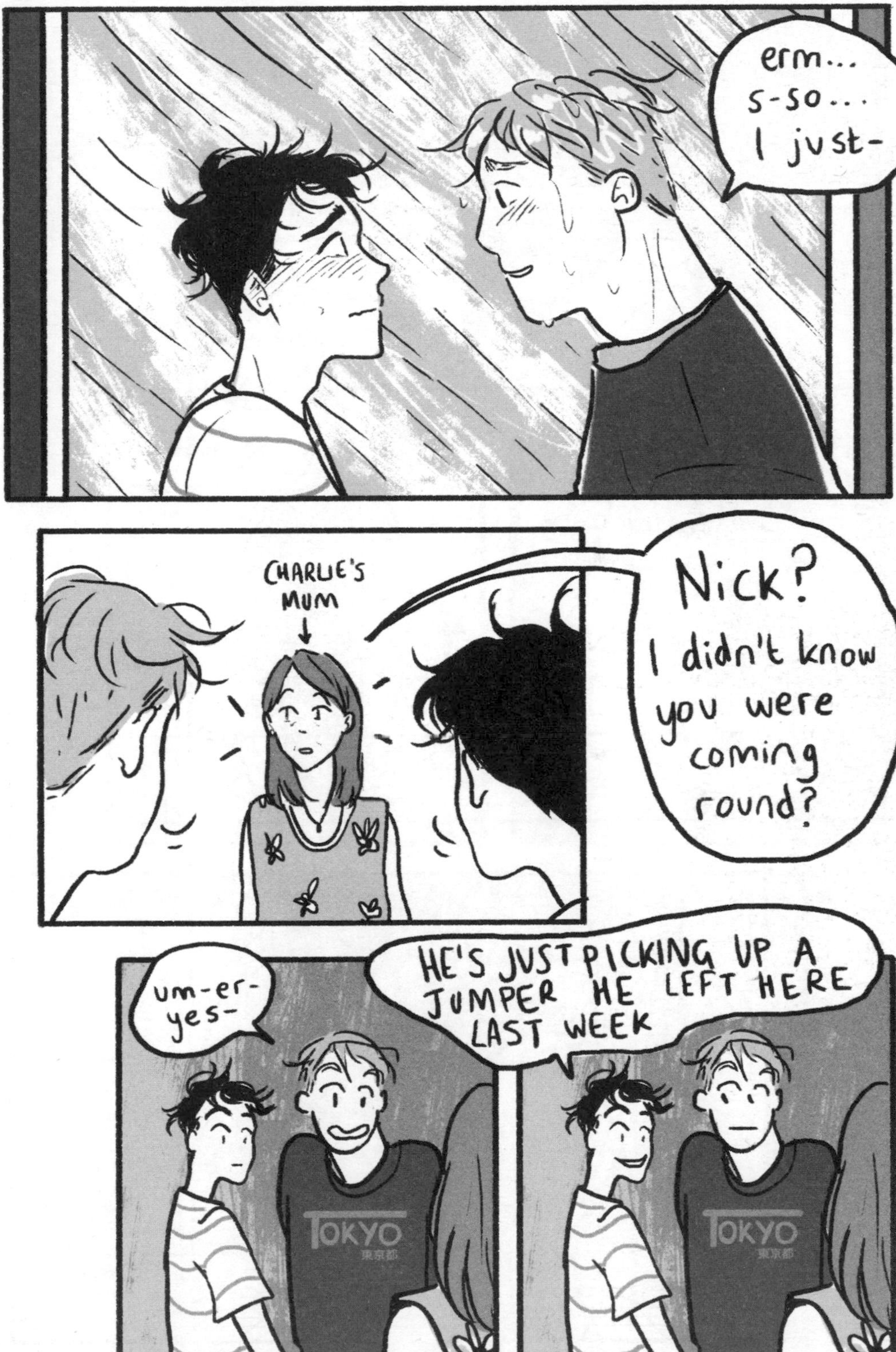
erm... s-so... I just-
CHARLIE'S MUM
Nick? I didn't know you were coming round?
um-er-yes-
HE'S JUST PICKING UP A JUMPER HE LEFT HERE LAST WEEK
TOKYO 東京都
TOKYO 東京都

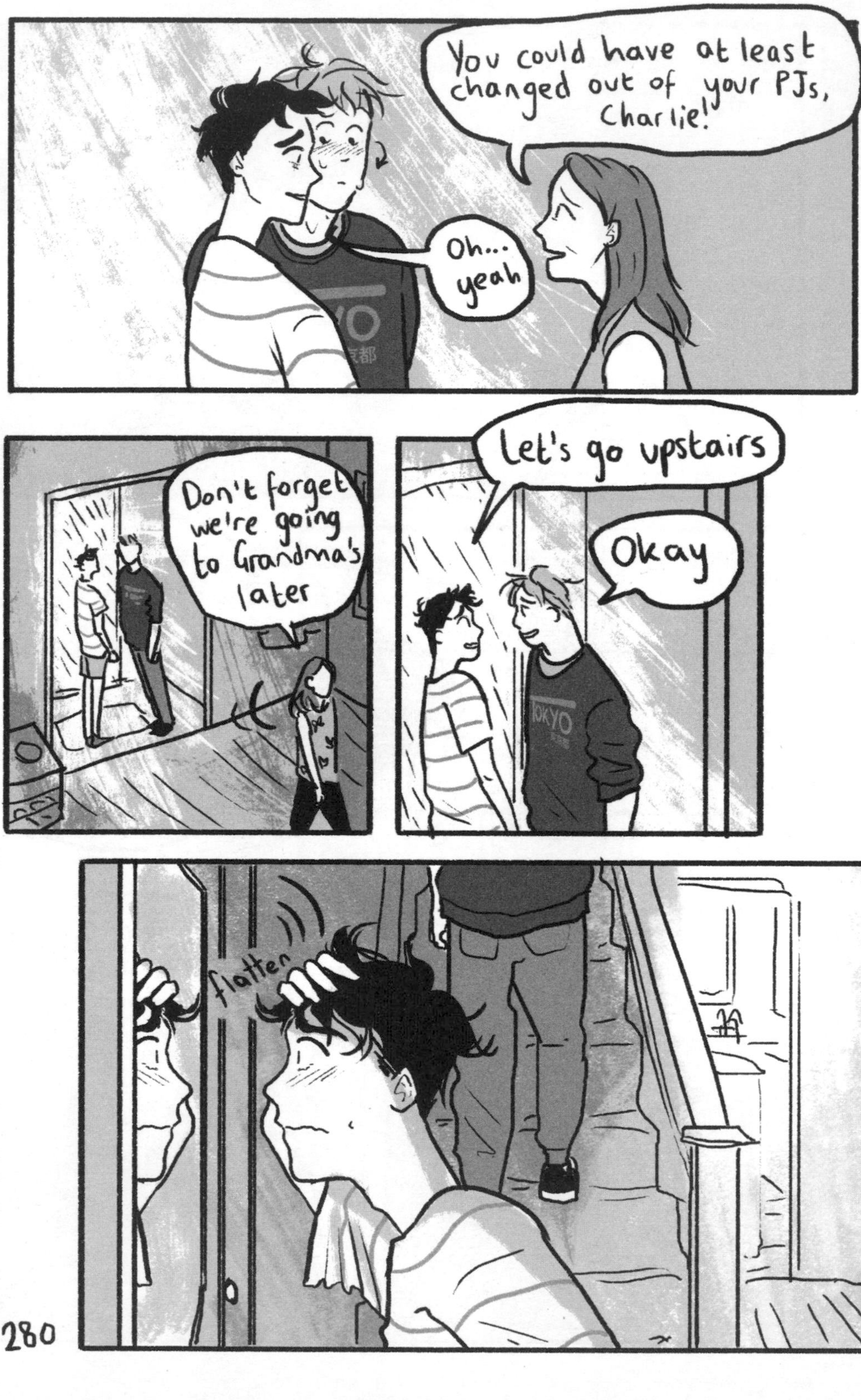
You could have at least changed out of your PJs, Charlie!
Oh... yeah
Don't forget we're going to Grandma's later
Let's go upstairs
Okay
flatten

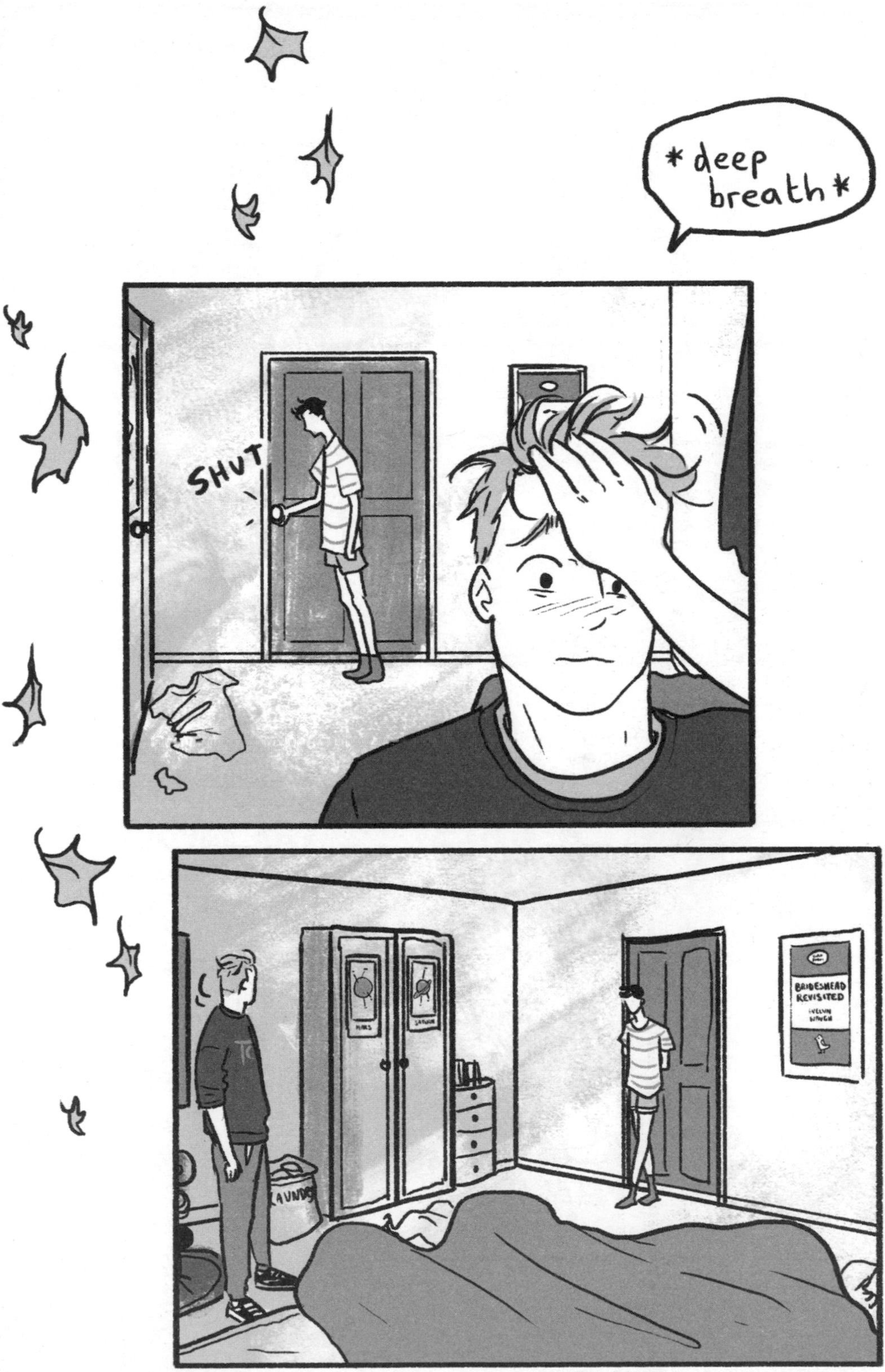
deep breath
SHUT
BRIDESHEAD REVISITED

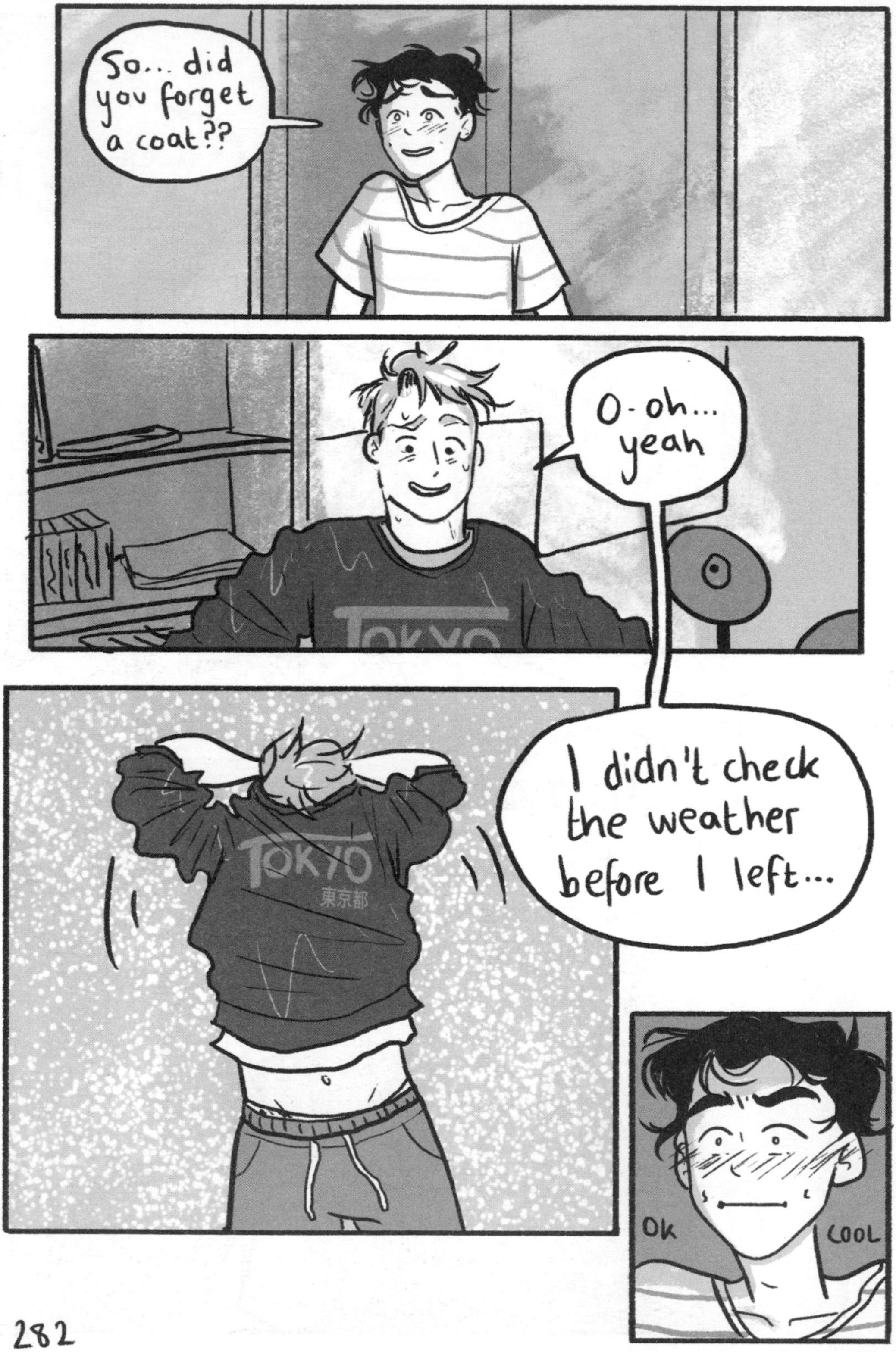
So... did you forget a coat??
O-oh... yeah
I didn't check the weather before I left...
TOKYO
東京都
OK
COOL

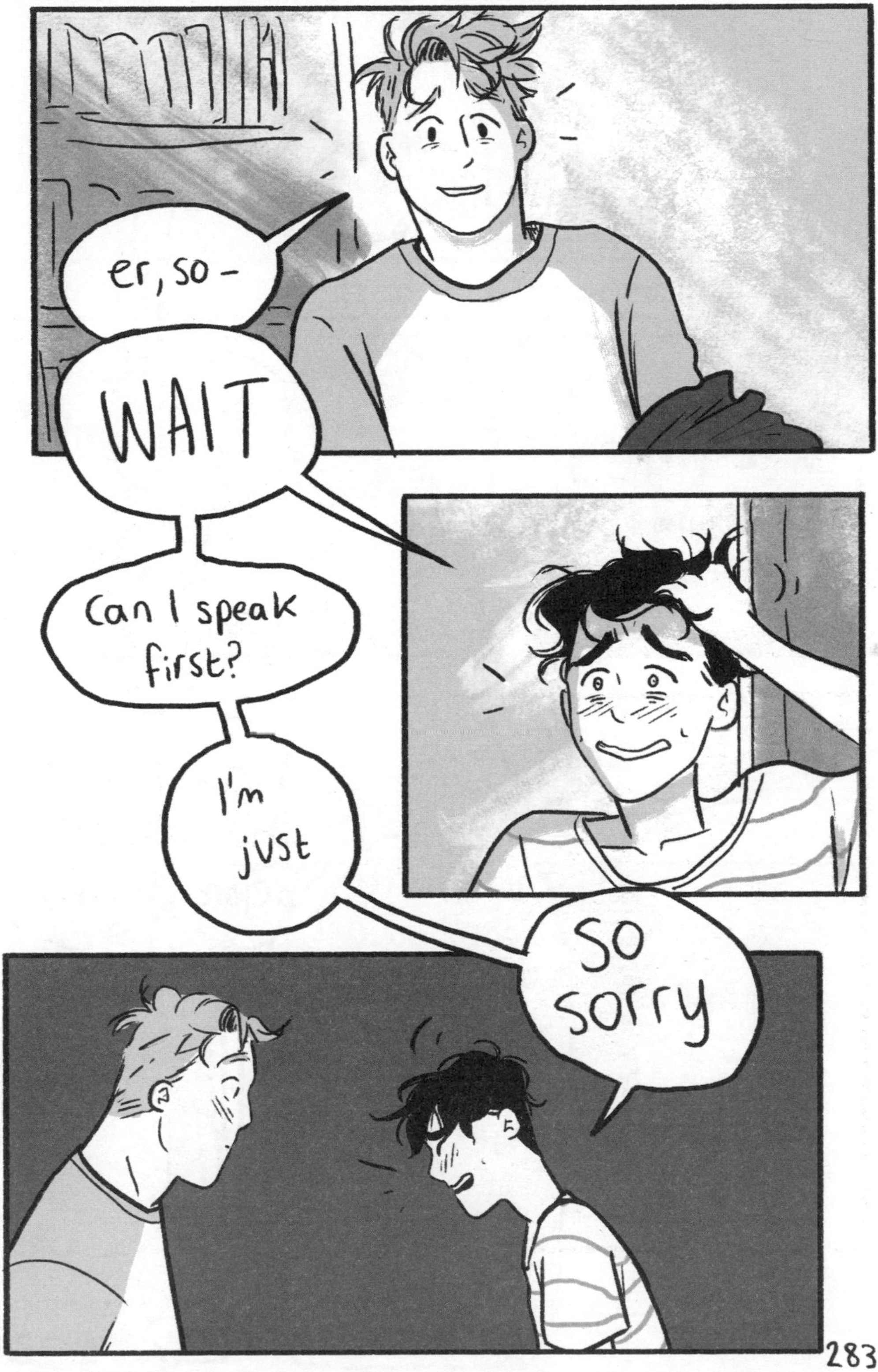
er, so -
WAIT
Can I speak first?
I'm just
So sorry

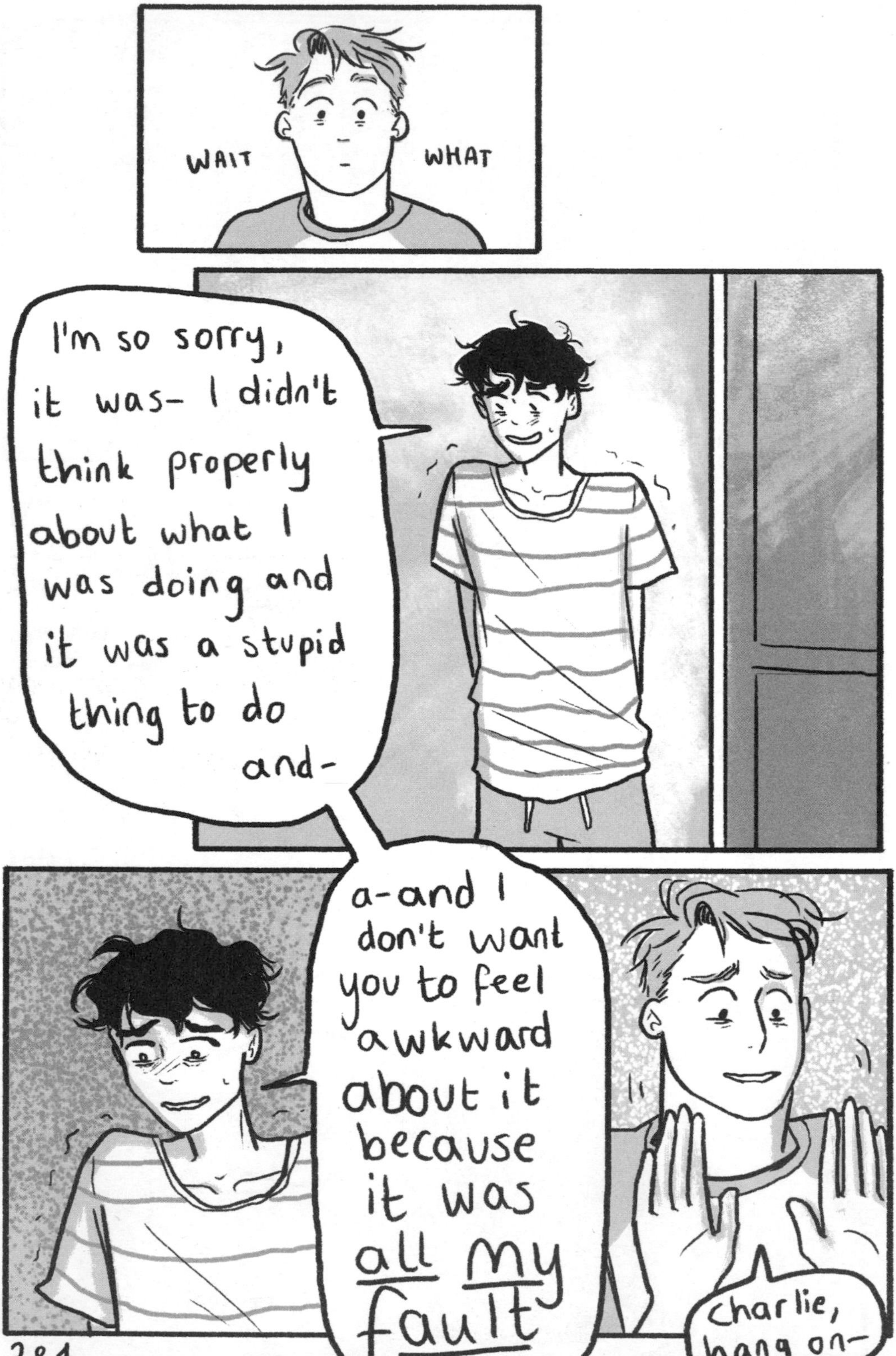
WAIT
WHAT
I'm so sorry, it was- I didn't think properly about what I was doing and it was a stupid thing to do and-
a-and I don't want you to feel awkward about it because it was all my fault
Charlie, hang on-

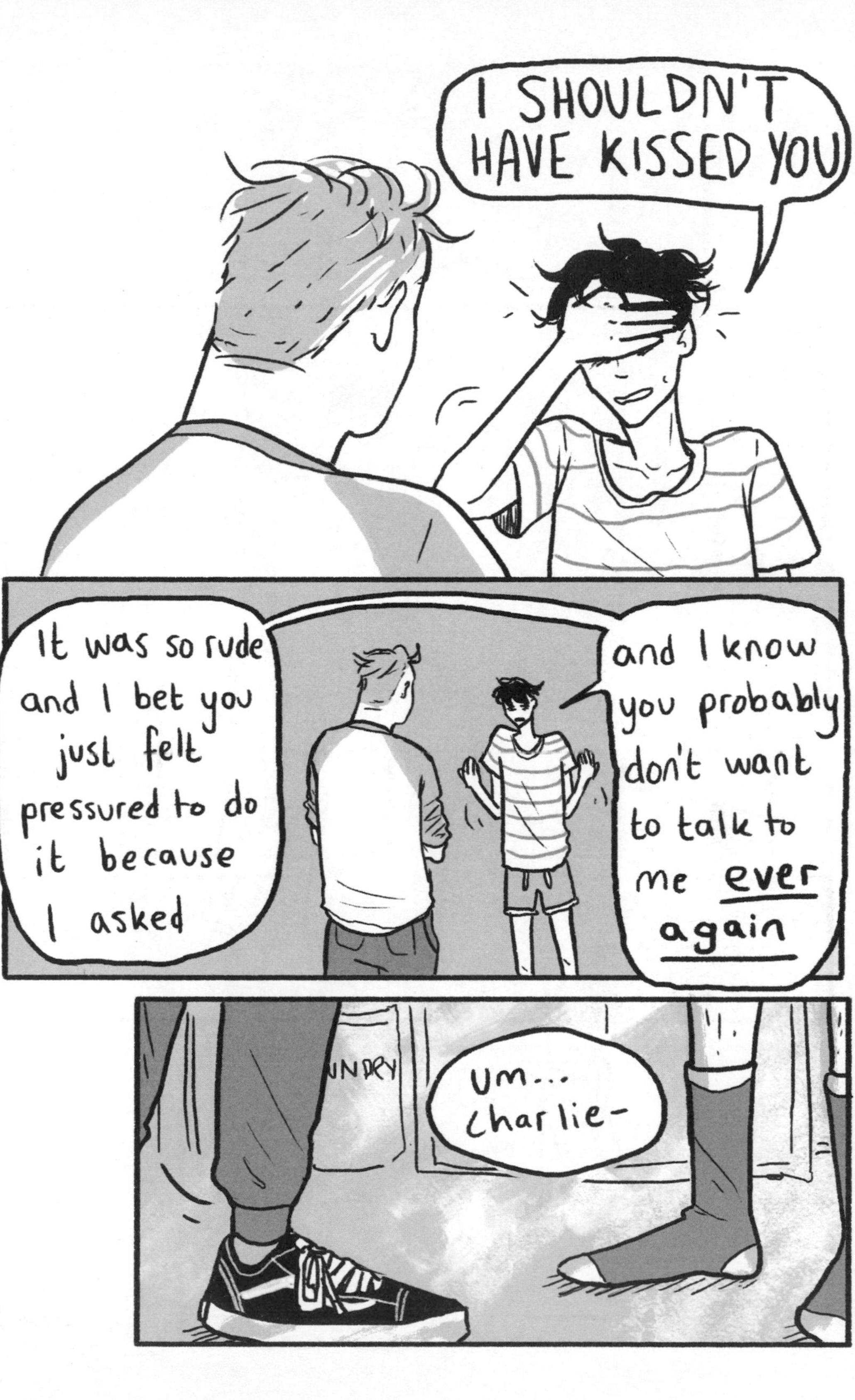
I SHOULDN'T HAVE KISSED YOU
It was so rude and I bet you just felt pressured to do it because I asked
and I know you probably don't want to talk to me ever again
UNDRY
Um... Charlie-

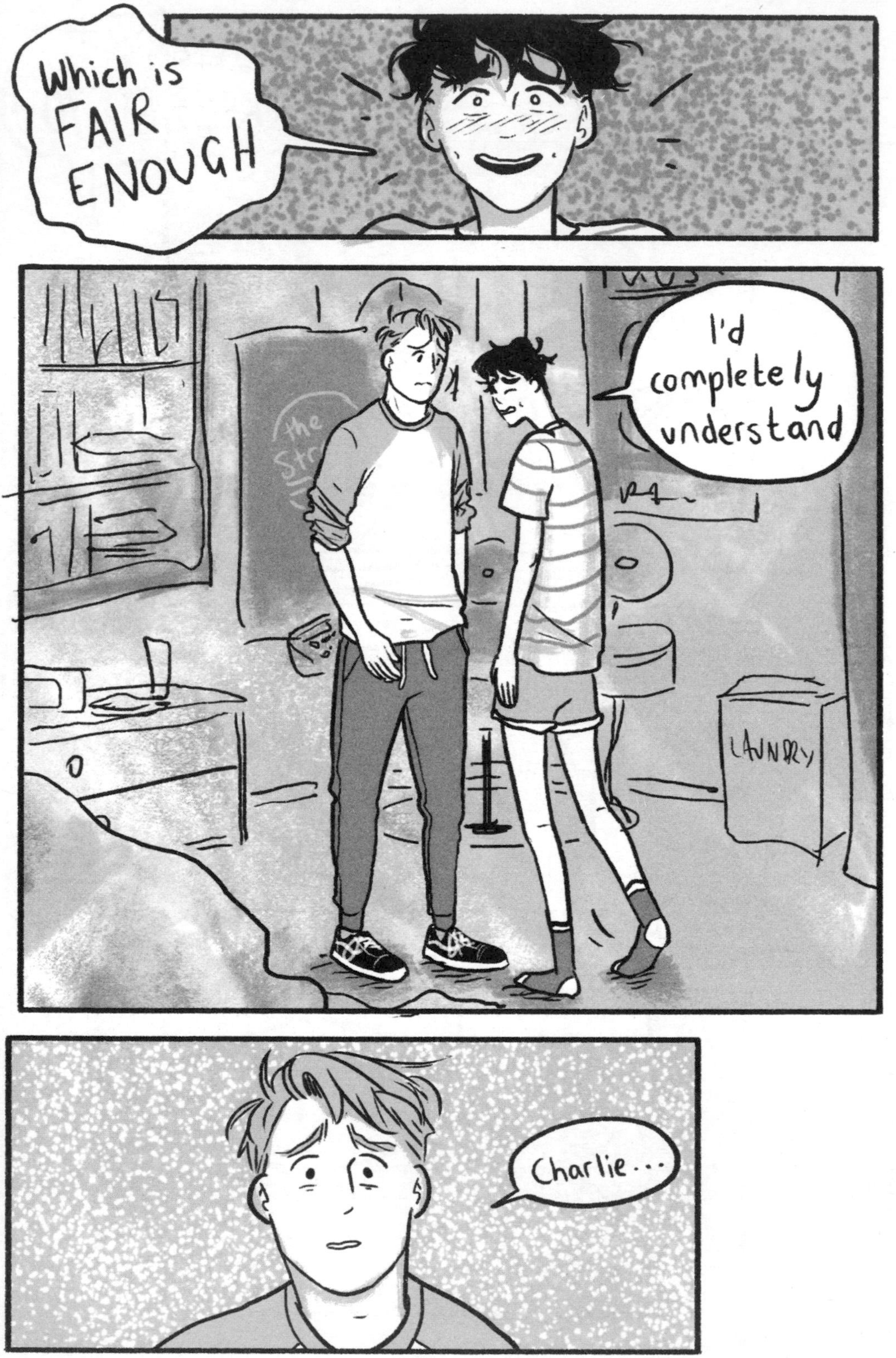
Which is FAIR ENOUGH
I'd completely understand
LAUNDRY
Charlie...

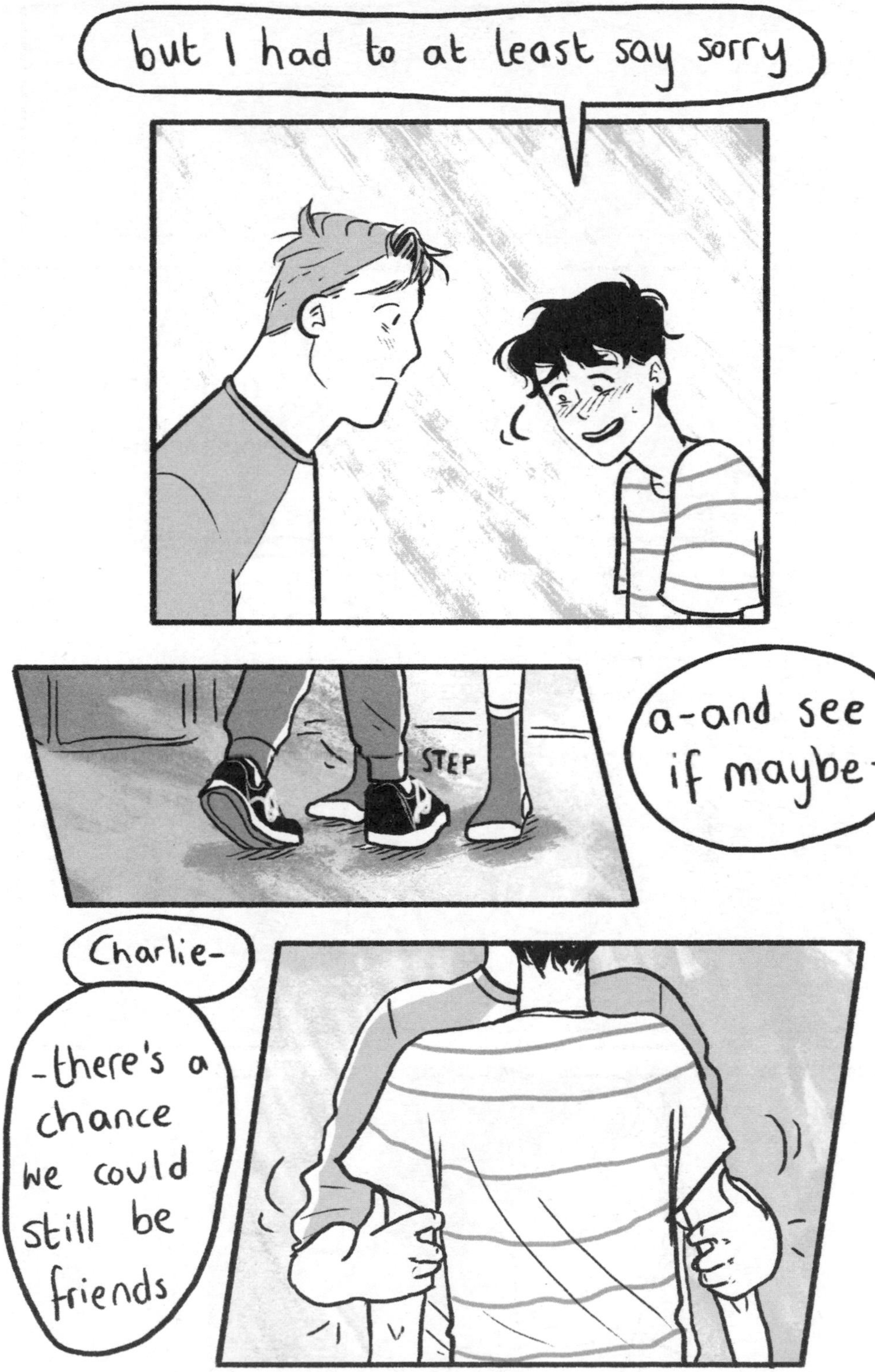
but I had to at least say sorry
a-and see if maybe-
STEP
Charlie-
-there's a chance we could still be friends

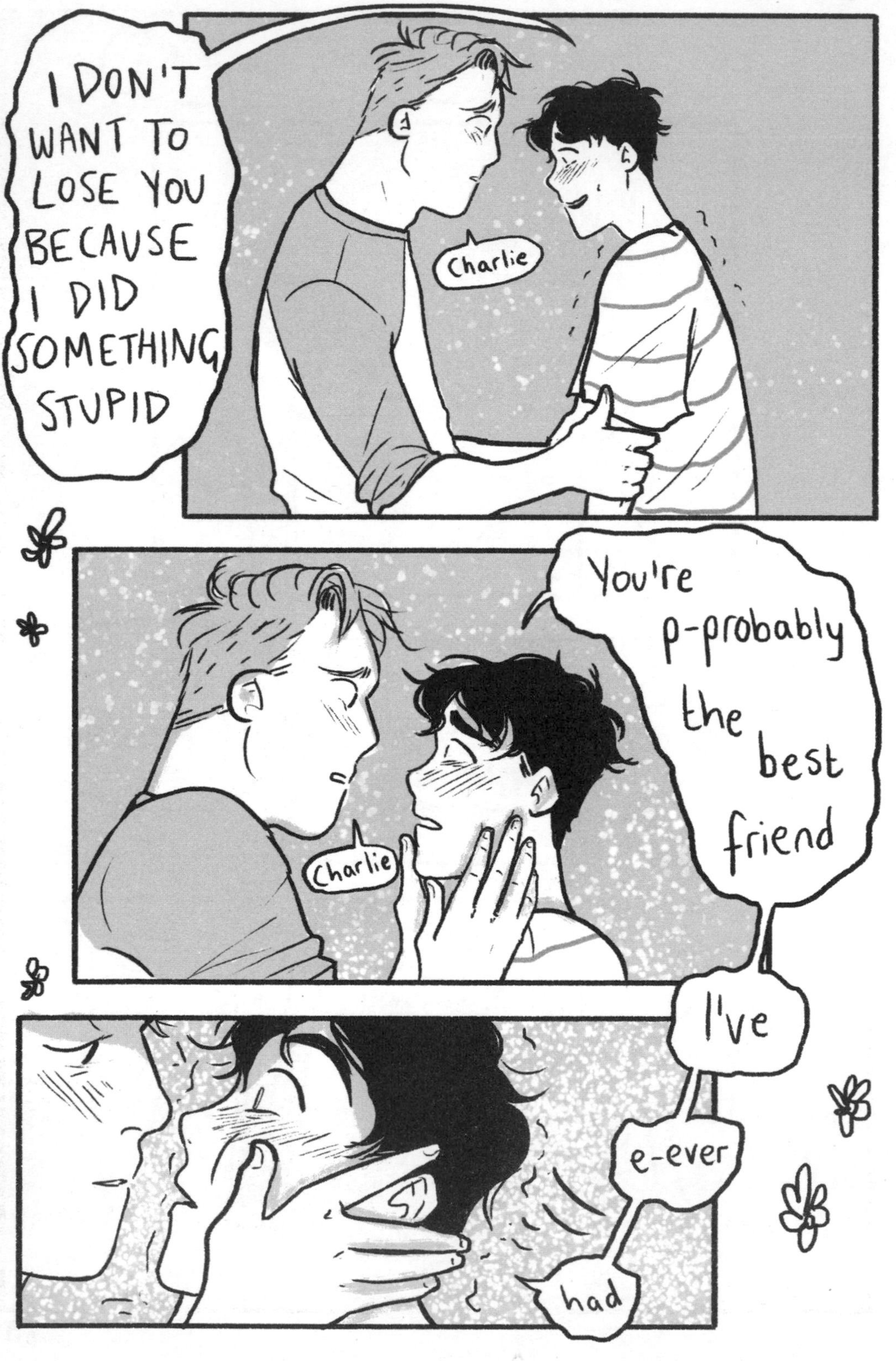
I DON'T WANT TO LOSE YOU BECAUSE I DID SOMETHING STUPID
Charlie
Charlie
You're p-probably the best friend
I've
e-ever
had

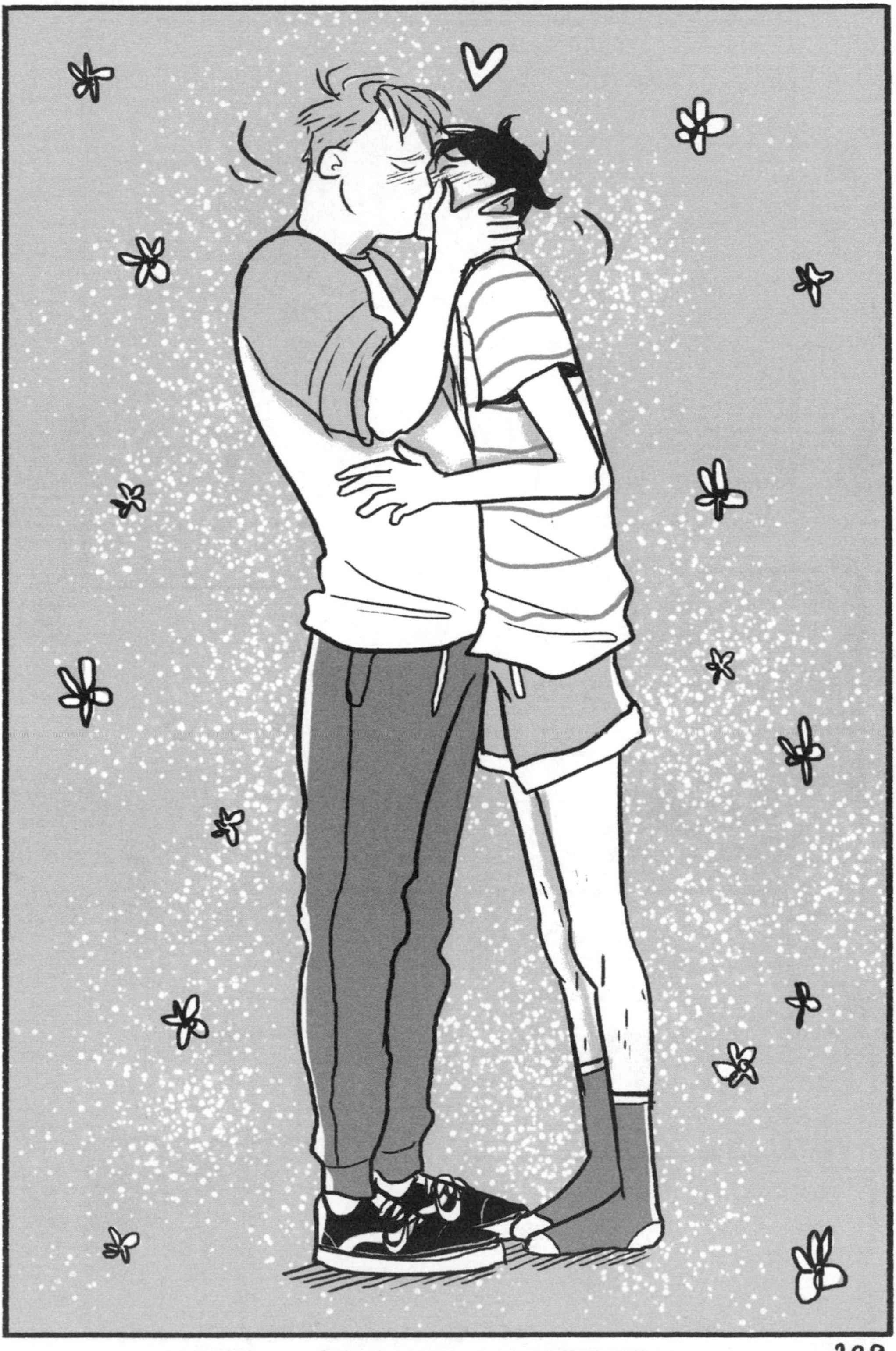

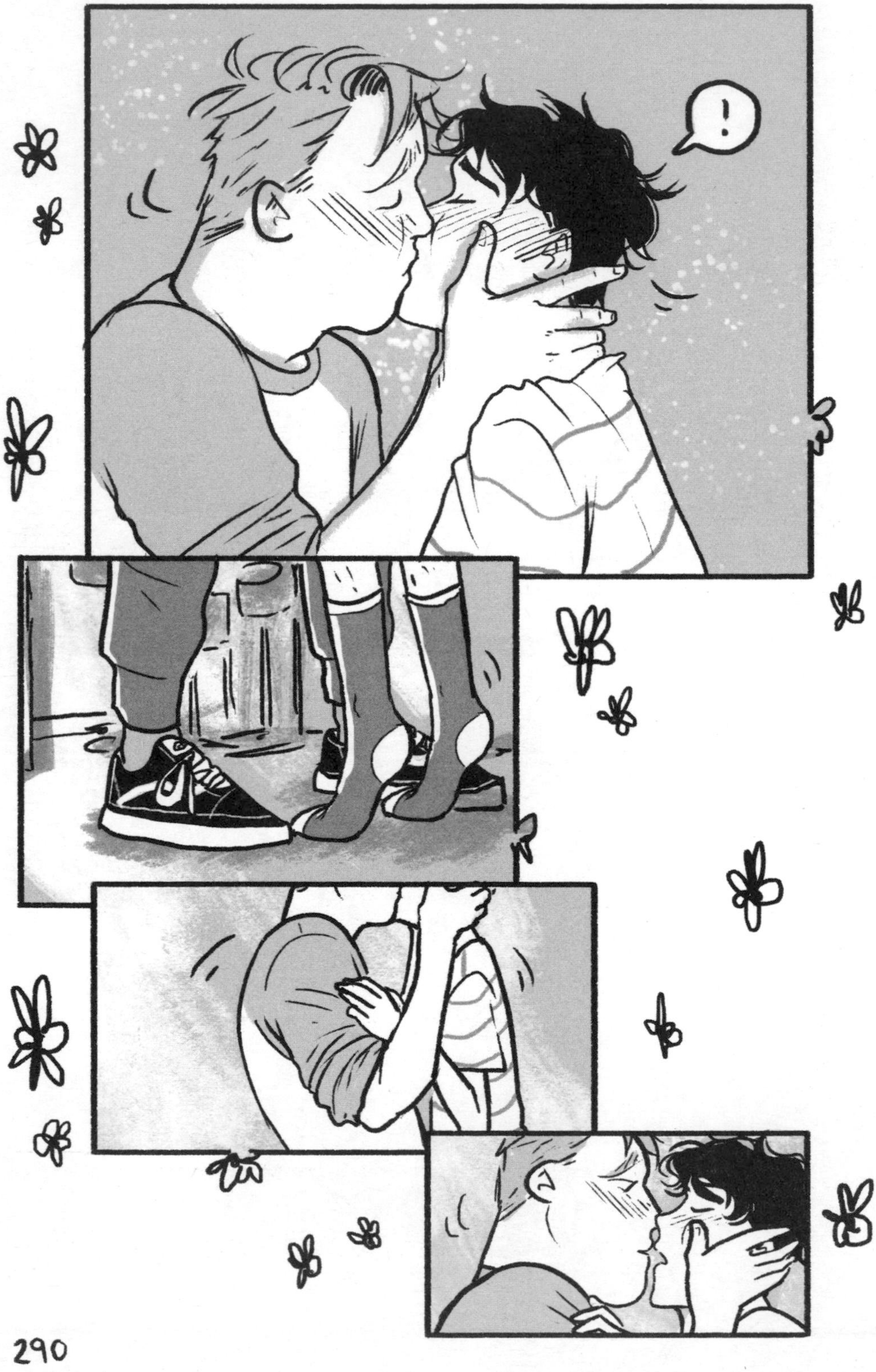
!

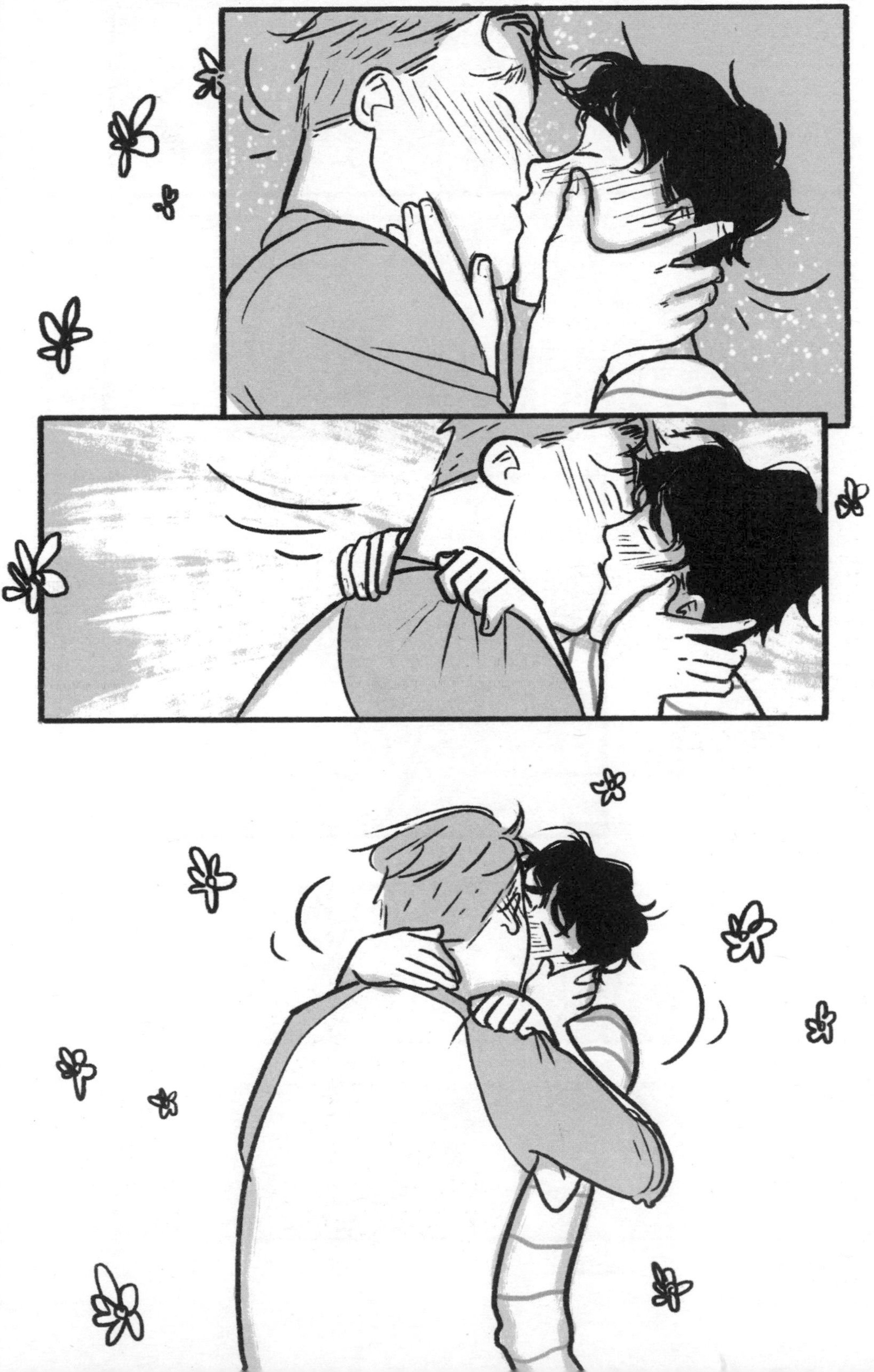

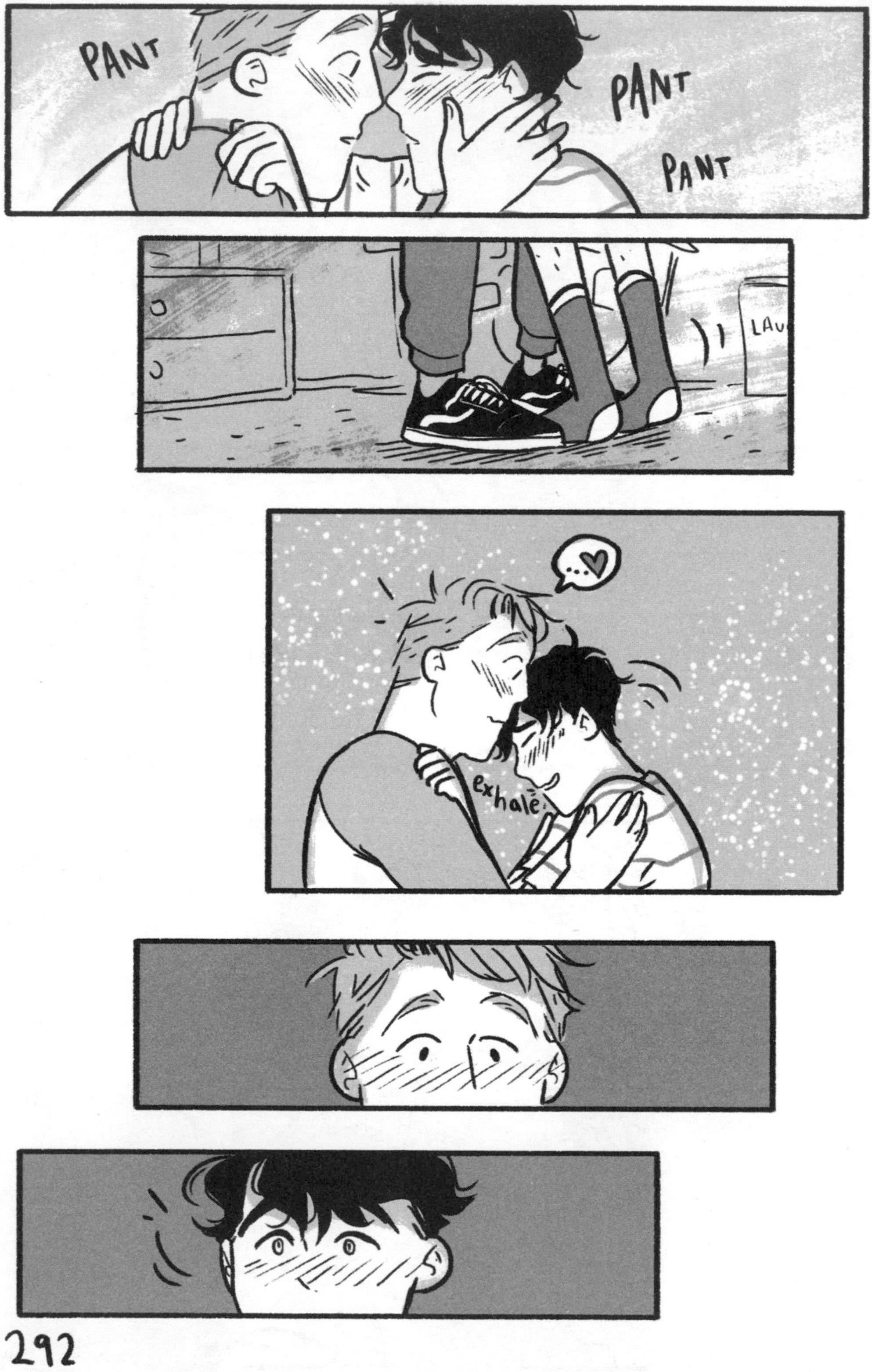
PANT
PANT
PANT
LAU
exhale

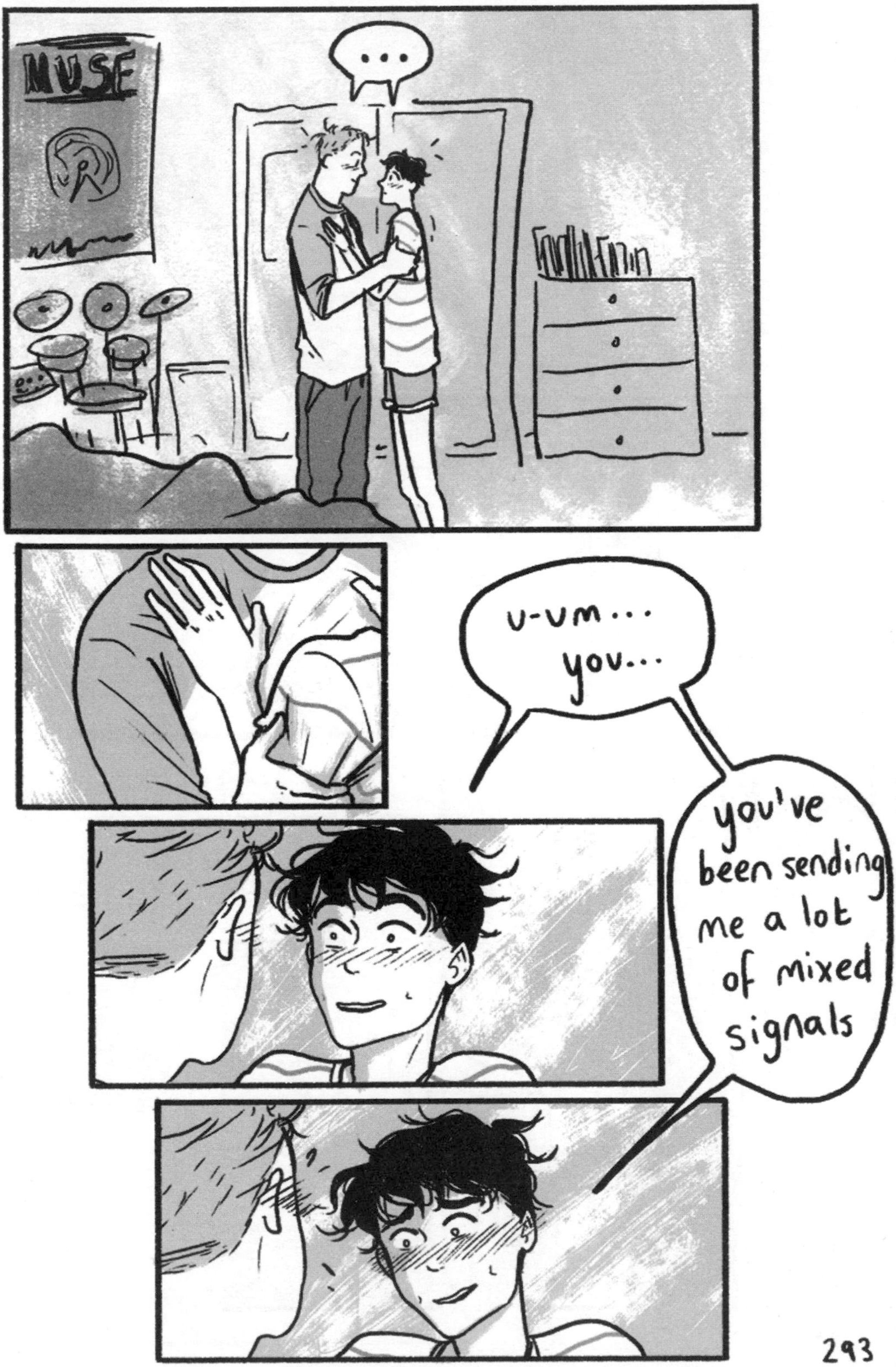
...
MUSE
u-um...
you...
you've been sending me a lot of mixed signals

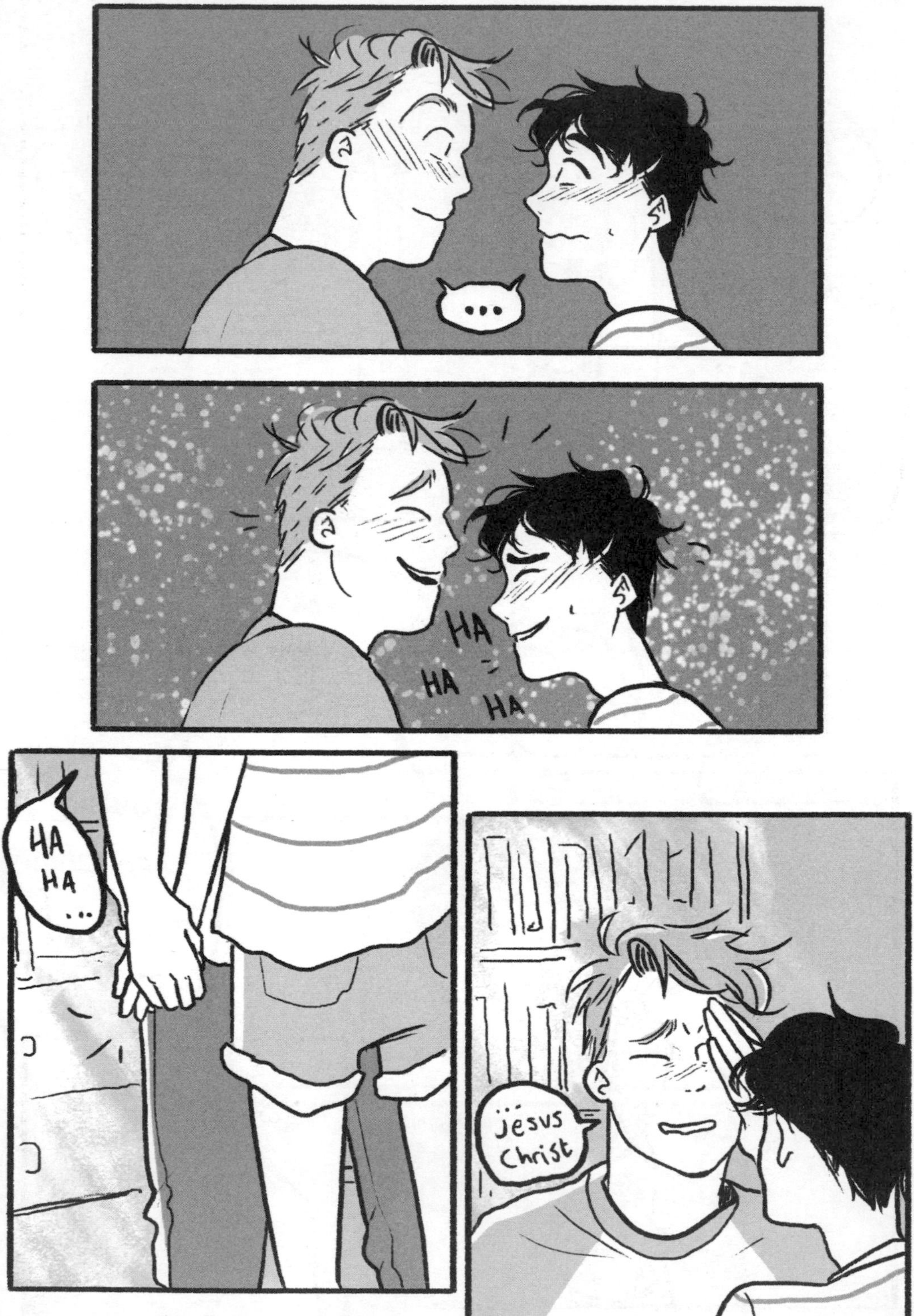
...
HA
HA
HA
HA HA ...
... Jesus Christ

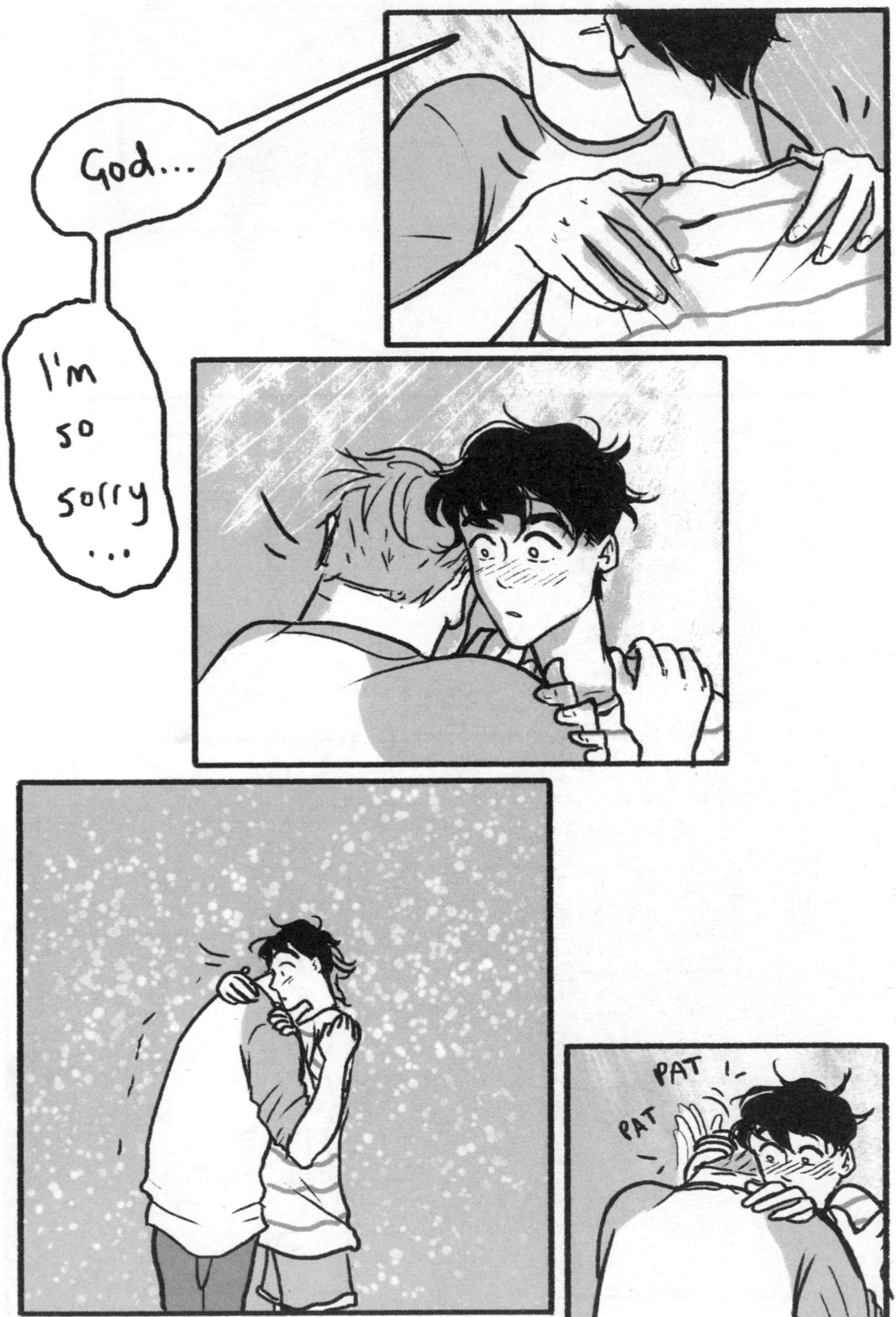
God...
I'm so sorry ...
PAT
PAT

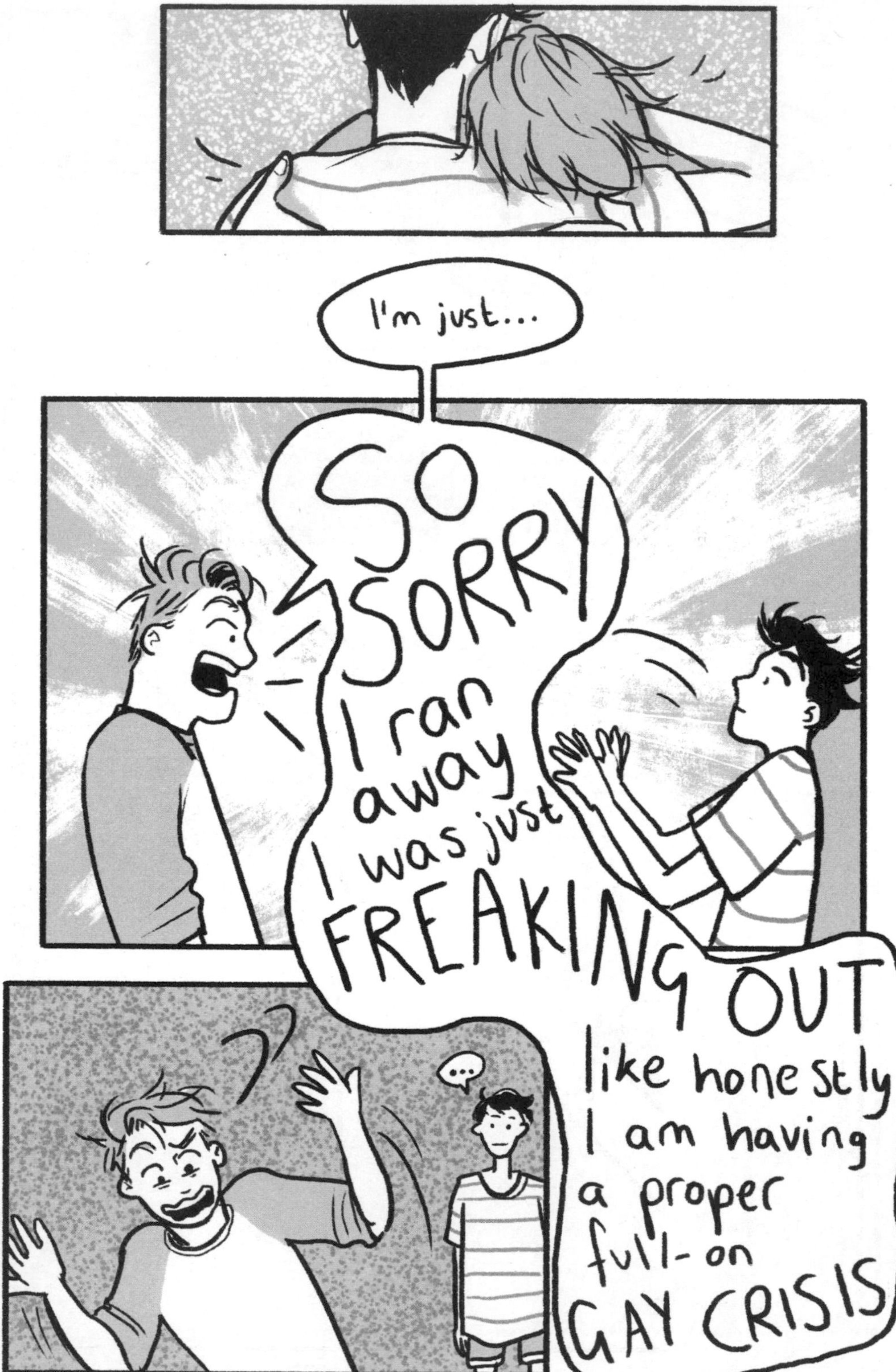
I'm just...
SO SORRY I ran away I was just FREAKING OUT like honestly I am having a proper full-on GAY CRISIS
...

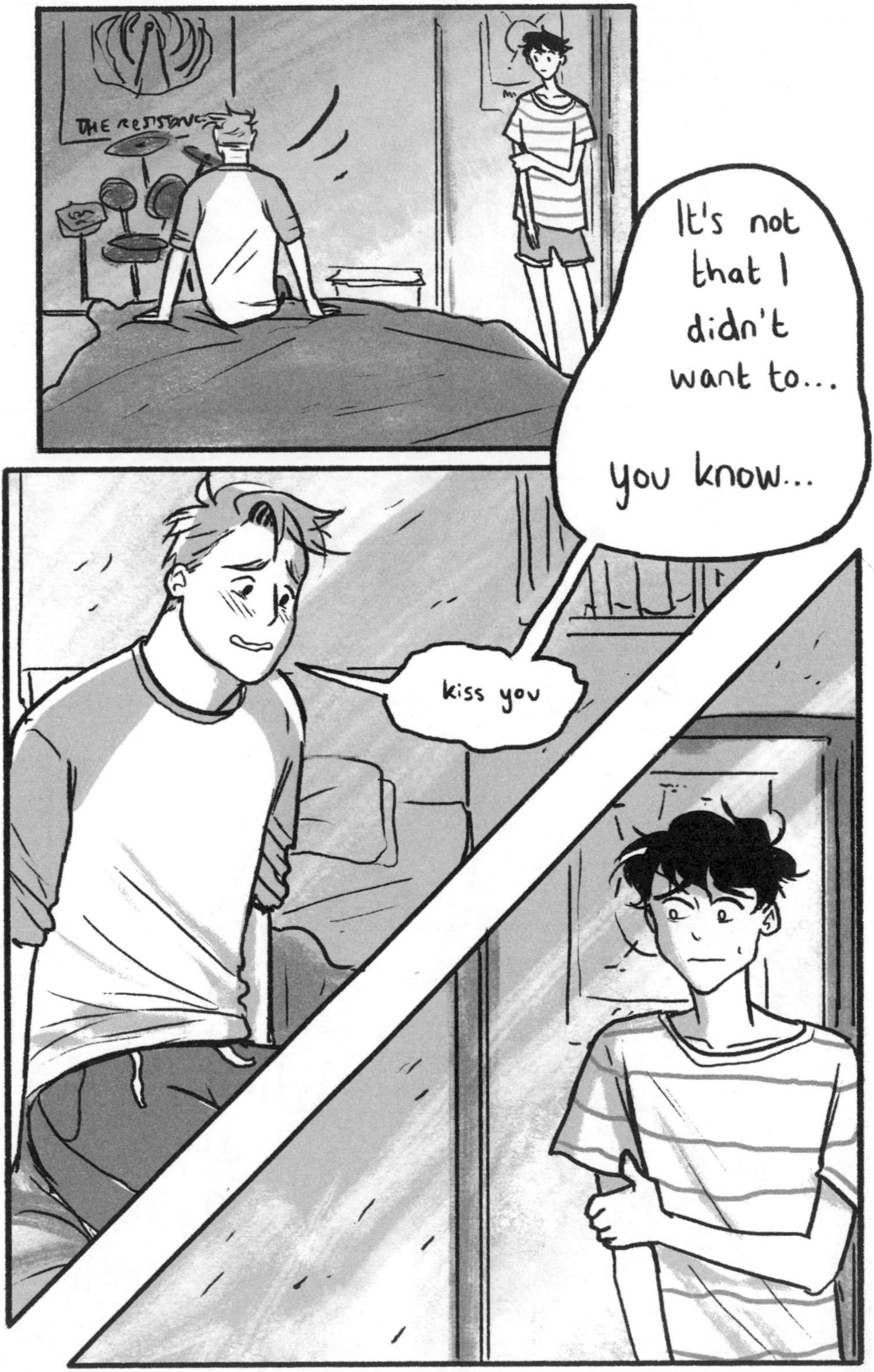
THE RESISTANCE
It's not that I didn't want to...
you know...
kiss you

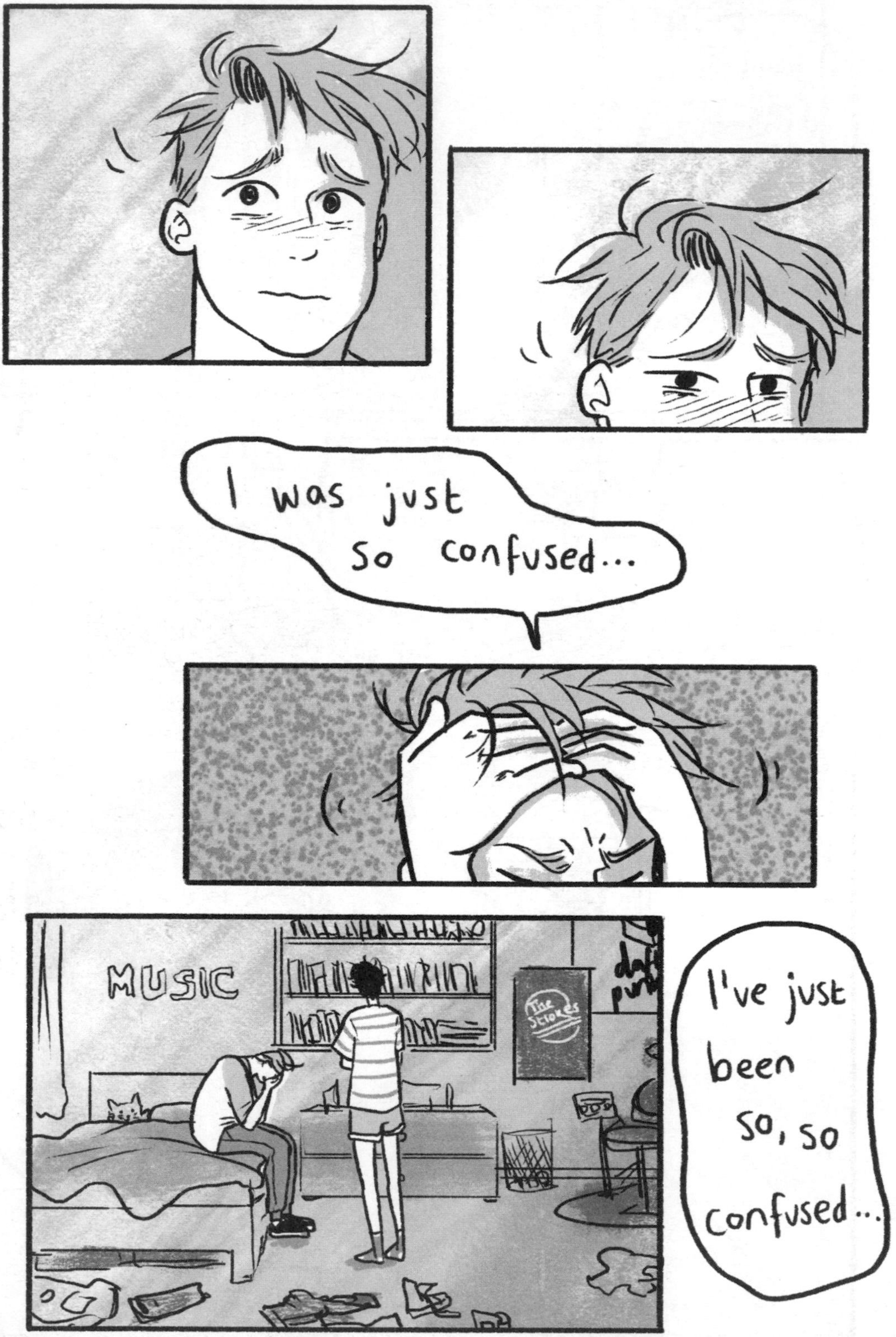
I was just so confused...
MUSIC
The Strokes
I've just been so, so confused...

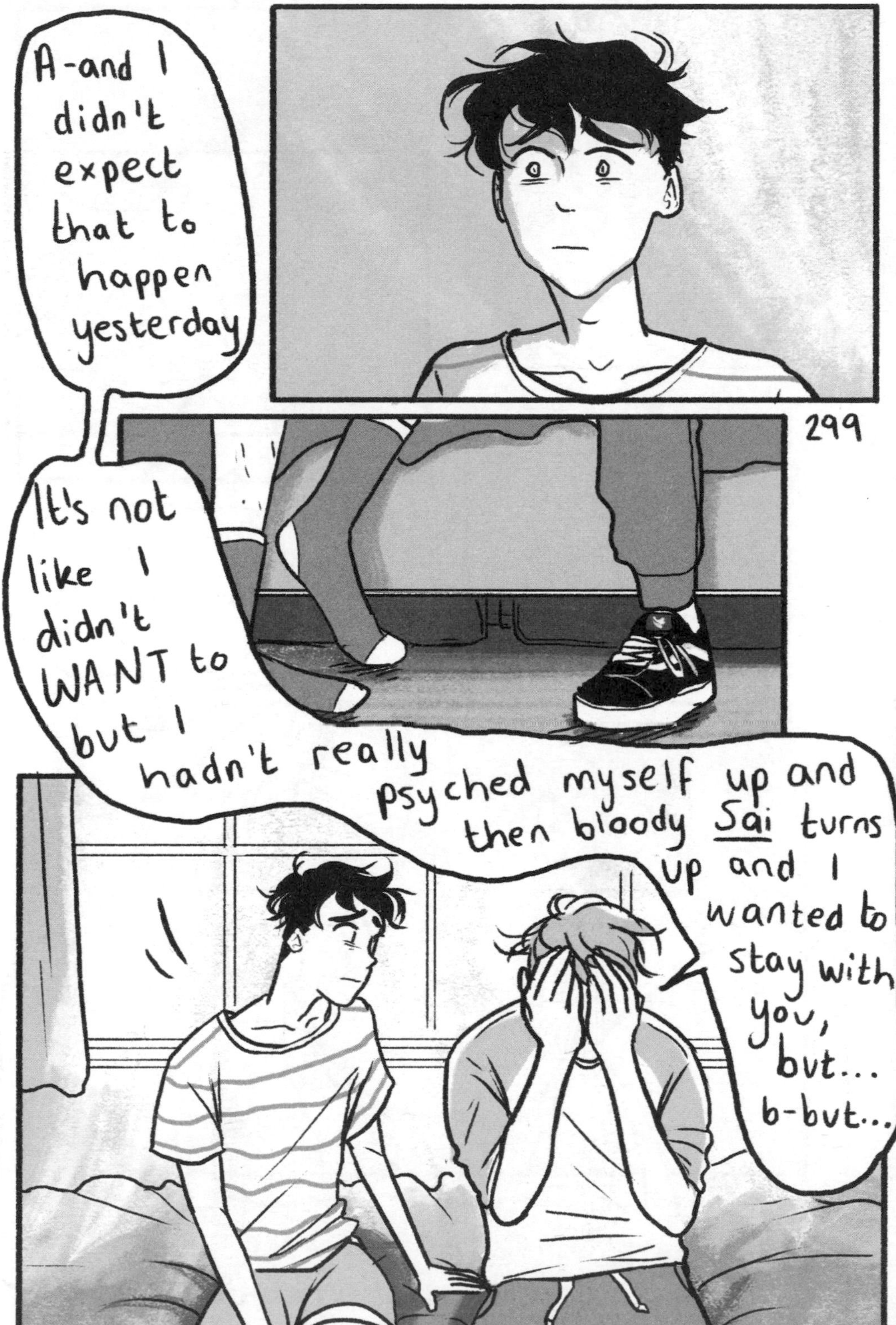
A-and I didn't expect that to happen yesterday
It's not like I didn't WANT to but I hadn't really psyched myself up and then bloody Sai turns up and I wanted to stay with you, but... b-but...

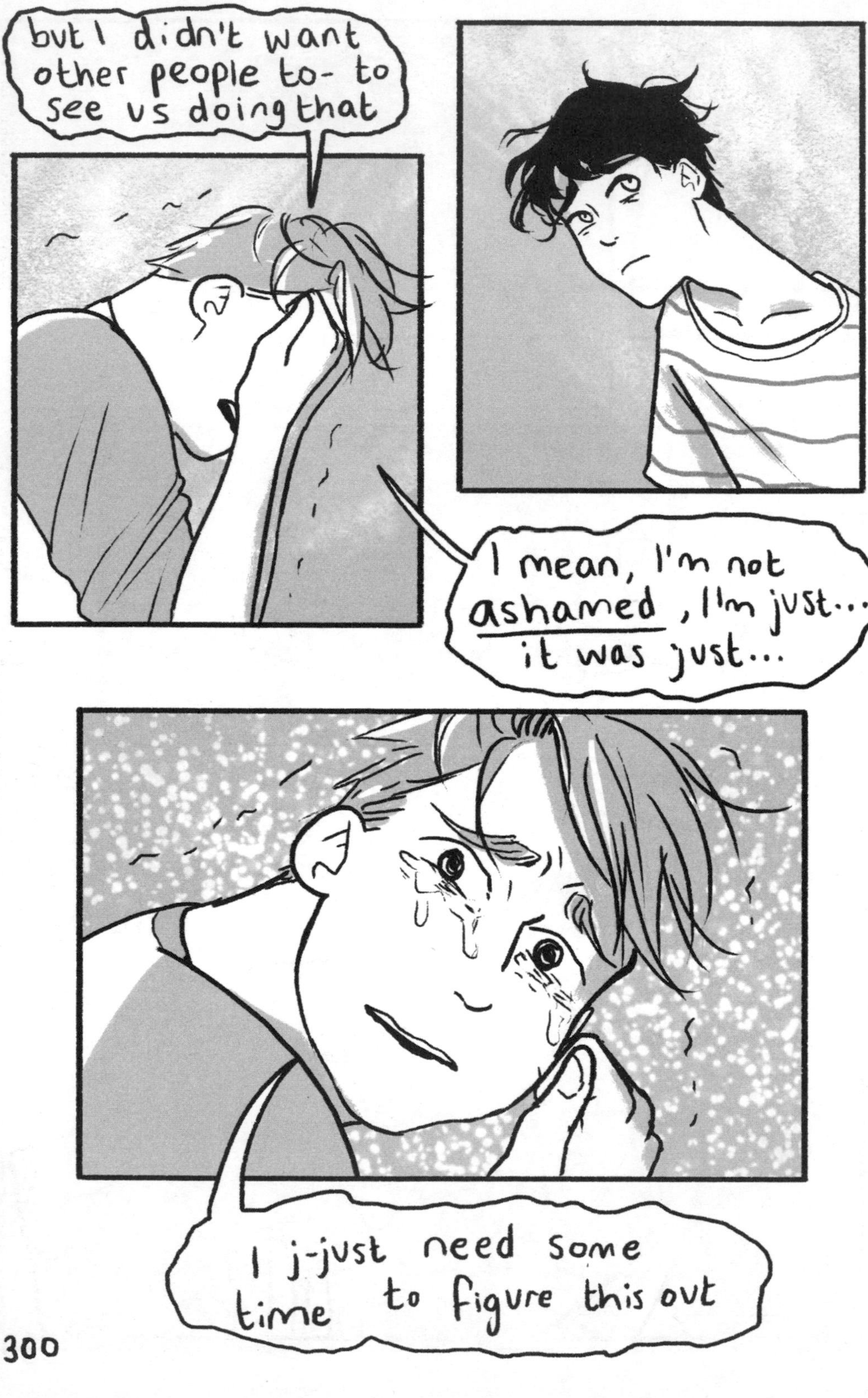
but I didn't want other people to- to see us doing that
I mean, I'm not ashamed, I'm just... it was just...
I j-just need some time to figure this out

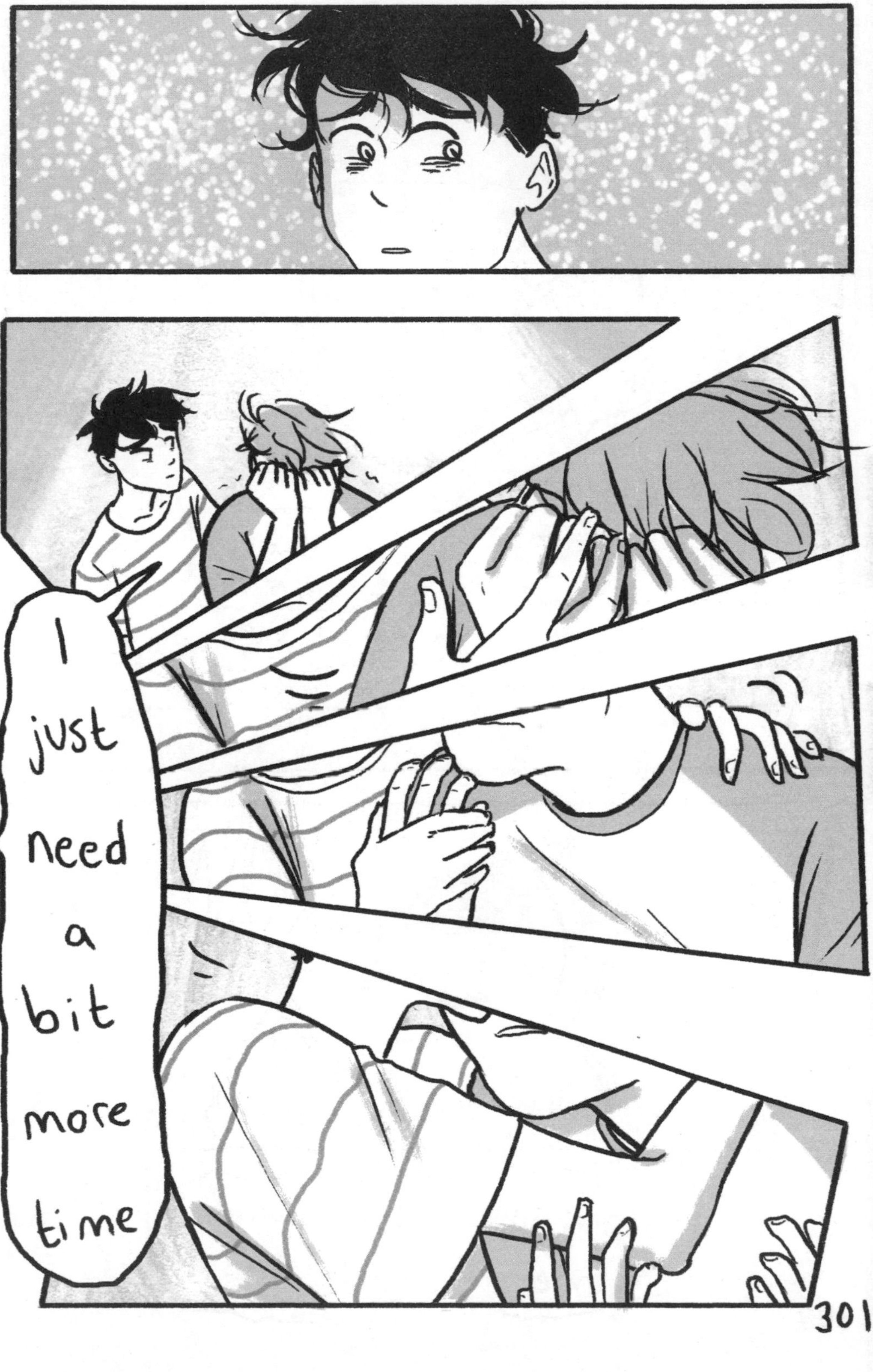
I just need a bit more time

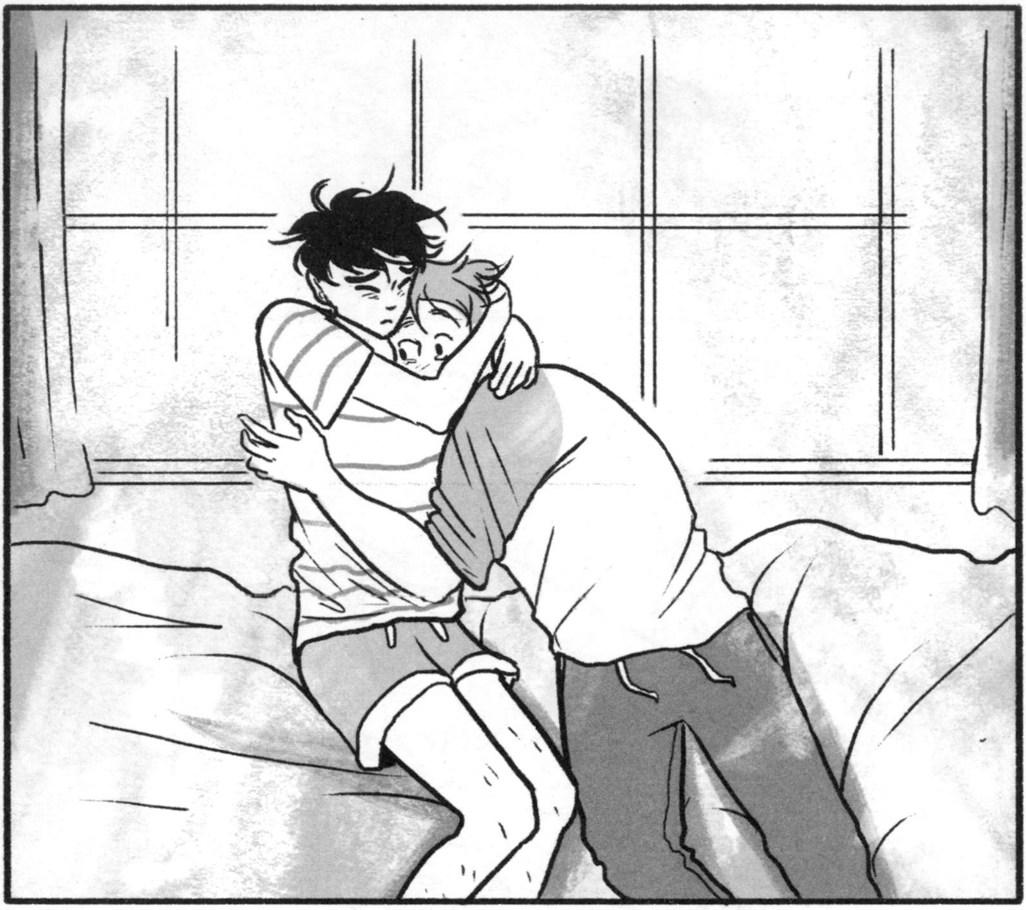

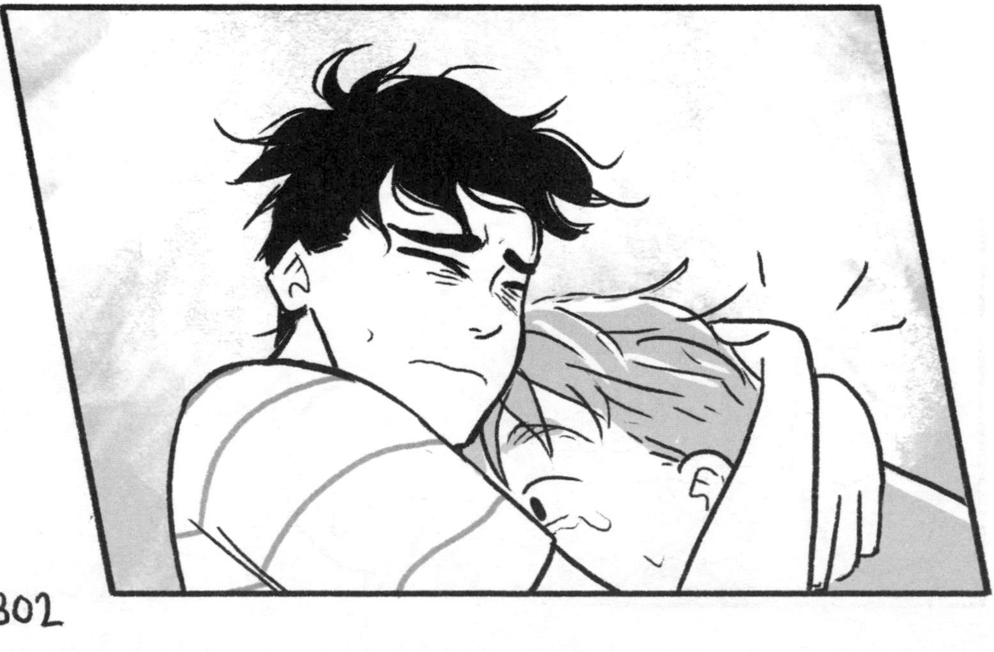

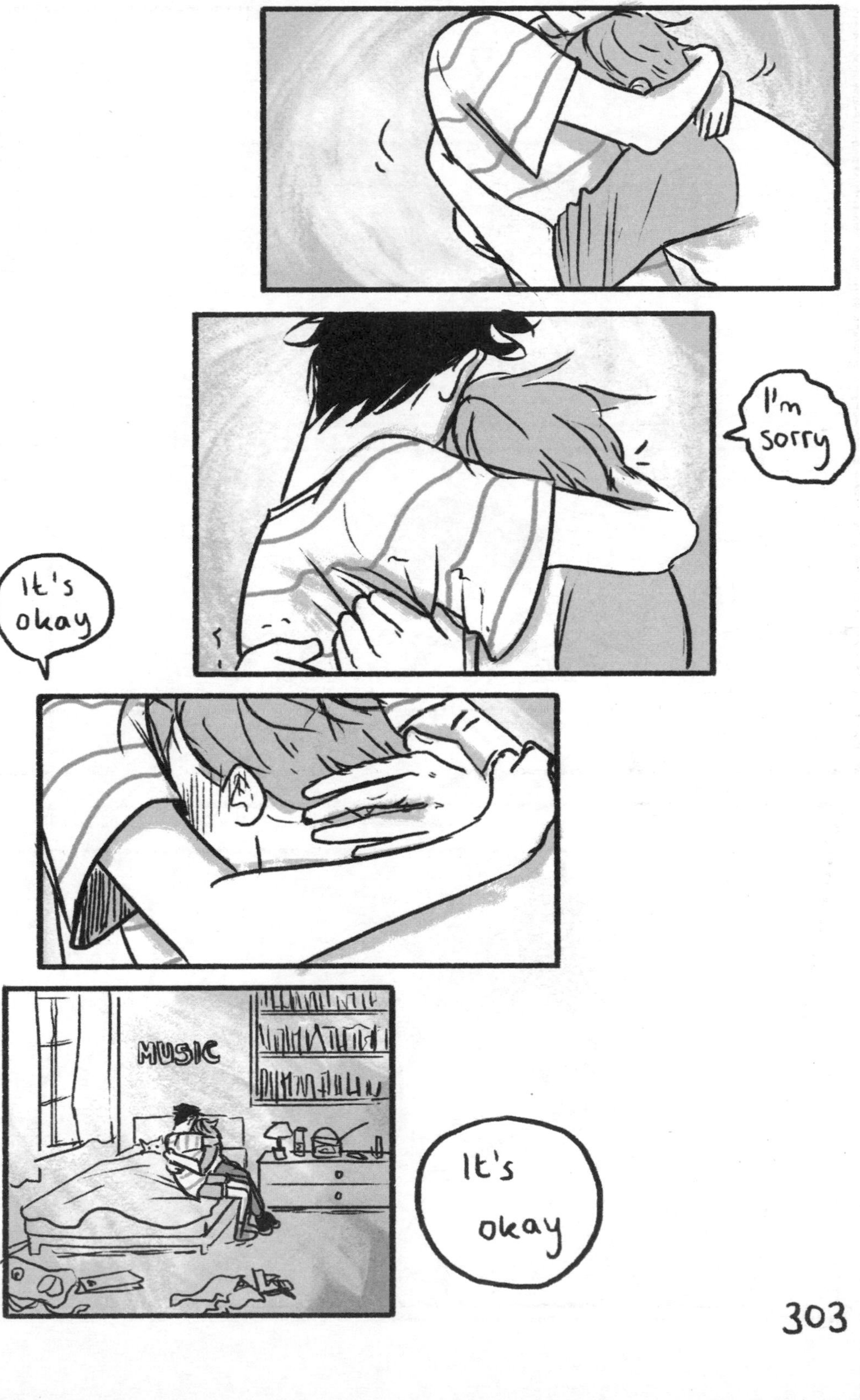
I'm sorry
It's okay
MUSIC
It's okay

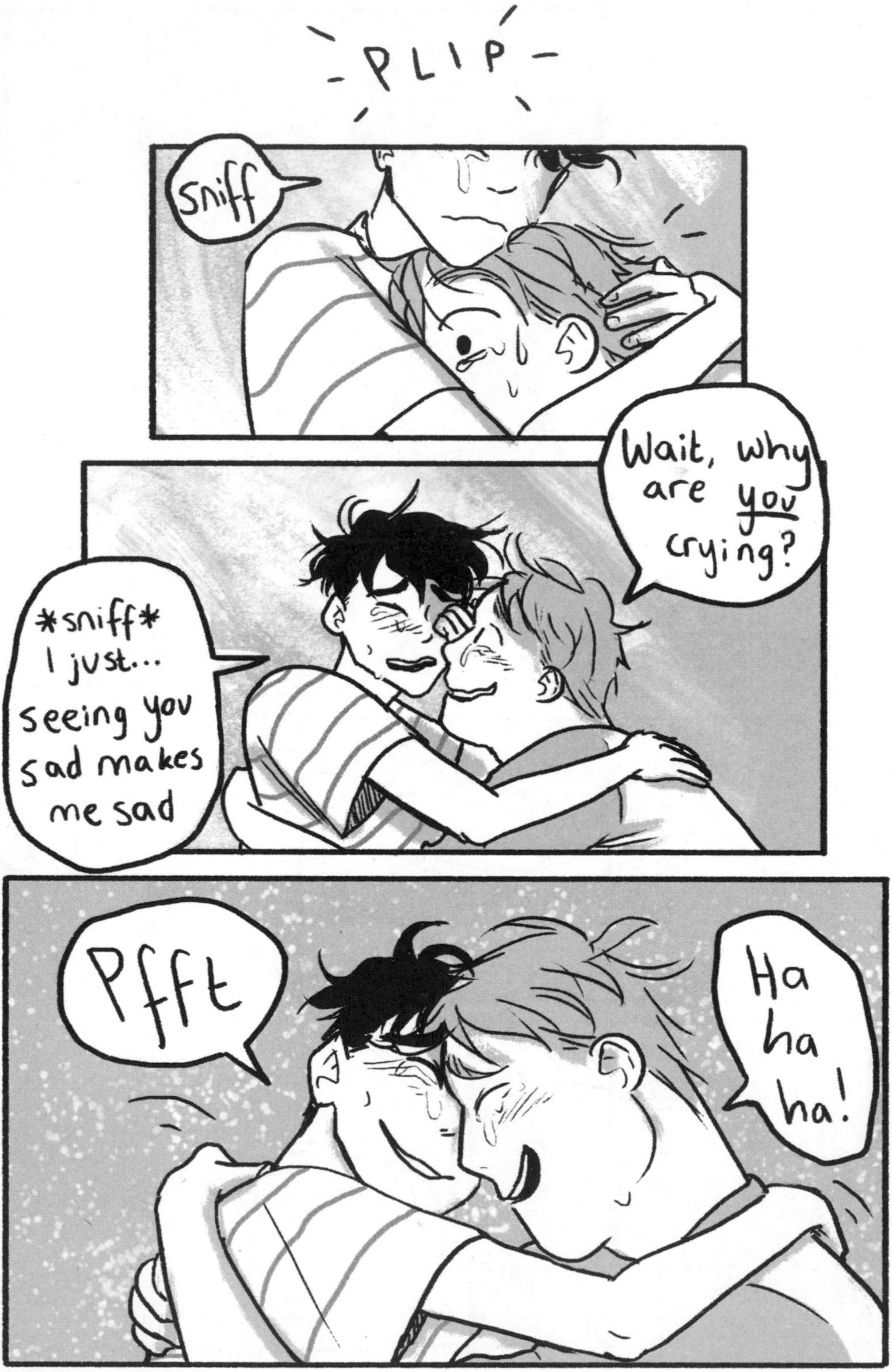
PLIP
Sniff
Wait, why are you crying?
sniff I just... seeing you sad makes me sad
Pfft
Ha ha ha!

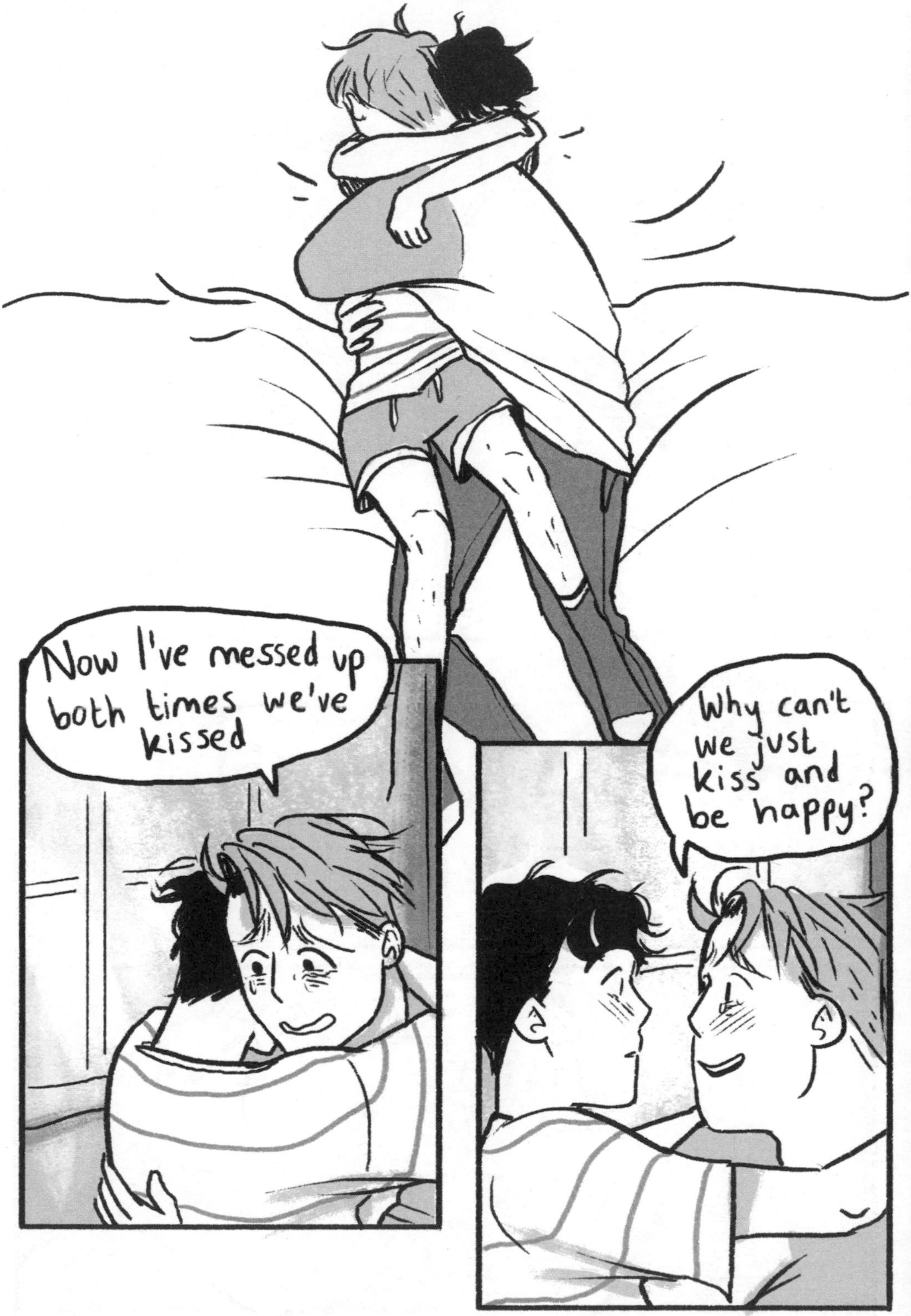

Now I've messed up both times we've kissed
Why can't we just kiss and be happy?

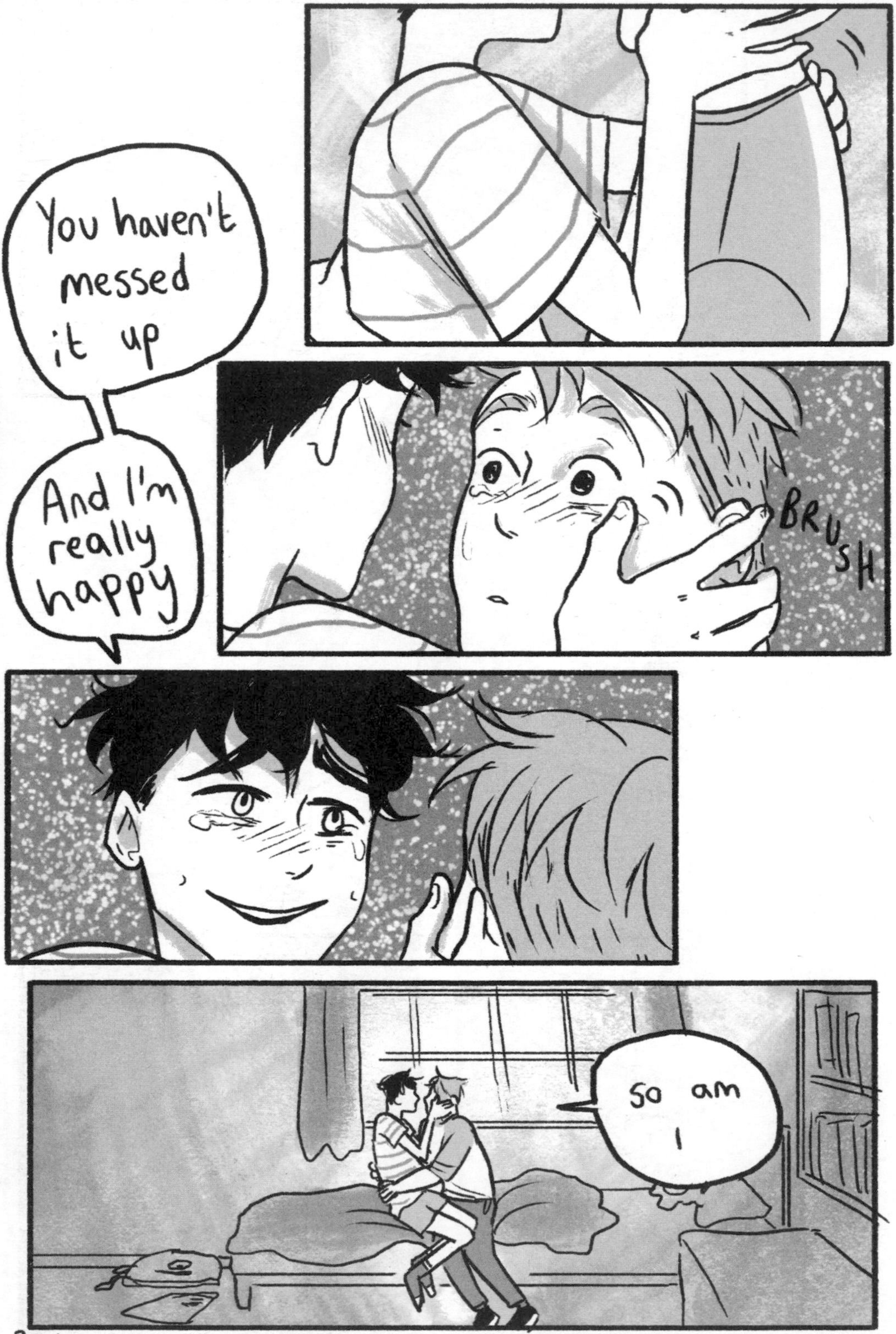
You haven't messed it up
And I'm really happy
BRUSH
so am I

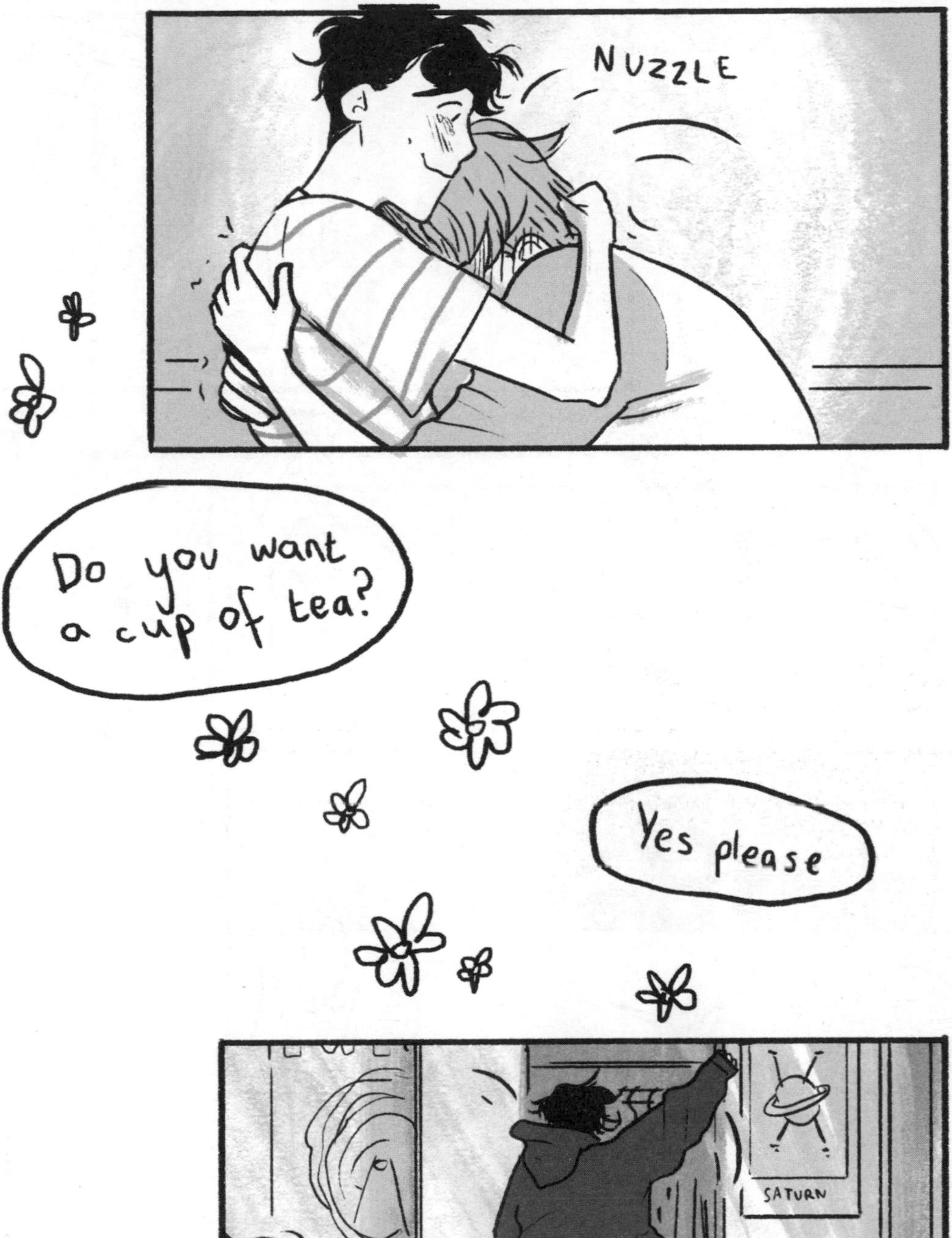
NUZZLE
Do you want a cup of tea?
Yes please
SATURN

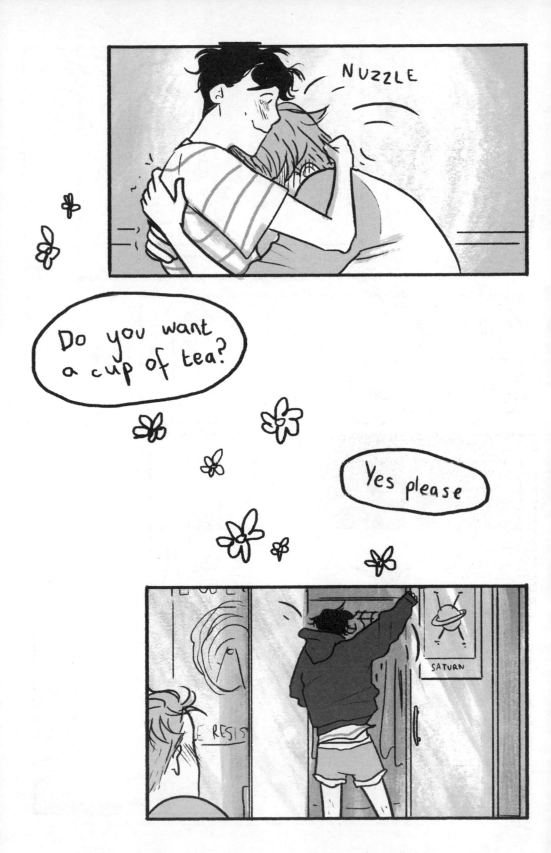

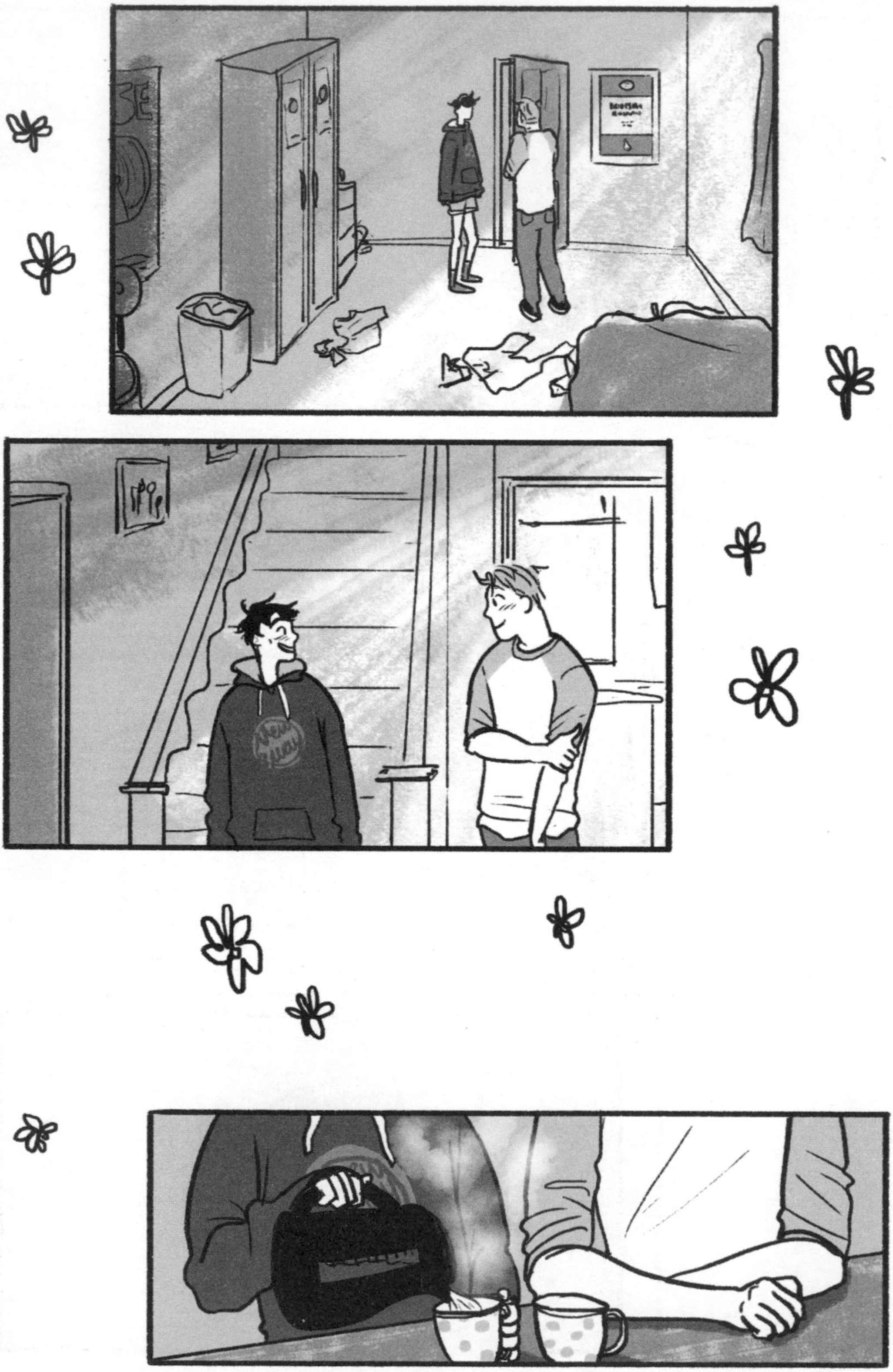

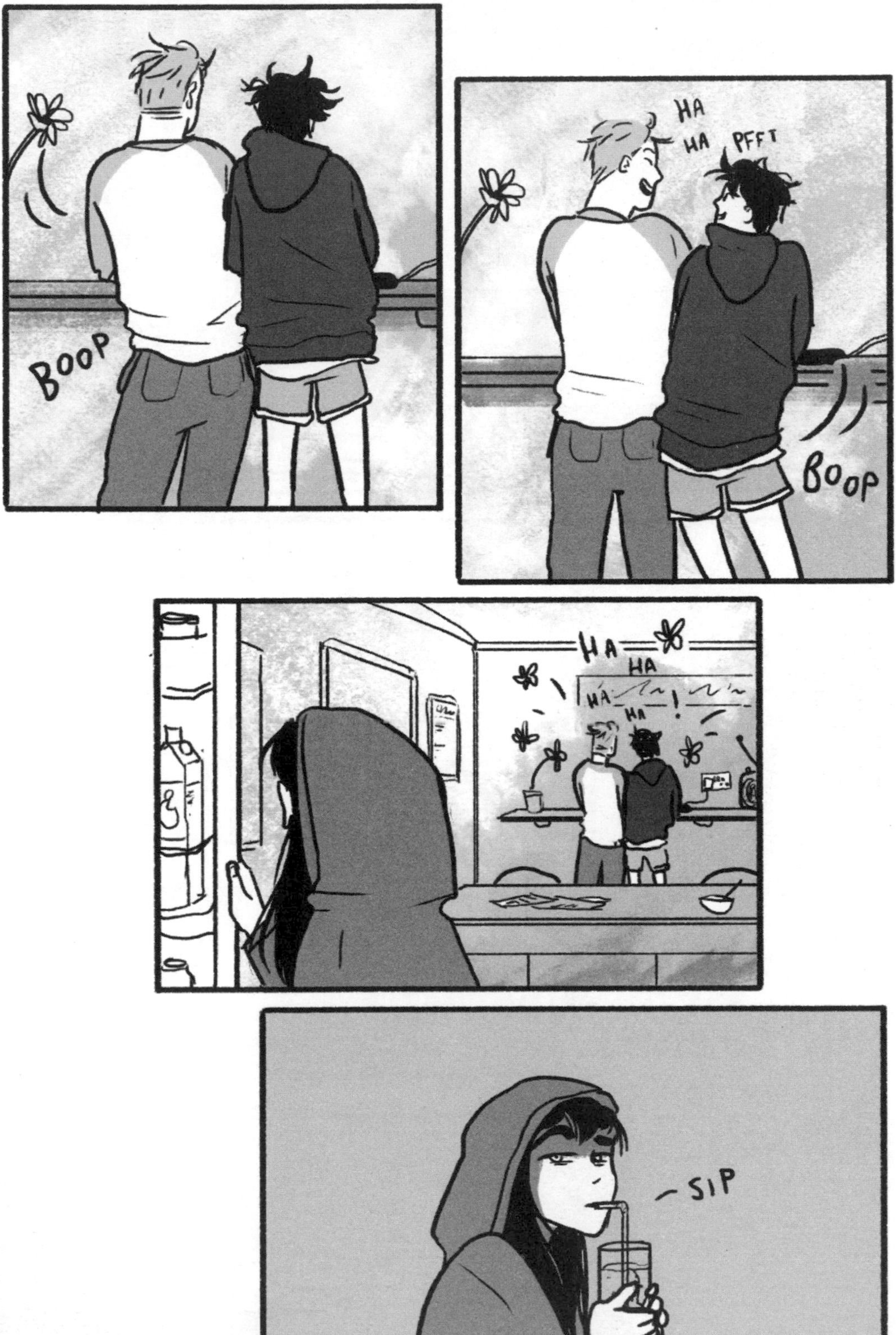
BOOP
HA
HA
PFFT
BOOP
HA
HA
HA
HA
SIP

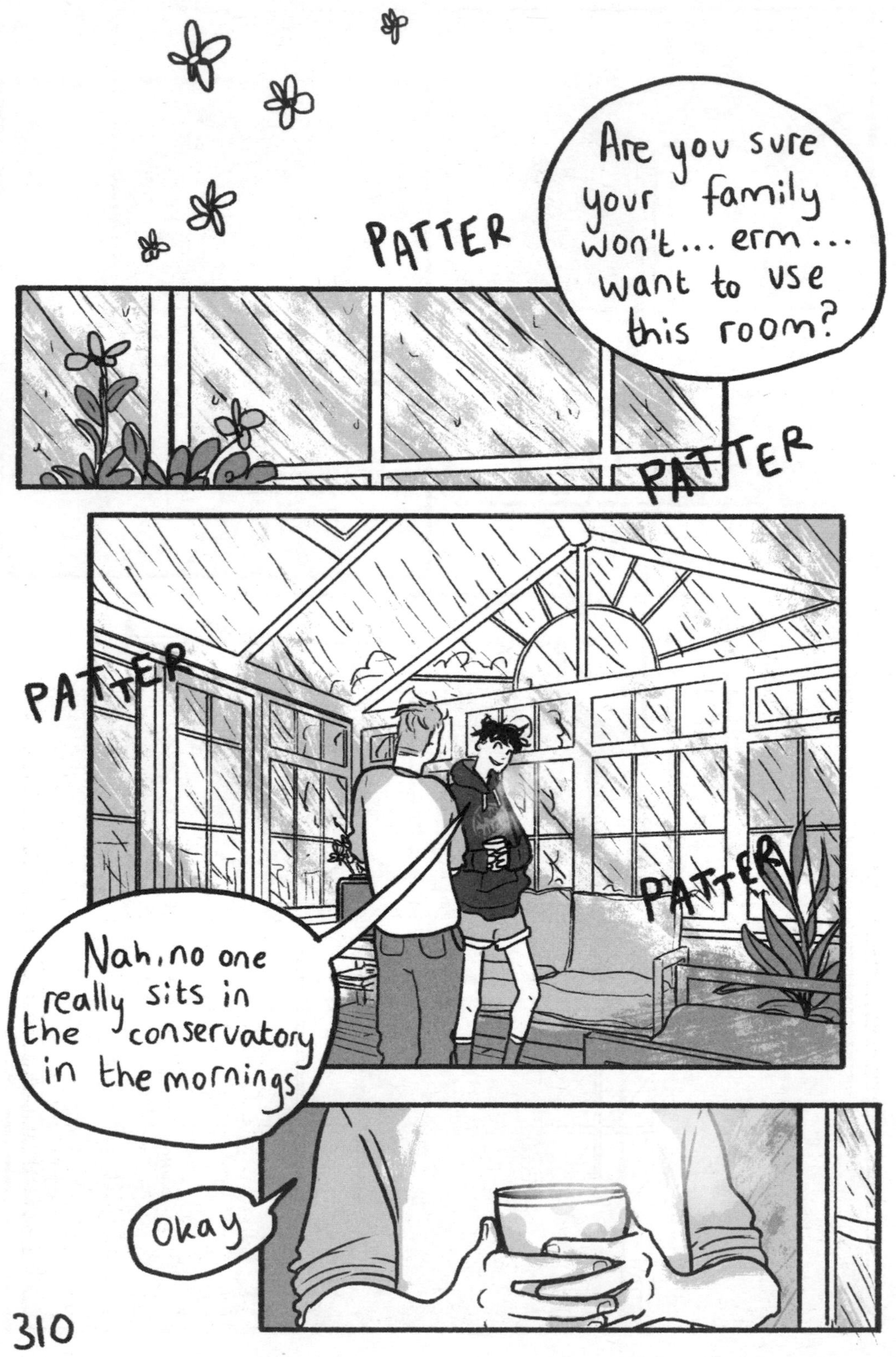
PATTER
Are you sure your family won't... erm... want to use this room?
PATTER
PATTER
PATTER
Nah, no one really sits in the conservatory in the mornings
Okay

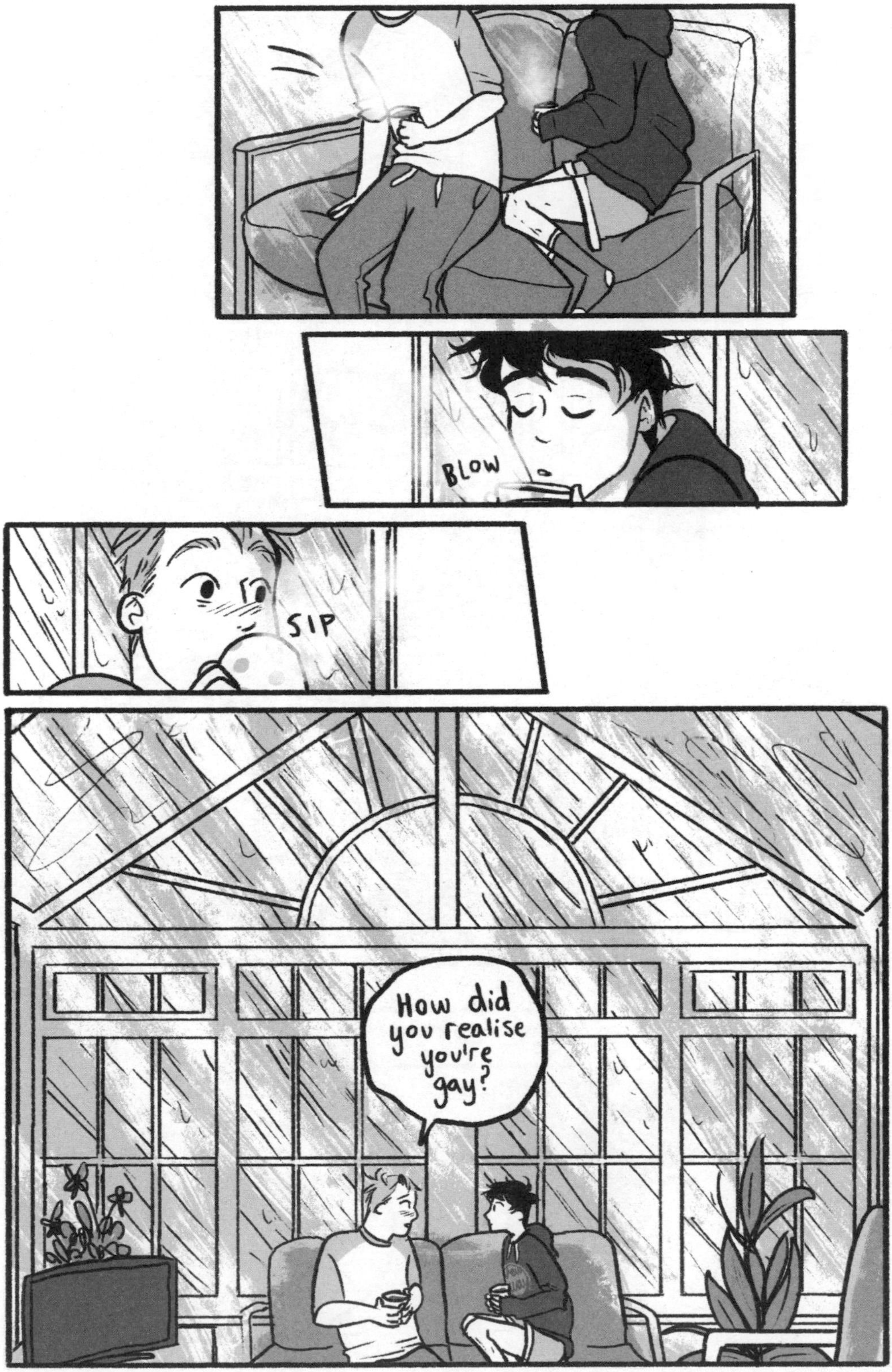
BLOW
SIP
How did you realise you're gay?

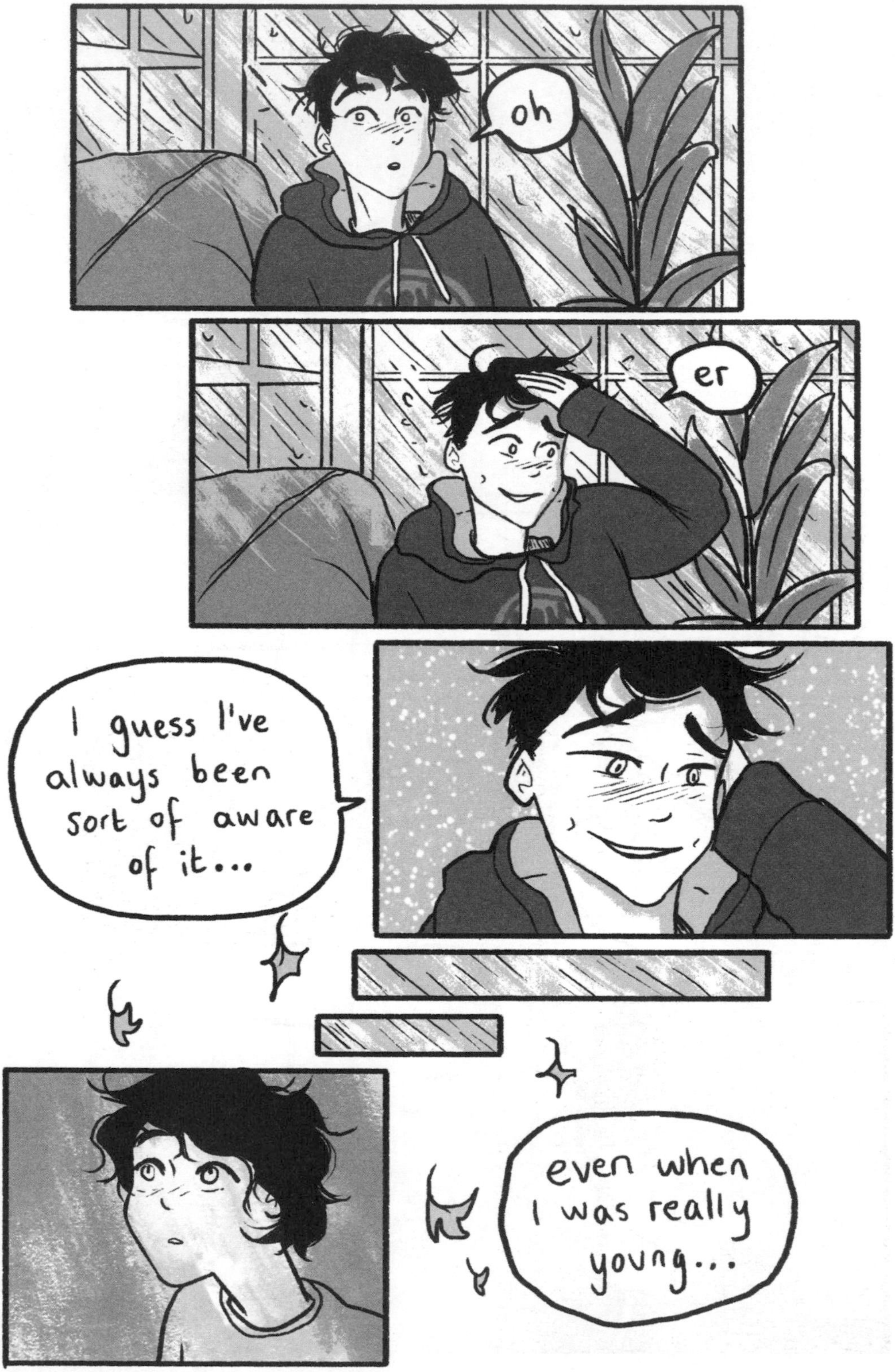
oh
er
I guess I've always been sort of aware of it...
even when I was really young...

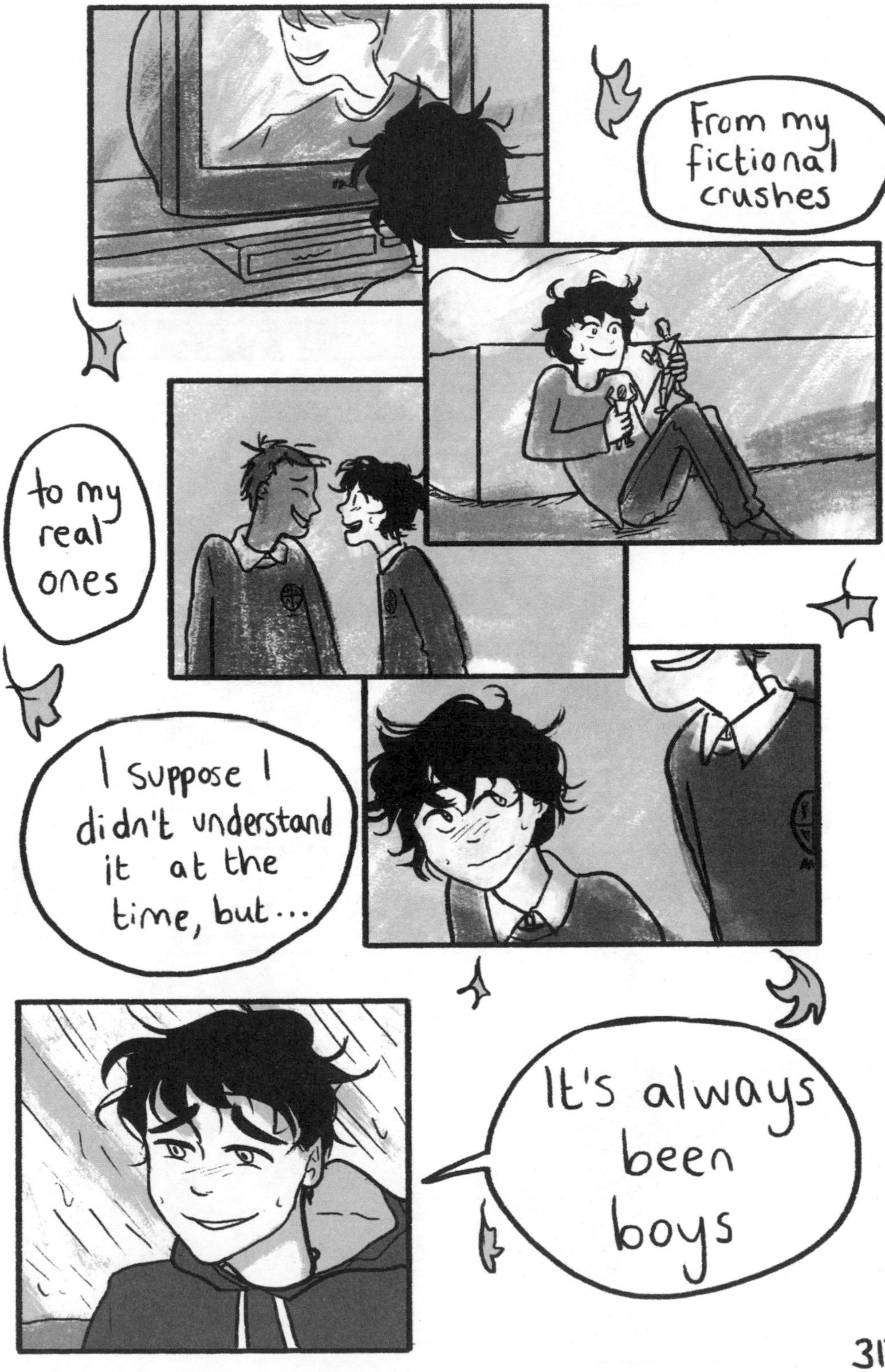
From my fictional crushes
to my real ones
I suppose I didn't understand it at the time, but...
It's always been boys

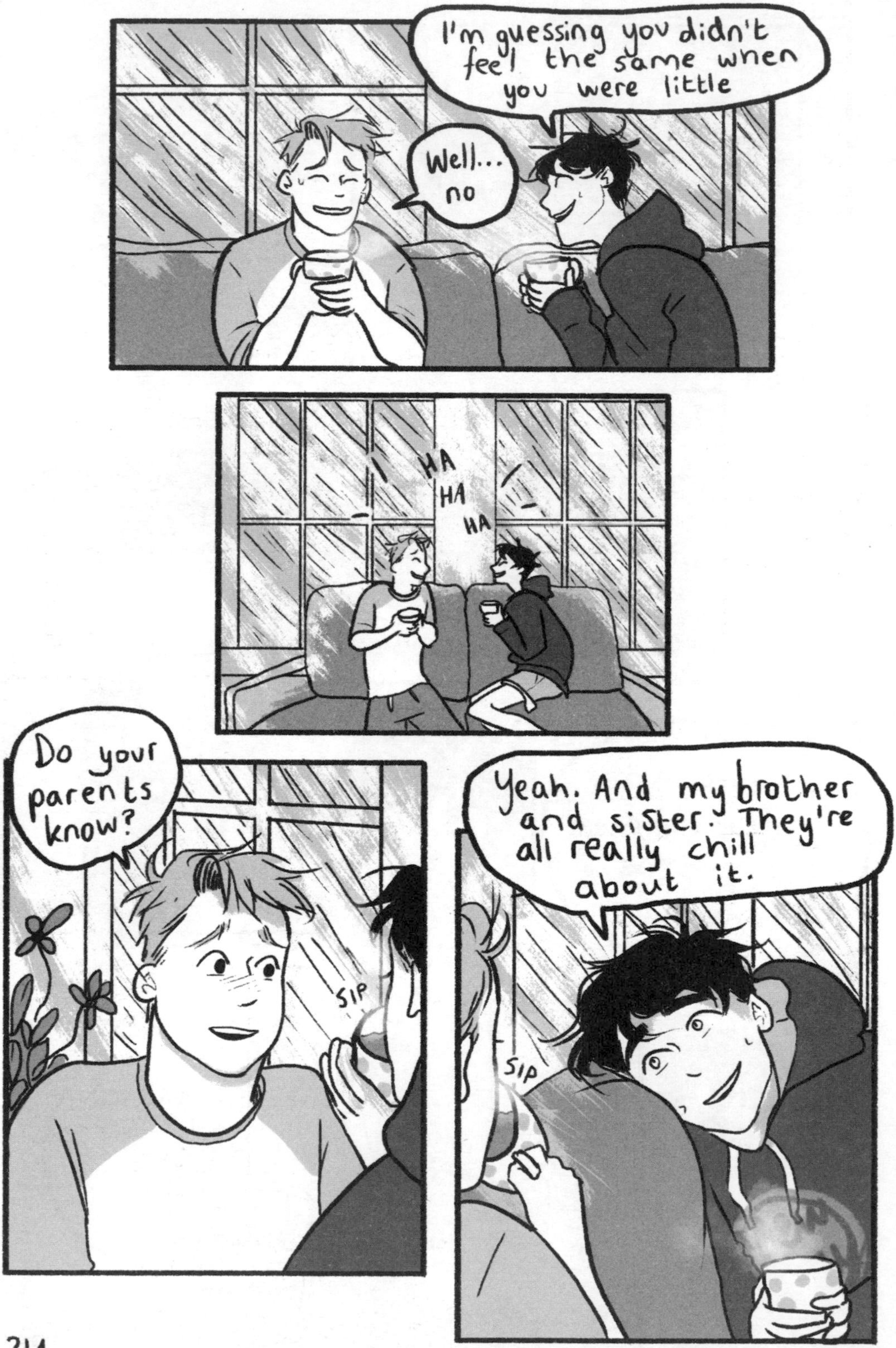
I'm guessing you didn't feel the same when you were little
Well... no
HA HA HA
Do your parents know?
SIP
Yeah. And my brother and sister. They're all really chill about it.
SIP

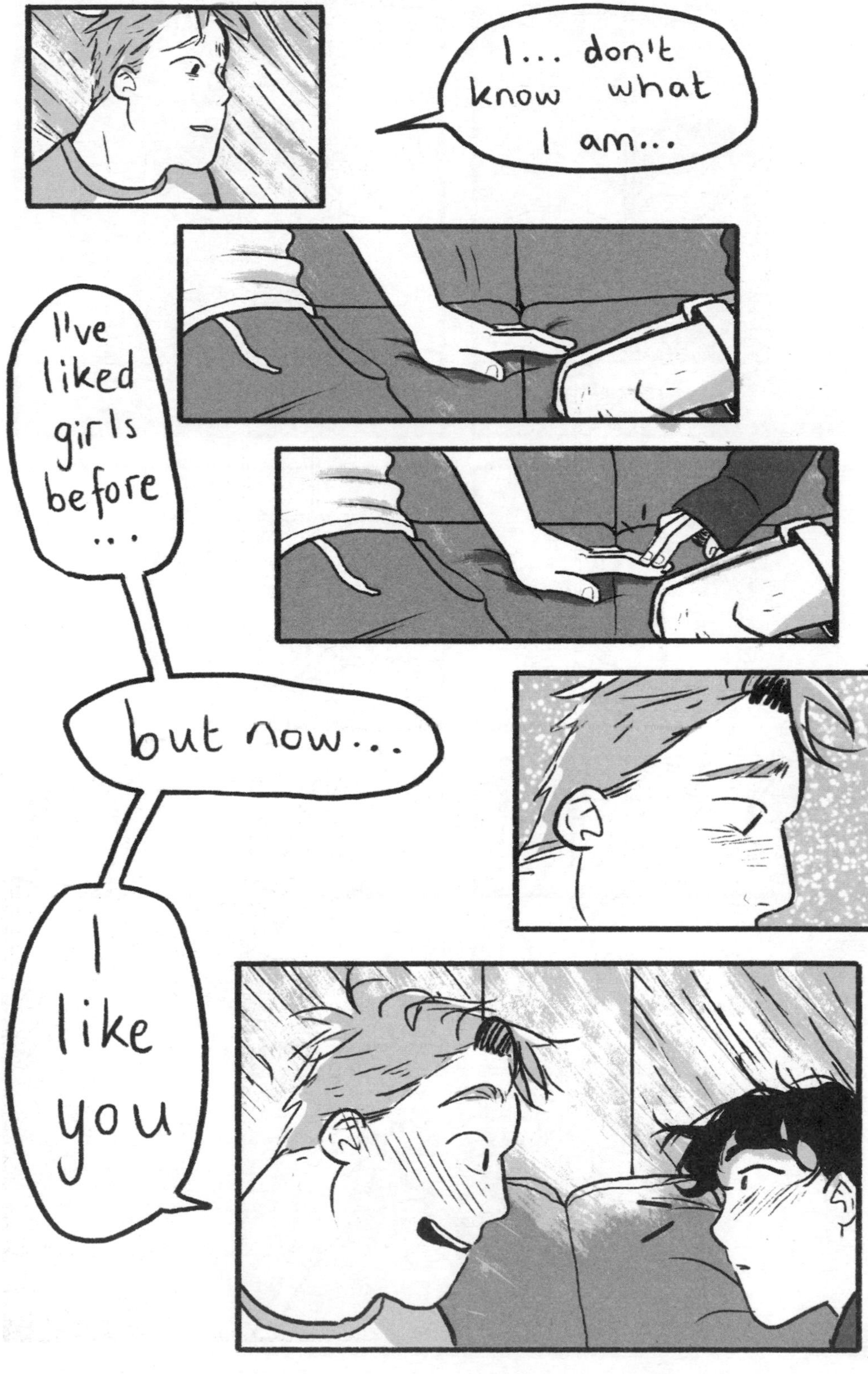
I... don't know what I am...
I've liked girls before...
but now...
I like you

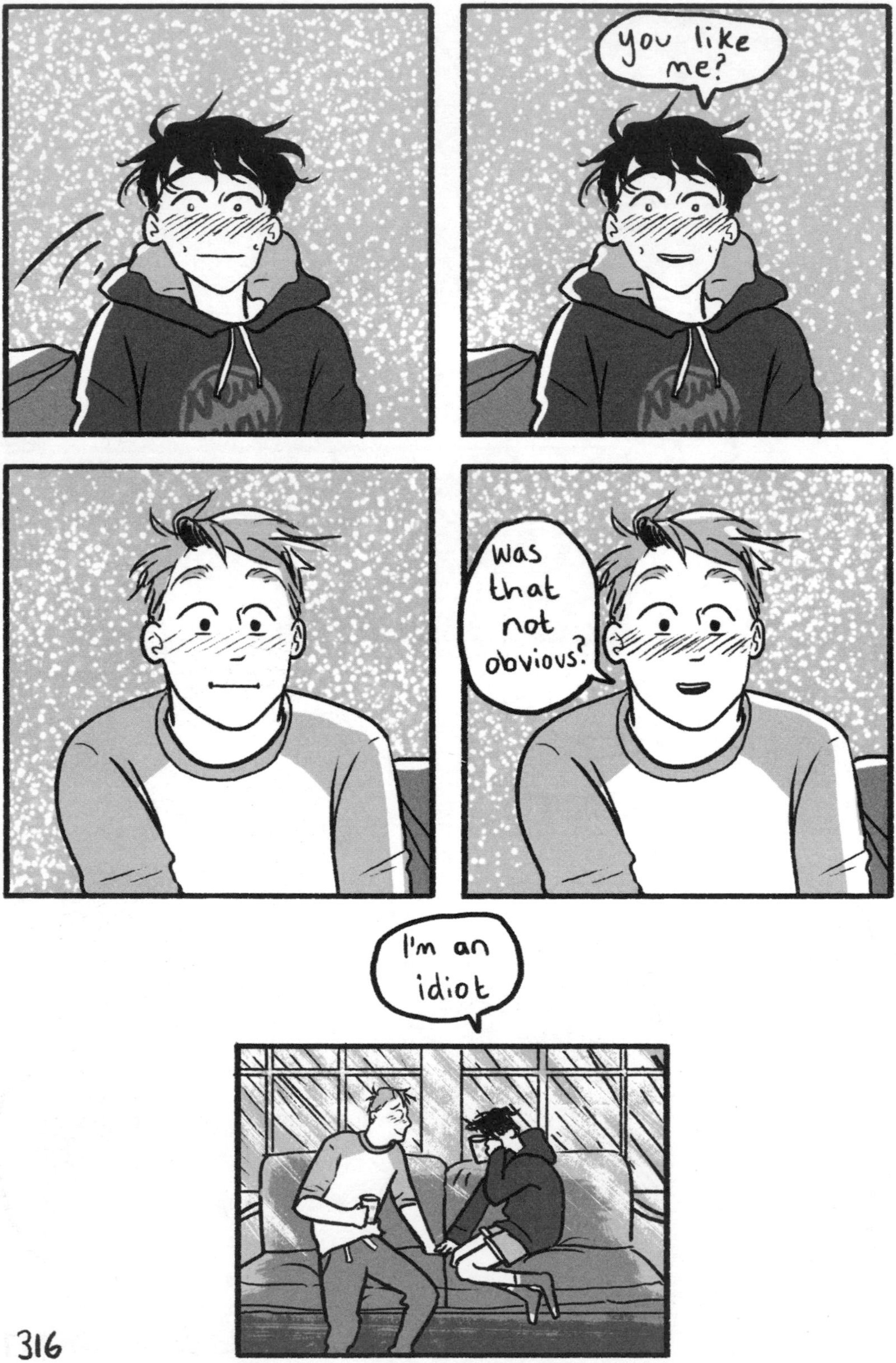
you like me?
Was that not obvious?
I'm an idiot

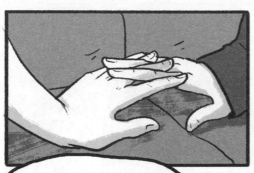

I thought... I just really liked you as a friend... a **best** friend... because, like, I want to hang out with you all the time and I just love everything about you...

but I kept wanting to... I don't know... hug you and hold your hand

and then yesterday, when you suggested it, I- I really wanted to kiss you

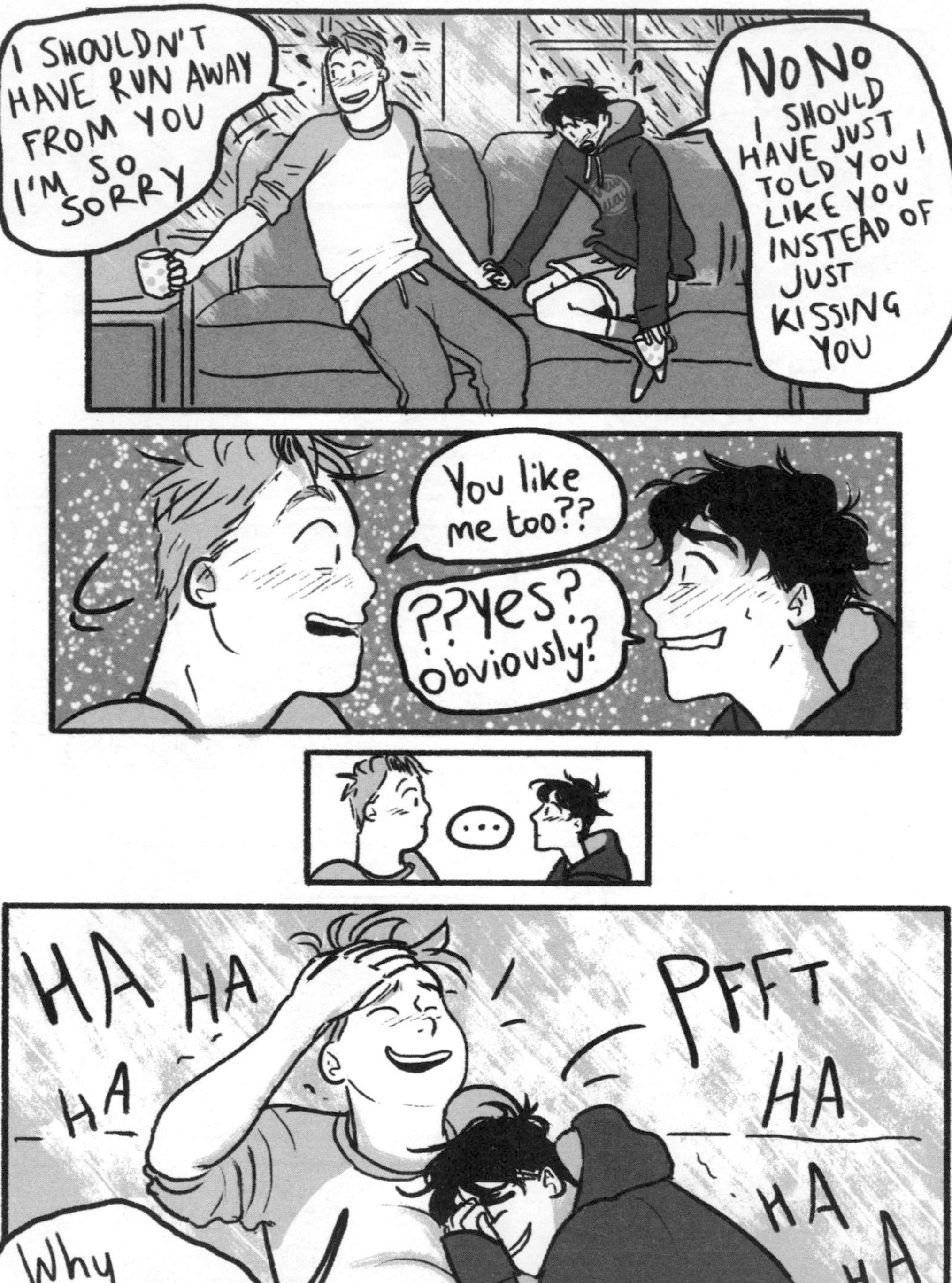
I SHOULDN'T HAVE RUN AWAY FROM YOU I'M SO SORRY
NO NO I SHOULD HAVE JUST TOLD YOU I LIKE YOU INSTEAD OF JUST KISSING YOU
You like me too??
??yes? obviously?
...
HA HA HA
PFFT HA HA HA
Why are we like this??

FSSSSH

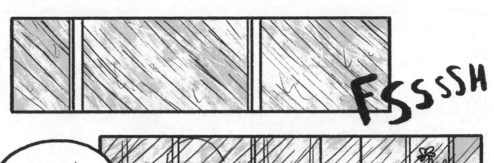

I would have said something sooner, but I convinced myself you were straight.

I don't know what I am now

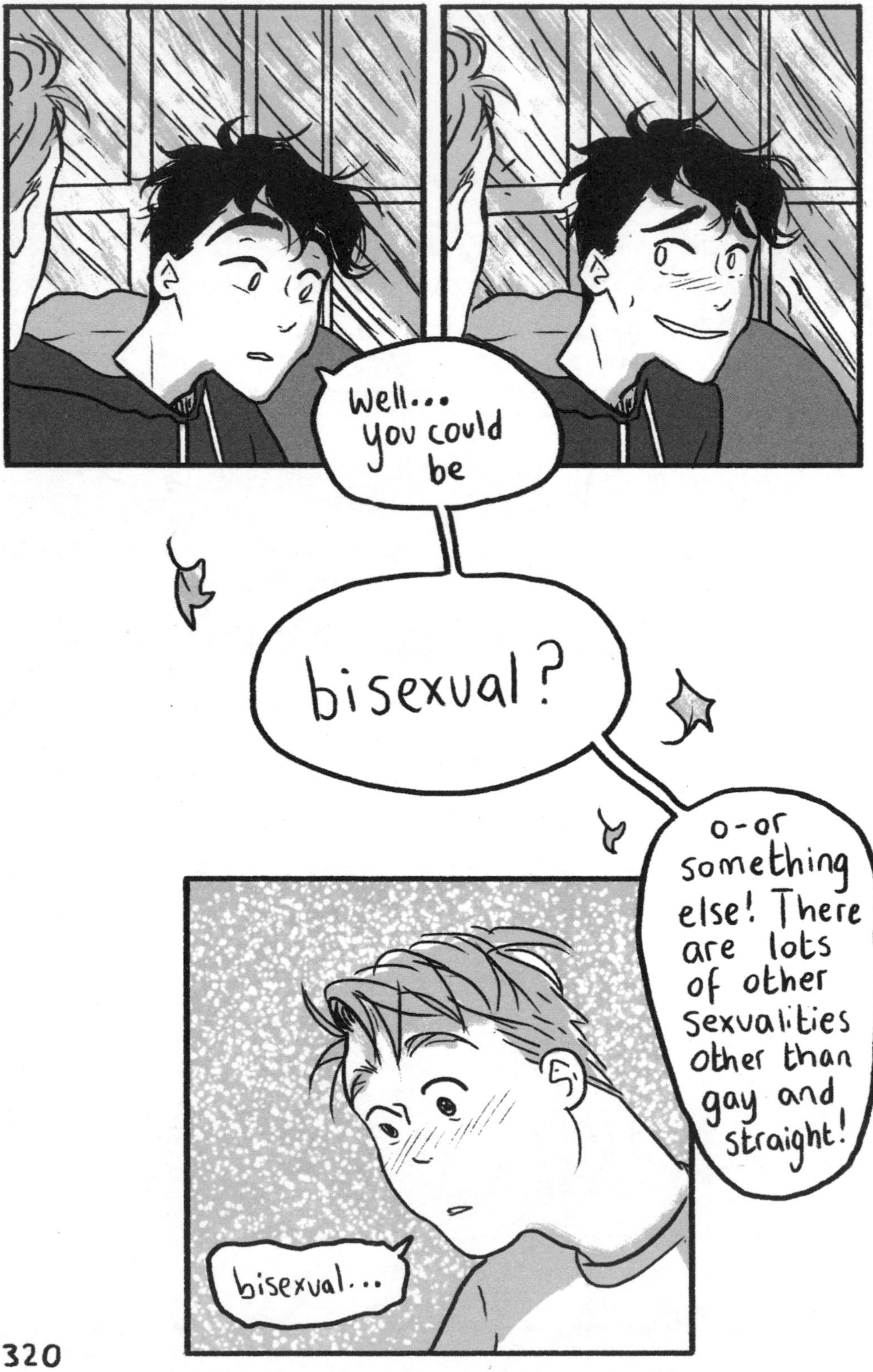
Well...
you could
be
bisexual?
o-or
something
else! There
are lots
of other
sexualities
other than
gay and
straight!
bisexual...

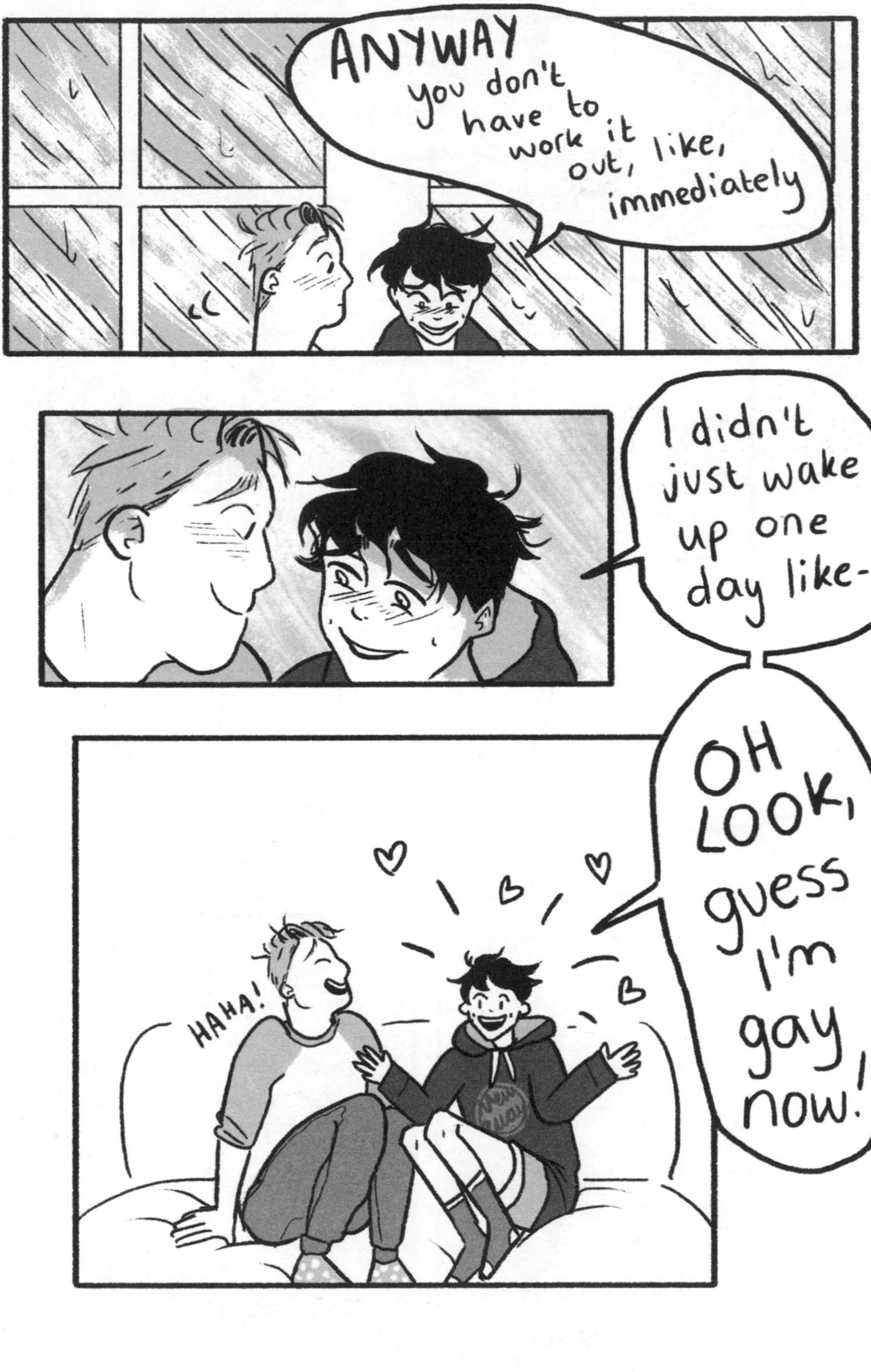
ANYWAY you don't have to work it out, like, immediately
I didn't just wake up one day like-
OH LOOK, guess I'm gay now!
HAHA!

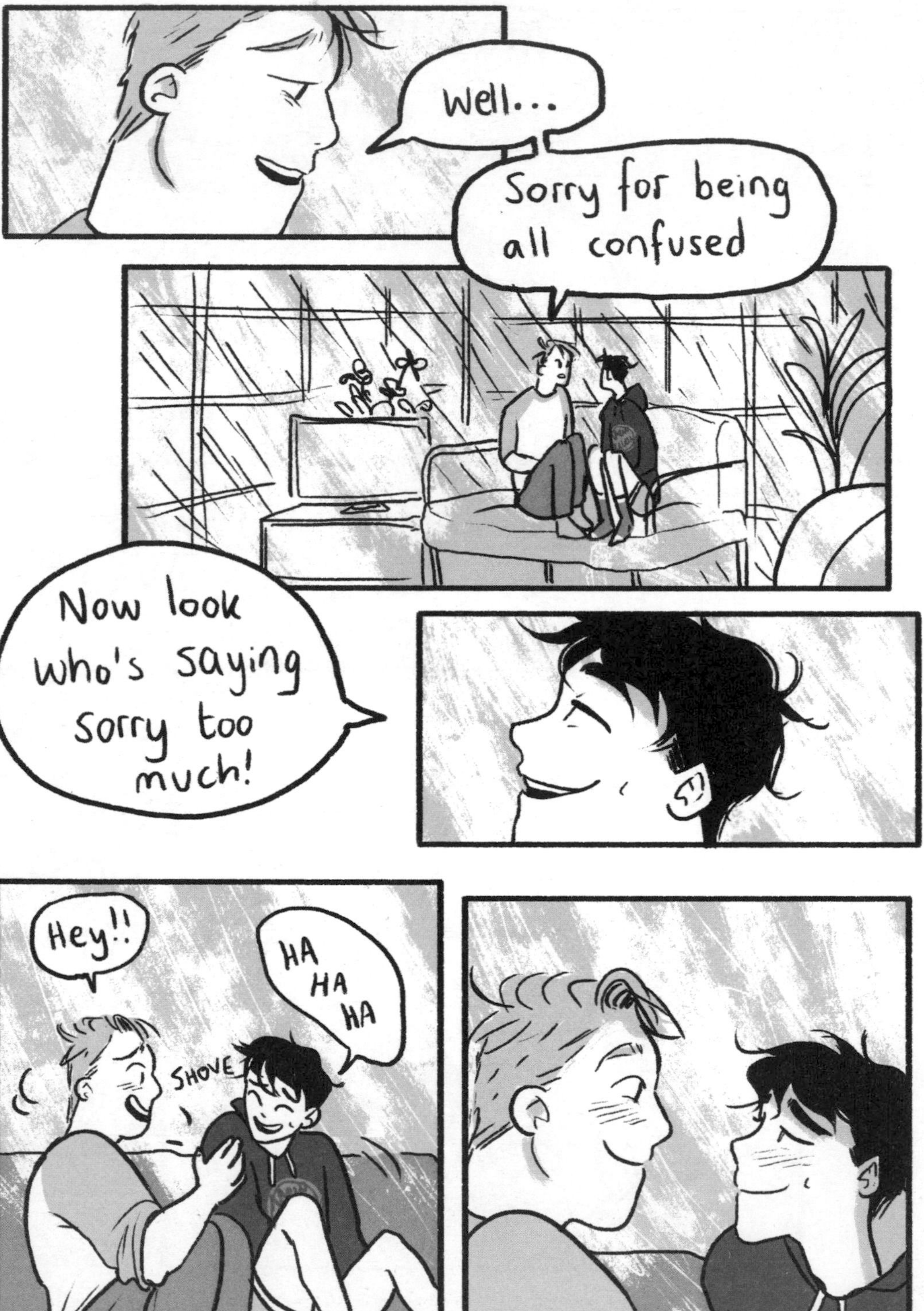
Well...
Sorry for being all confused
Now look who's saying sorry too much!
Hey!!
HA HA HA
SHOVE

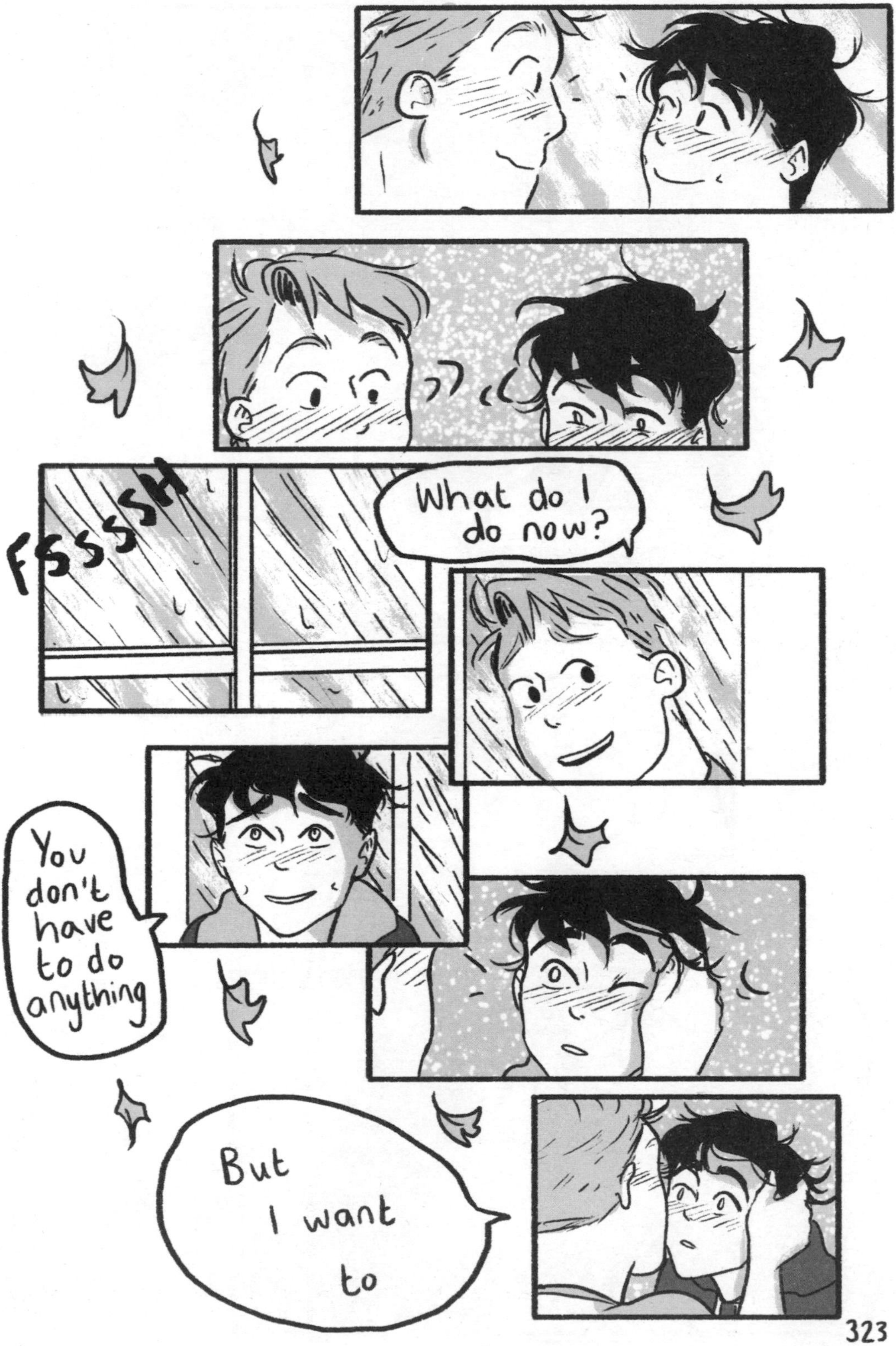
FSSSSH
What do I do now?
You don't have to do anything
But I want to

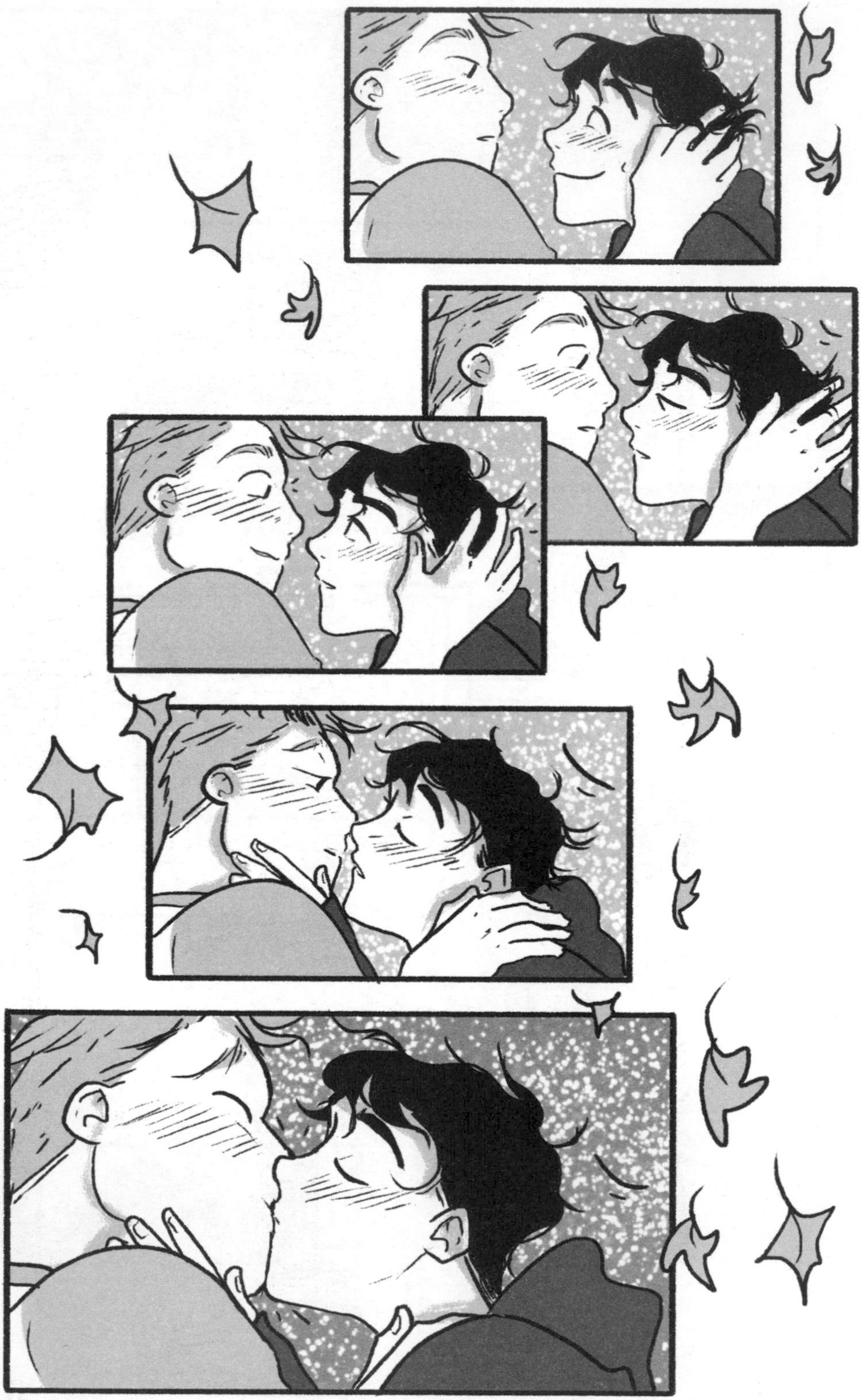

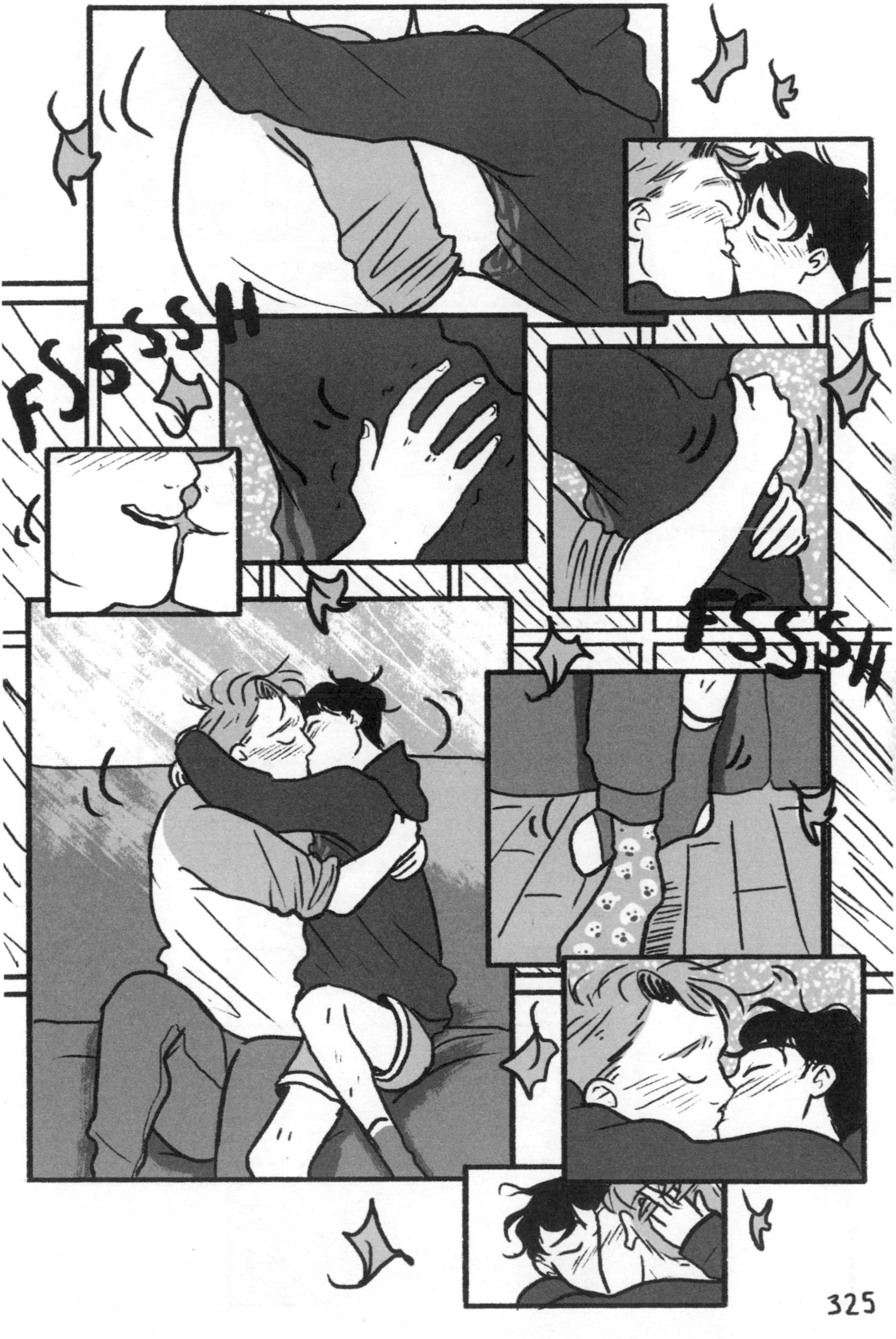
FSSSSH
FSSSH

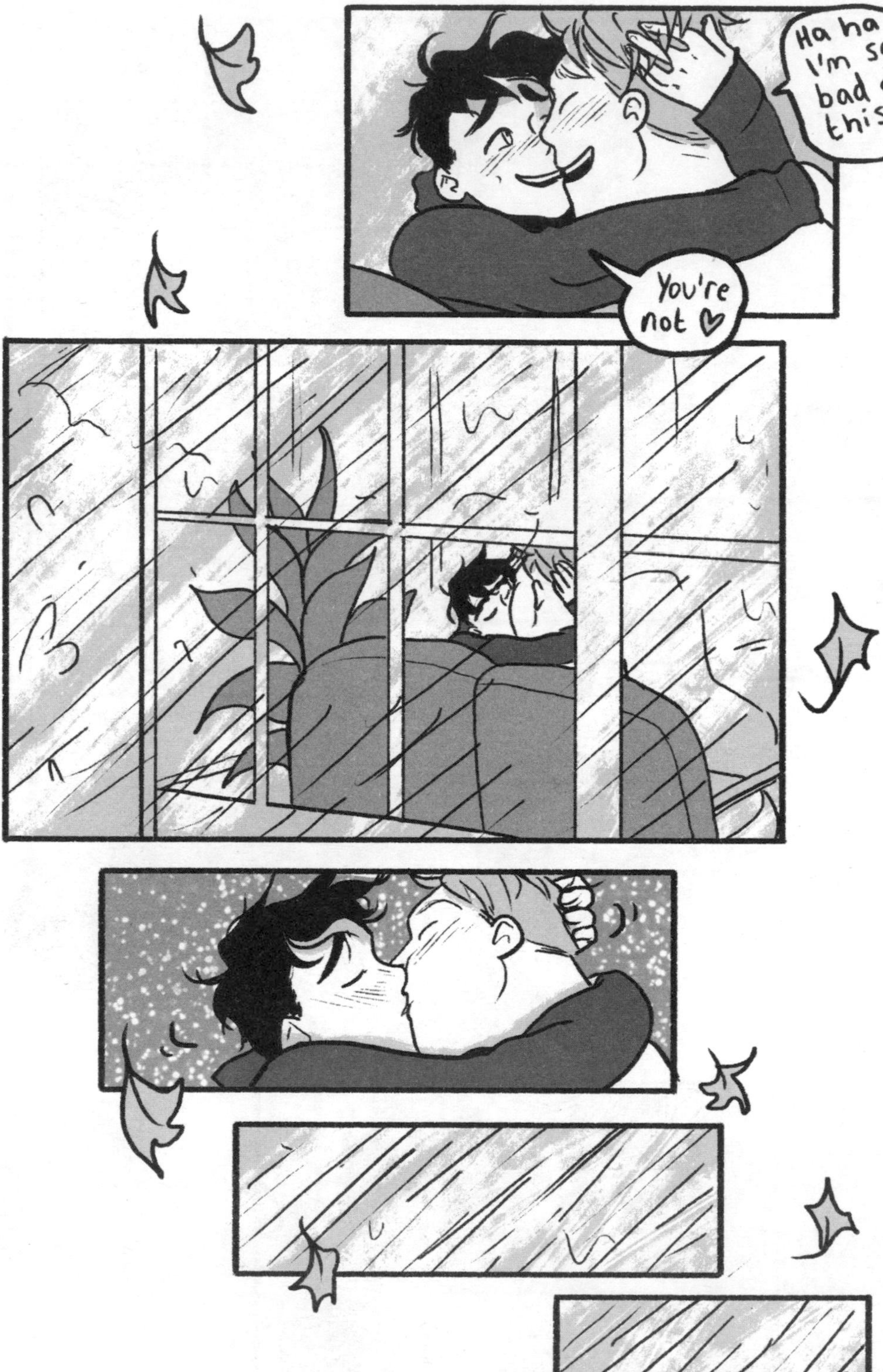
Ha ha I'm so bad at this
You're not ♥

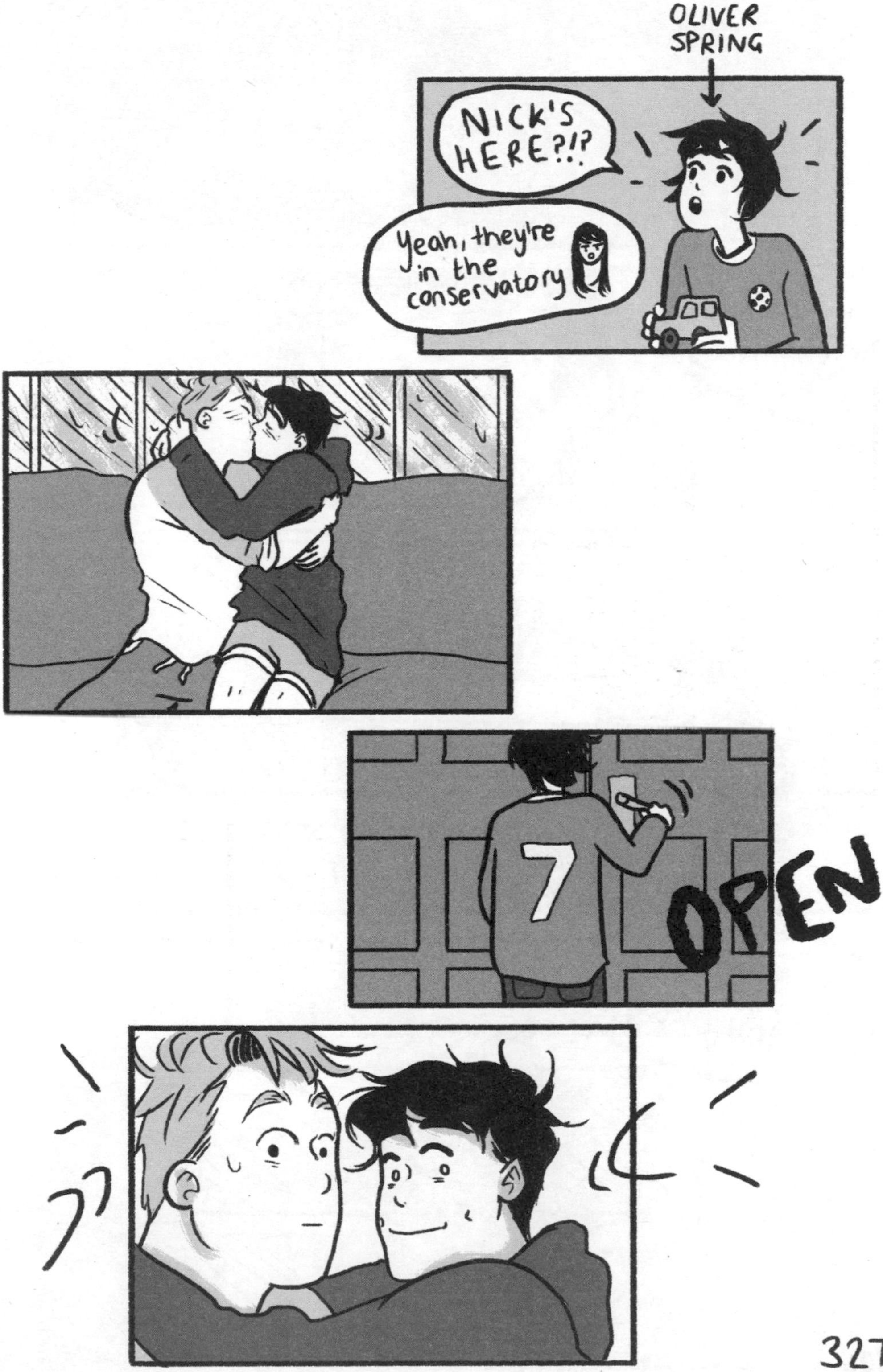
OLIVER SPRING
NICK'S HERE?!?
Yeah, they're in the conservatory
OPEN

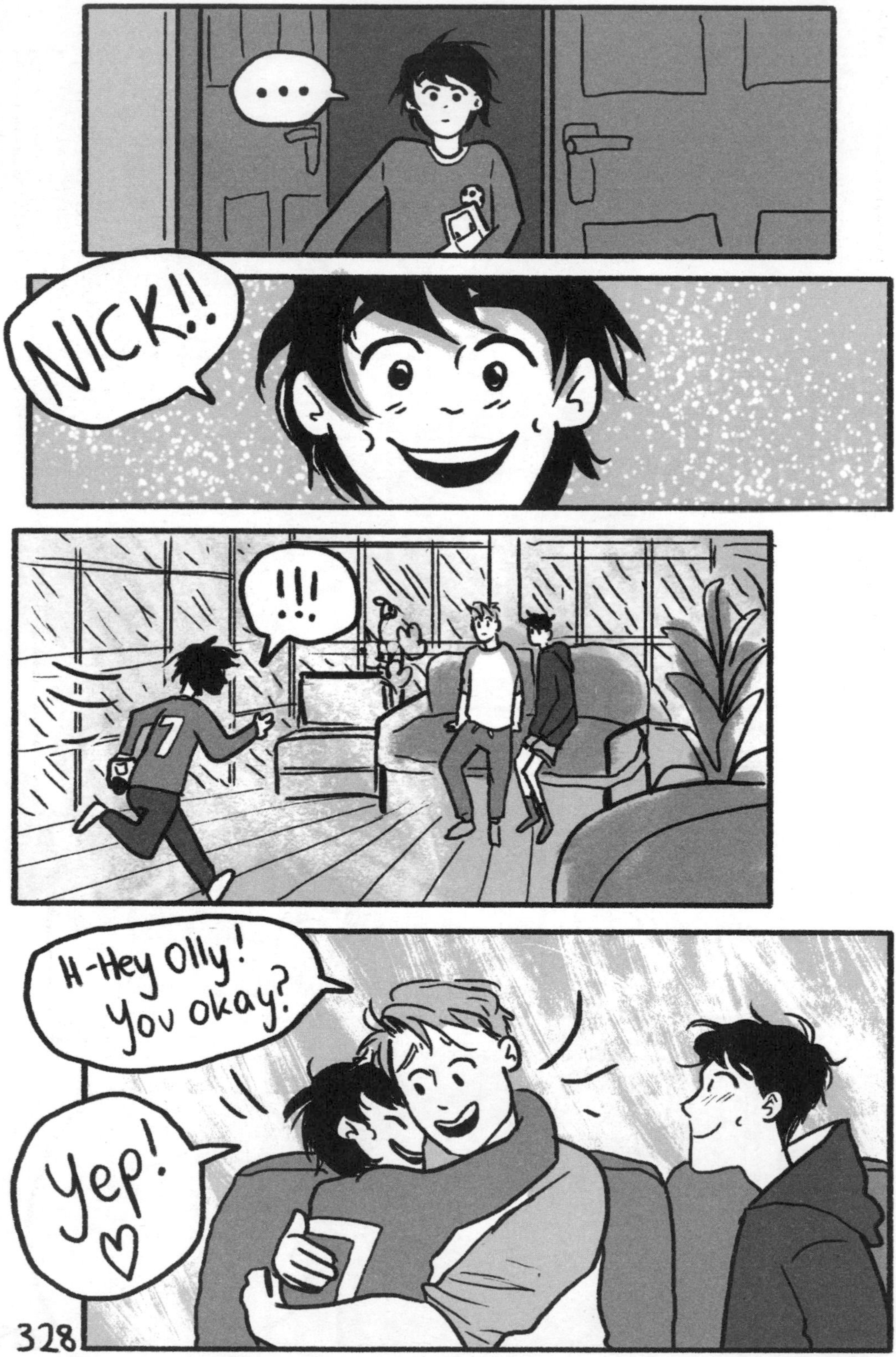
...
NICK!!
!!!
H-Hey Olly! You okay?
Yep! ♡

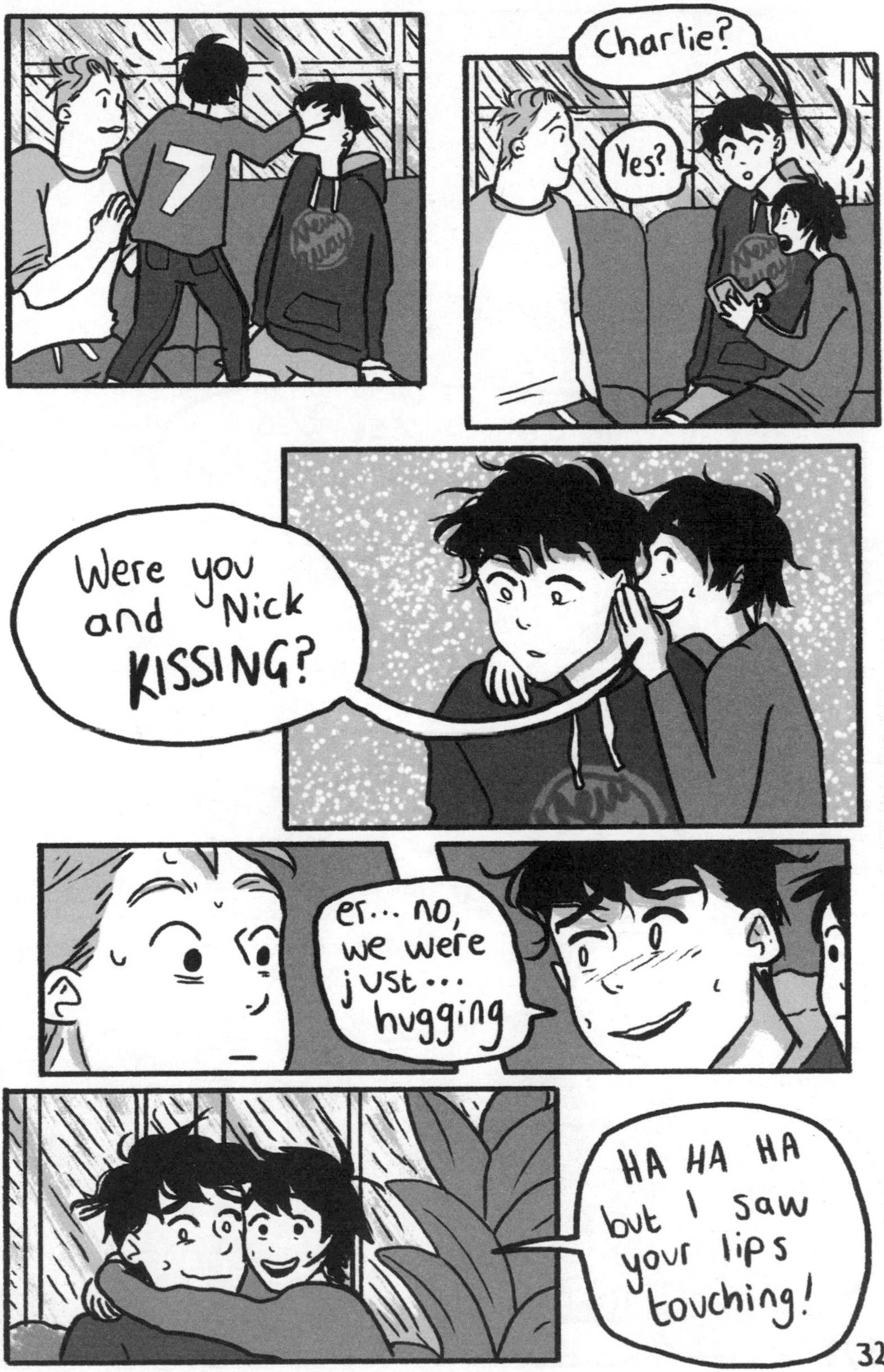
Charlie?
Yes?
Were you and Nick KISSING?
er... no, we were just... hugging
HA HA HA but I saw your lips touching!

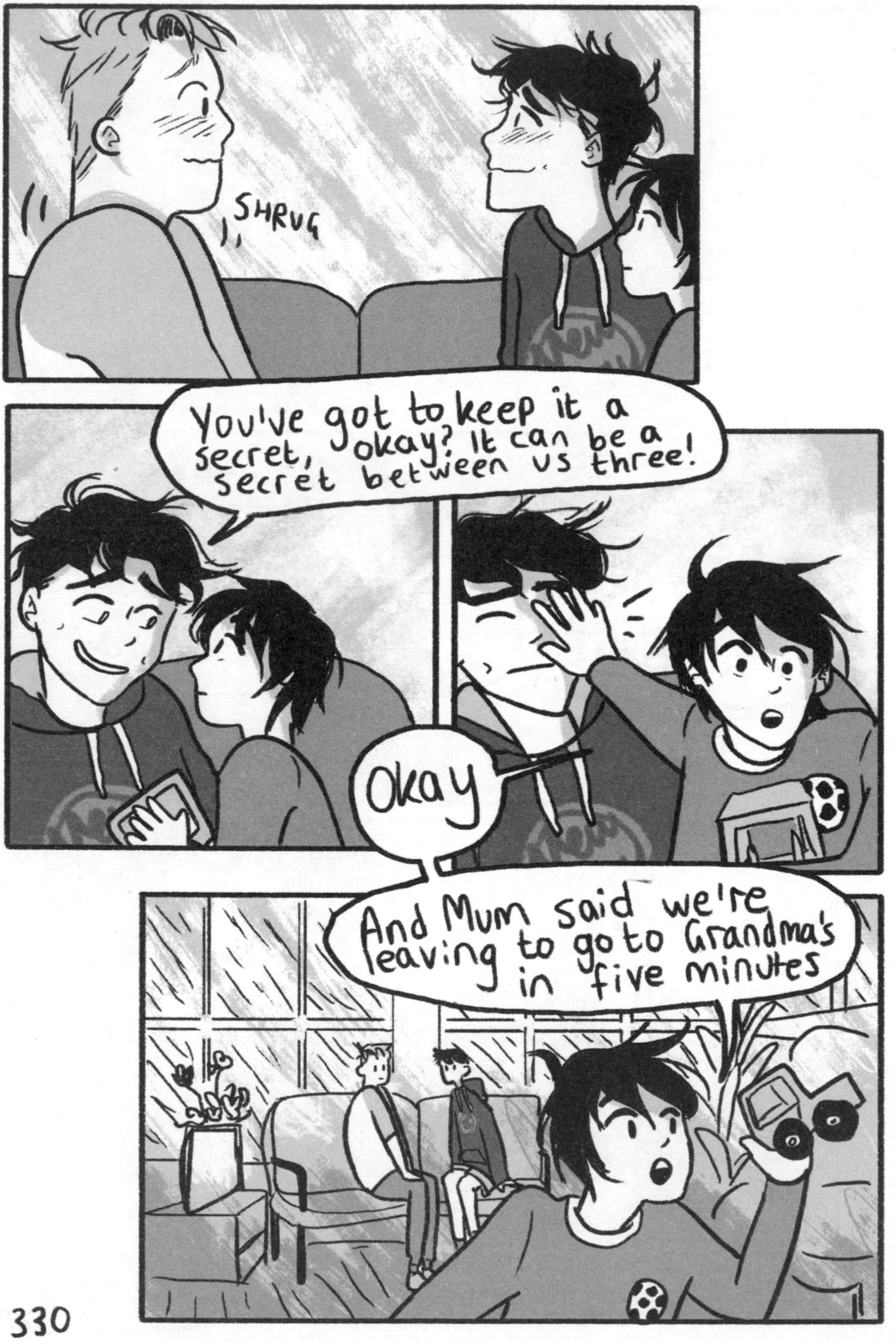
SHRUG
You've got to keep it a secret, okay? It can be a secret between us three!
Okay
And Mum said we're leaving to go to Grandma's in five minutes

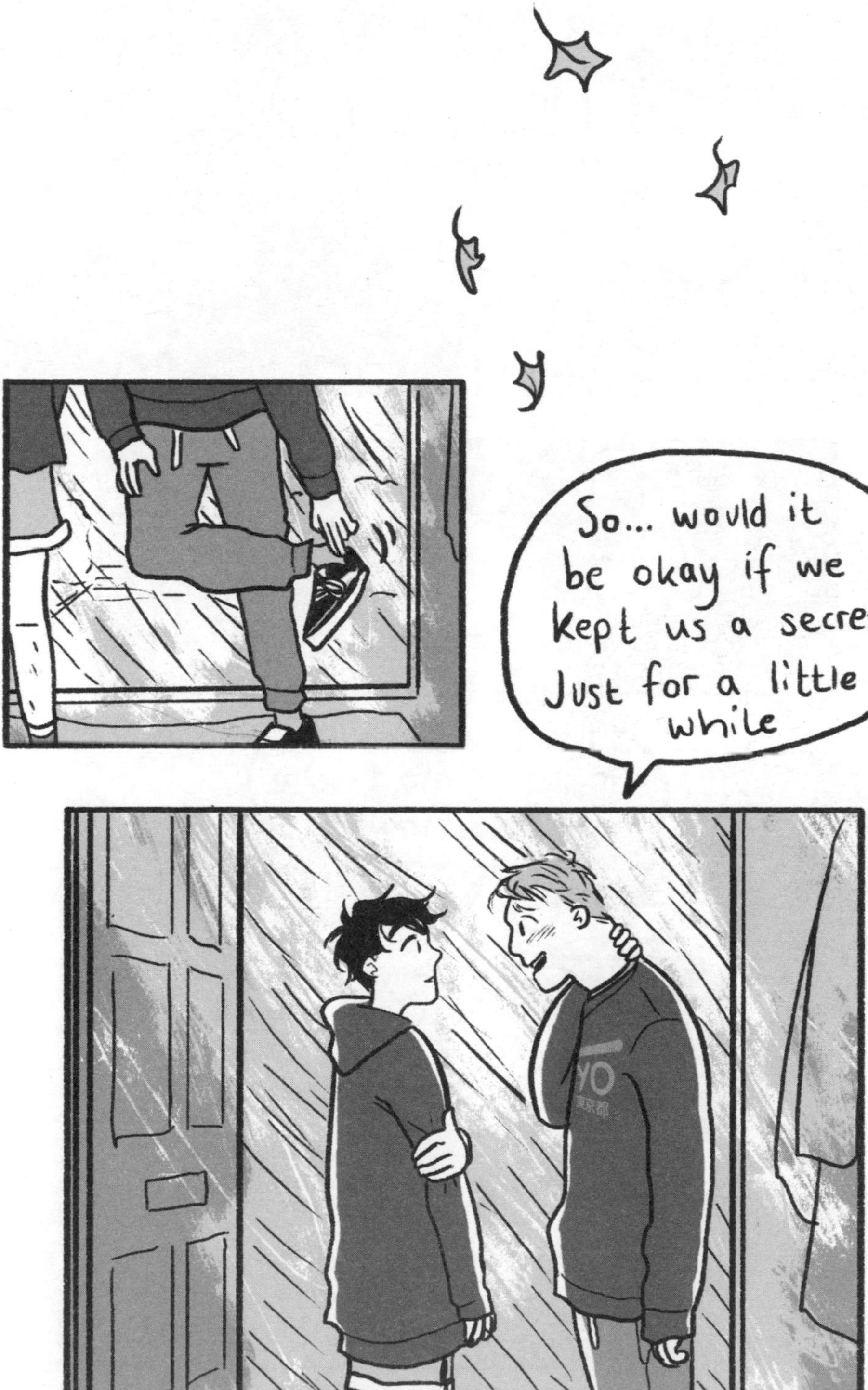
So... would it be okay if we kept us a secret? Just for a little while

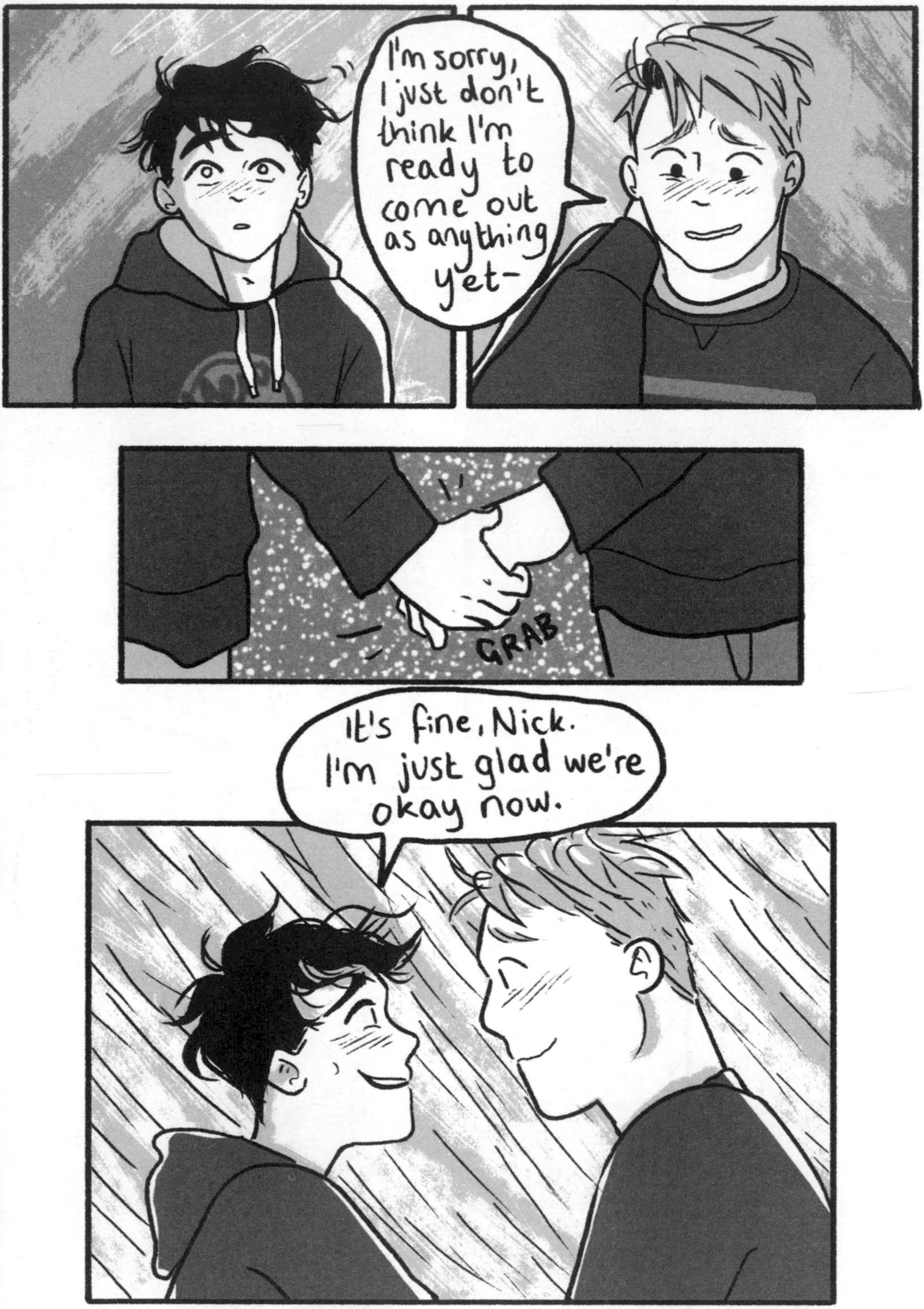
I'm sorry, I just don't think I'm ready to come out as anything yet-
GRAB
It's fine, Nick. I'm just glad we're okay now.

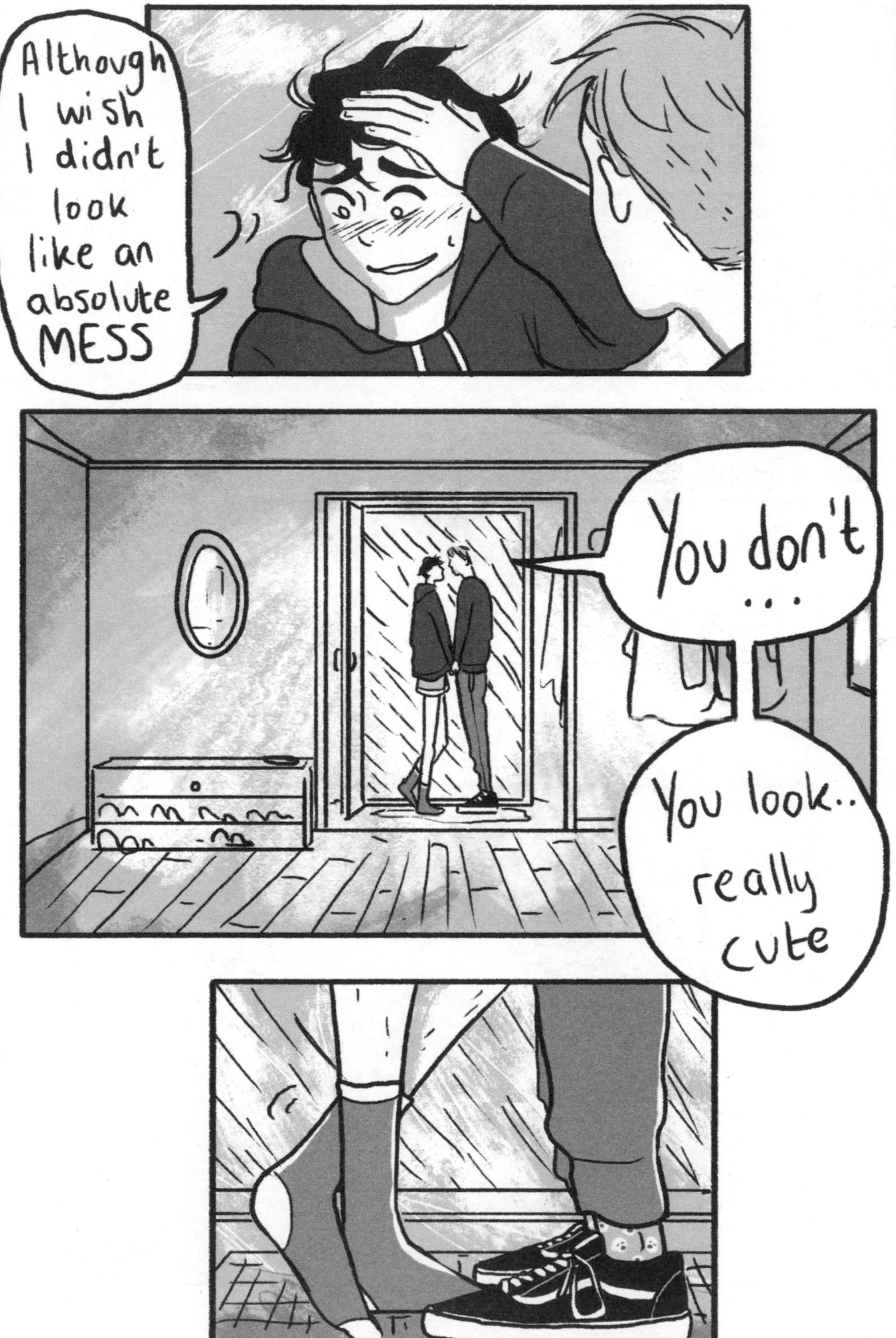
Although I wish I didn't look like an absolute MESS
You don't ...
You look.. really cute

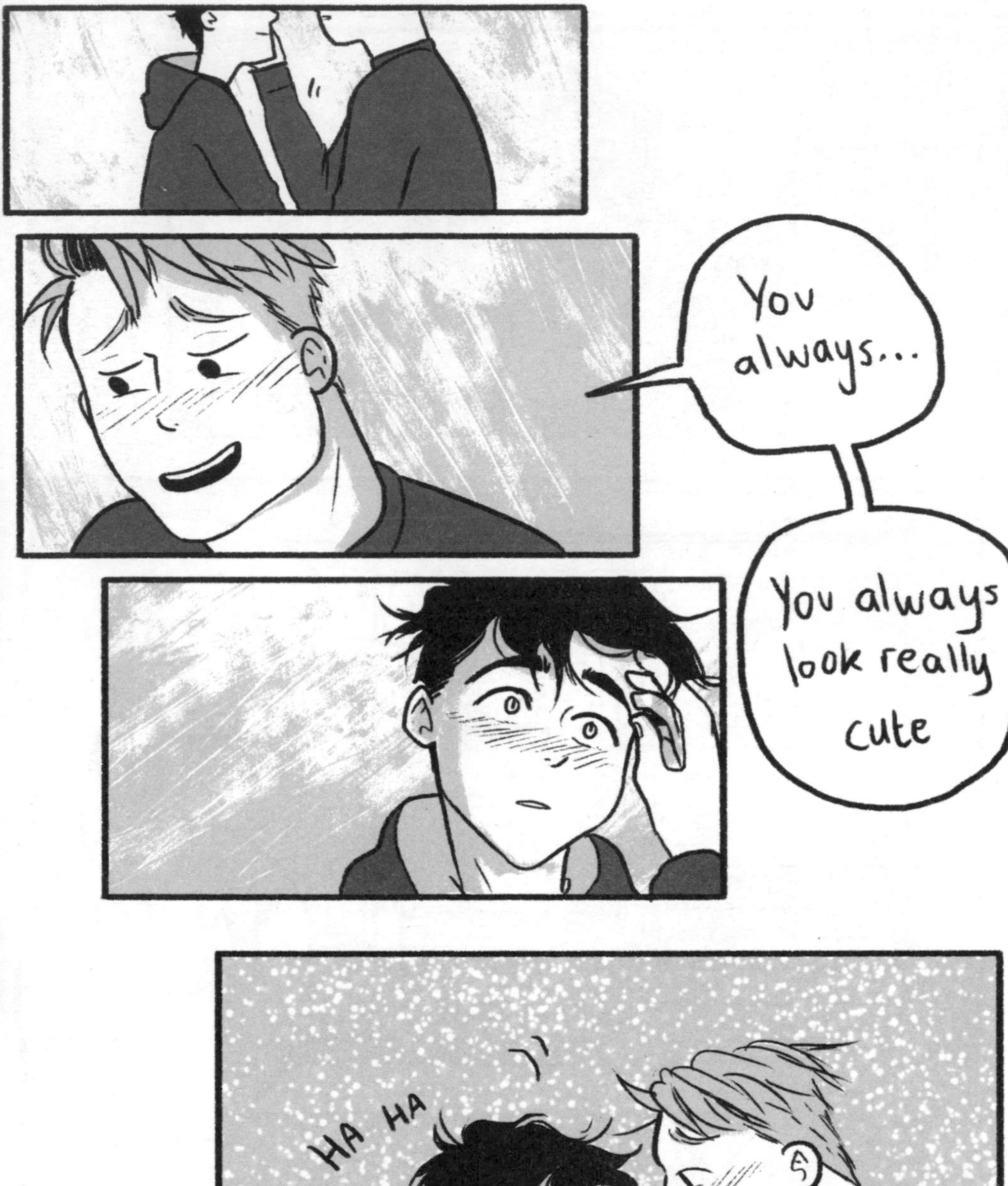
You always...
You always look really cute
HA HA HA

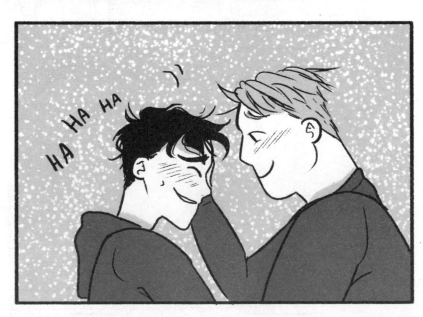

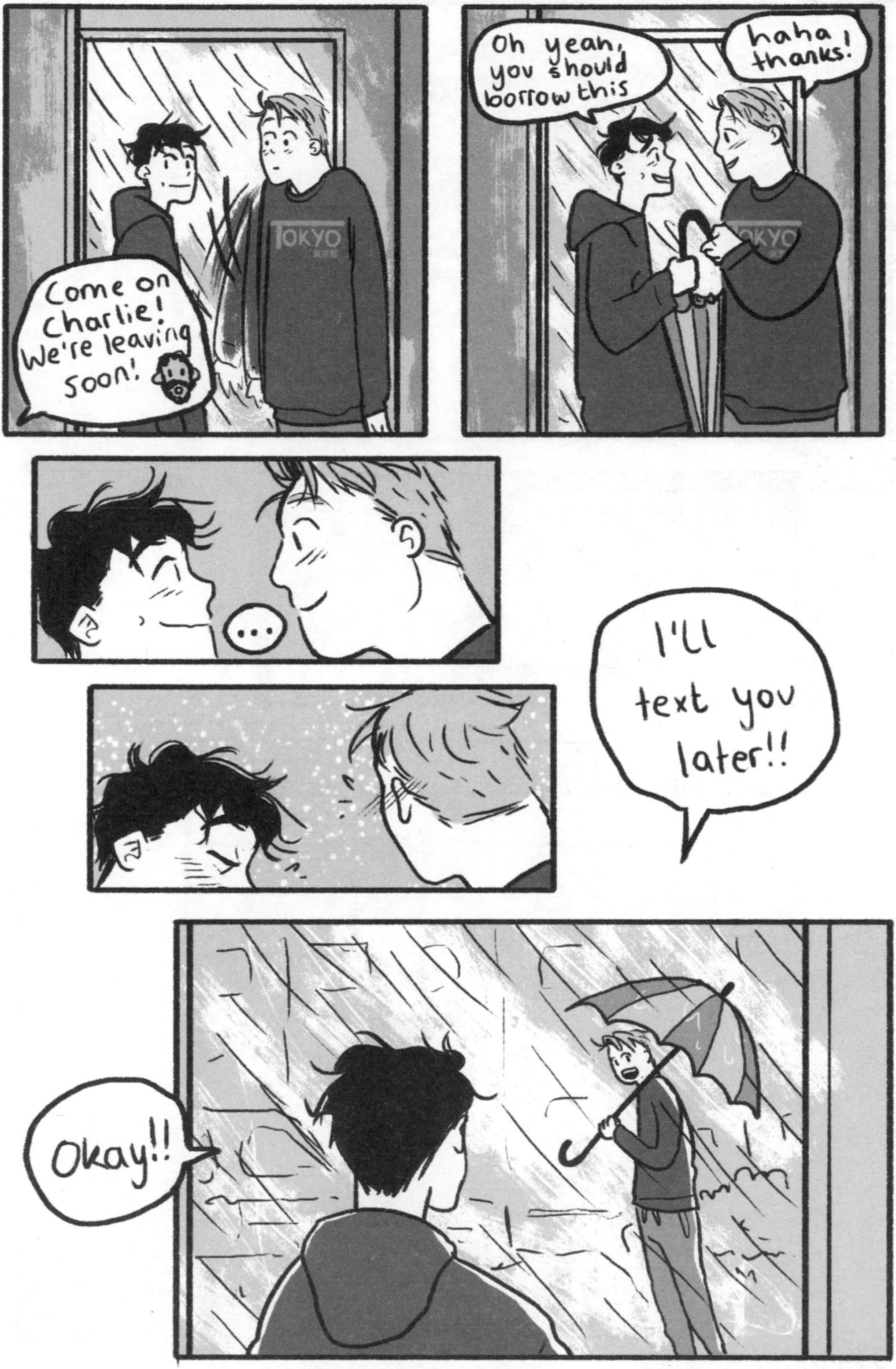
Come on Charlie! We're leaving soon!
Oh yeah, you should borrow this
haha thanks!
...
I'll text you later!!
Okay!!

PATTER

PATTER

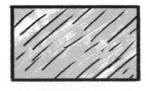

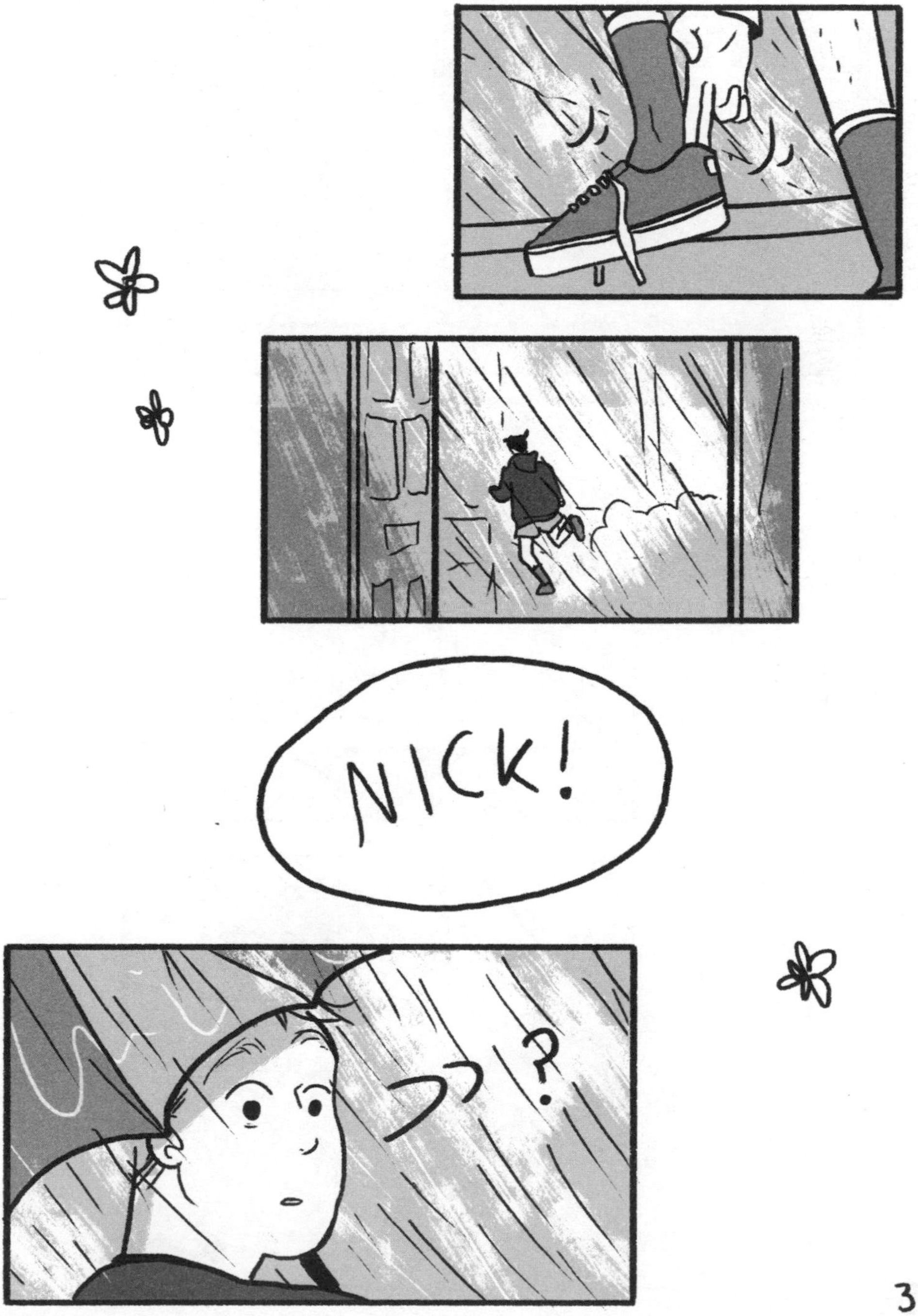
NICK!

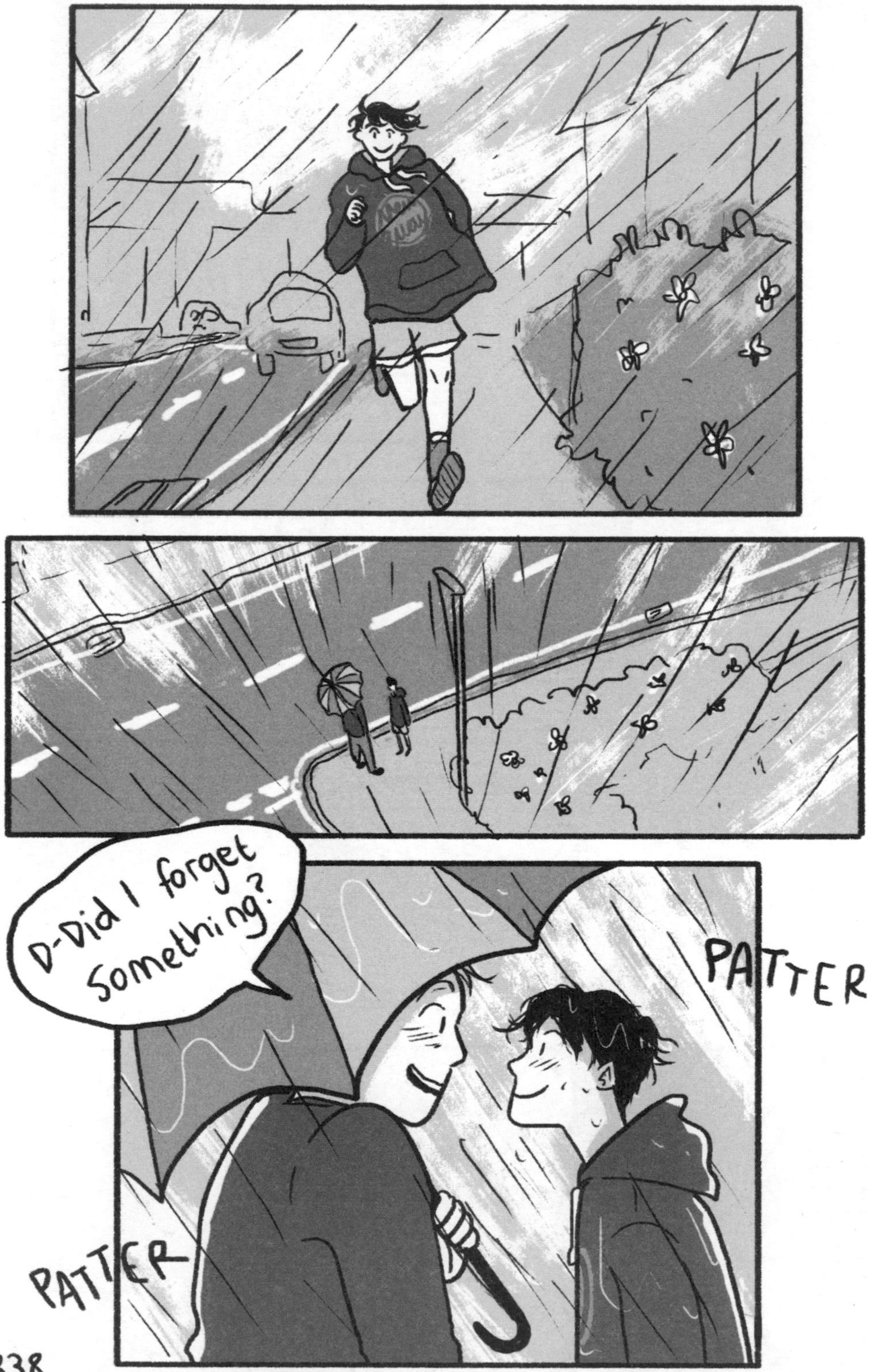
D-Did I forget something?
PATTER
PATTER

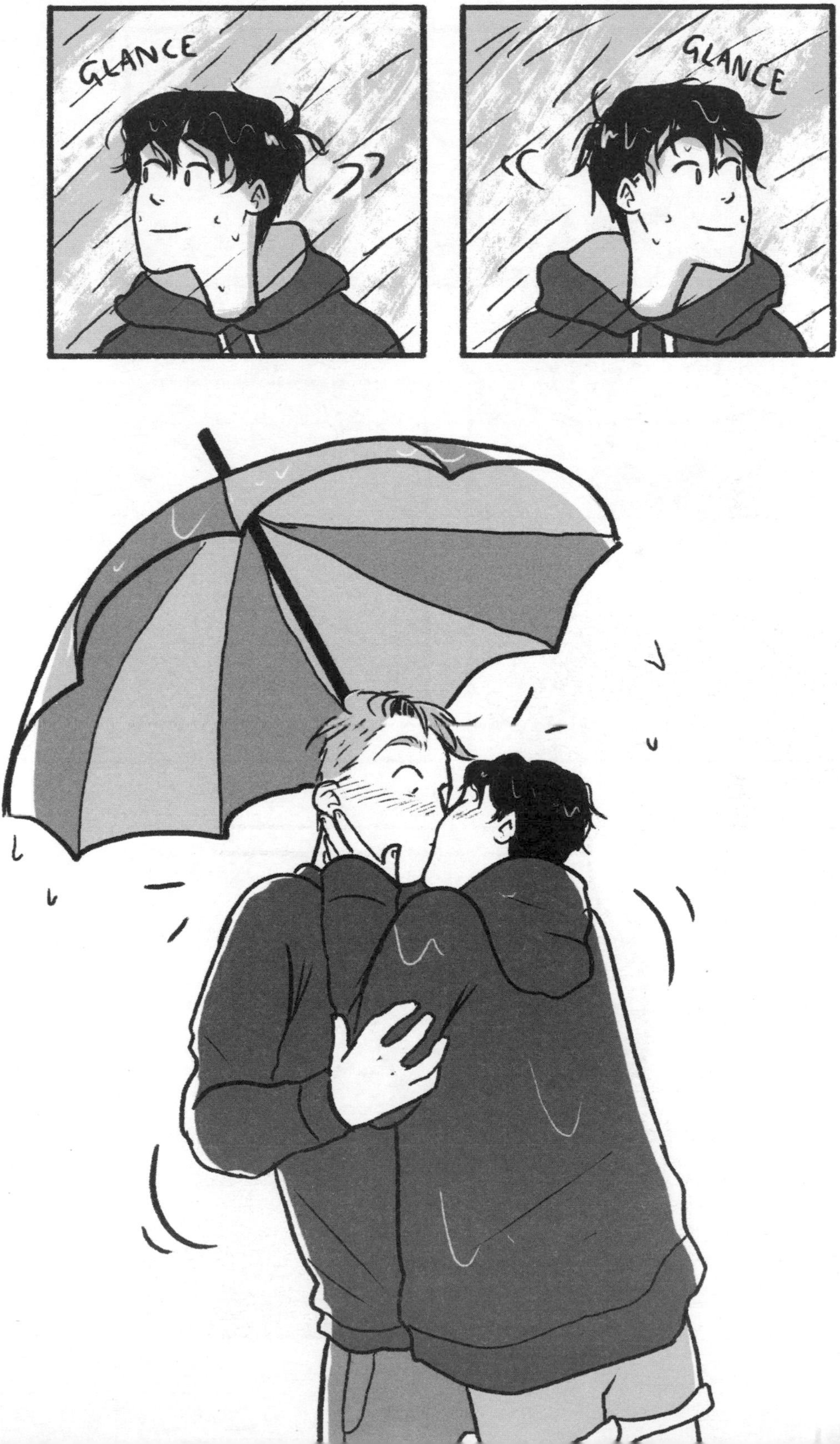
GLANCE
GLANCE

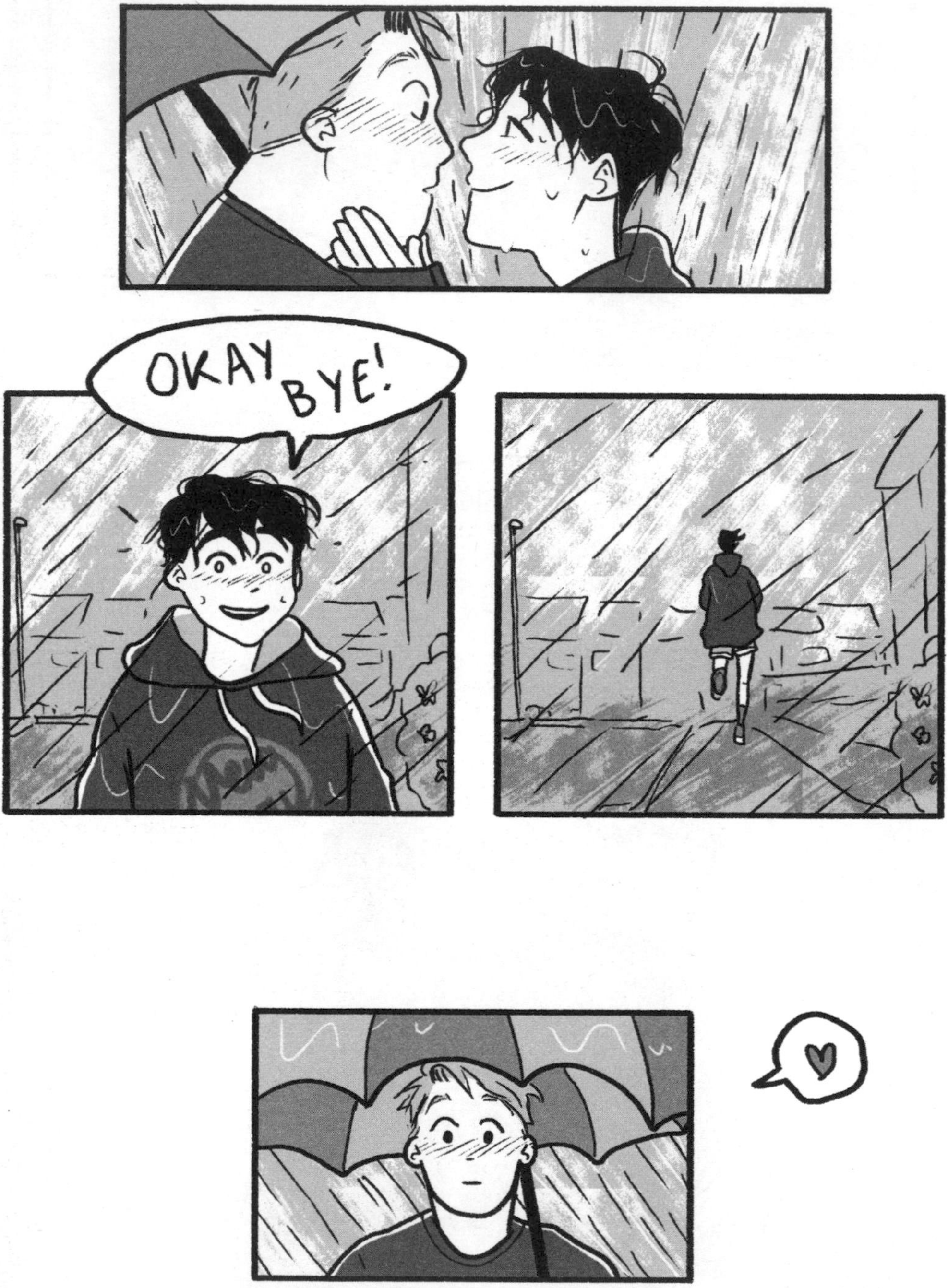
OKAY BYE!

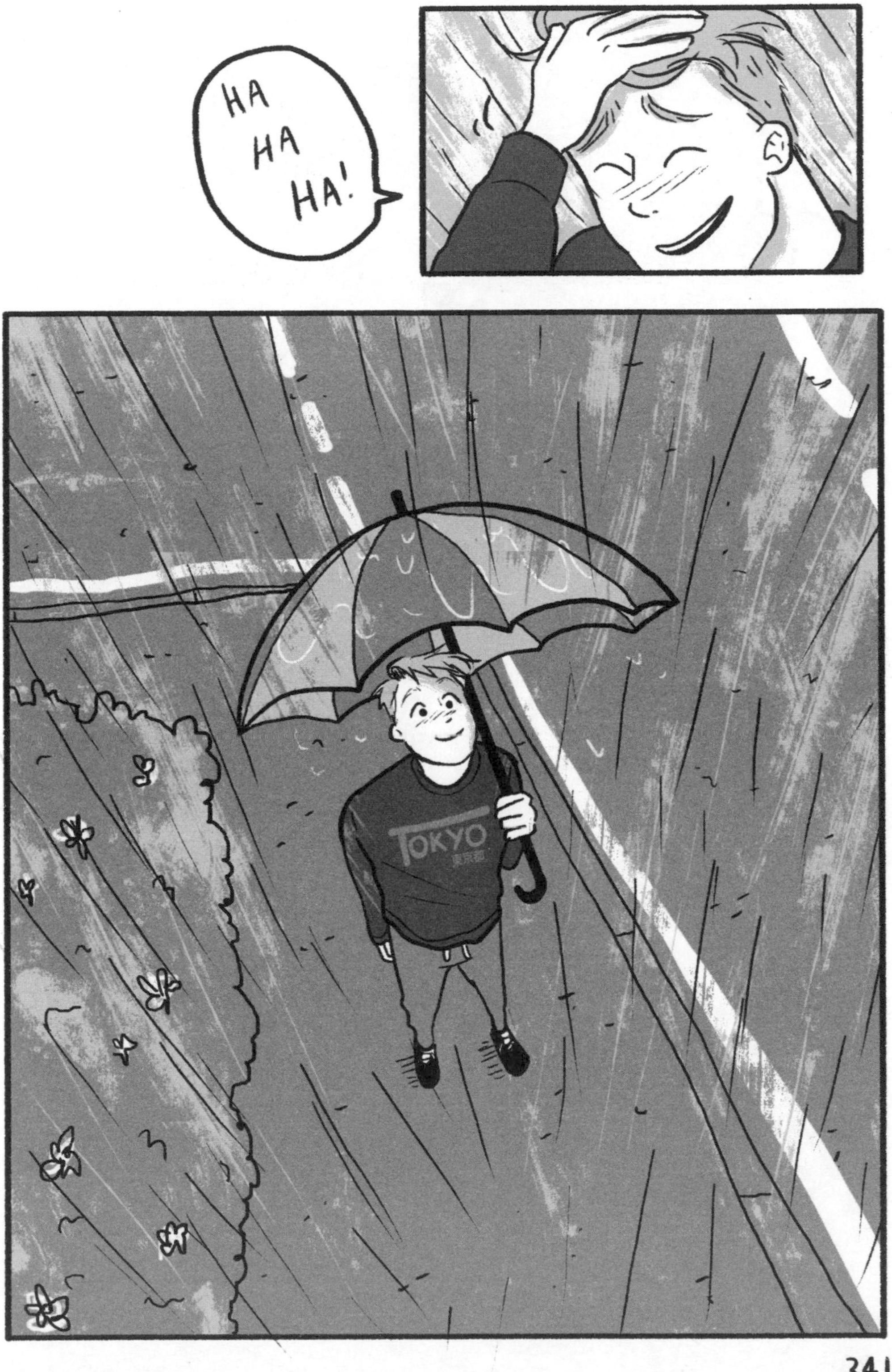
HA HA HA!
TOKYO
東京都

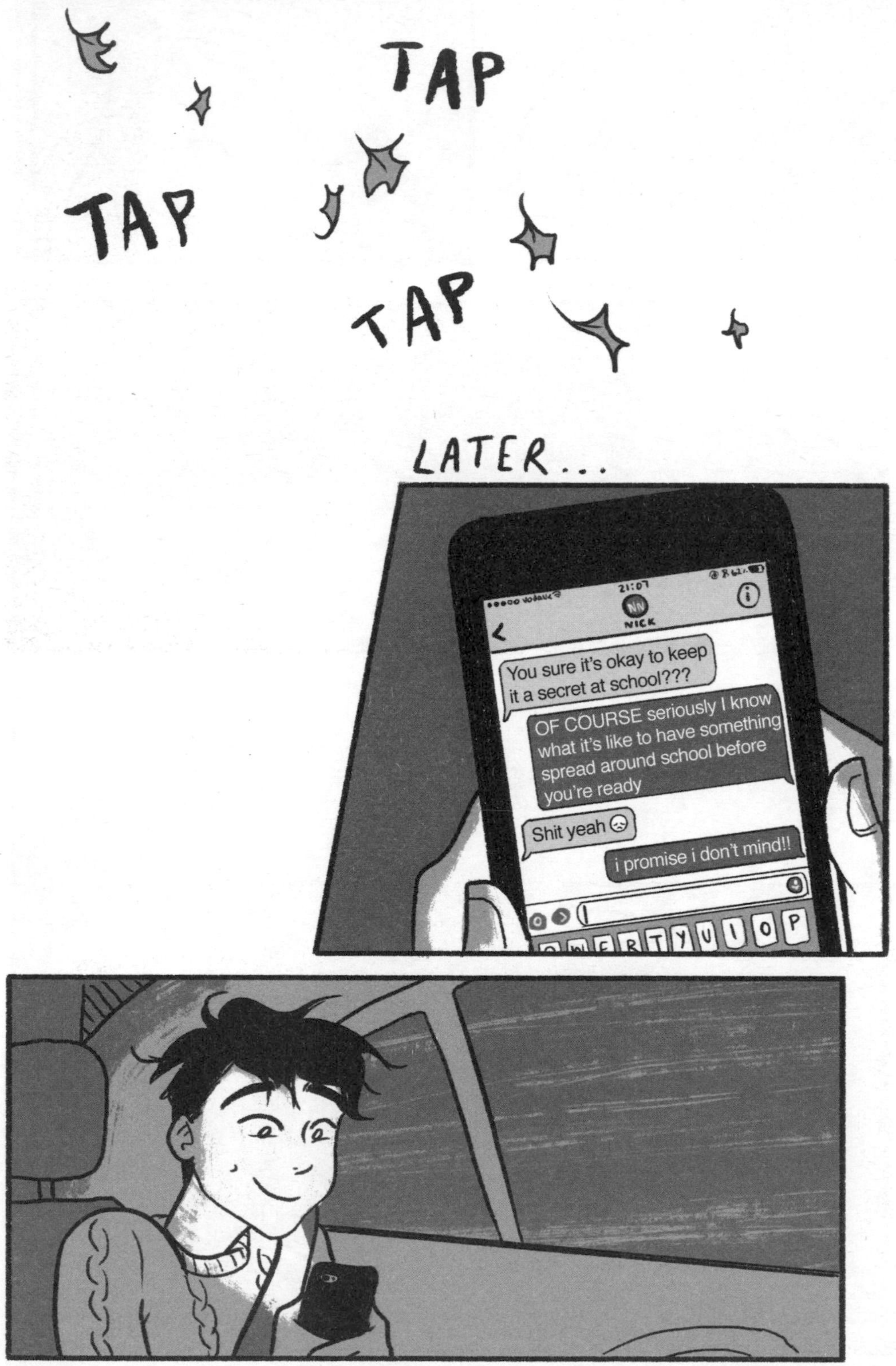
TAP
TAP
TAP
LATER...
21:07
NICK
You sure it's okay to keep it a secret at school???
OF COURSE seriously I know what it's like to have something spread around school before you're ready
Shit yeah
i promise i don't mind!!

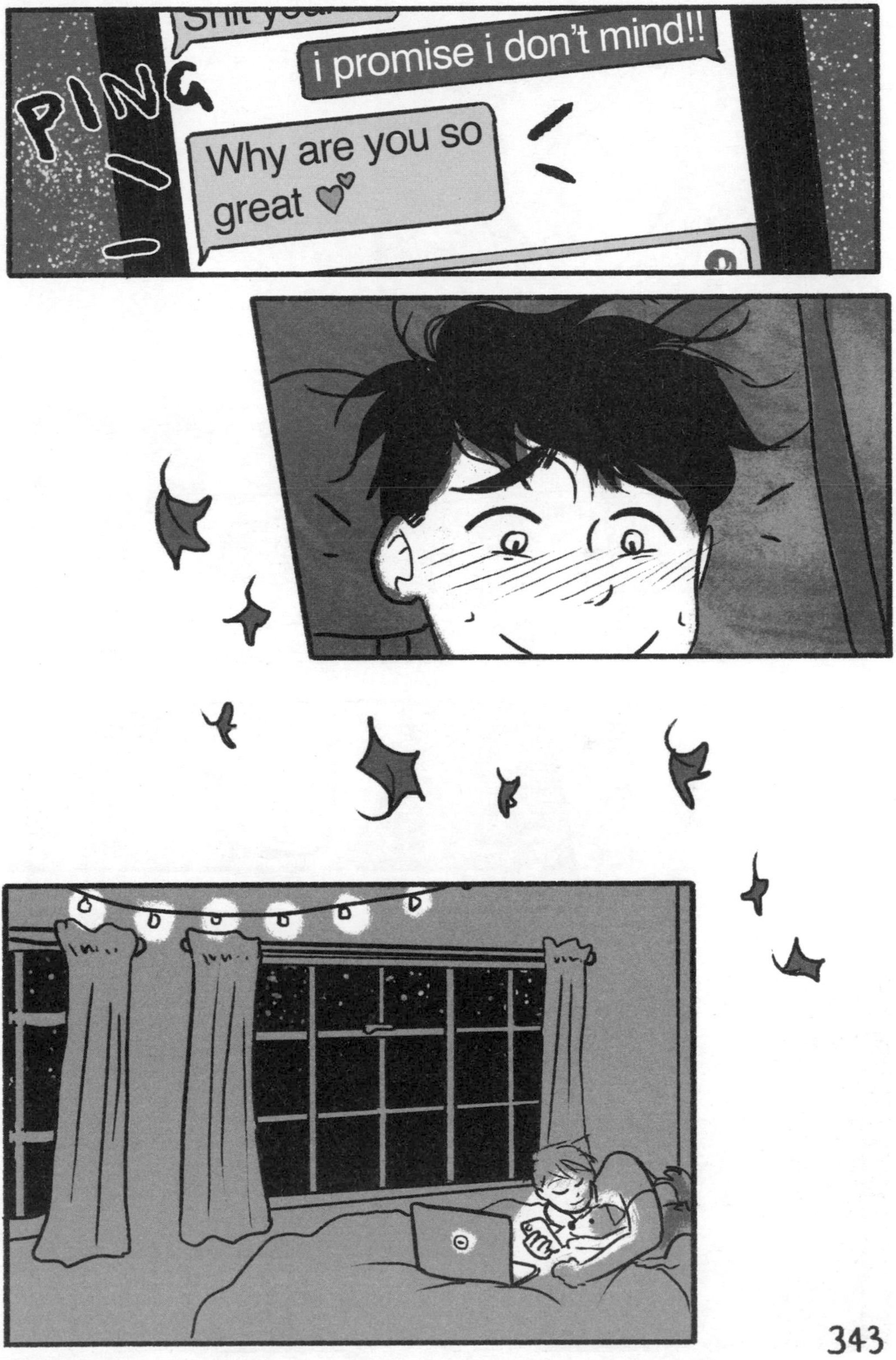
i promise i don't mind!!
PING
Why are you so great

PING

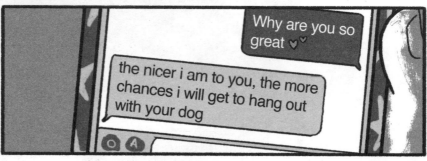

Why are you so great ♡♡

the nicer i am to you, the more chances i will get to hang out with your dog

HA HA

SNAP

SEND

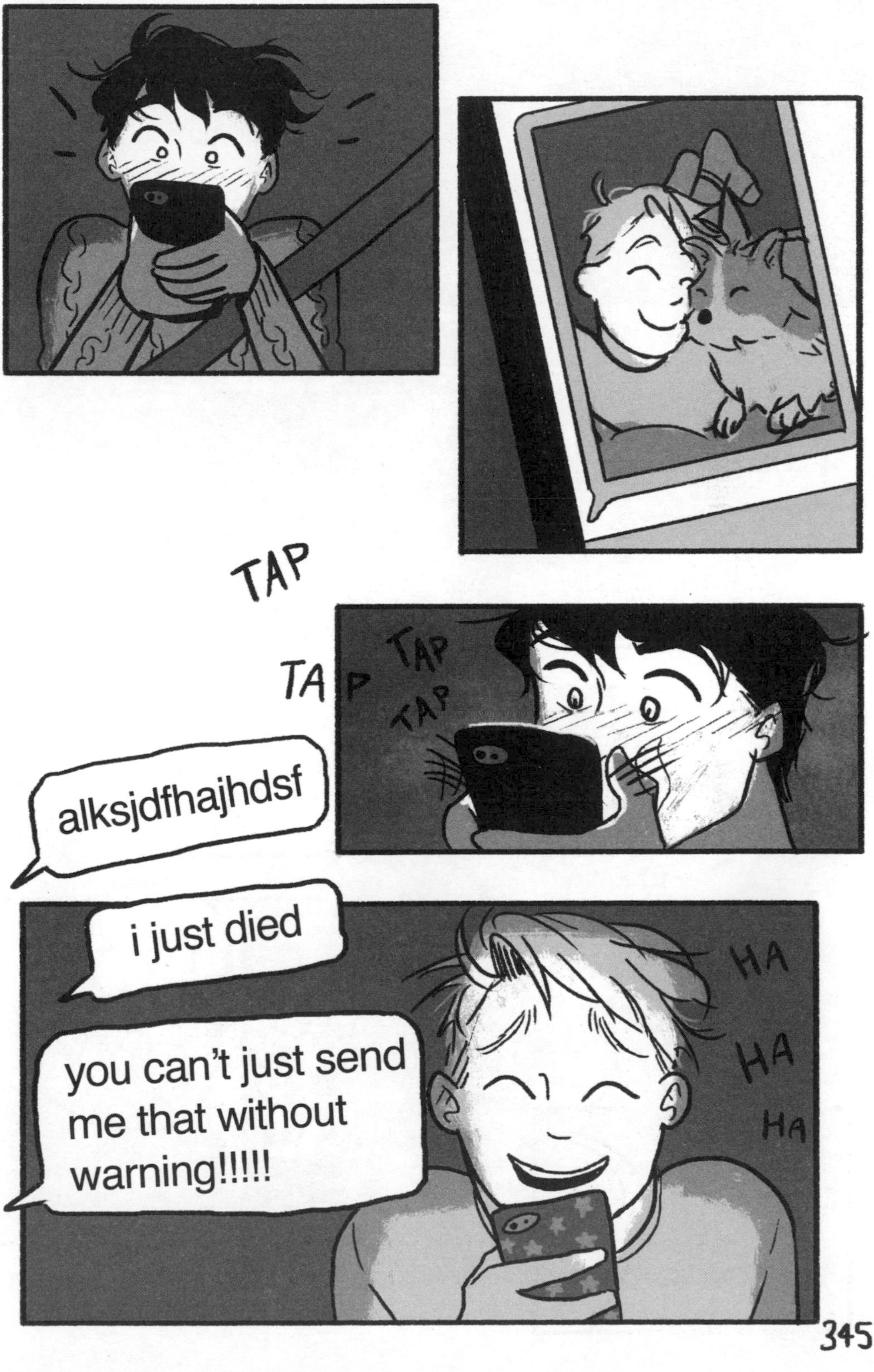
TAP
TAP
TAP TAP
alksjdfhajhdsf
i just died
you can't just send me that without warning!!!!!
HA
HA
HA

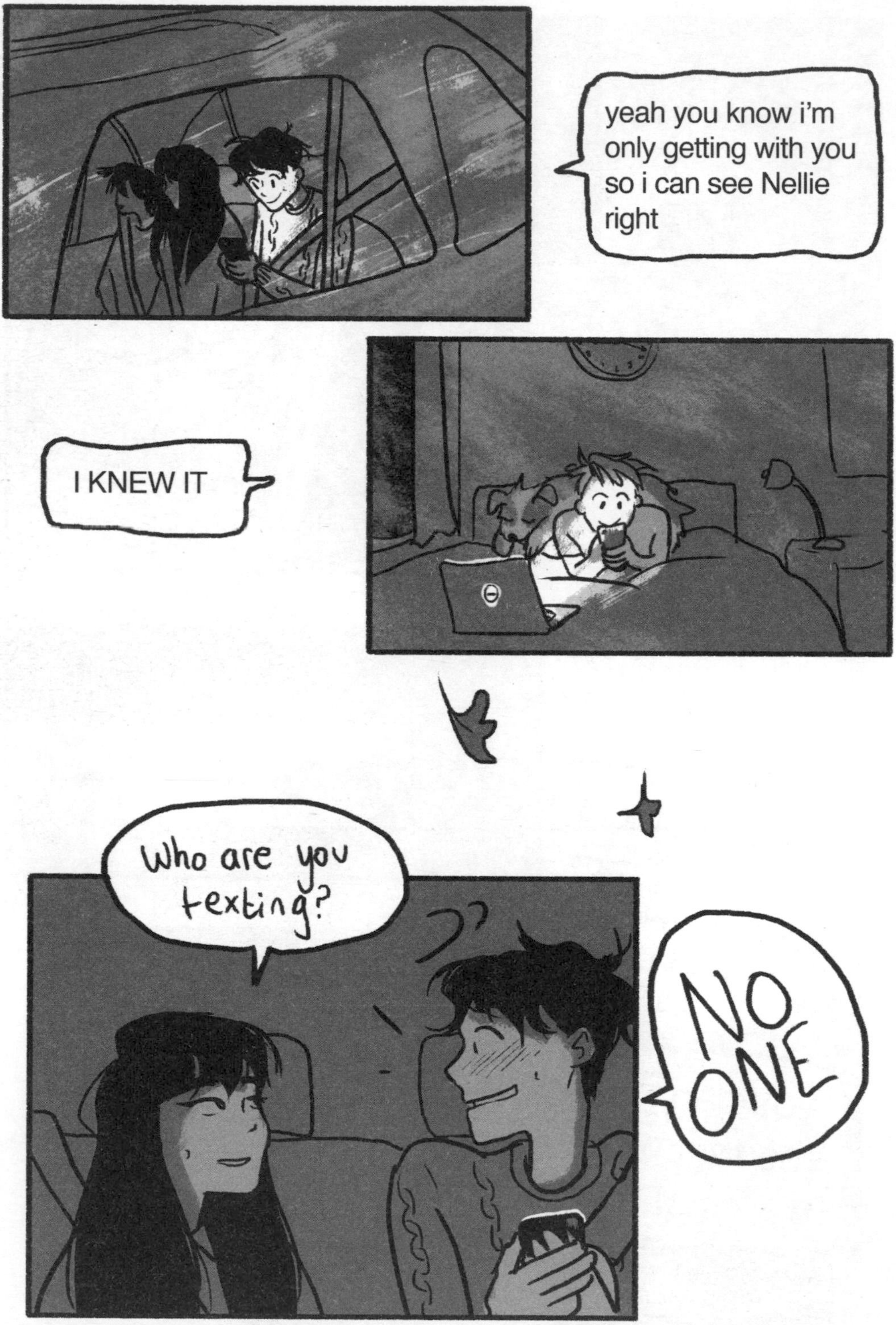
yeah you know i'm only getting with you so i can see Nellie right
I KNEW IT
Who are you texting?
NO ONE

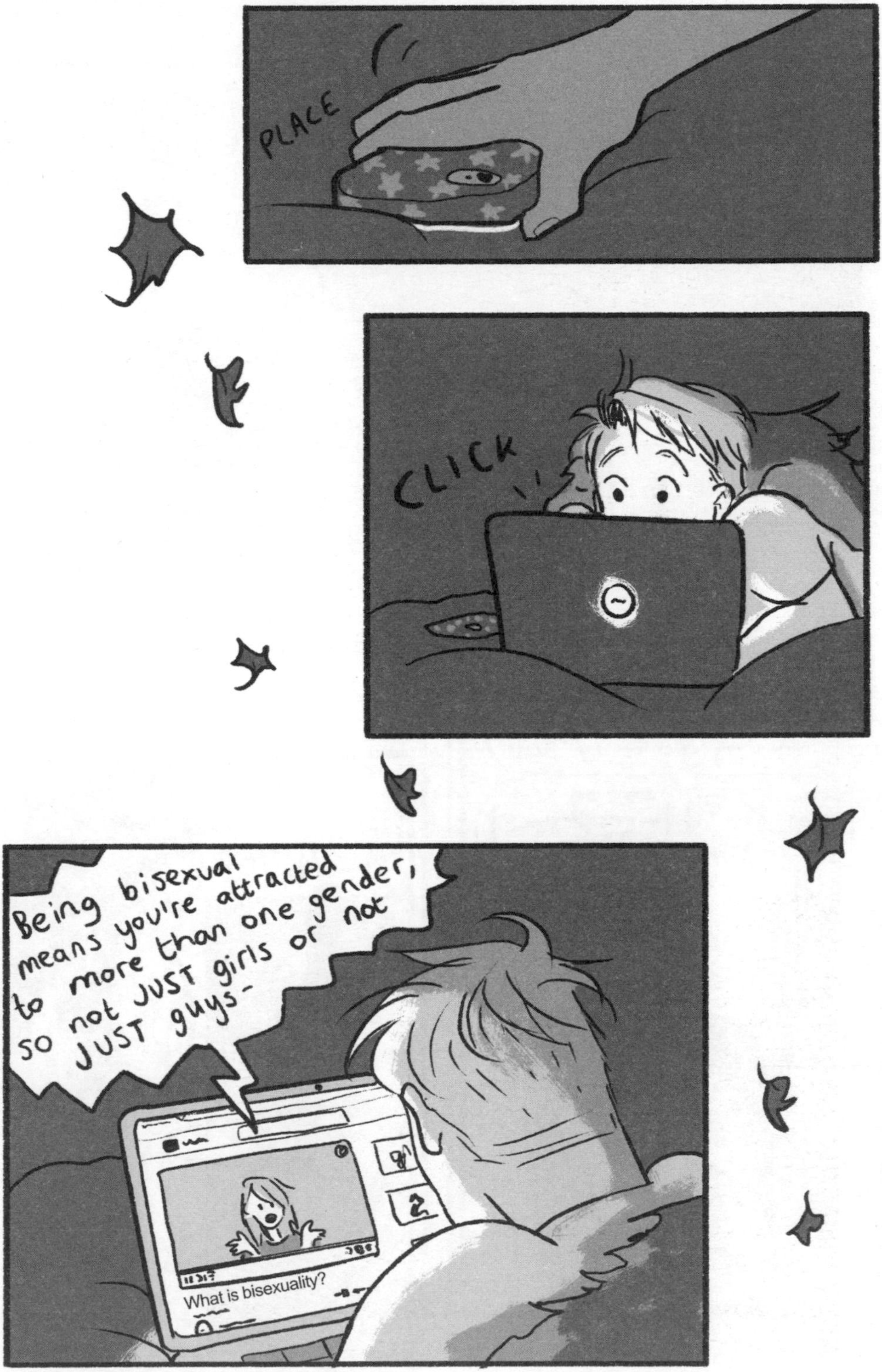
PLACE
CLICK
Being bisexual means you're attracted to more than one gender, so not JUST girls or not JUST guys-
What is bisexuality?

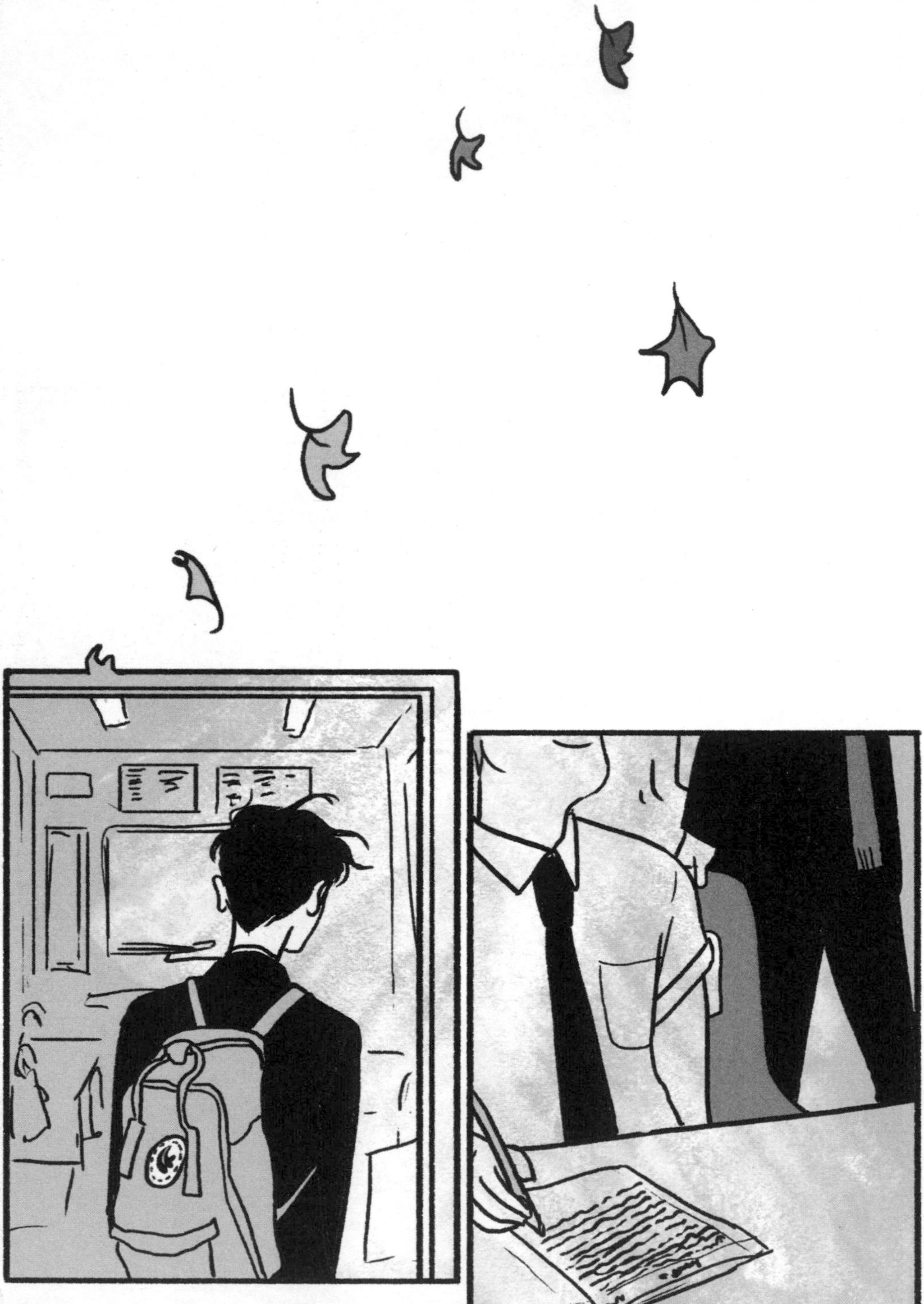

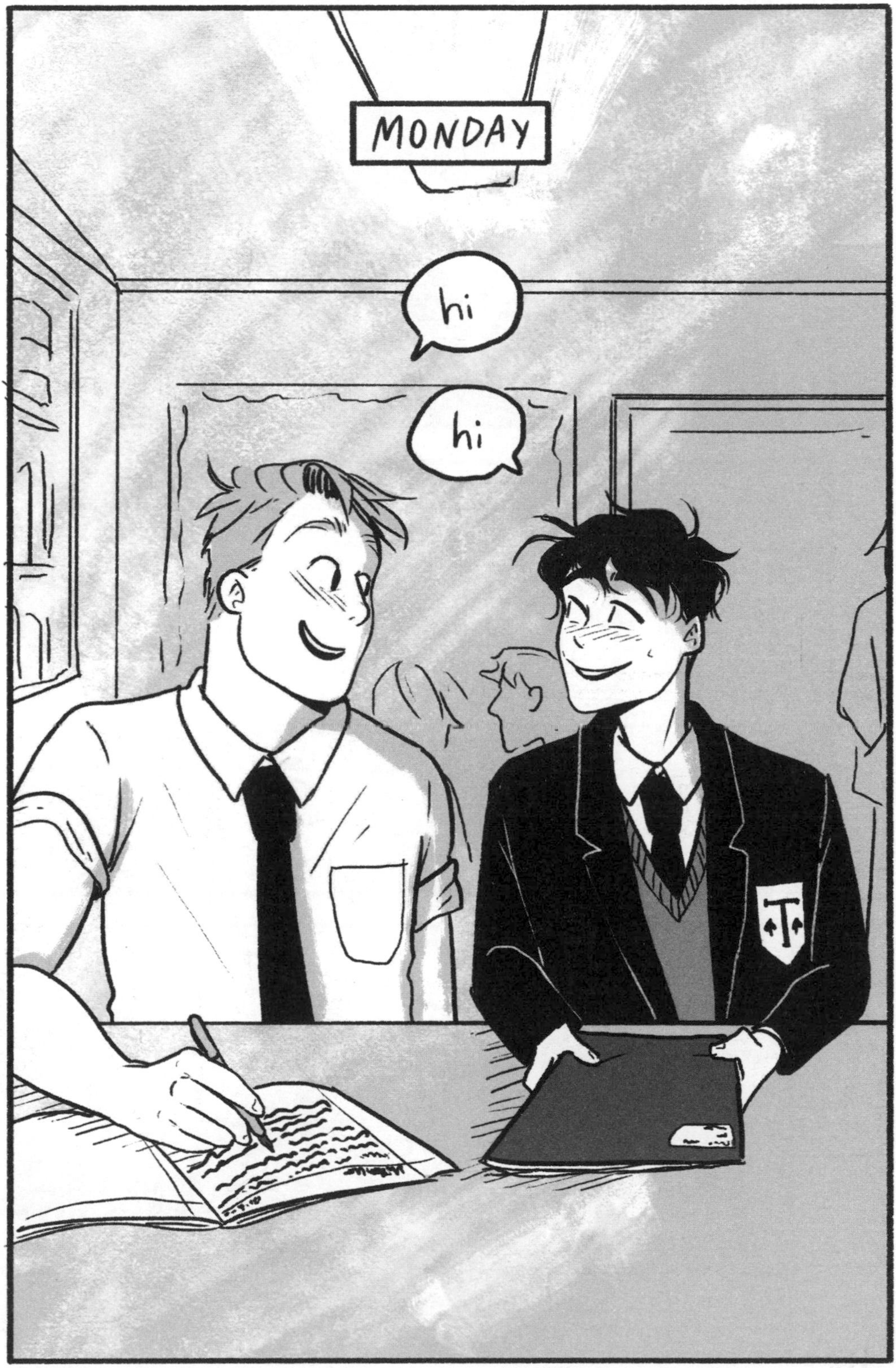
MONDAY
hi
hi

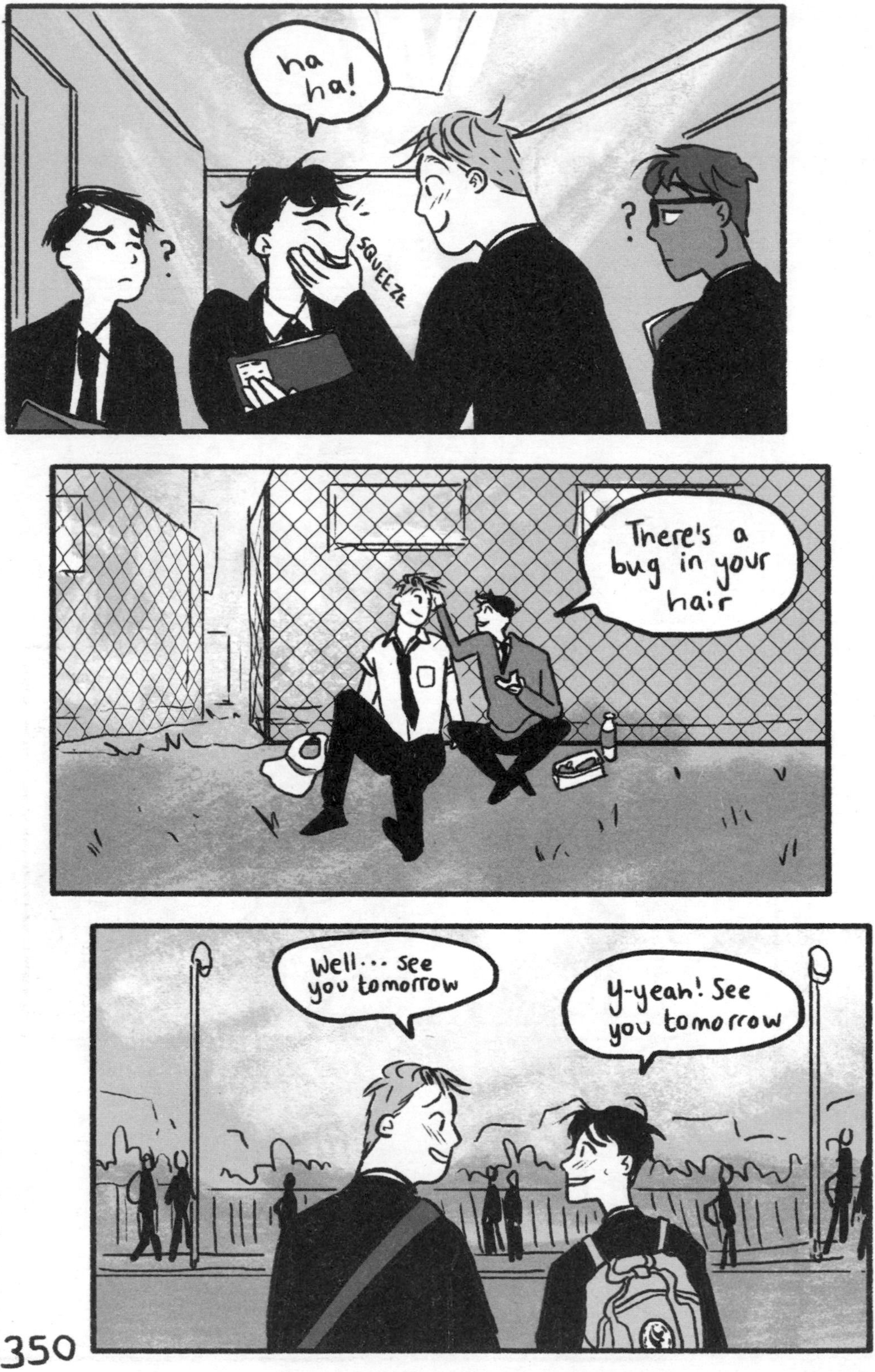
ha ha!
SQUEEZE
?
?
There's a bug in your hair
Well... see you tomorrow
Y-yeah! See you tomorrow

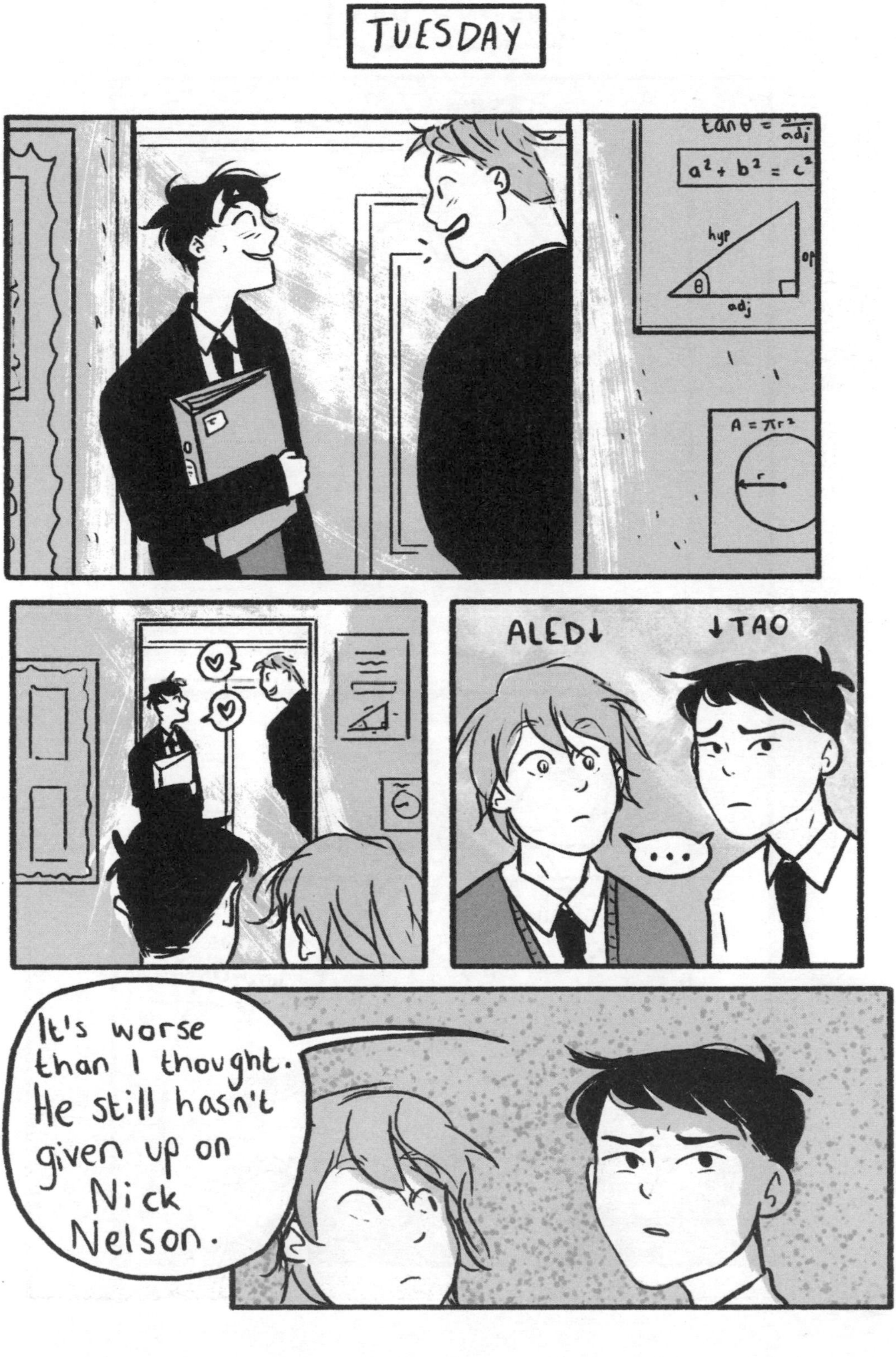
TUESDAY
a² + b² = c²
hyp
adj
A = πr²
ALED↓
↓TAO
...
It's worse than I thought. He still hasn't given up on Nick Nelson.

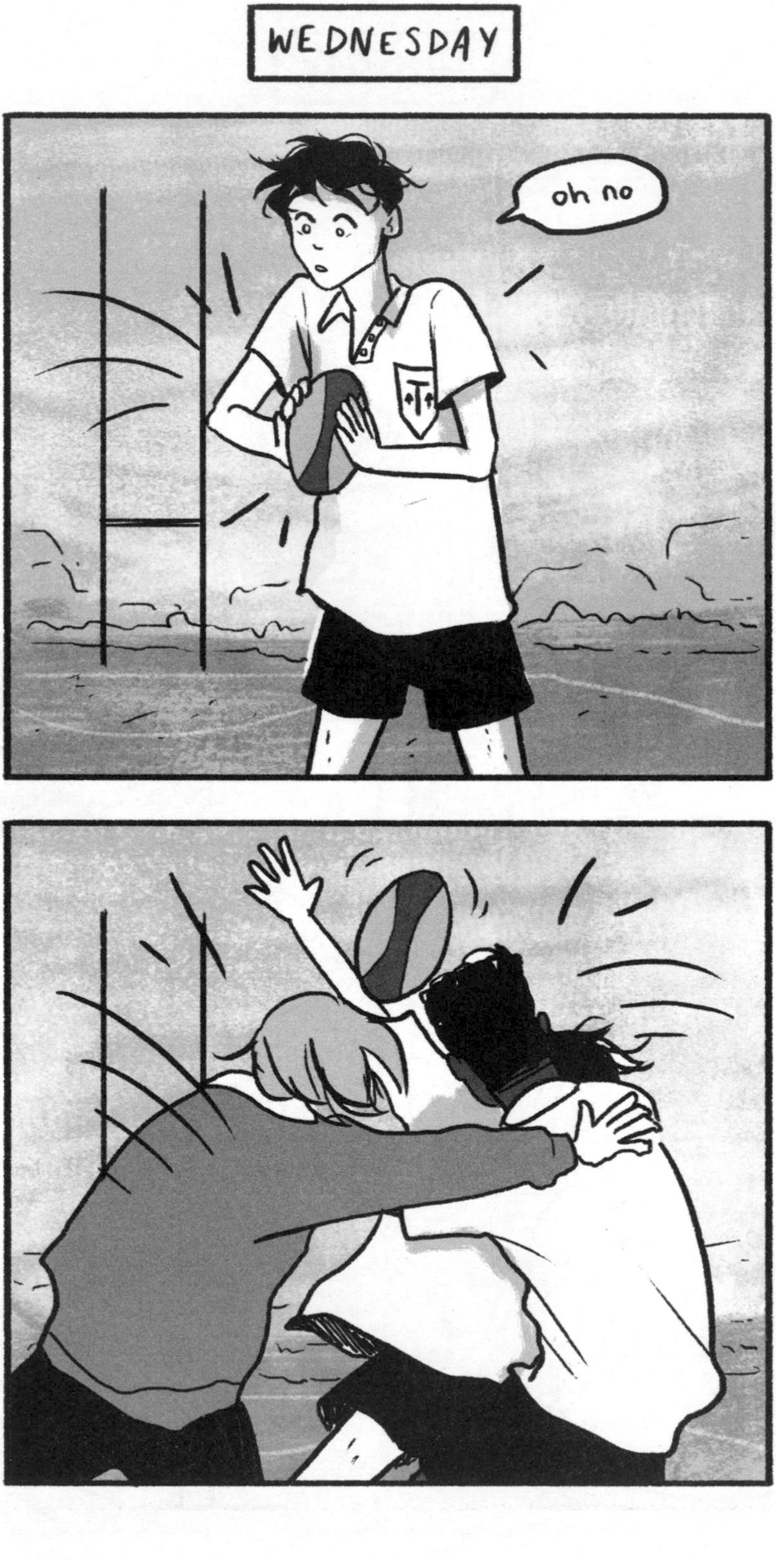
WEDNESDAY
oh no

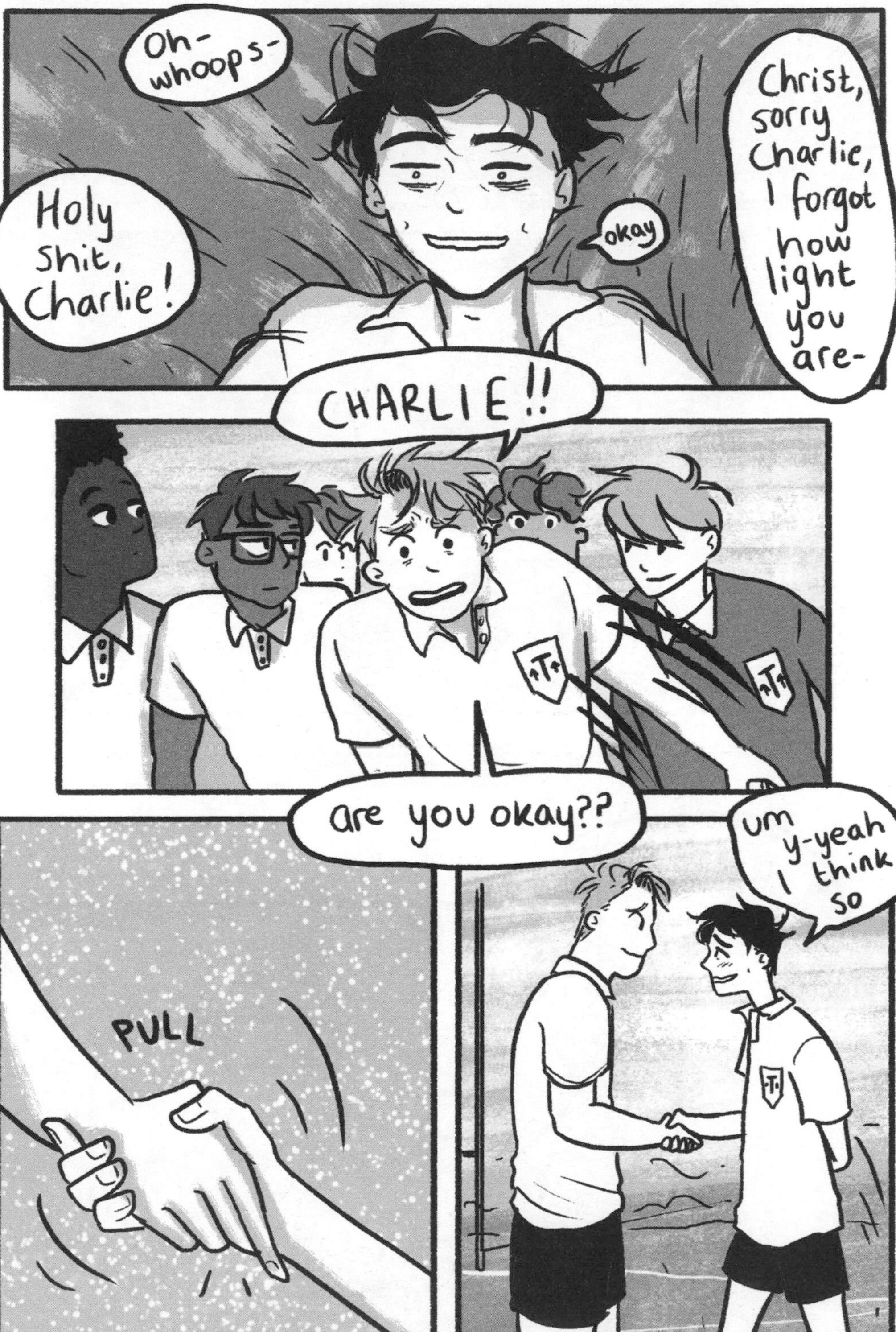

Oh- whoops-
Holy shit, Charlie!
okay
Christ, sorry Charlie, I forgot how light you are-
CHARLIE!!
are you okay??
PULL
um y-yeah I think so

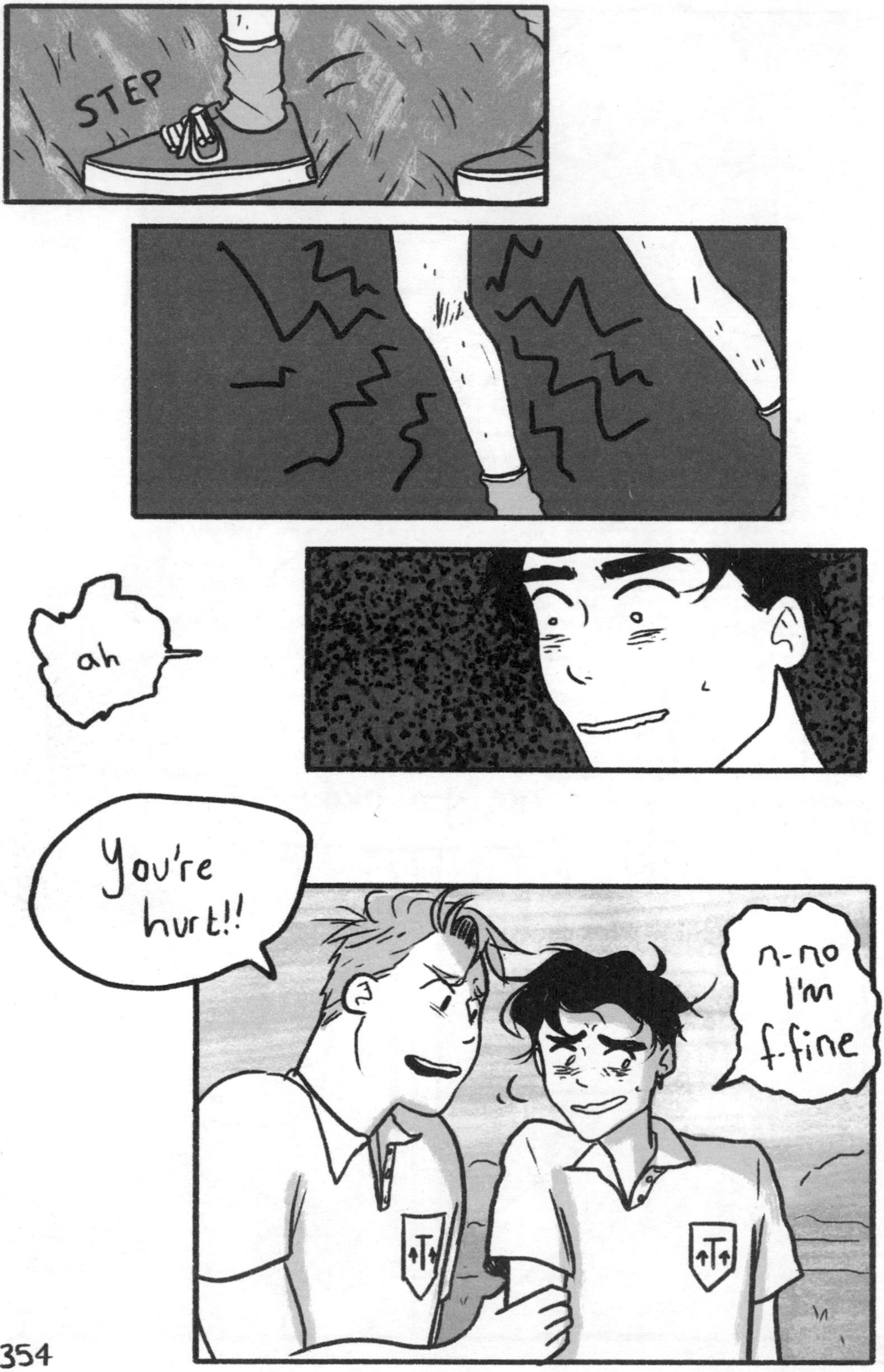
STEP
ah
You're hurt!!
n-no I'm f-fine

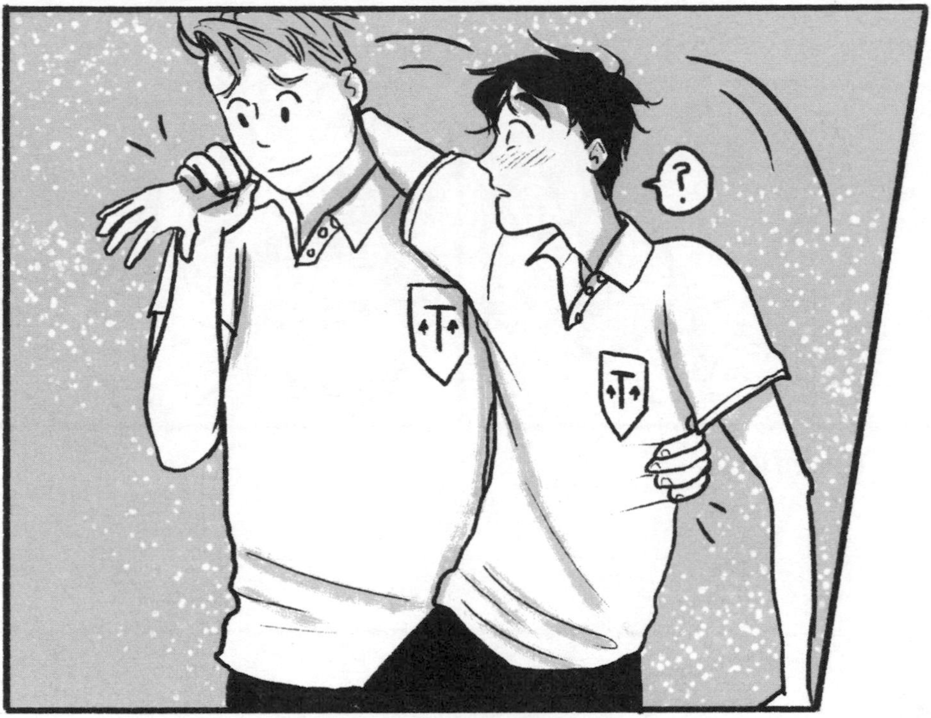
?

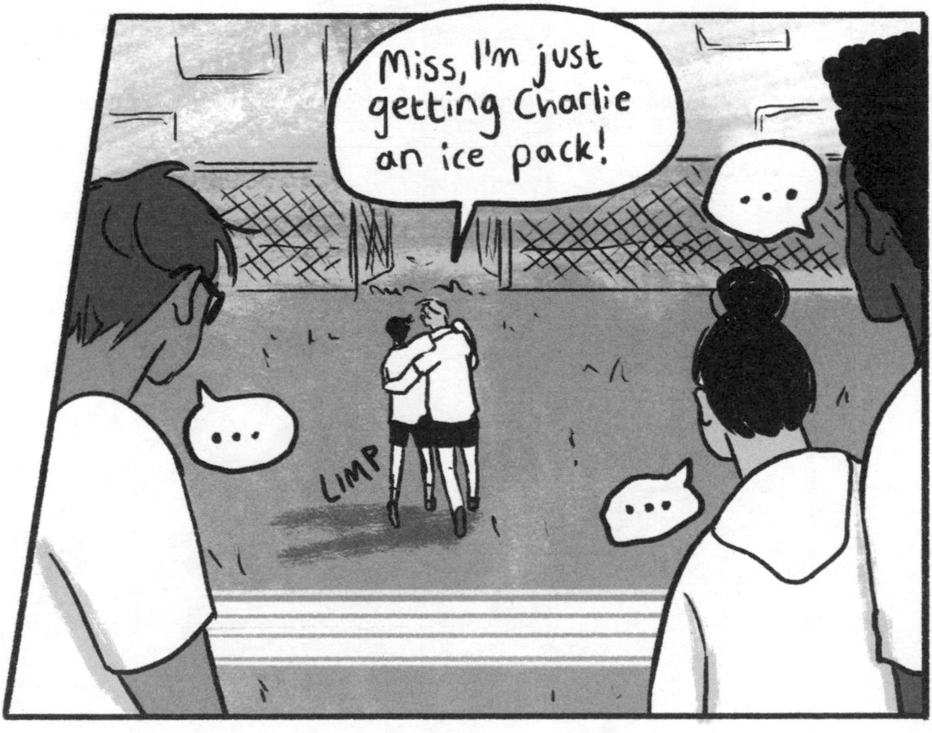
Miss, I'm just getting Charlie an ice pack!
...
...
...
LIMP

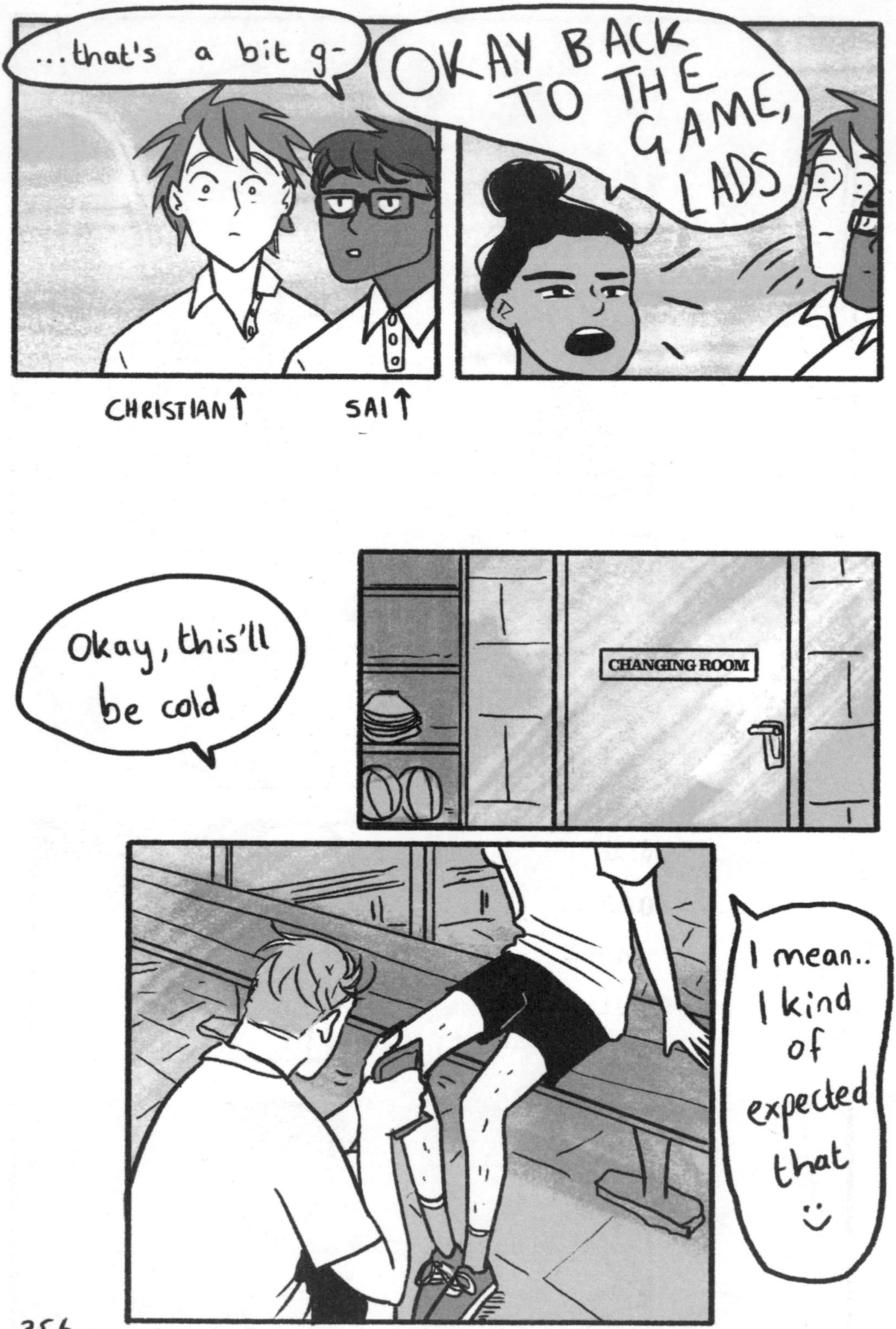

...that's a bit g-
OKAY BACK TO THE GAME, LADS
CHRISTIAN↑
SAI↑
Okay, this'll be cold
CHANGING ROOM
I mean.. I kind of expected that :)

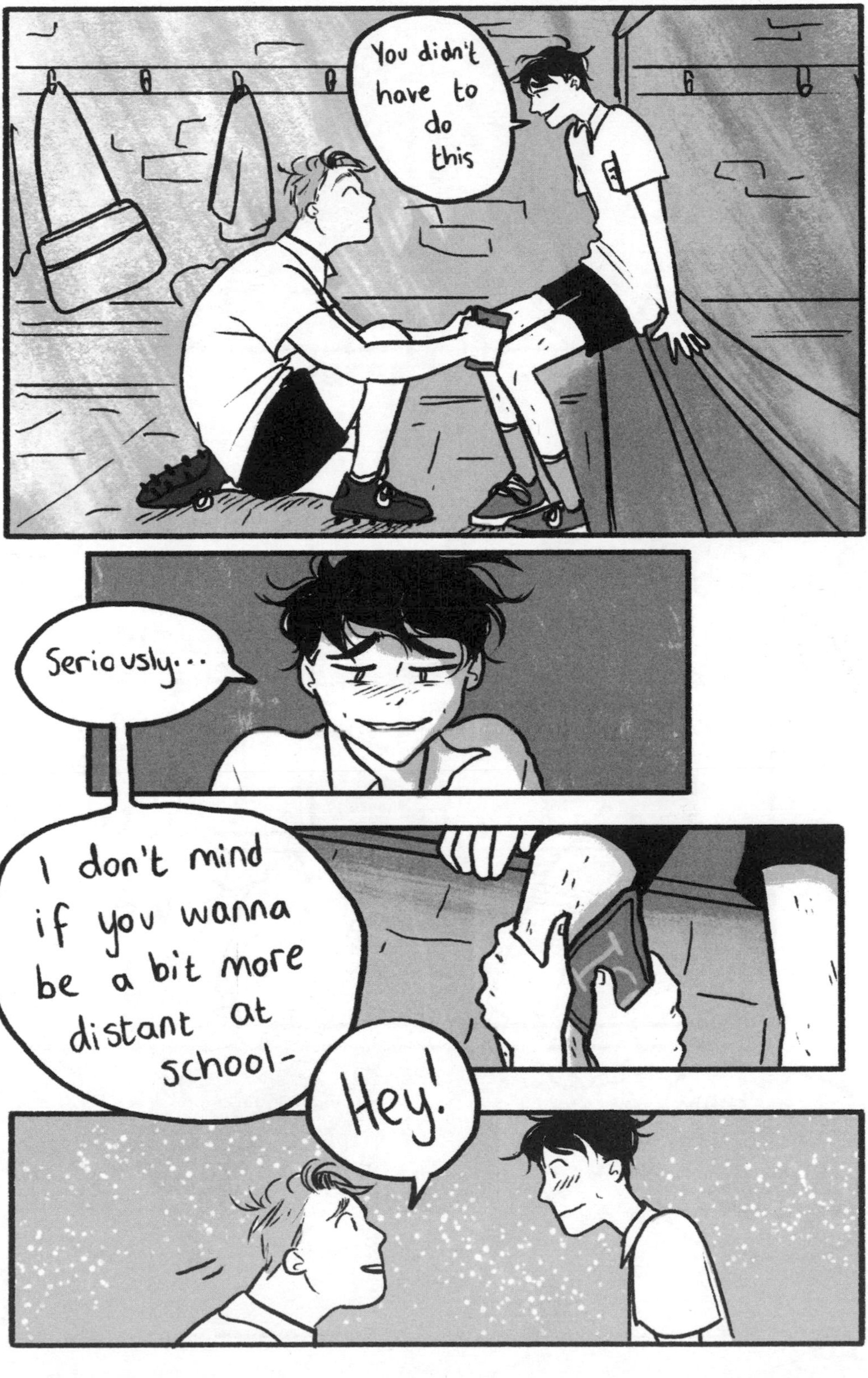
You didn't have to do this
Seriously...
I don't mind if you wanna be a bit more distant at school-
Hey!

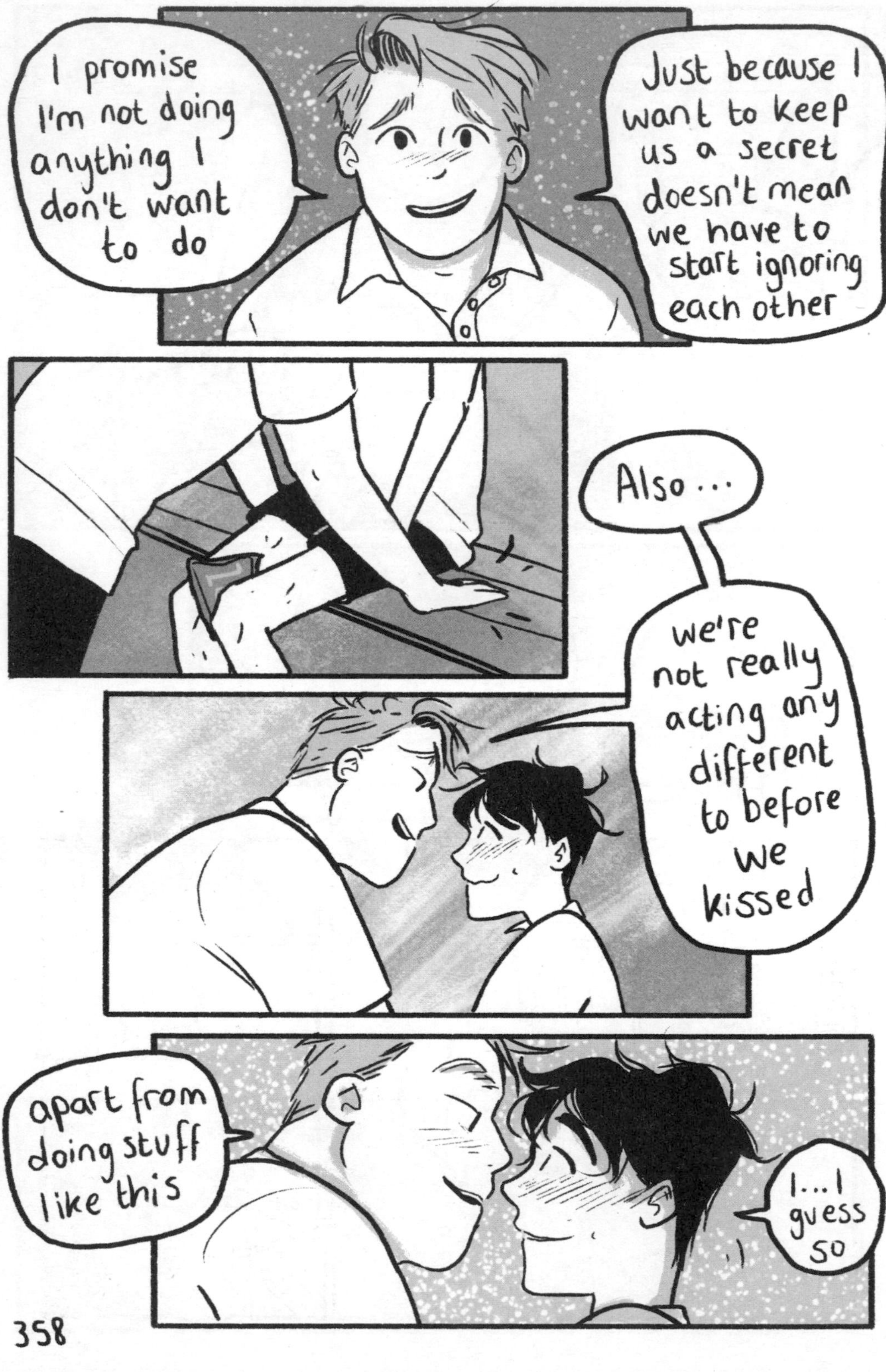
I promise I'm not doing anything I don't want to do
Just because I want to keep us a secret doesn't mean we have to start ignoring each other
Also...
we're not really acting any different to before we kissed
apart from doing stuff like this
I...I guess so

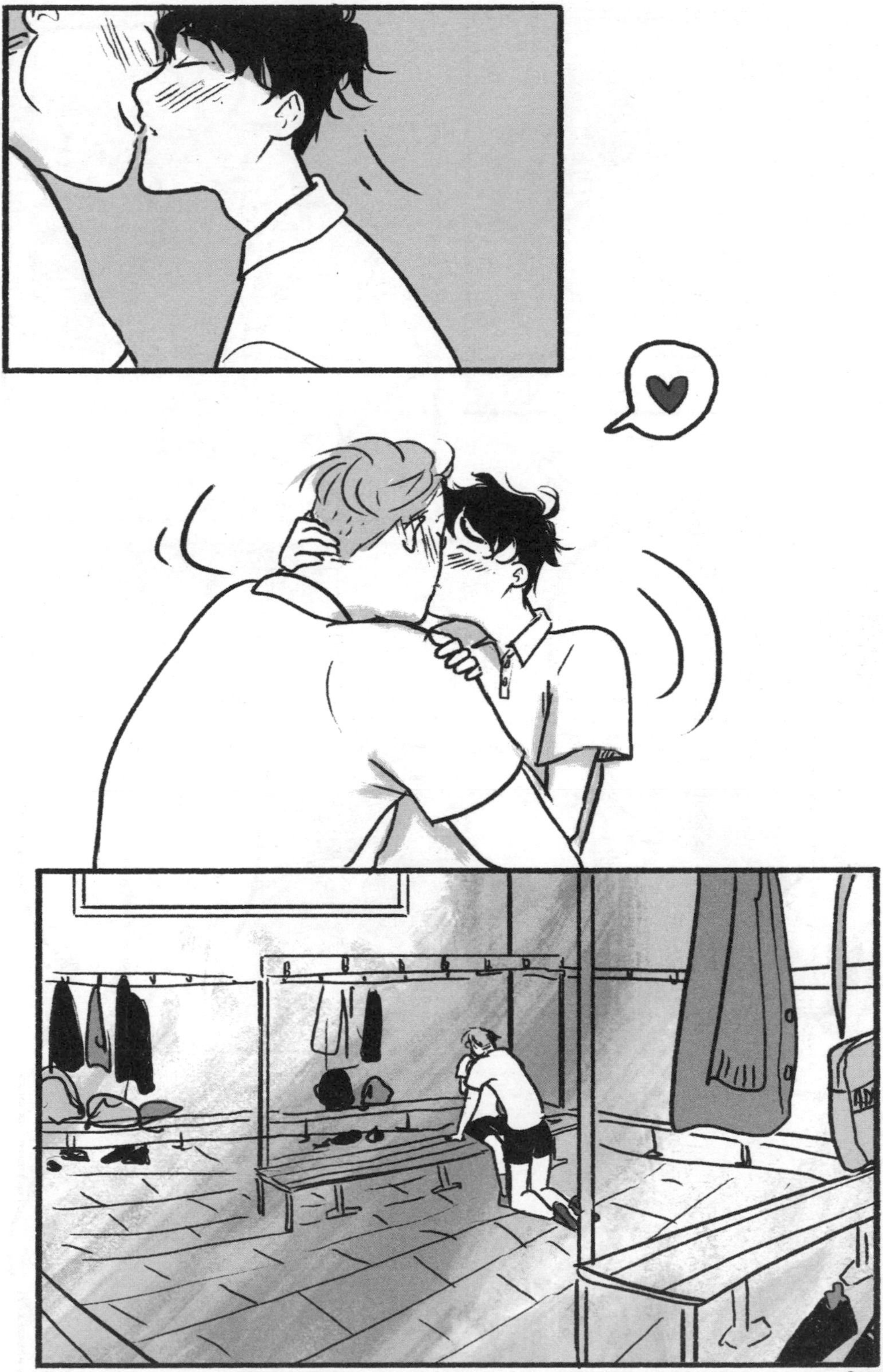

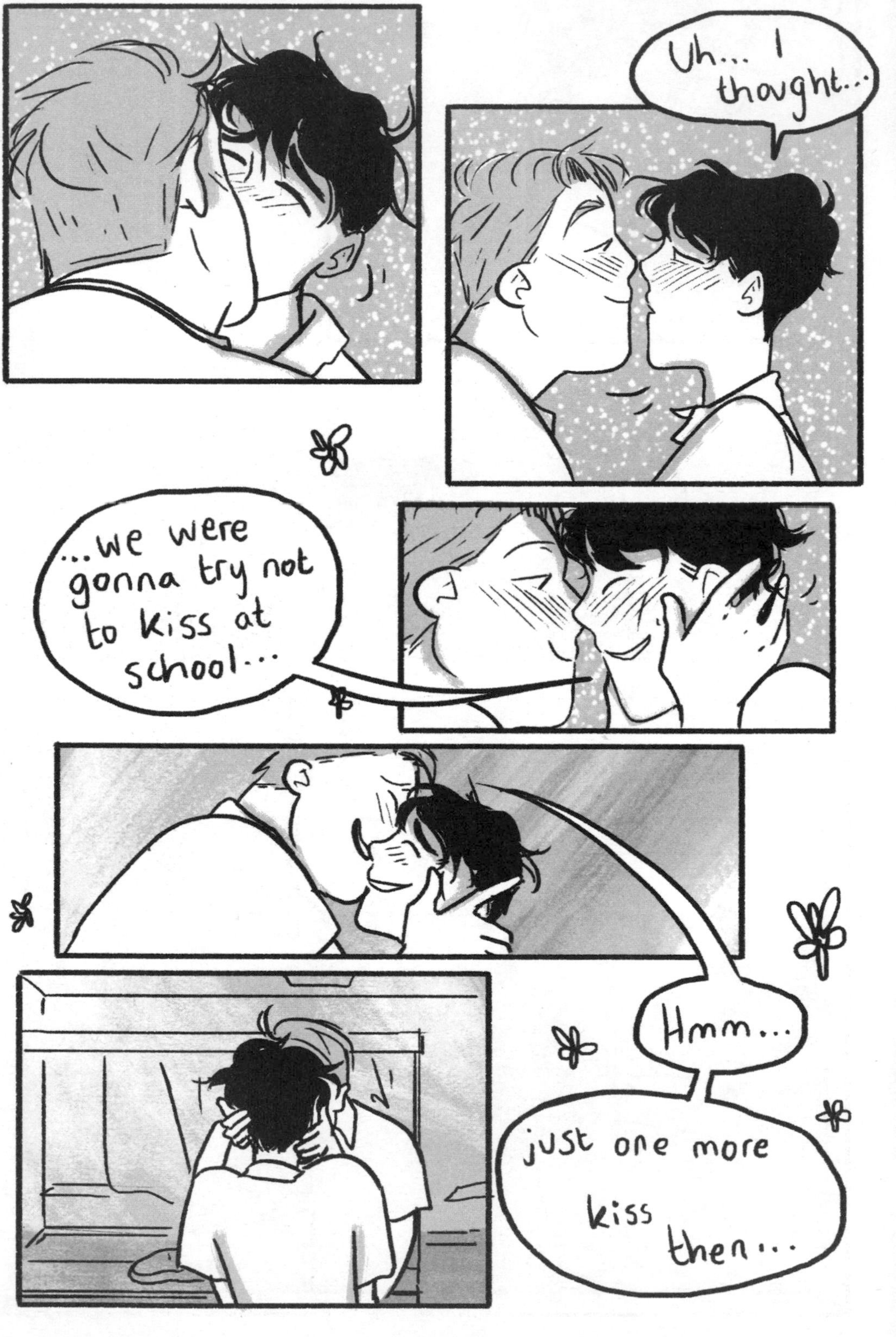
Uh... I thought...
...we were gonna try not to kiss at school...
Hmm...
just one more kiss then...

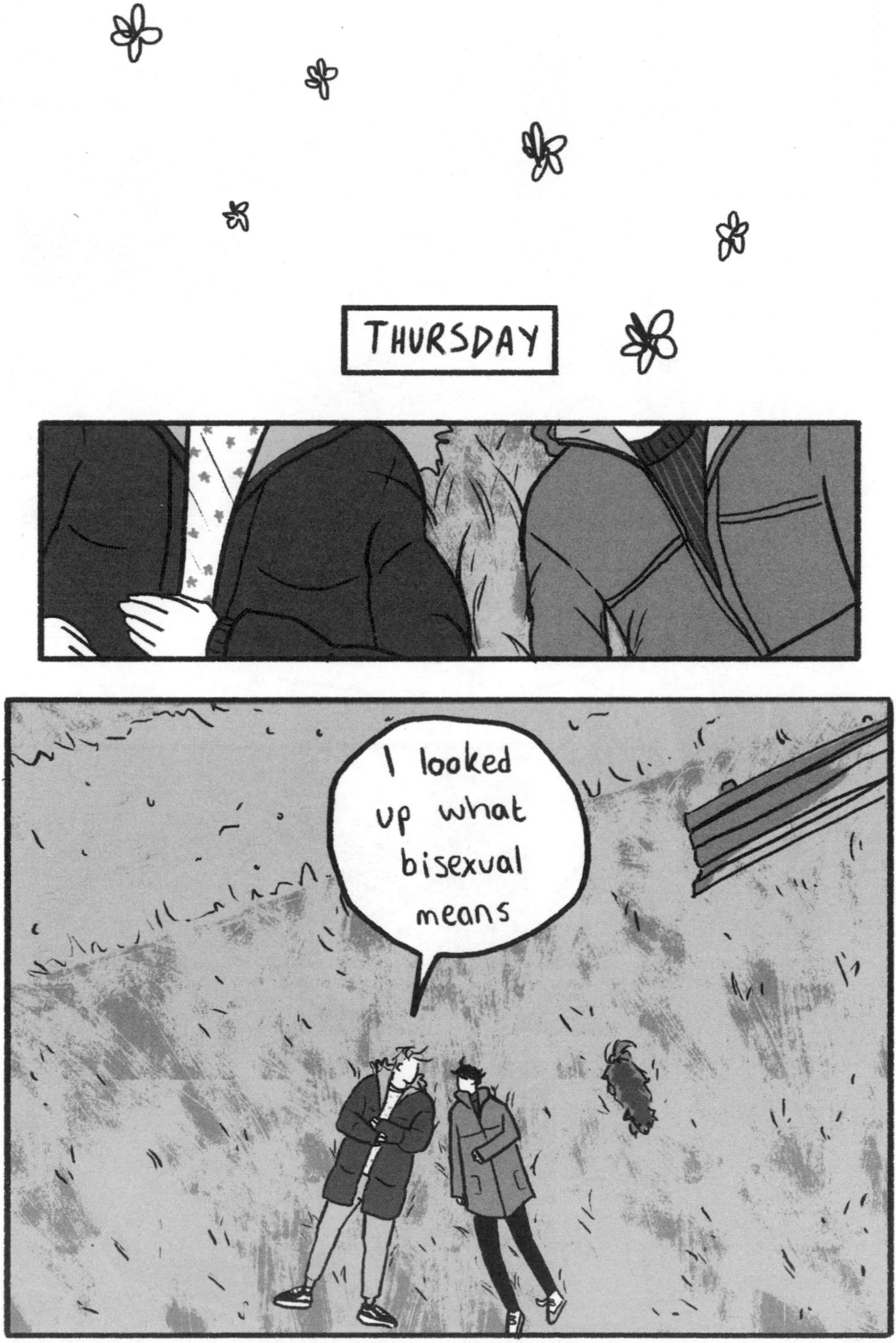
THURSDAY
I looked up what bisexual means

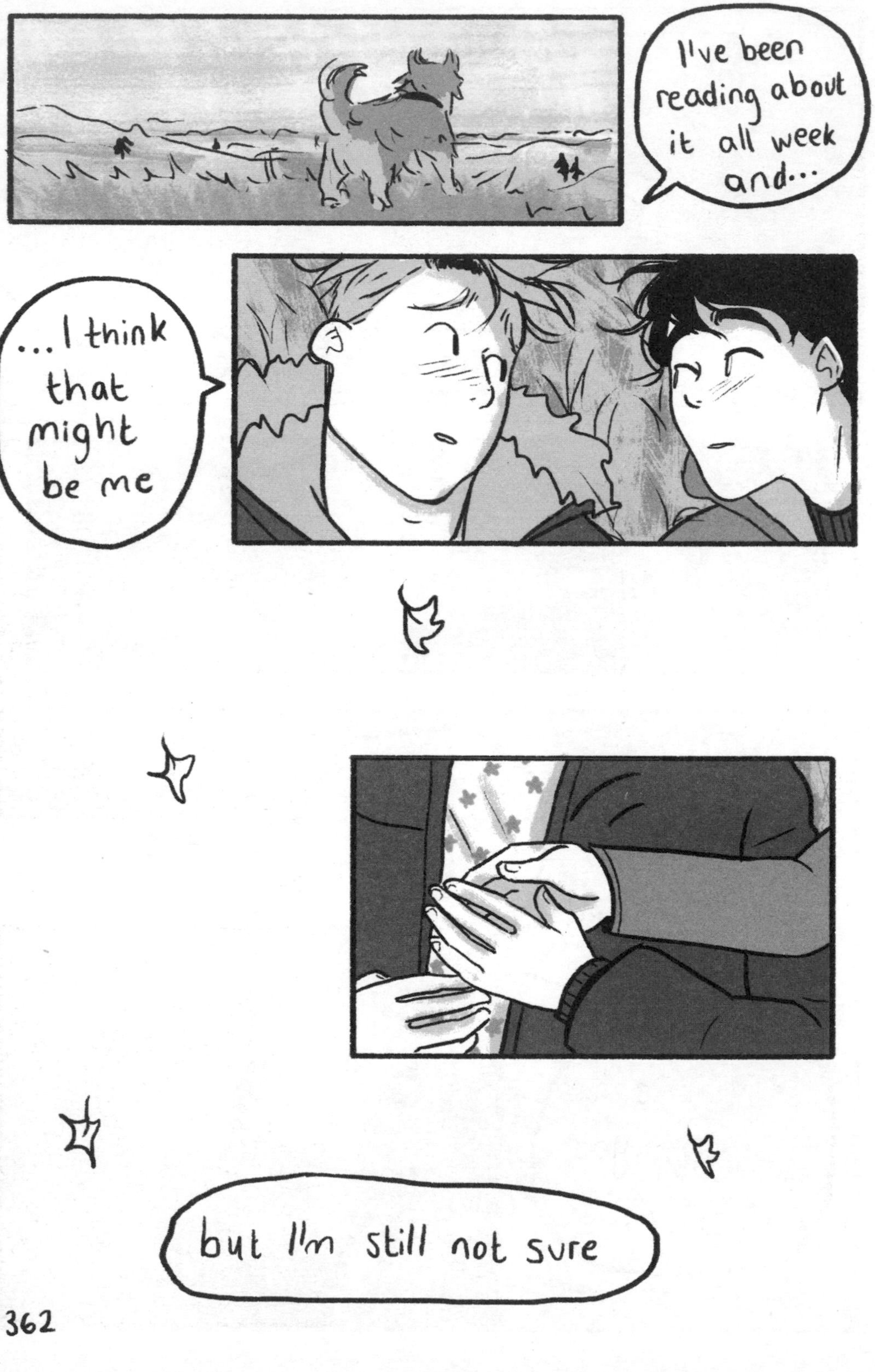
I've been reading about it all week and...
...I think that might be me
but I'm still not sure

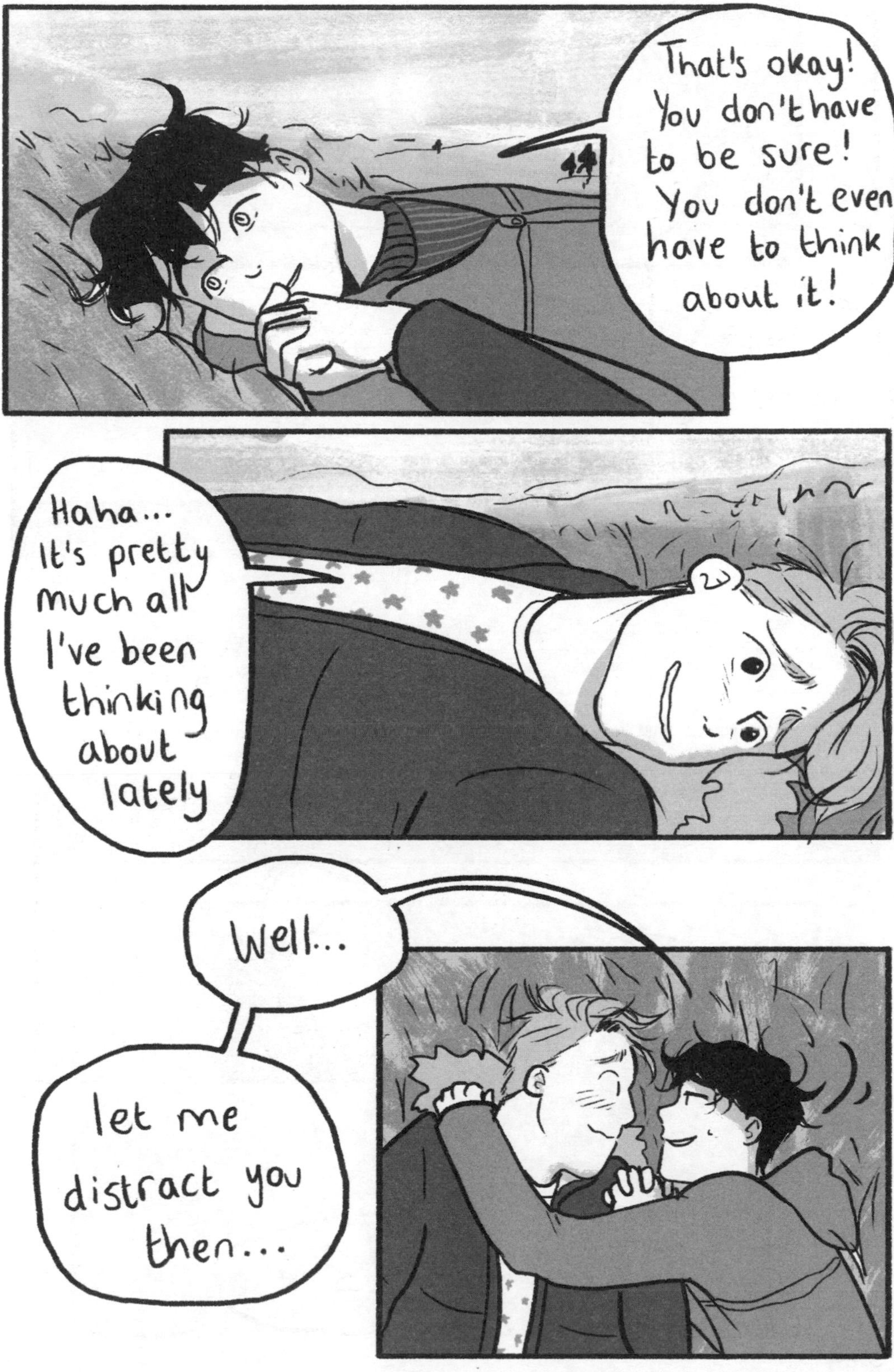
That's okay! You don't have to be sure! You don't even have to think about it!
Haha... It's pretty much all I've been thinking about lately
Well...
let me distract you then...

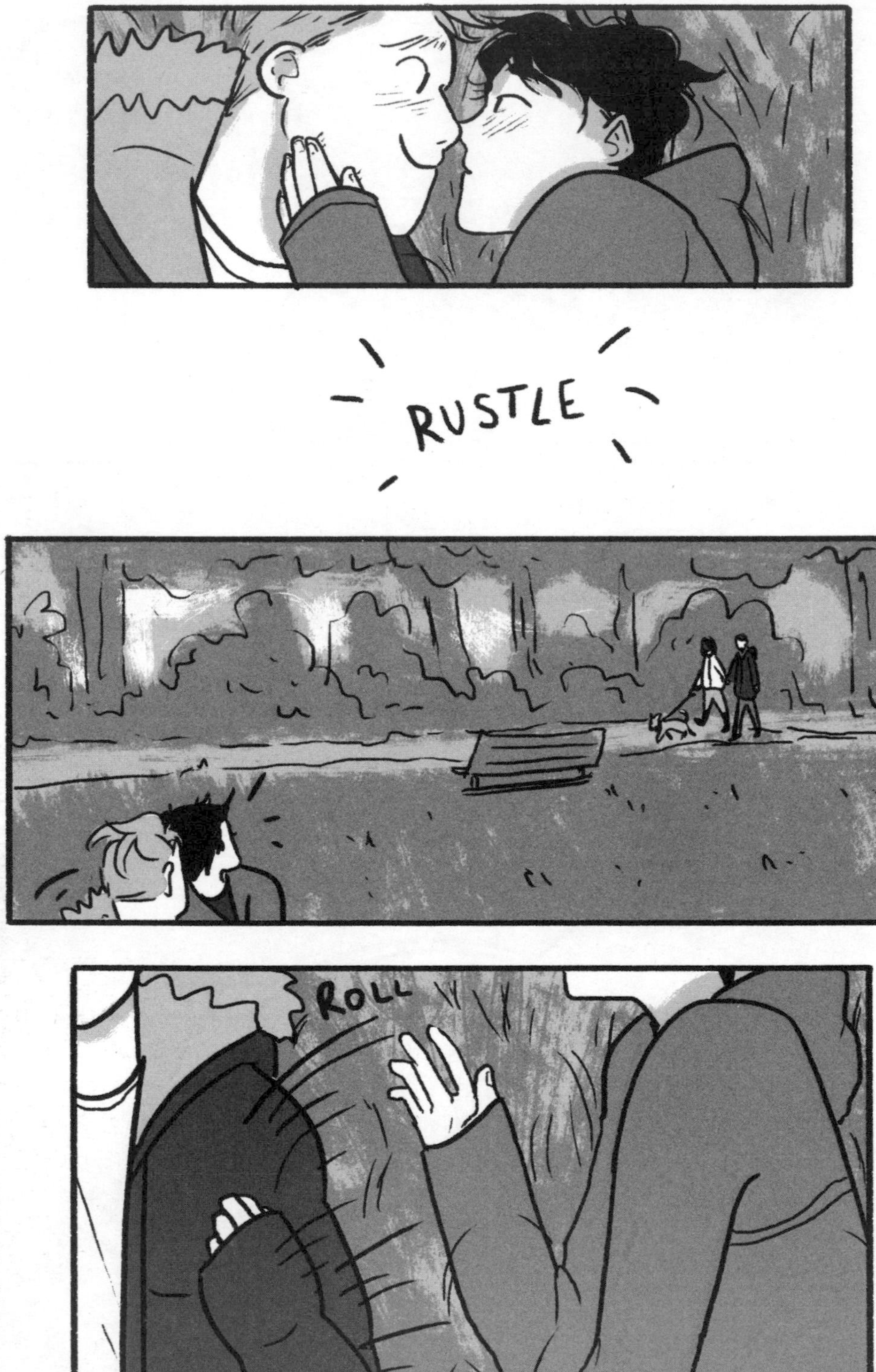
RUSTLE
ROLL

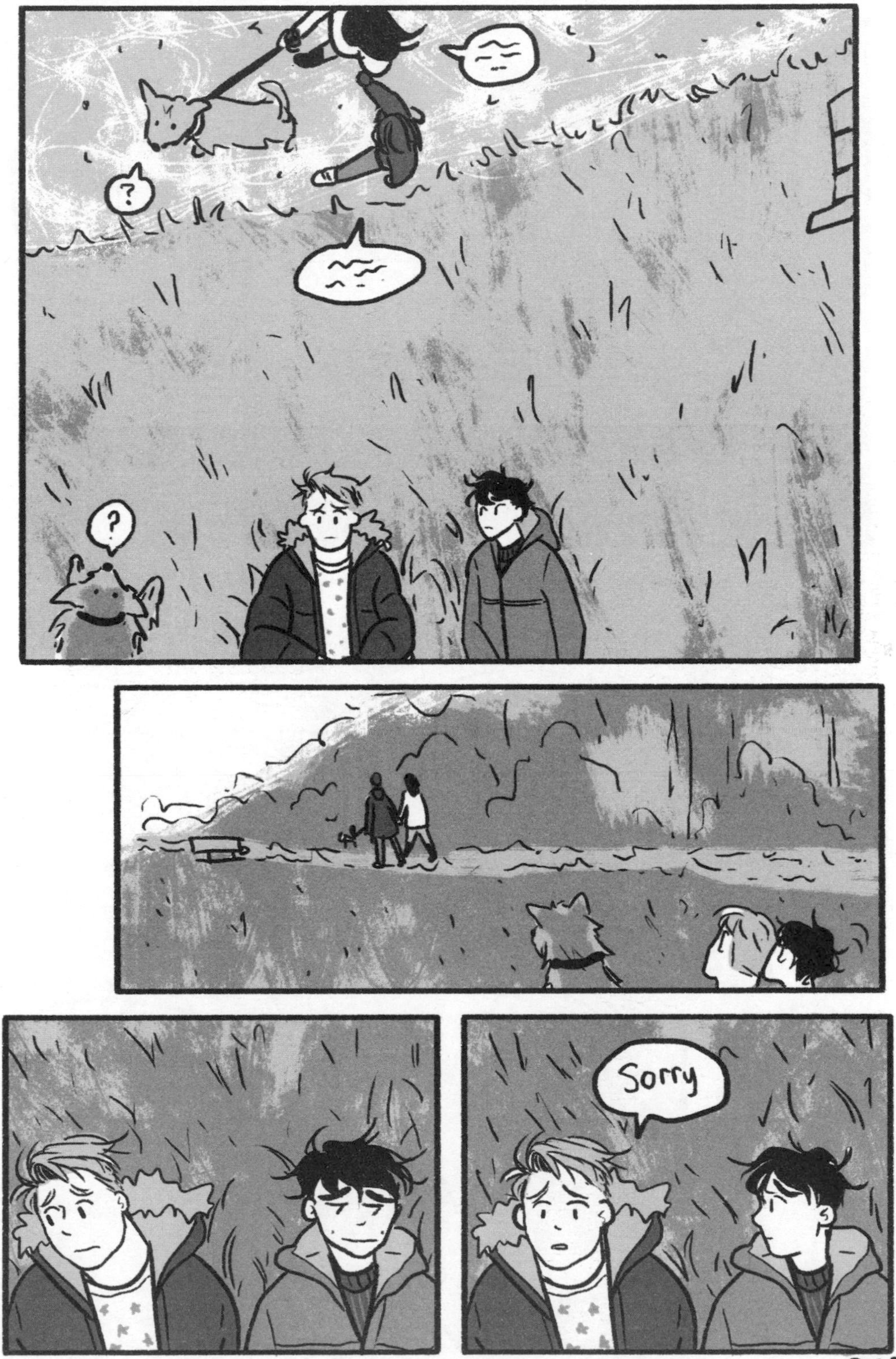
?
?
Sorry

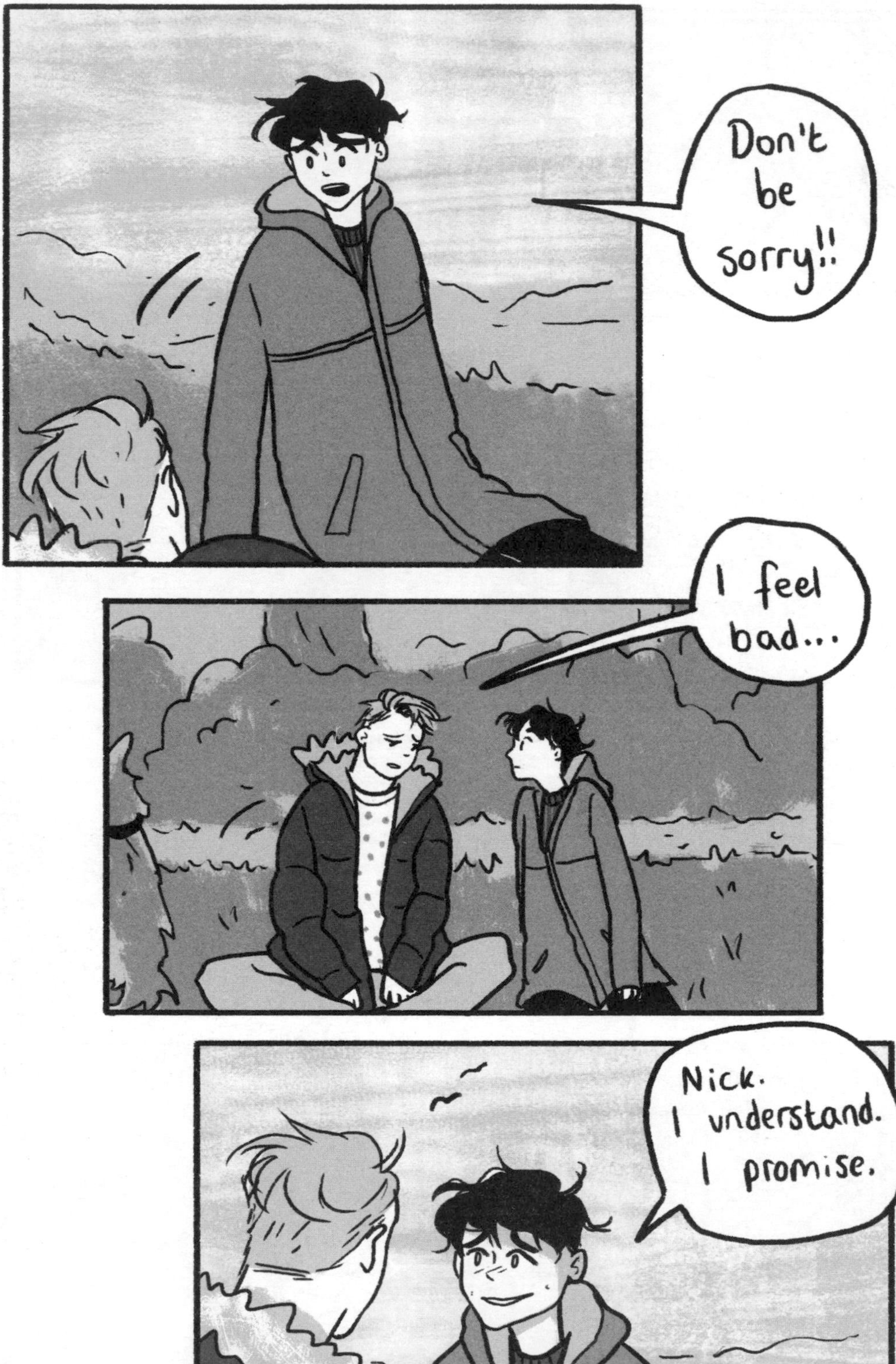
Don't be sorry!!
I feel bad...
Nick. I understand. I promise.

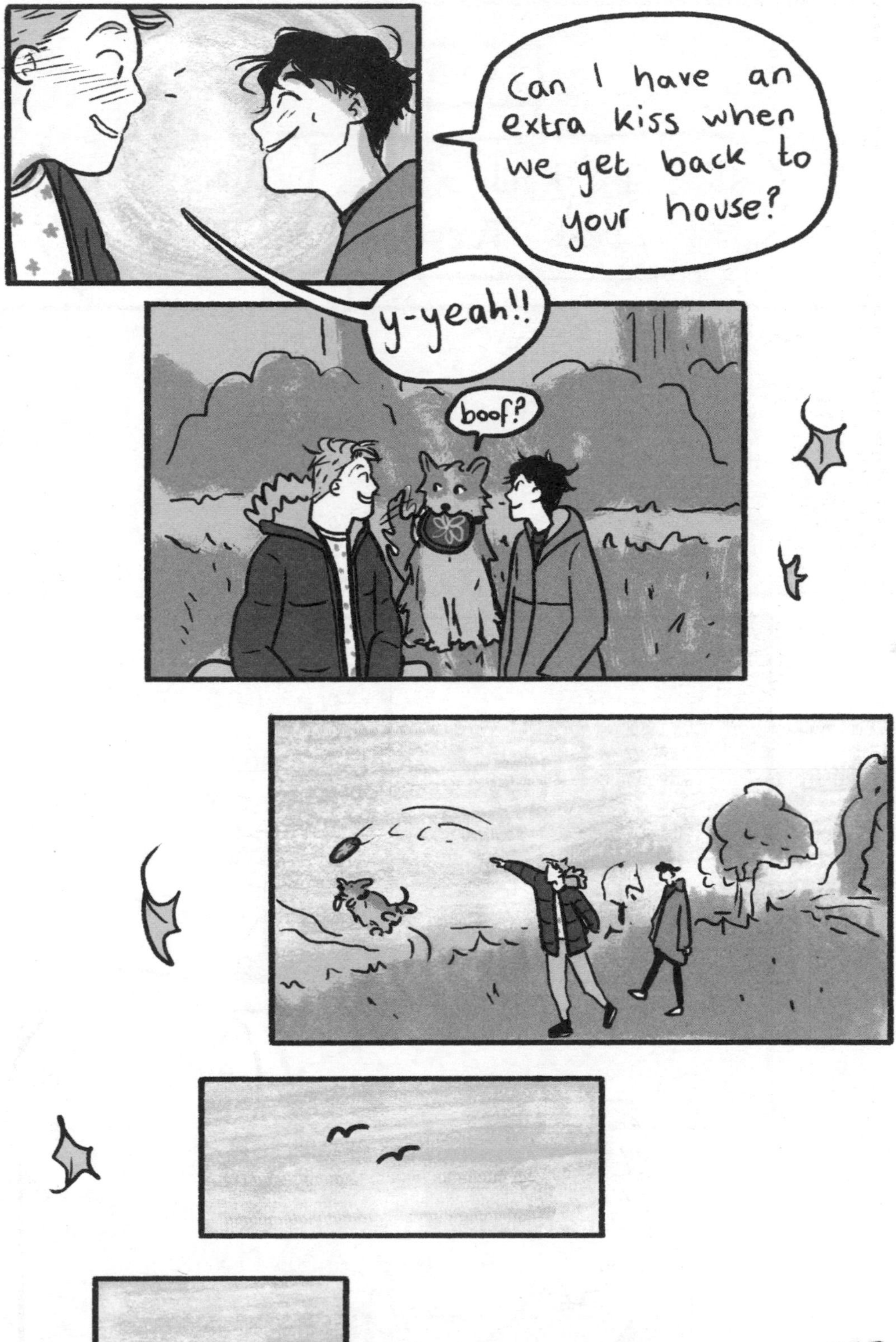
Can I have an extra kiss when we get back to your house?
y-yeah!!
boof?

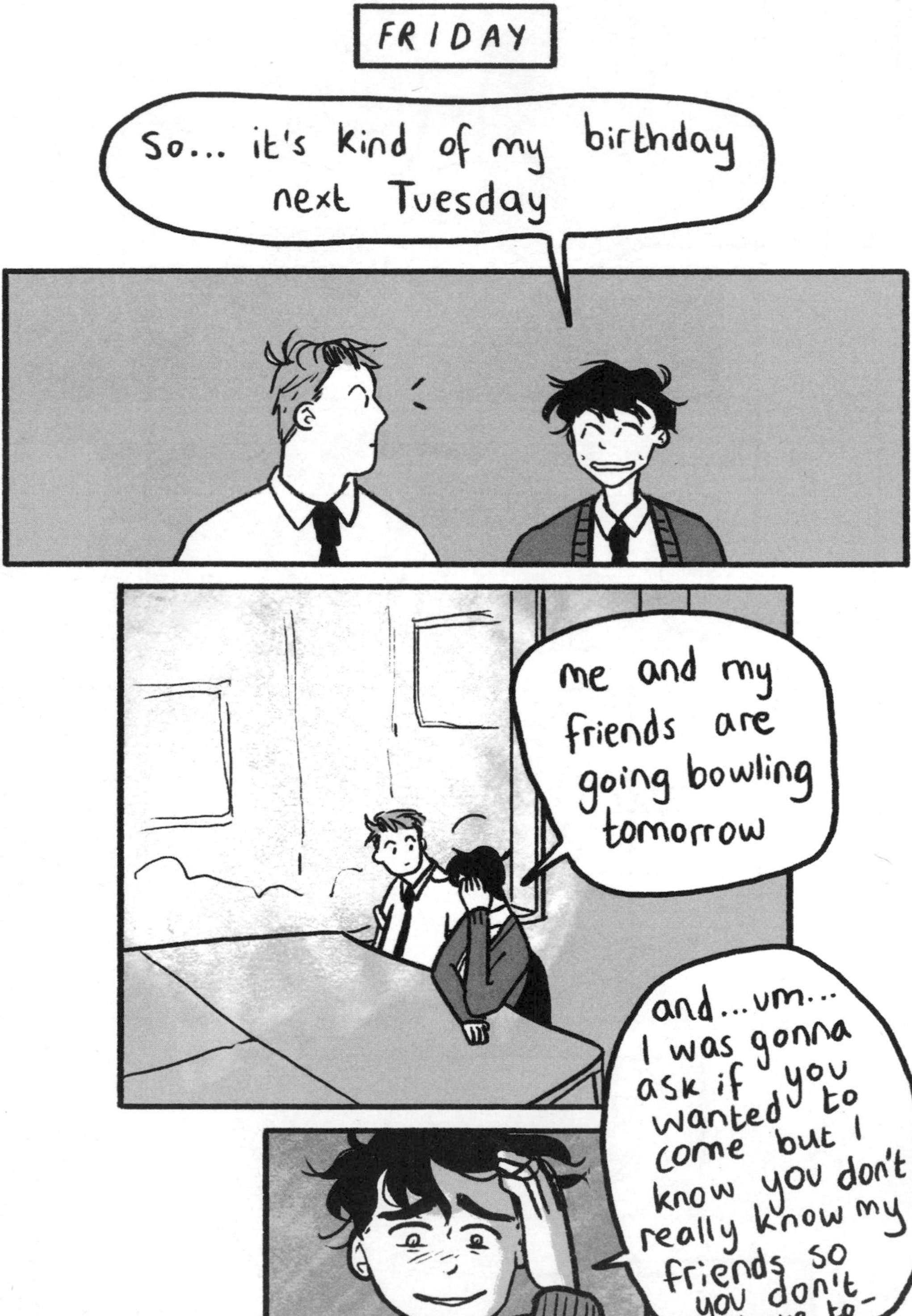
FRIDAY
So... it's kind of my birthday next Tuesday
me and my friends are going bowling tomorrow
and...um... I was gonna ask if you wanted to come but I know you don't really know my friends so you don't have to-

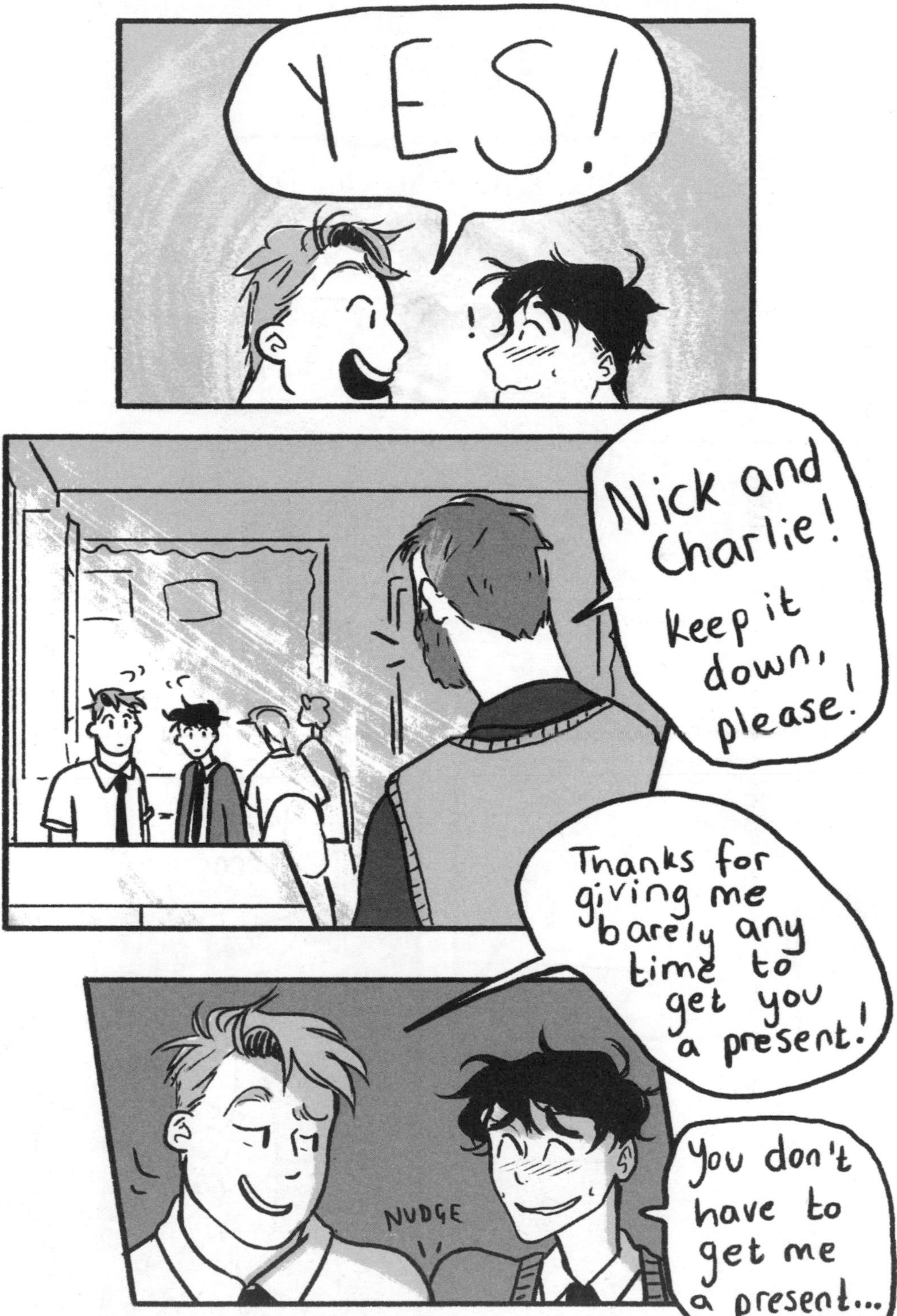
YES!
!
Nick and Charlie! Keep it down, please!
Thanks for giving me barely any time to get you a present!
NUDGE
You don't have to get me a present...

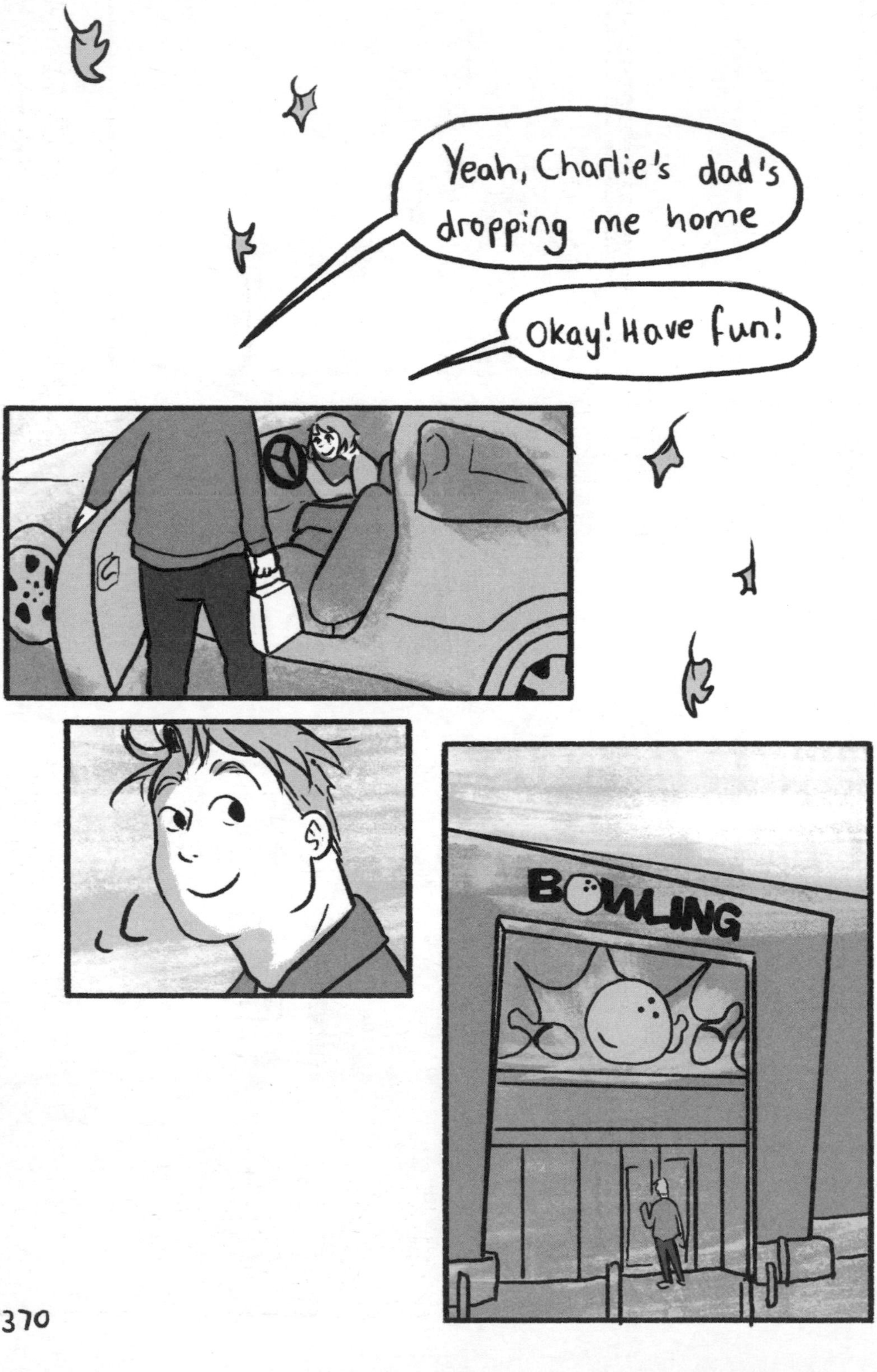
Yeah, Charlie's dad's dropping me home
Okay! Have fun!
BOWLING

SHUT
PUSH
Hey!
RECEPTION
15

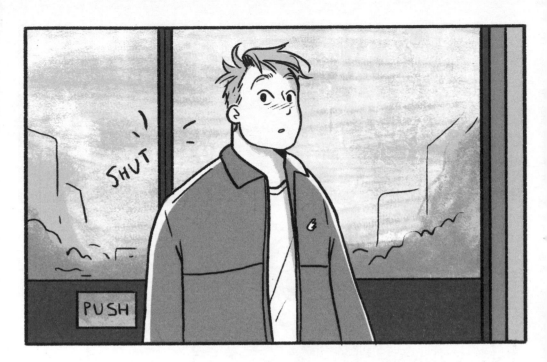

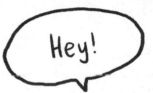

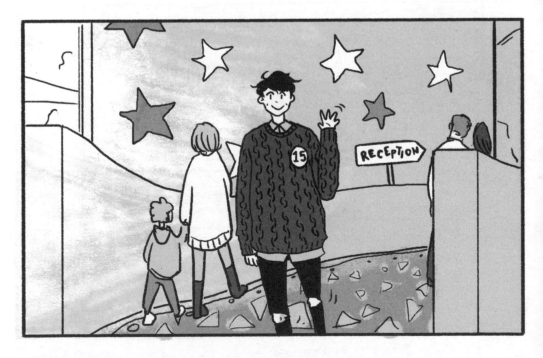

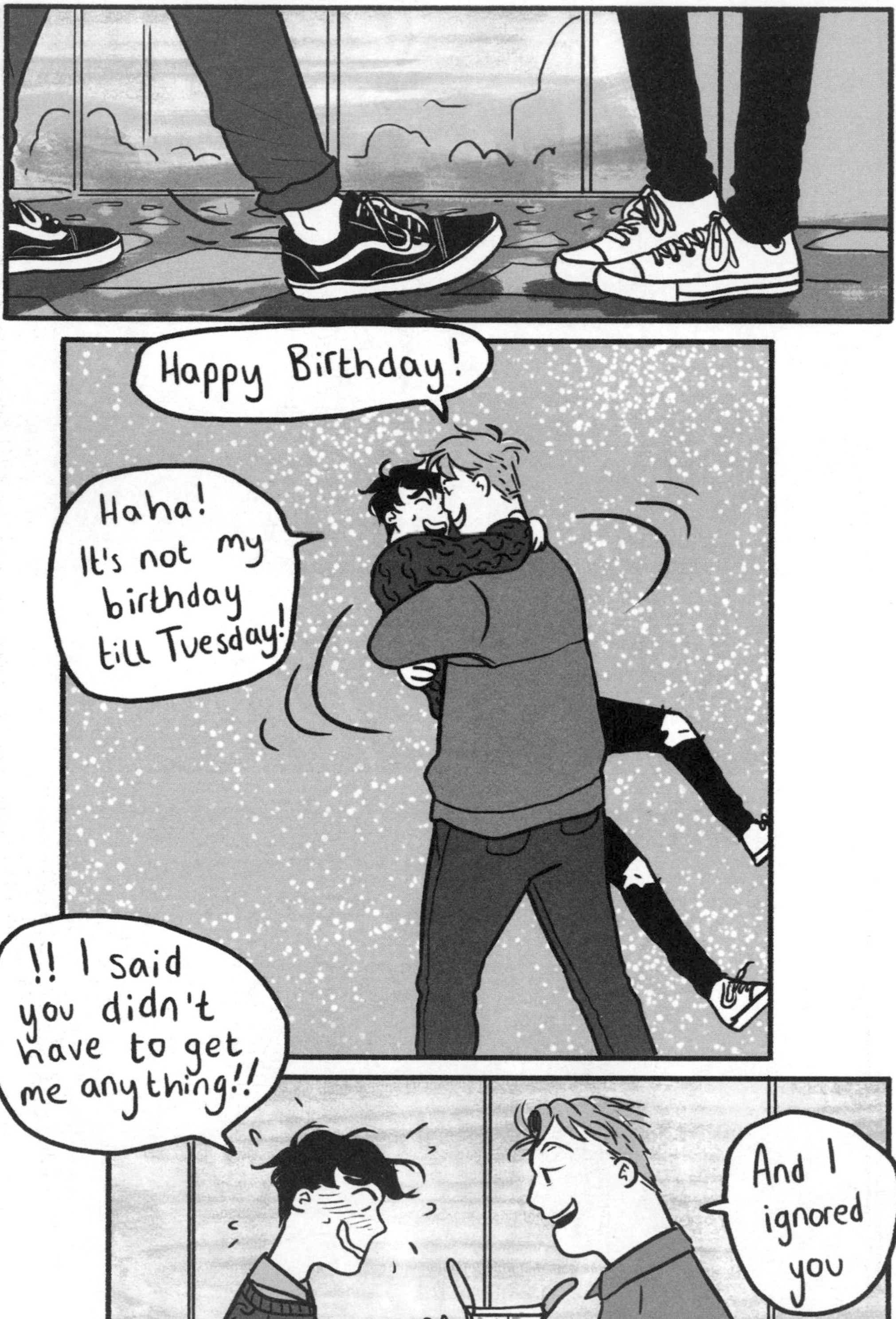
Happy Birthday!
Haha! It's not my birthday till Tuesday!
!! I said you didn't have to get me anything!!
And I ignored you

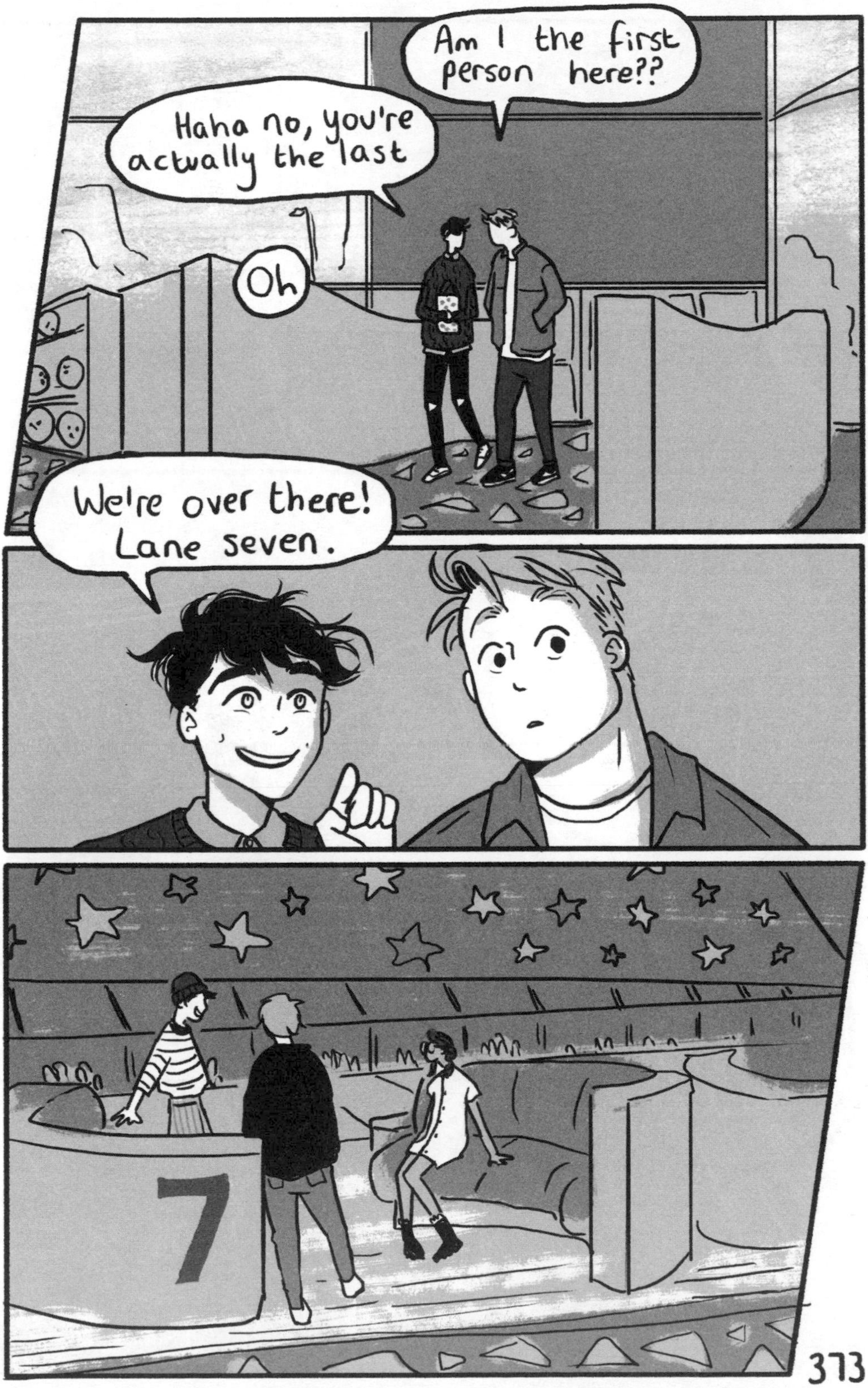
Am I the first person here??
Haha no, you're actually the last
Oh
We're over there! Lane seven.
7

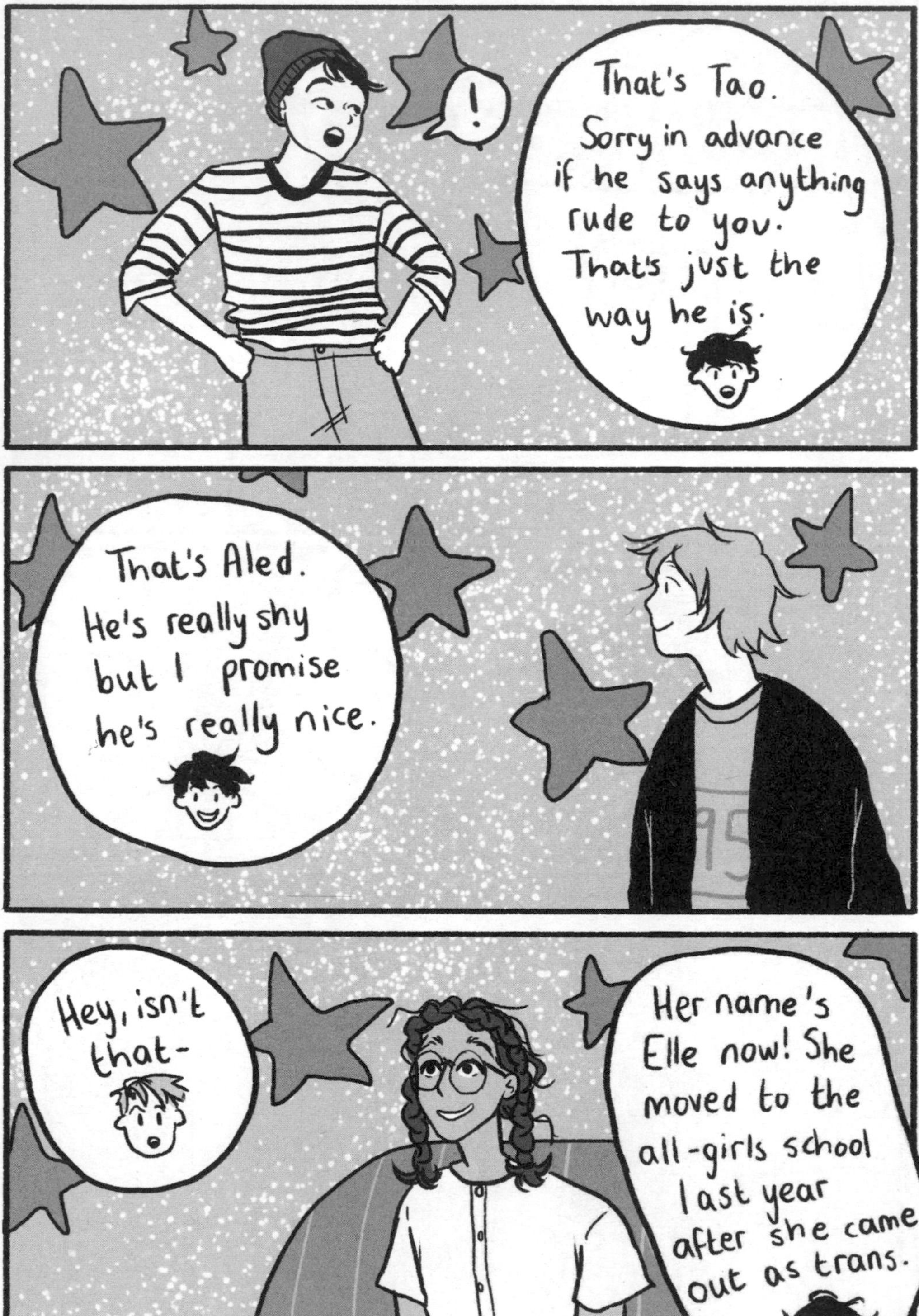
!
That's Tao. Sorry in advance if he says anything rude to you. That's just the way he is.
That's Aled. He's really shy but I promise he's really nice.
Hey, isn't that-
Her name's Elle now! She moved to the all-girls school last year after she came out as trans.

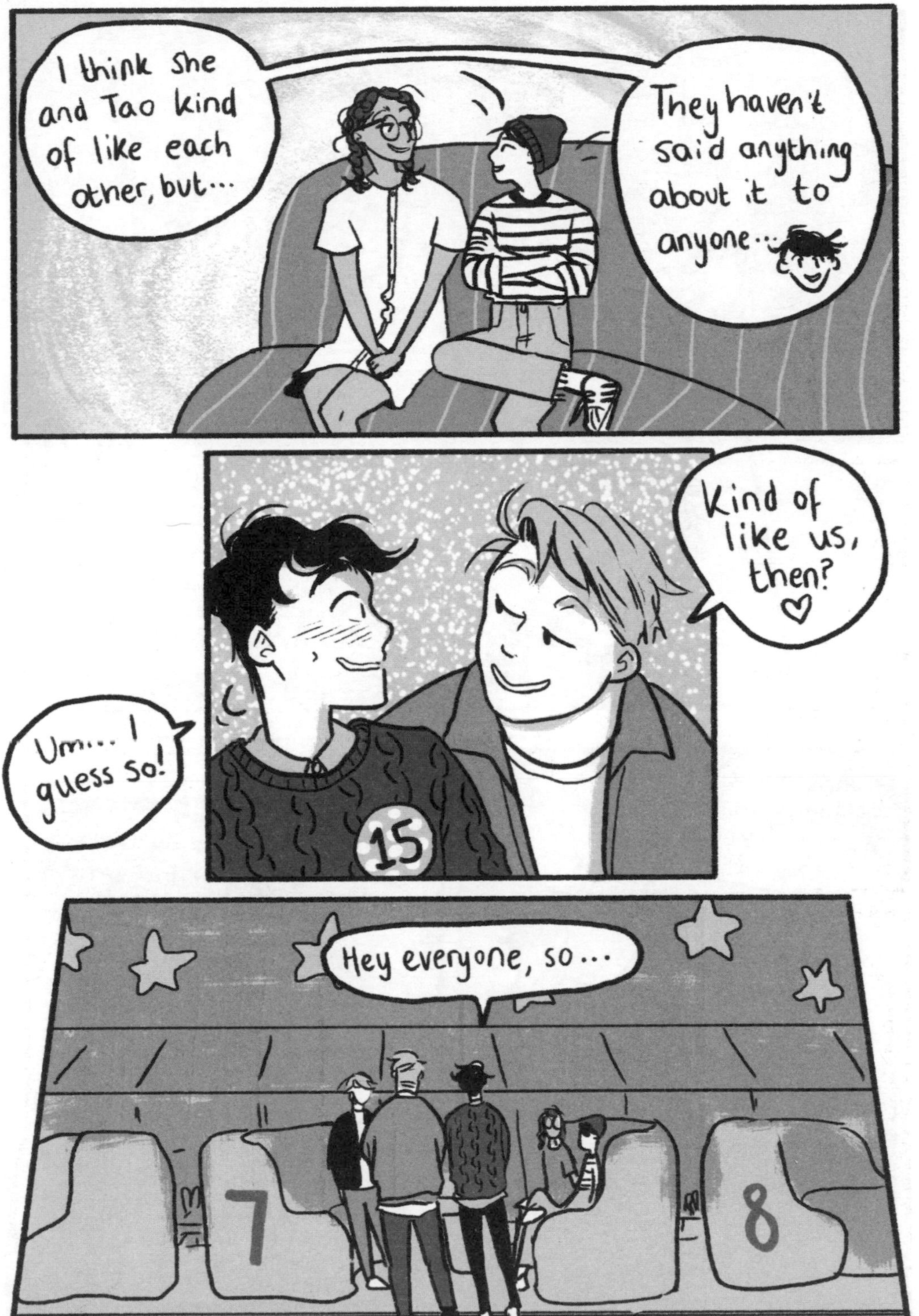
I think she and Tao kind of like each other, but...
They haven't said anything about it to anyone...
Kind of like us, then? ♡
Um... I guess so!
15
Hey everyone, so...
7
8

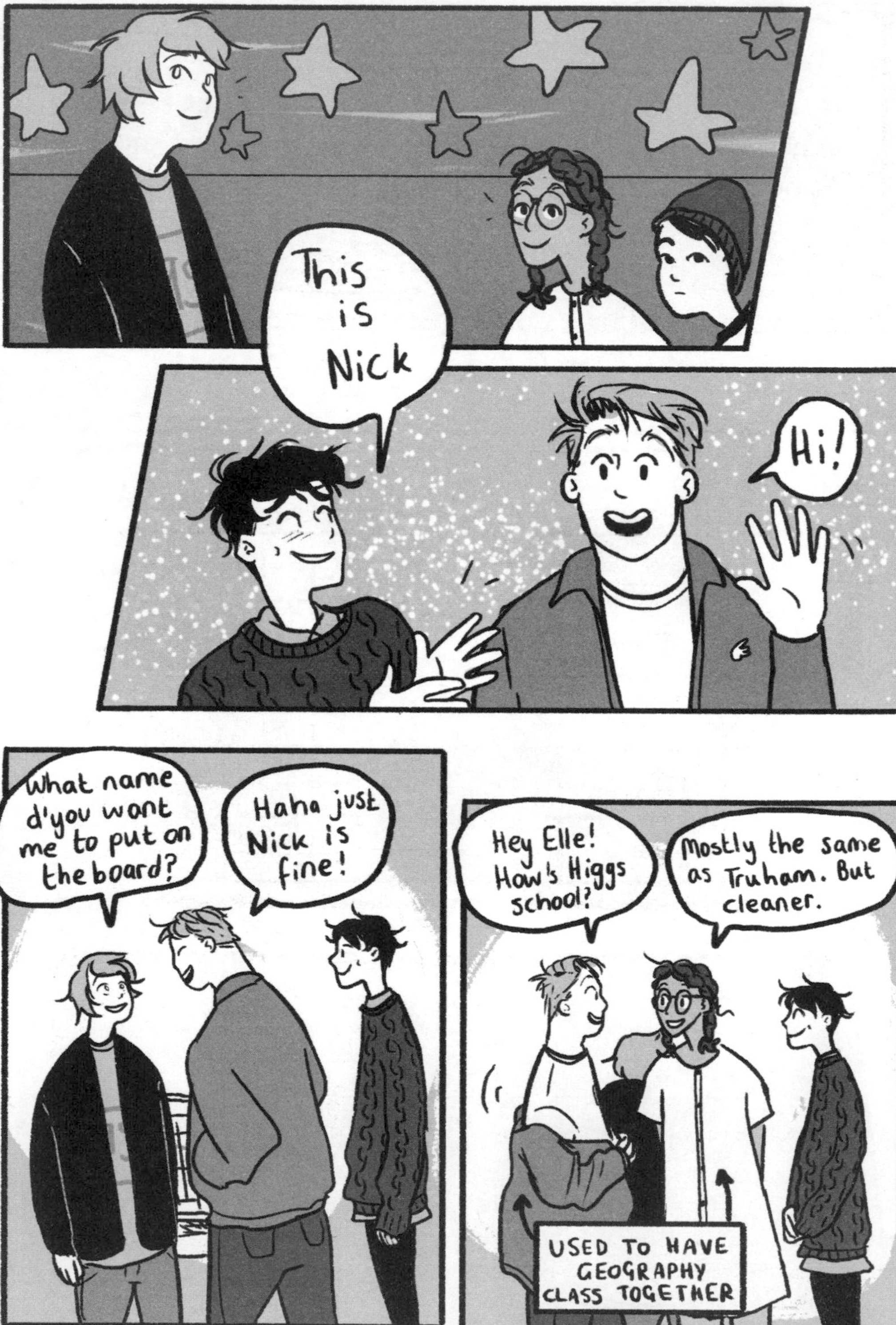
This is Nick
Hi!
What name d'you want me to put on the board?
Haha just Nick is fine!
Hey Elle! How's Higgs school?
Mostly the same as Truham. But cleaner.
USED TO HAVE GEOGRAPHY CLASS TOGETHER

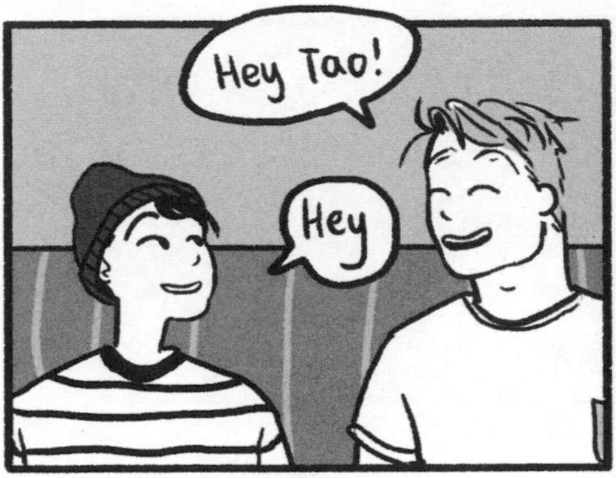
Hey Tao!
Hey

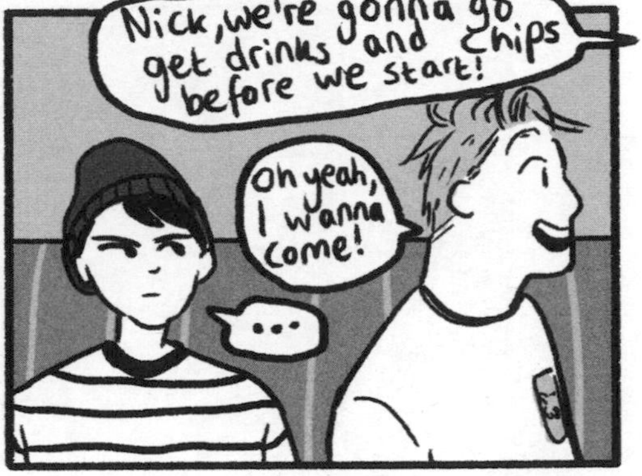
Nick, we're gonna go get drinks and chips before we start!
Oh yeah, I wanna come!
...

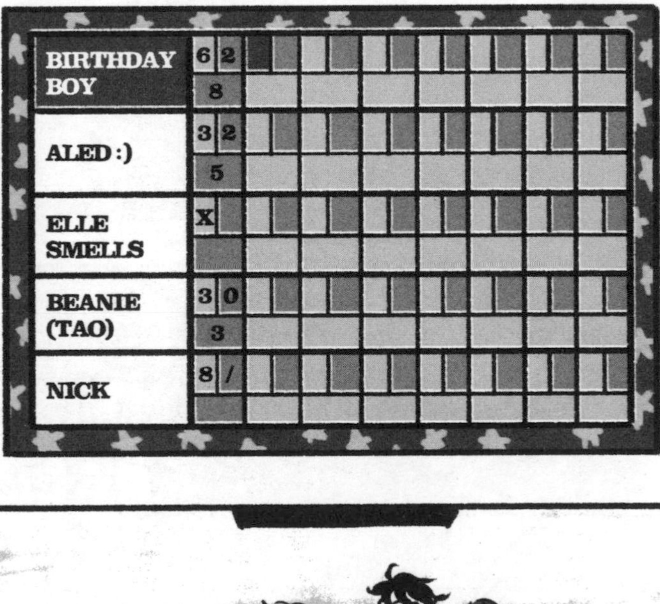
BIRTHDAY BOY
6 2
8
ALED :)
3 2
5
ELLE SMELLS
X
BEANIE (TAO)
3 0
3
NICK
8 /

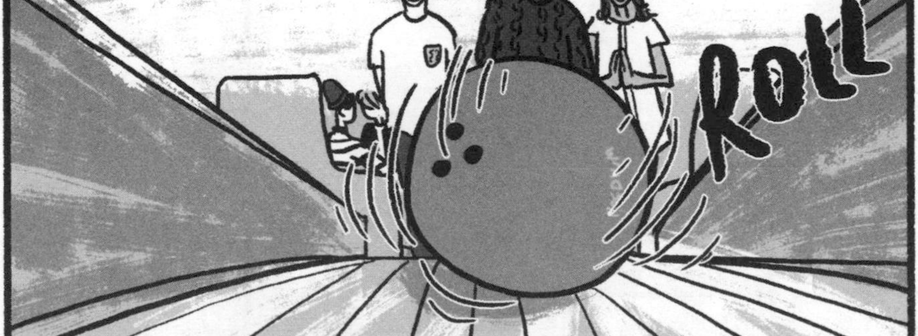
ROLL

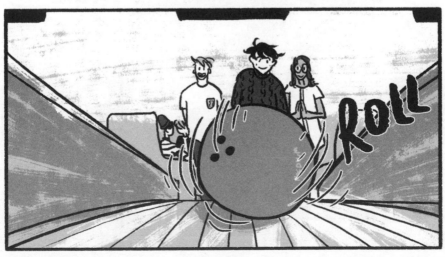

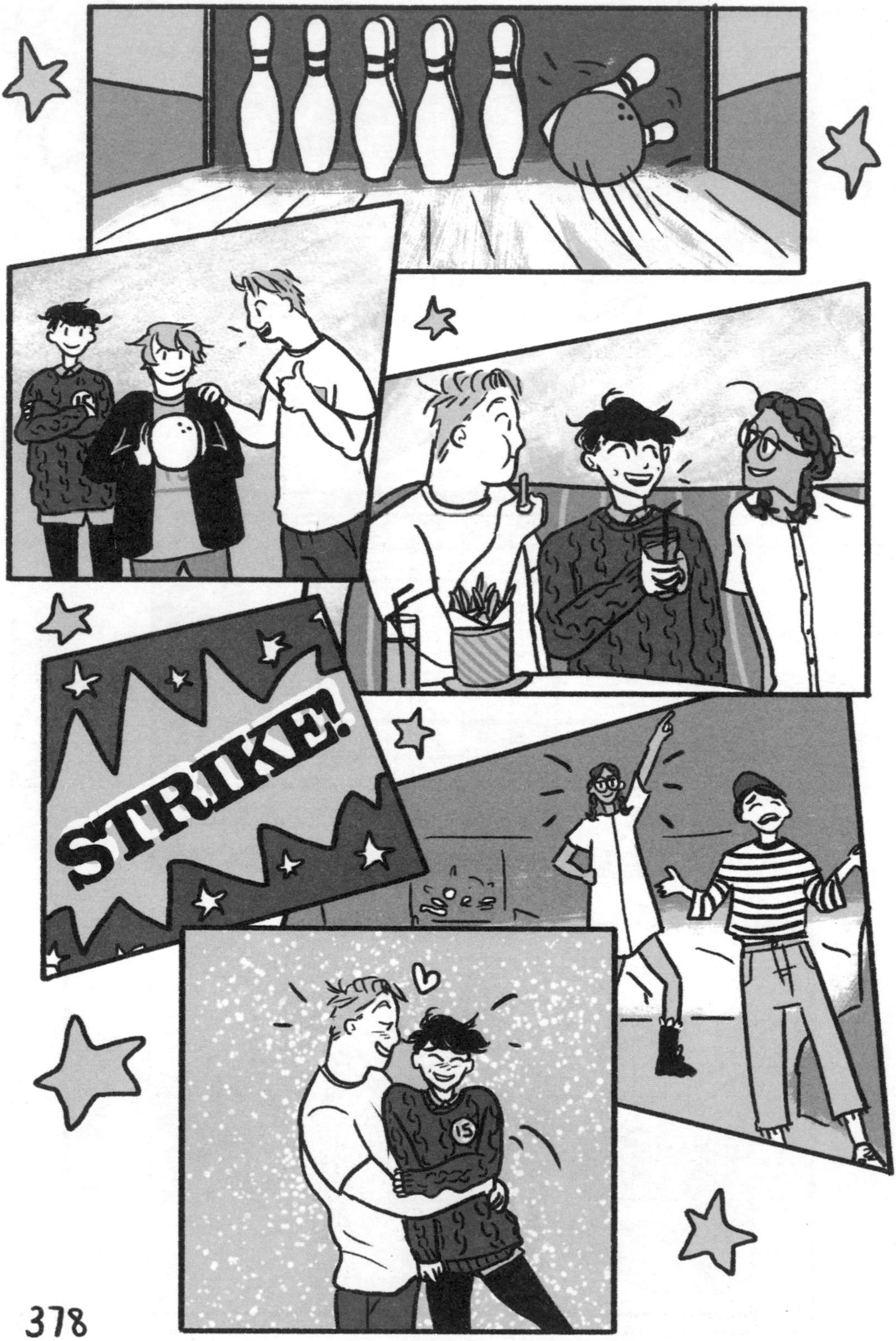
STRIKE!

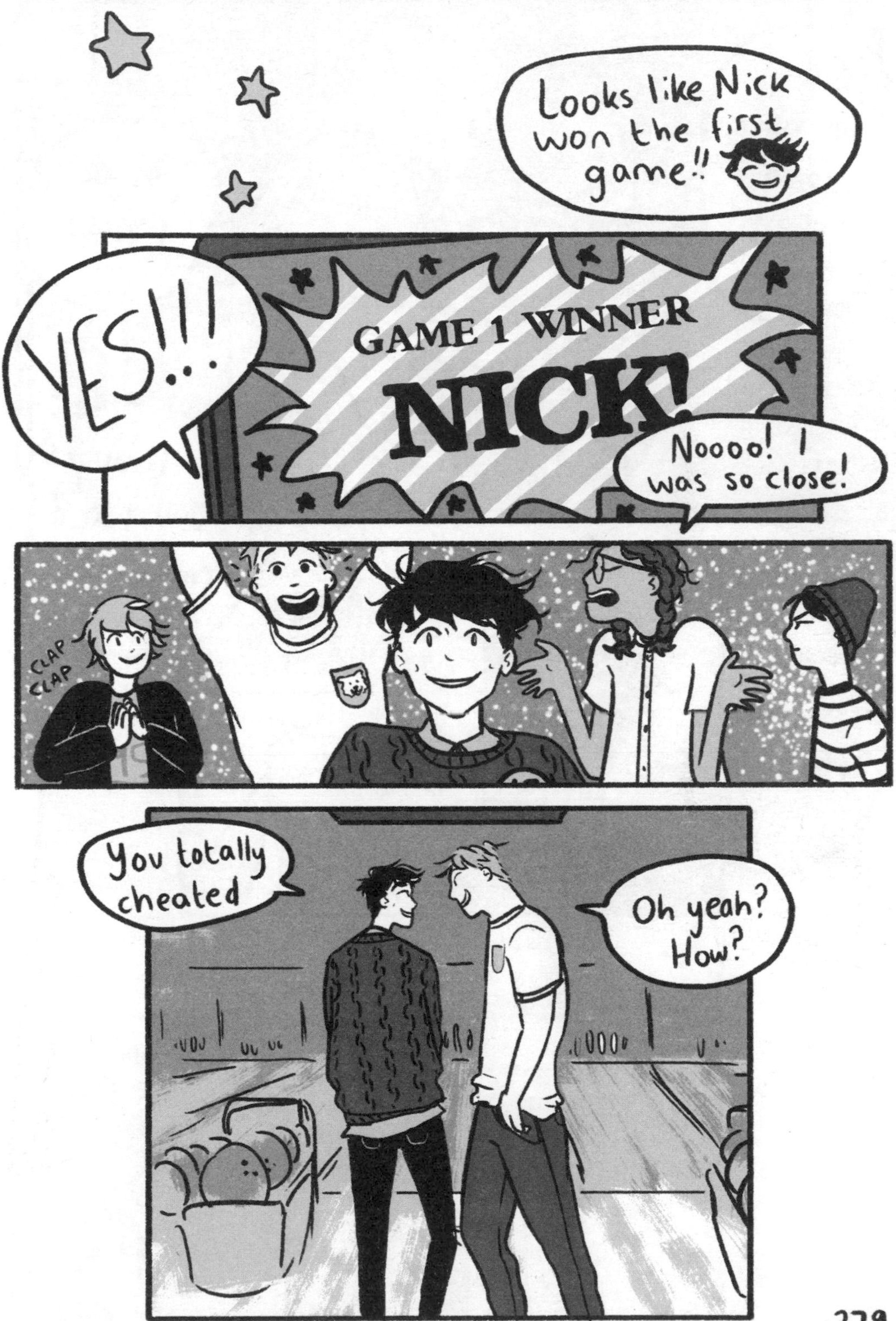
Looks like Nick won the first game!!
YES!!!...
GAME 1 WINNER
NICK!
Noooo! I was so close!
CLAP CLAP
You totally cheated
Oh yeah? How?

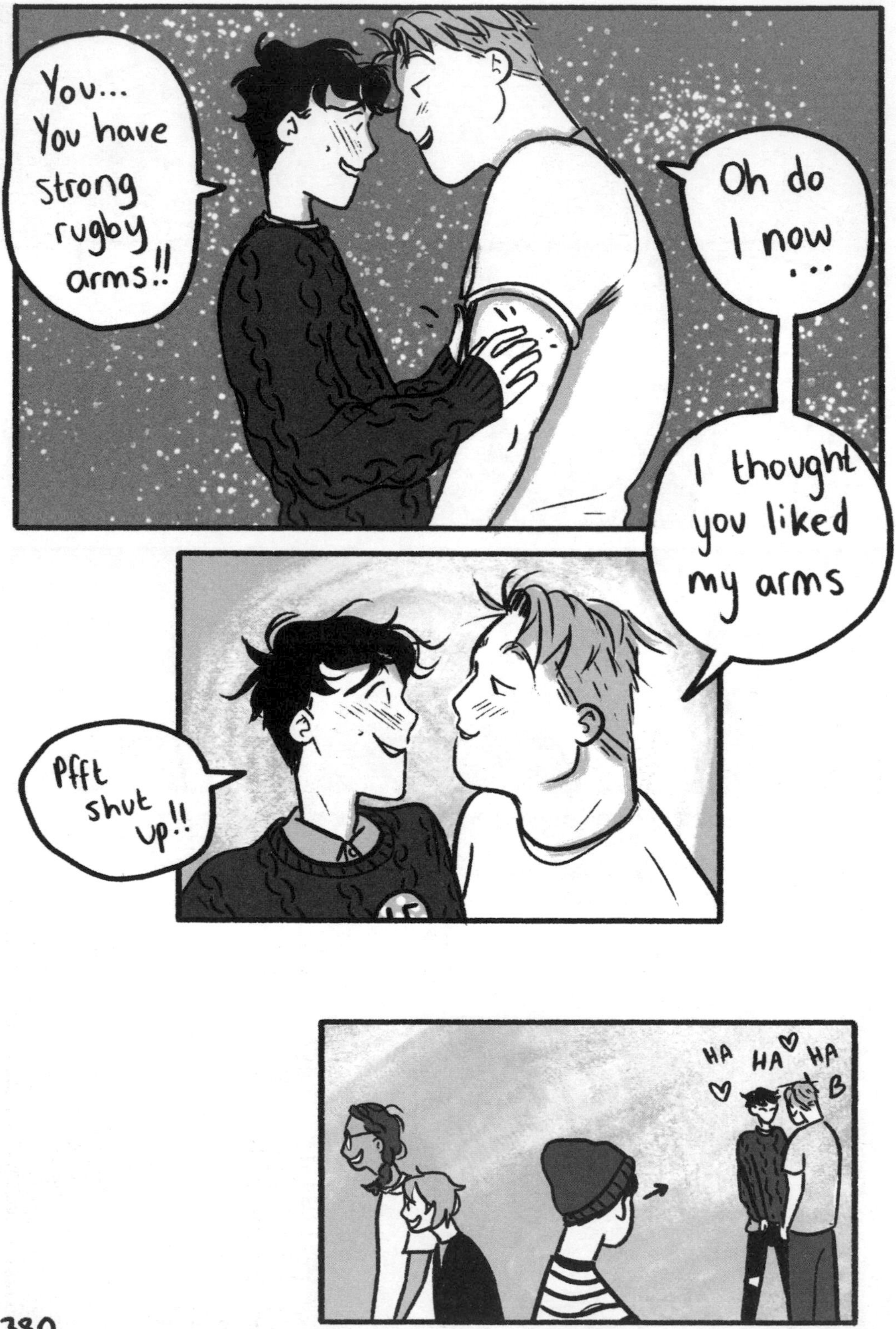
You... You have strong rugby arms!!
Oh do I now ...
I thought you liked my arms
Pfft shut up!!
HA HA HA
B

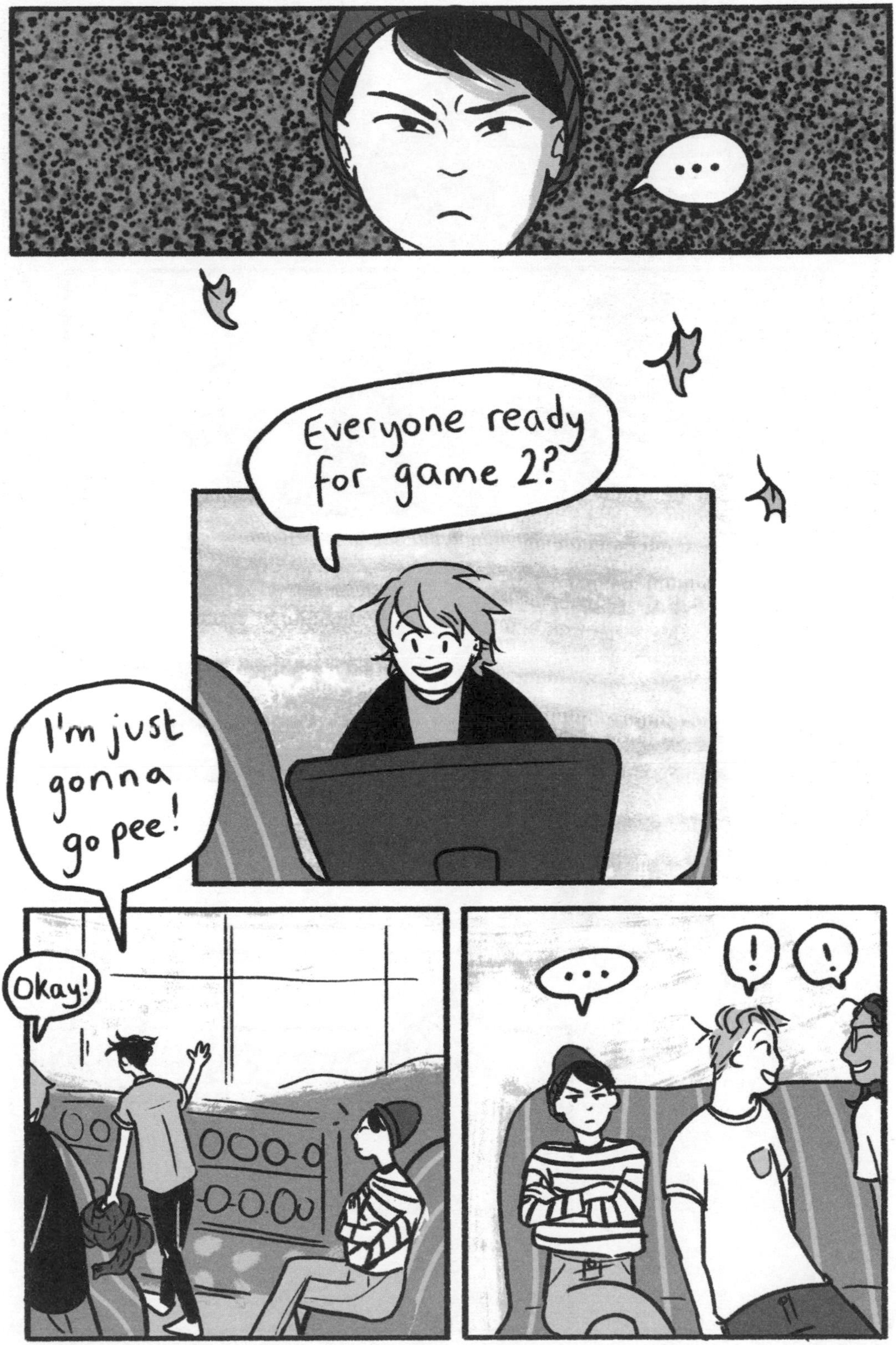
...
Everyone ready for game 2?
I'm just gonna go pee!
Okay!
...
!
!

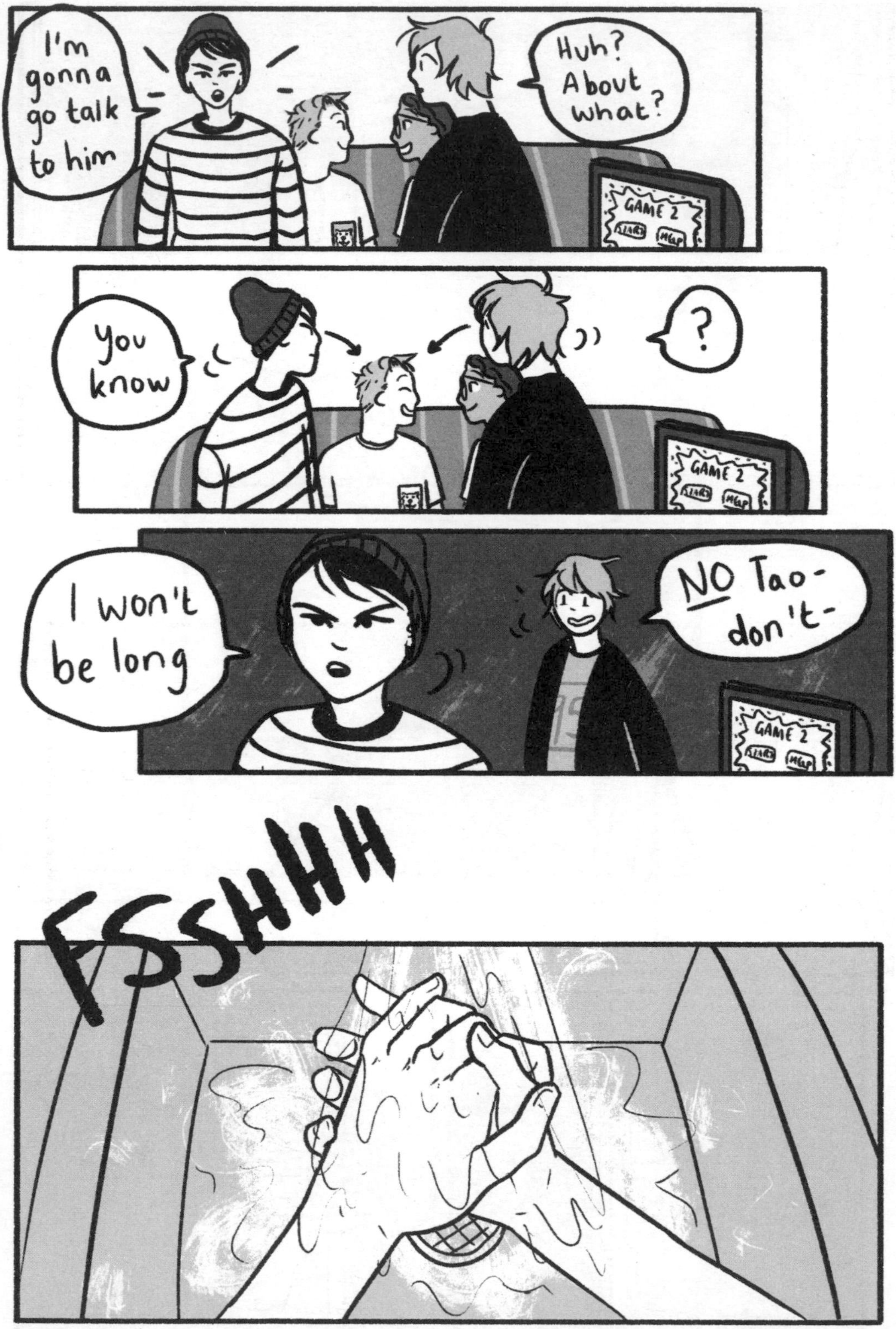
I'm gonna go talk to him
Huh? About what?
GAME 2
You know
?
GAME 2
I won't be long
NO Tao- don't-
GAME 2
FSSHHH

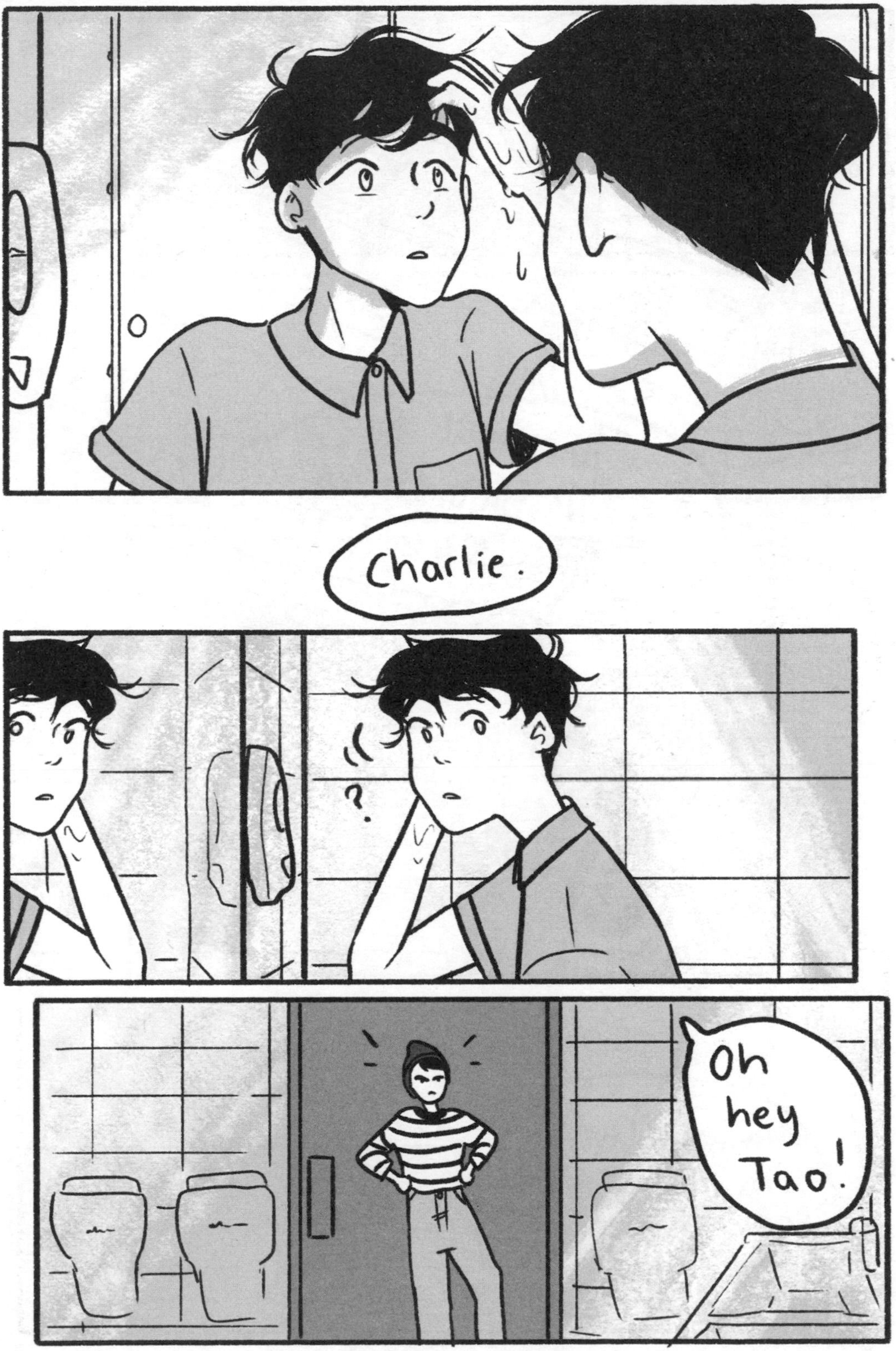
Charlie.
?
Oh hey Tao!

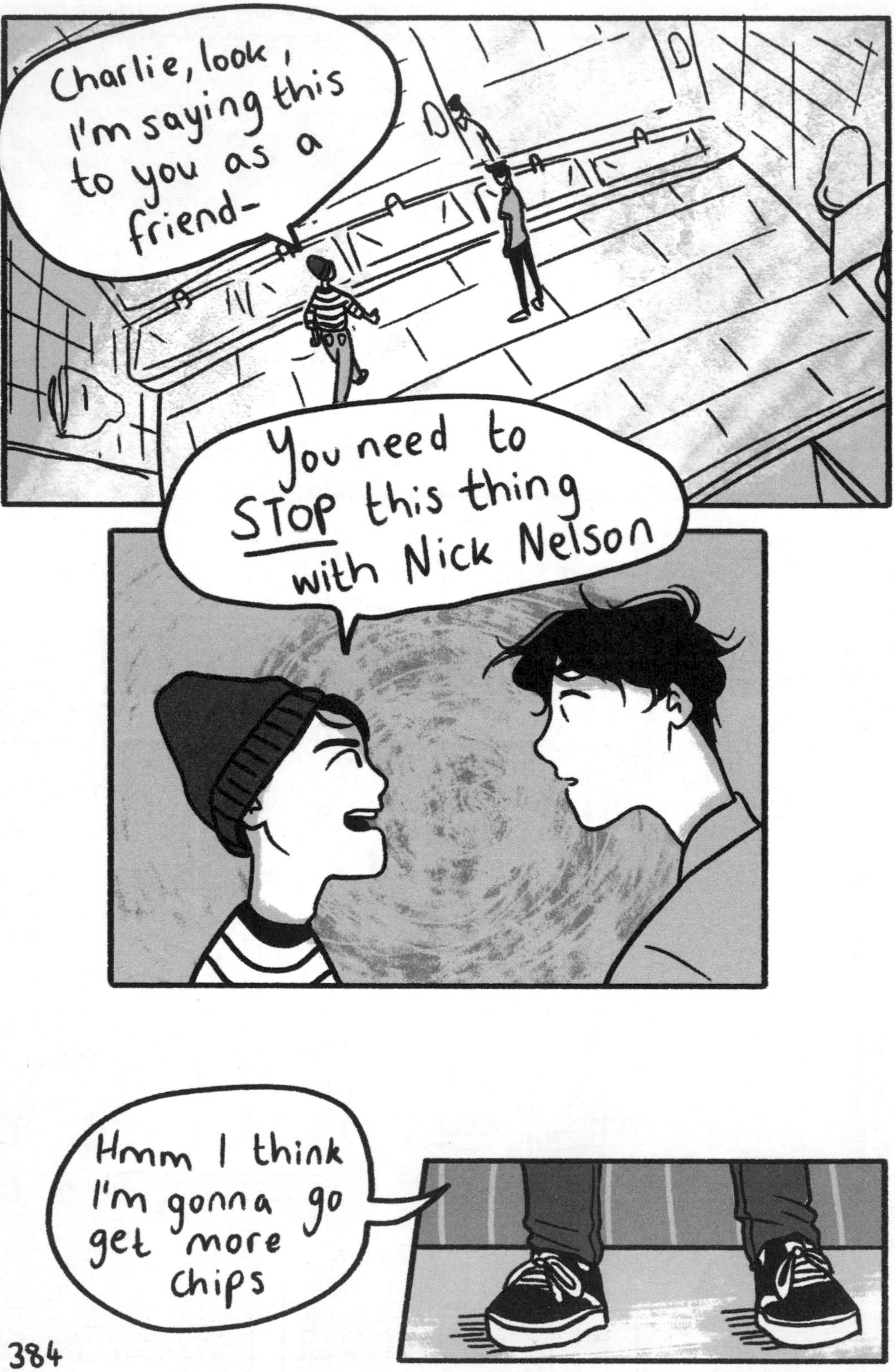
Charlie, look, I'm saying this to you as a friend-
You need to STOP this thing with Nick Nelson
Hmm I think I'm gonna go get more chips

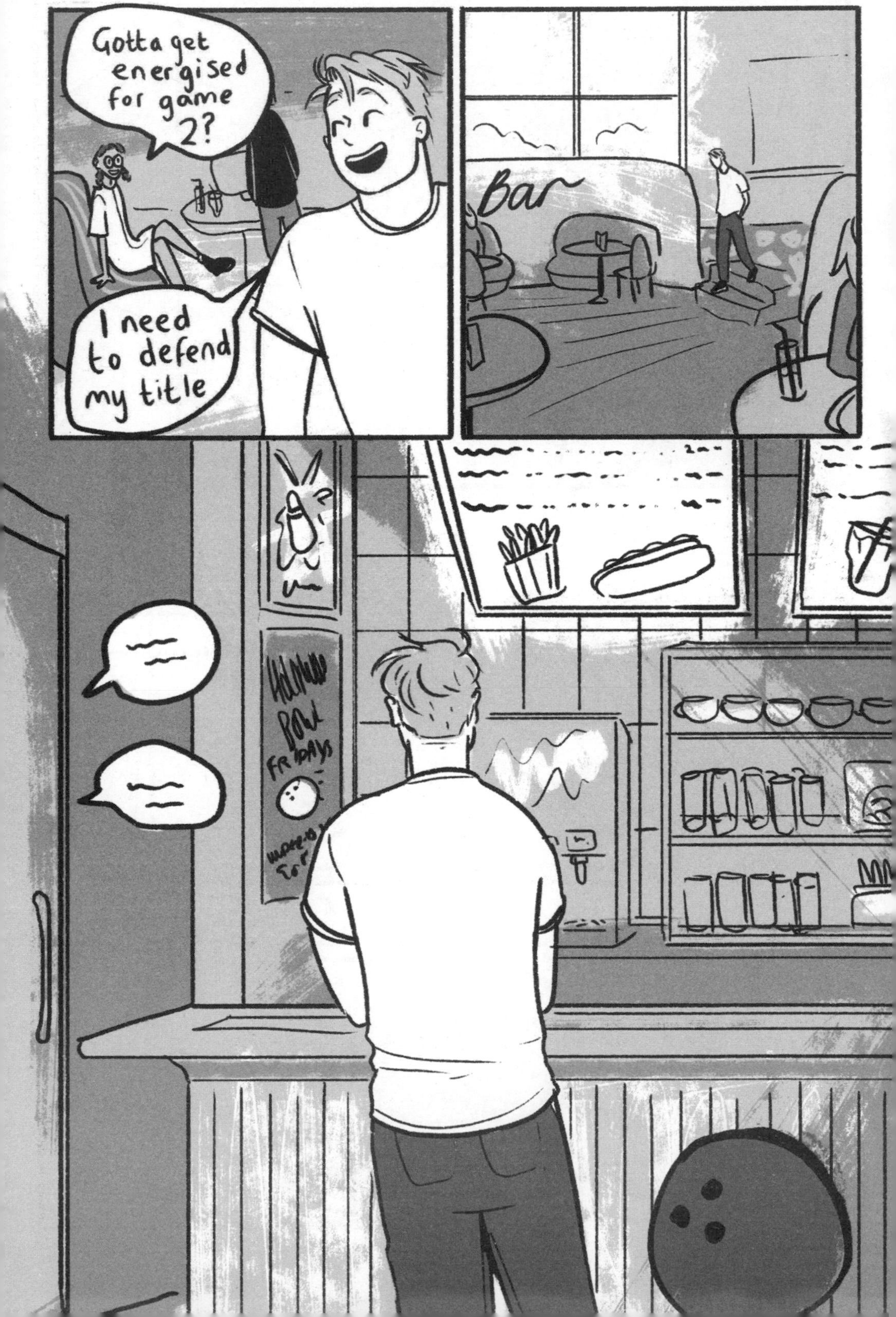
Gotta get energised for game 2?
I need to defend my title
Bar

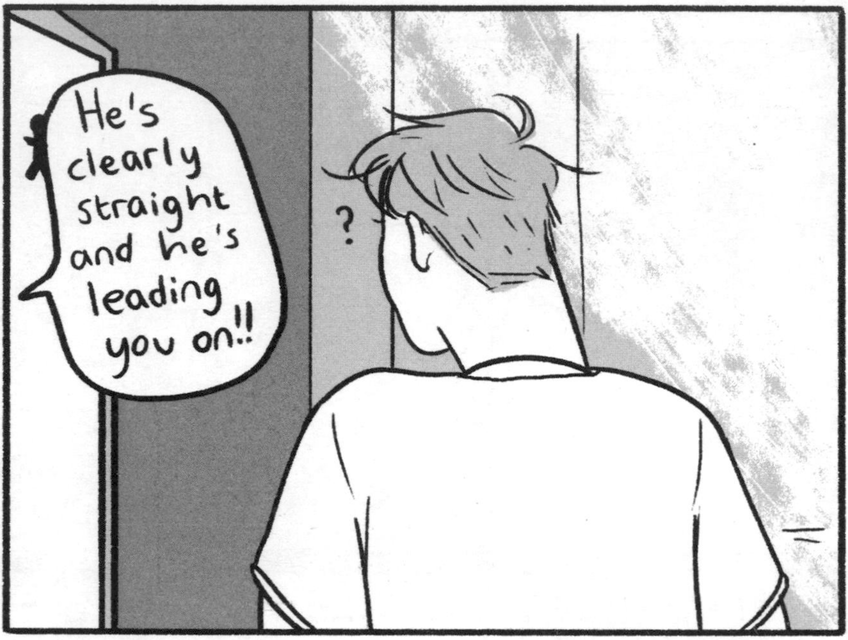
He's clearly straight and he's leading you on!!
?

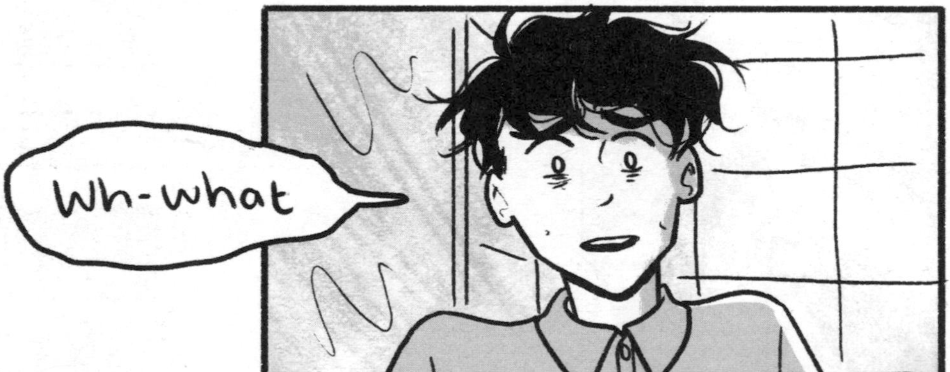
Wh-what

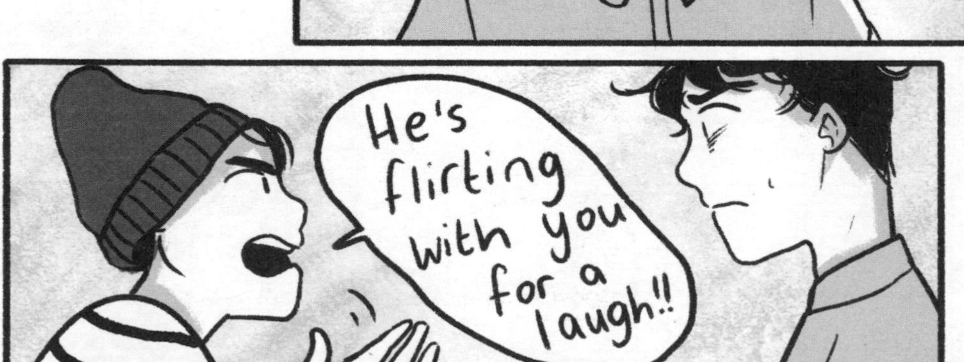
He's flirting with you for a laugh!!

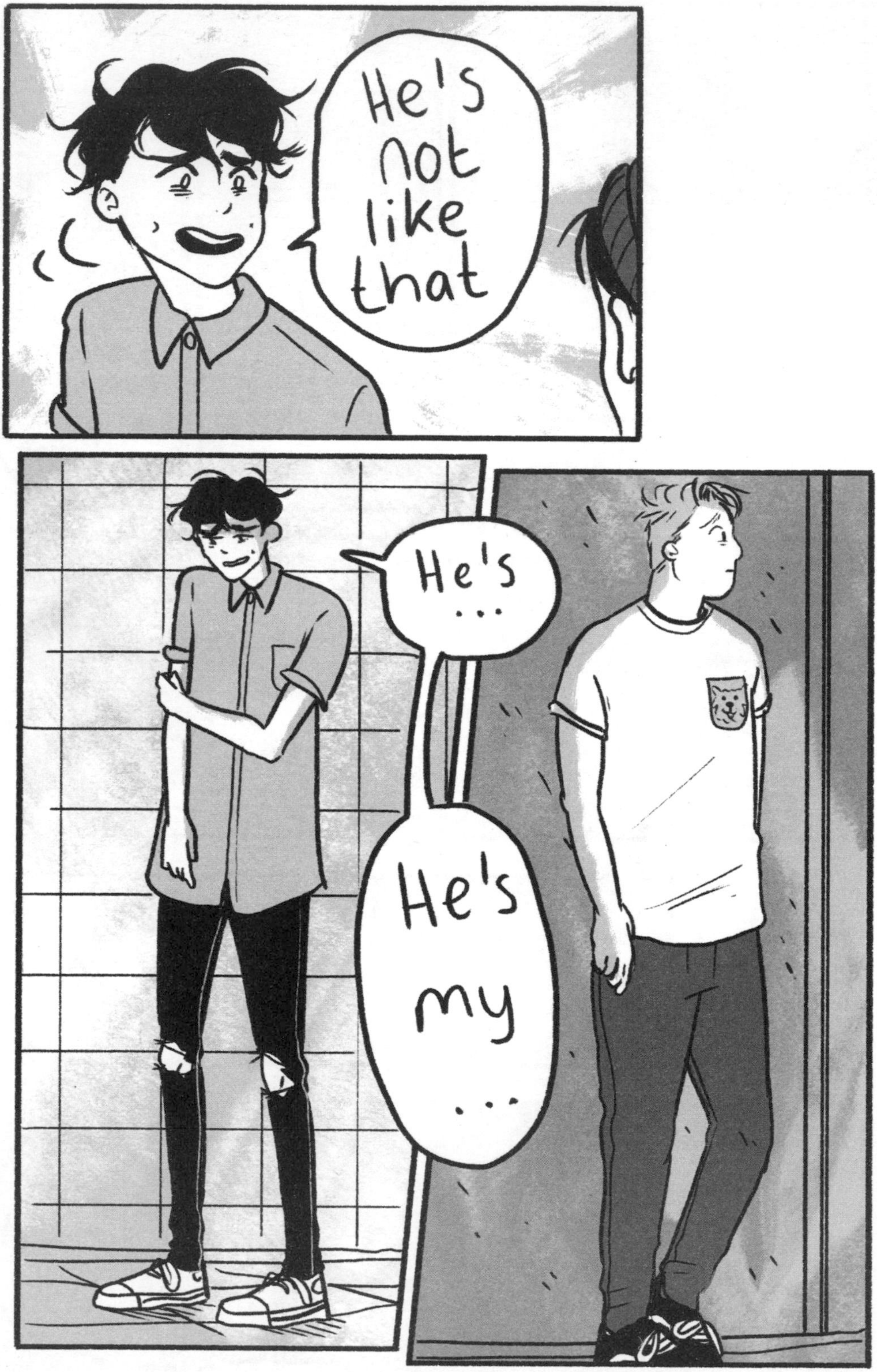
He's not like that
He's ...
He's my ...

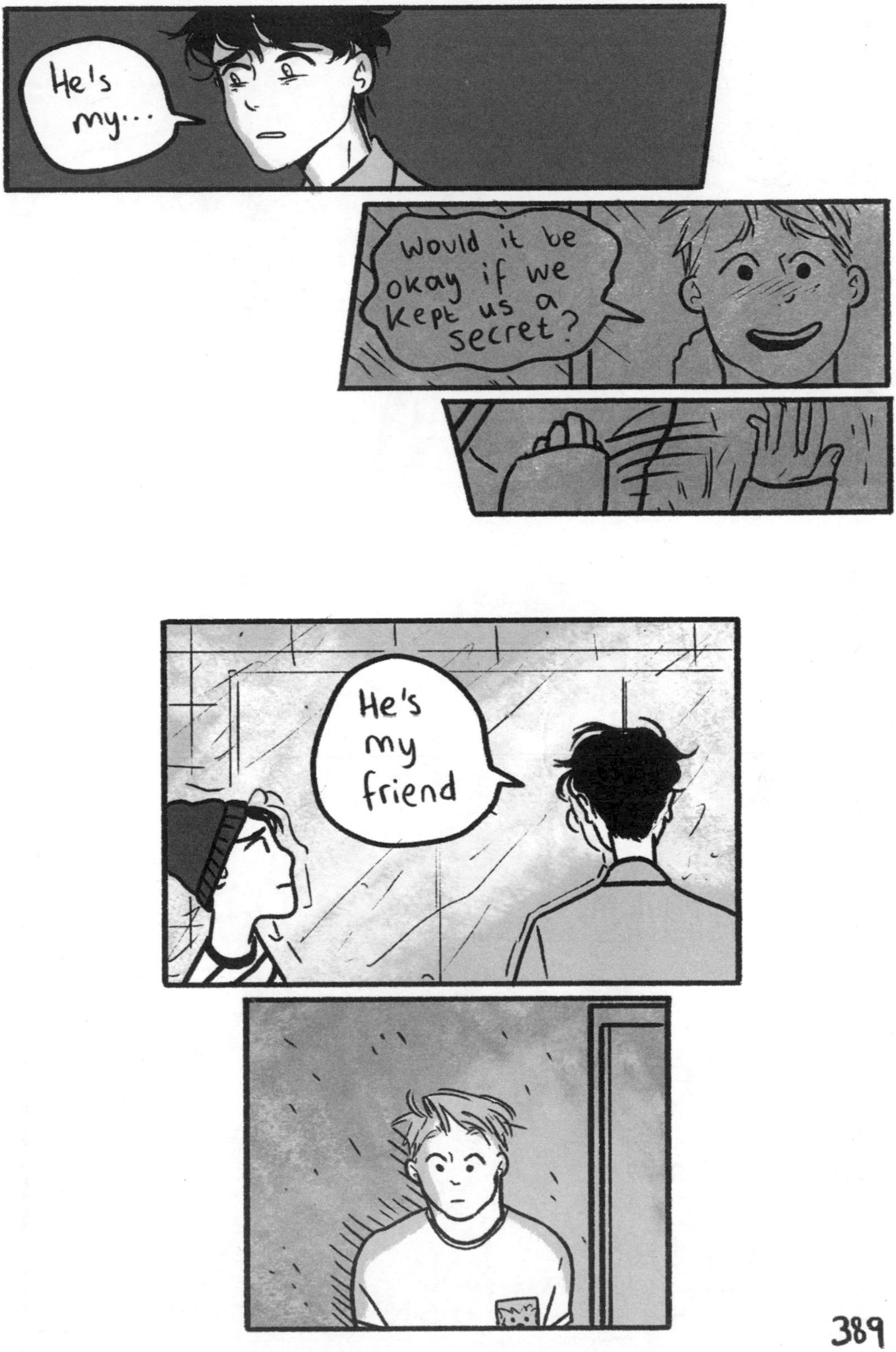
He's my...
Would it be okay if we kept us a secret?
He's my friend

390

391

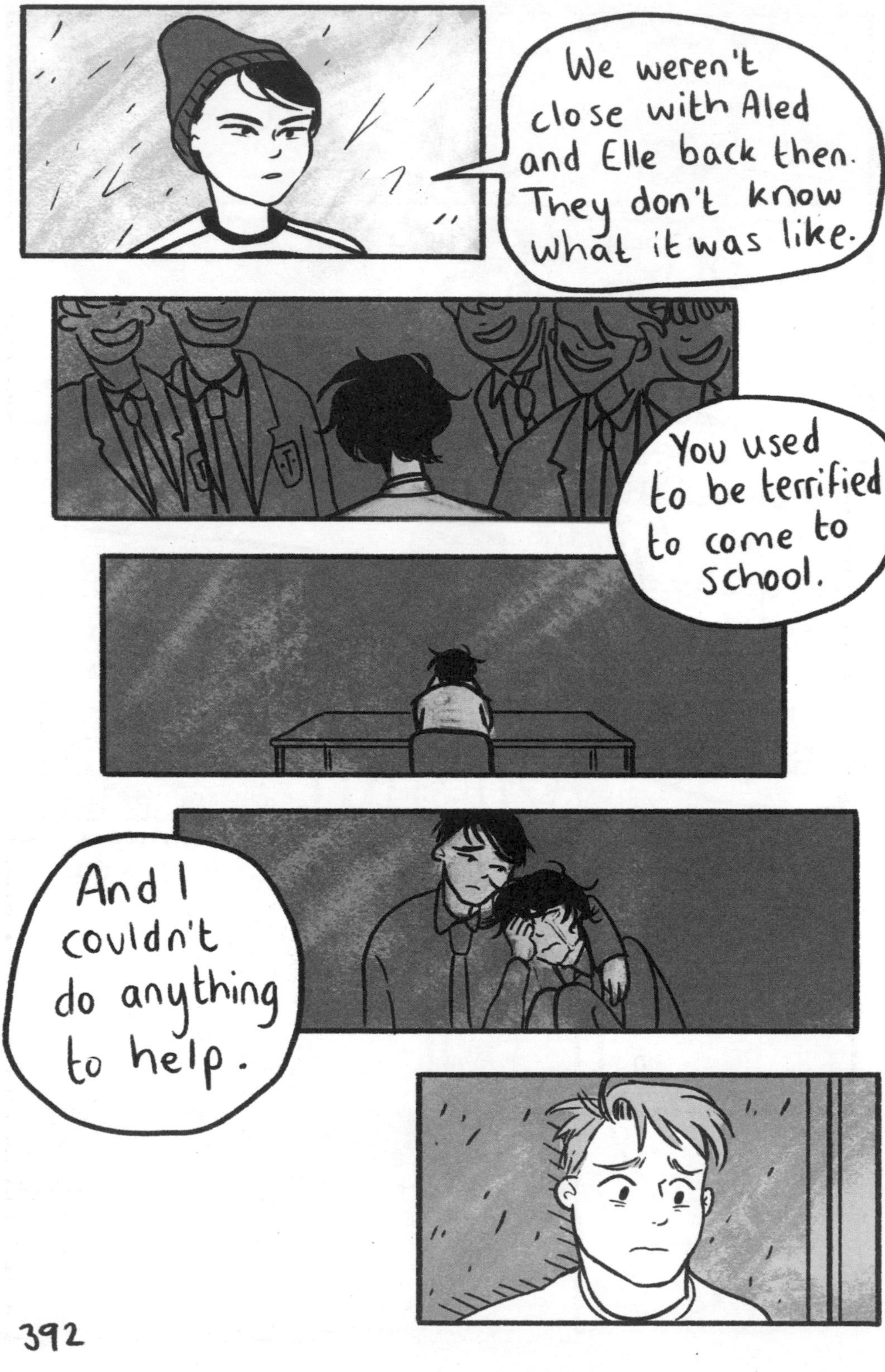
We weren't close with Aled and Elle back then. They don't know what it was like.
You used to be terrified to come to school.
And I couldn't do anything to help.

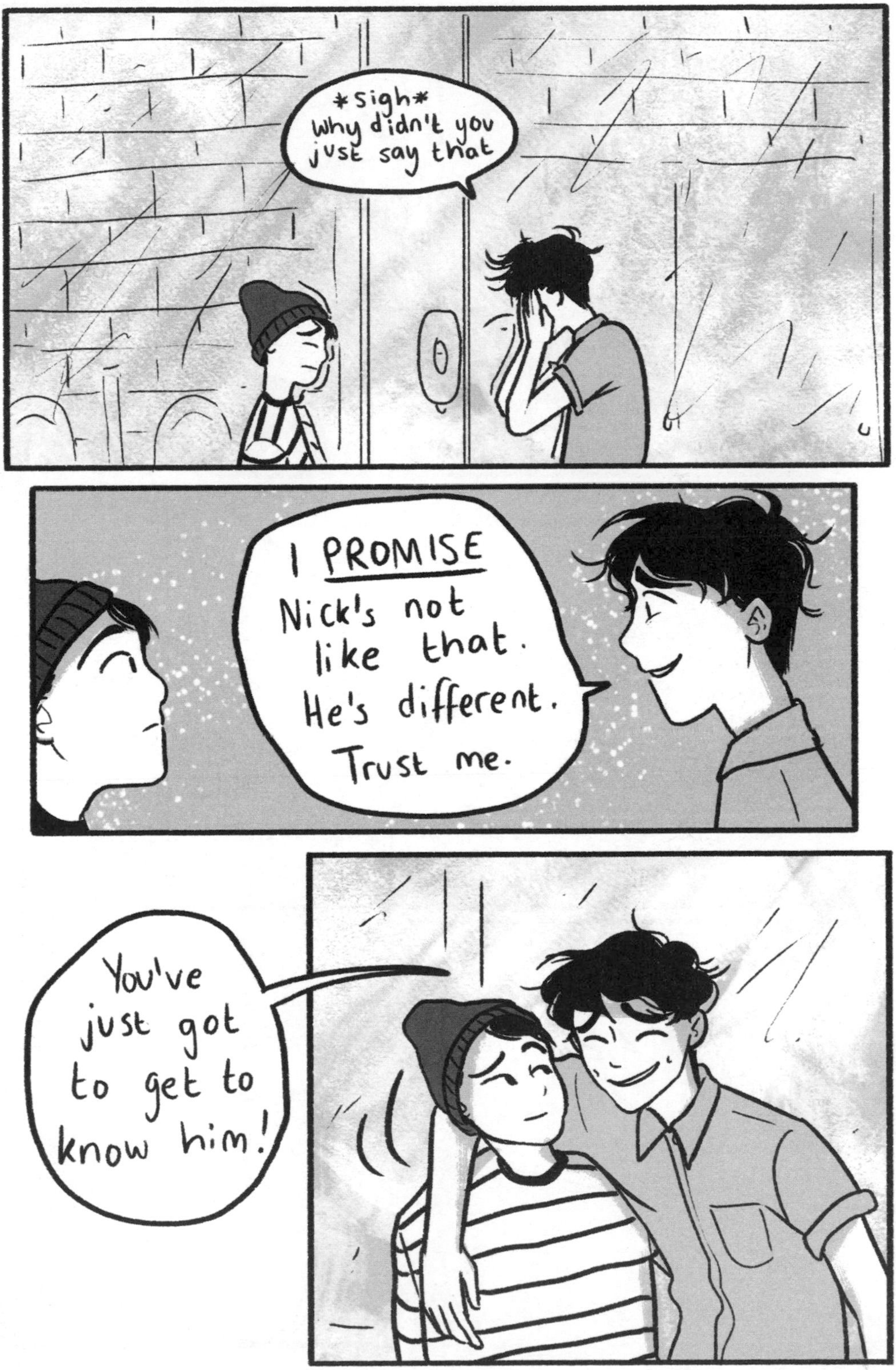
sigh
why didn't you just say that
I PROMISE Nick's not like that. He's different. Trust me.
You've just got to get to know him!

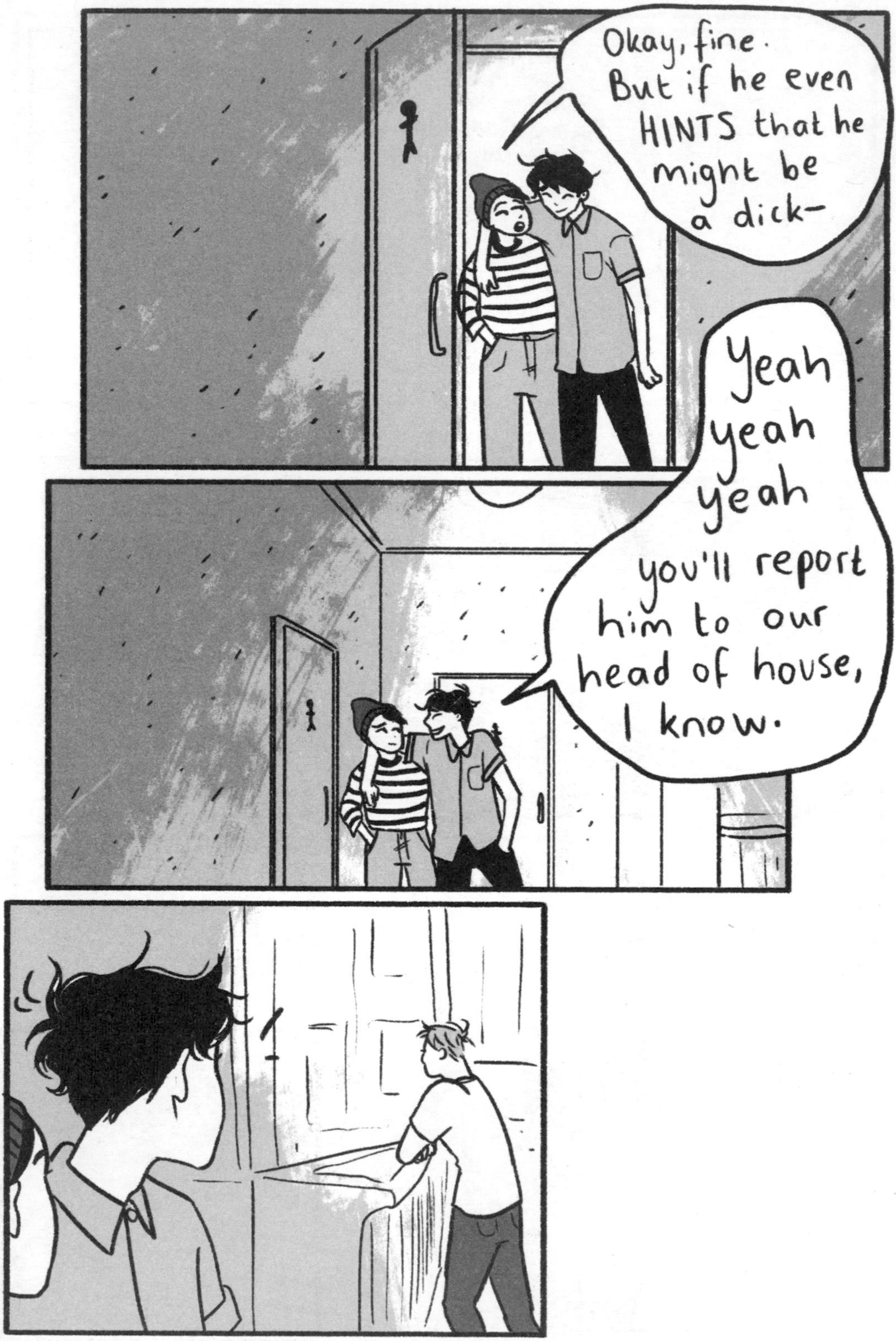
Okay, fine. But if he even HINTS that he might be a dick–
Yeah yeah yeah you'll report him to our head of house, I know.

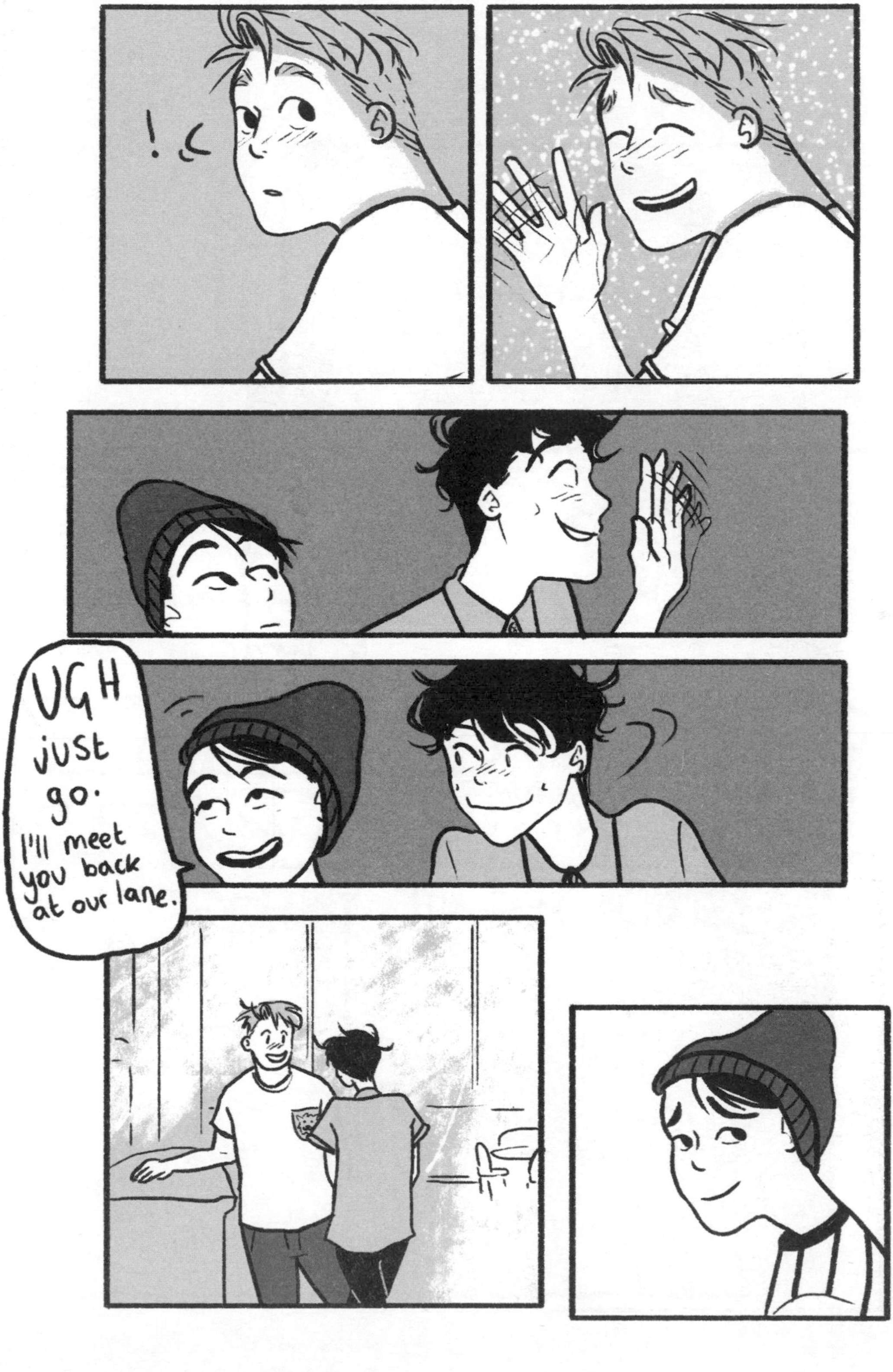
! c
UGH just go. I'll meet you back at our lane.

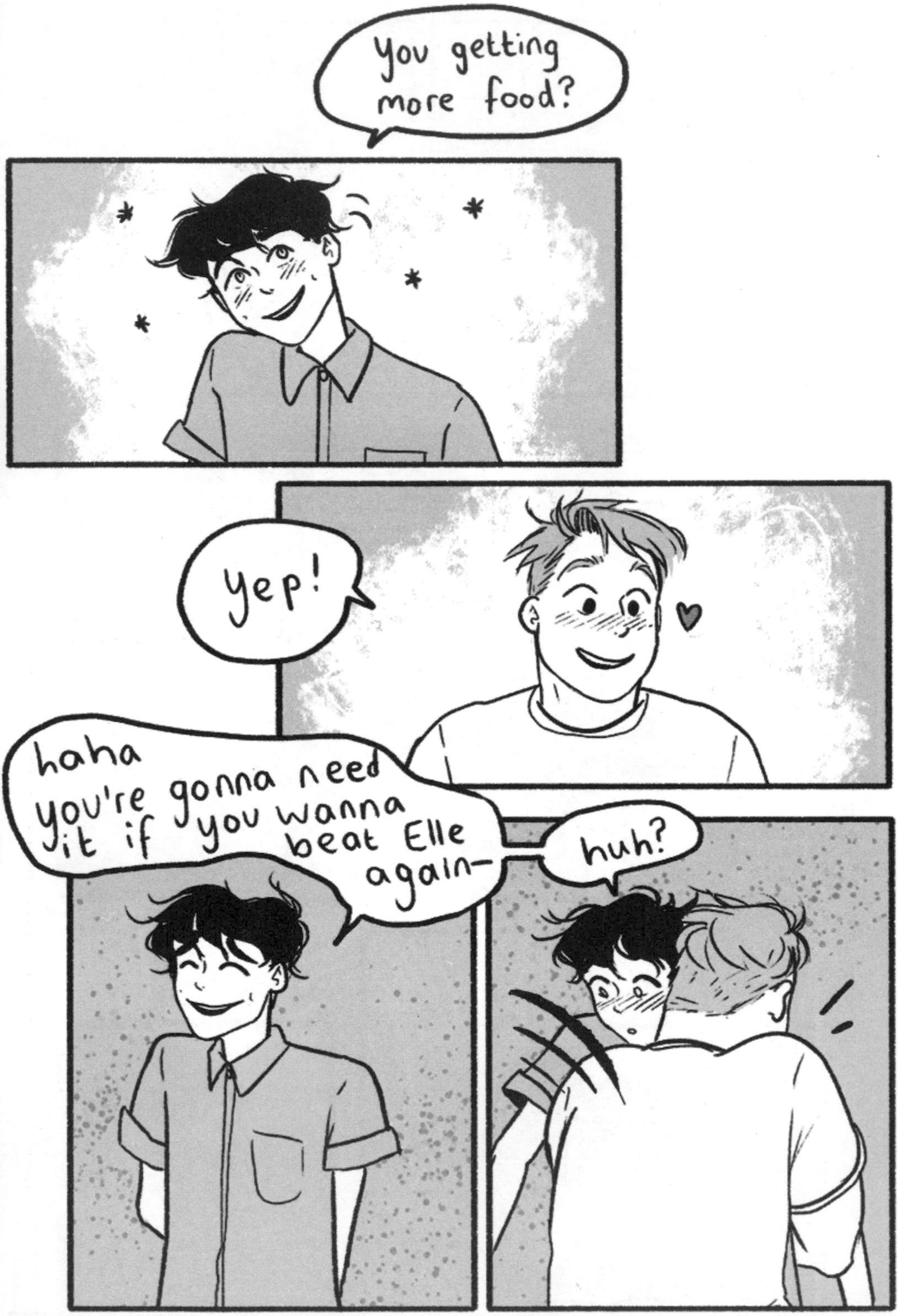
You getting more food?
Yep!
haha you're gonna need it if you wanna beat Elle again-
huh?

397

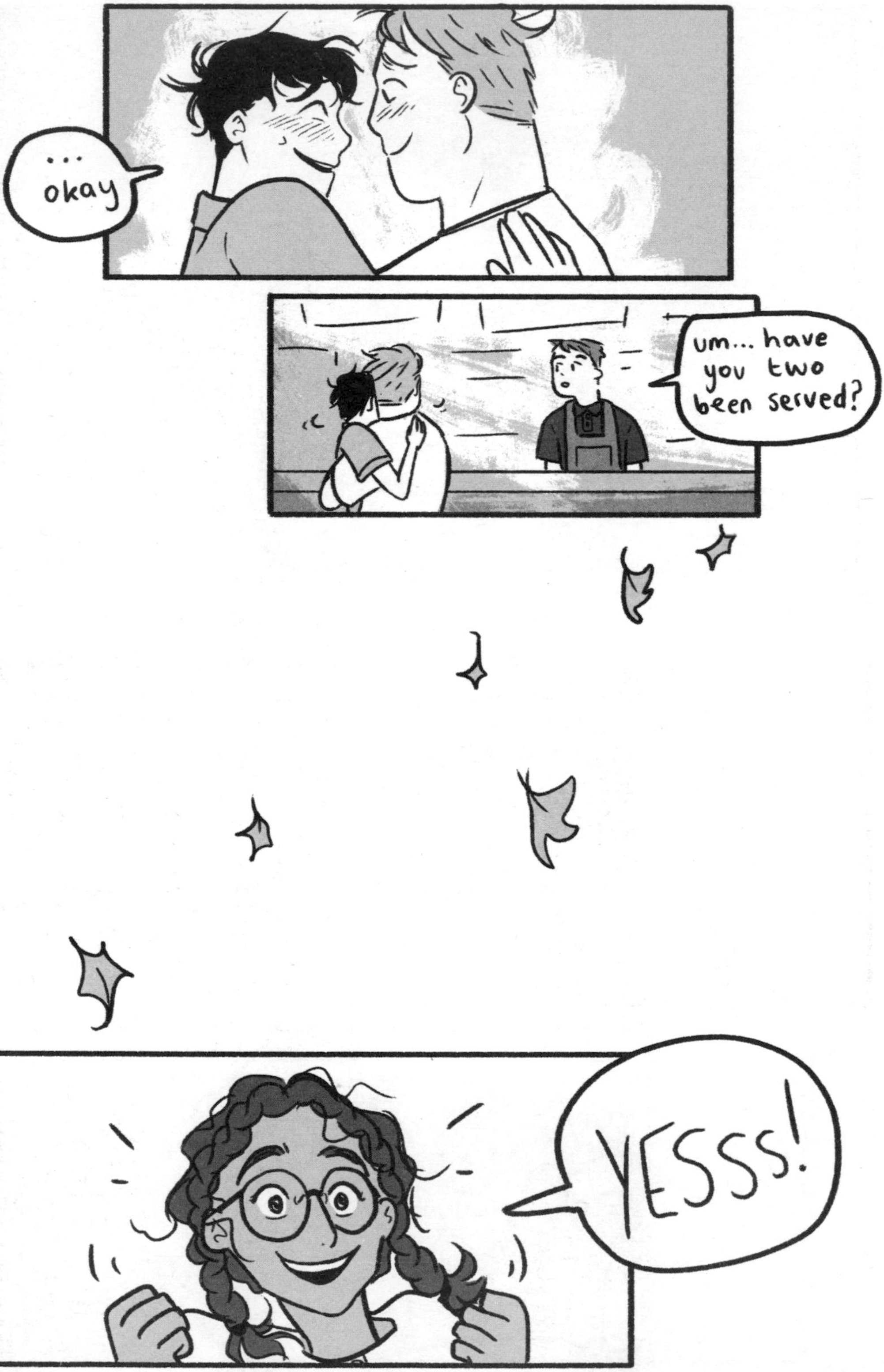
... okay
um... have you two been served?
YESSS!

HAPPY BIRTHDAY!
RIP
HAPPY BIRTHDAY!
Snow Day

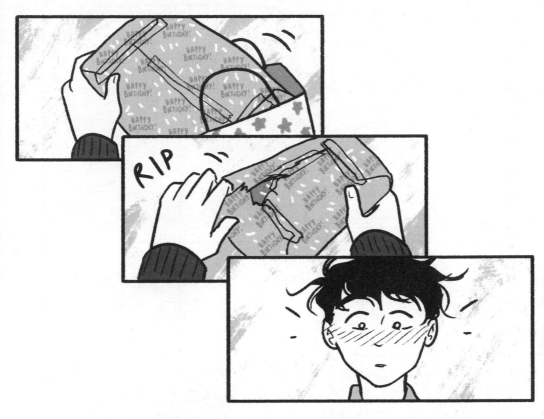

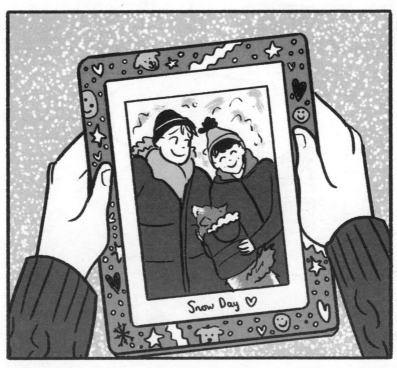

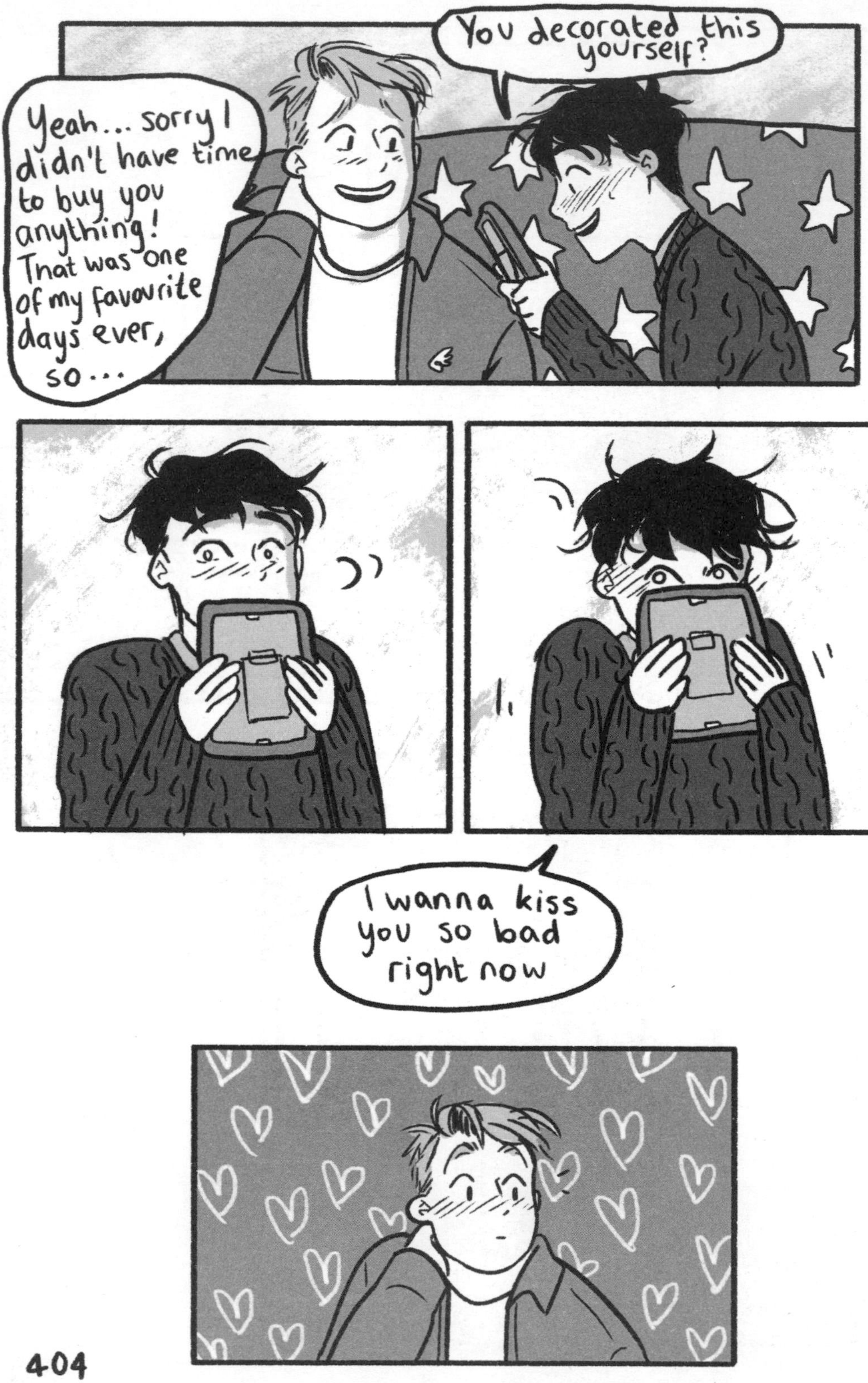
You decorated this yourself?
Yeah... sorry I didn't have time to buy you anything! That was one of my favourite days ever, so...
I wanna kiss you so bad right now

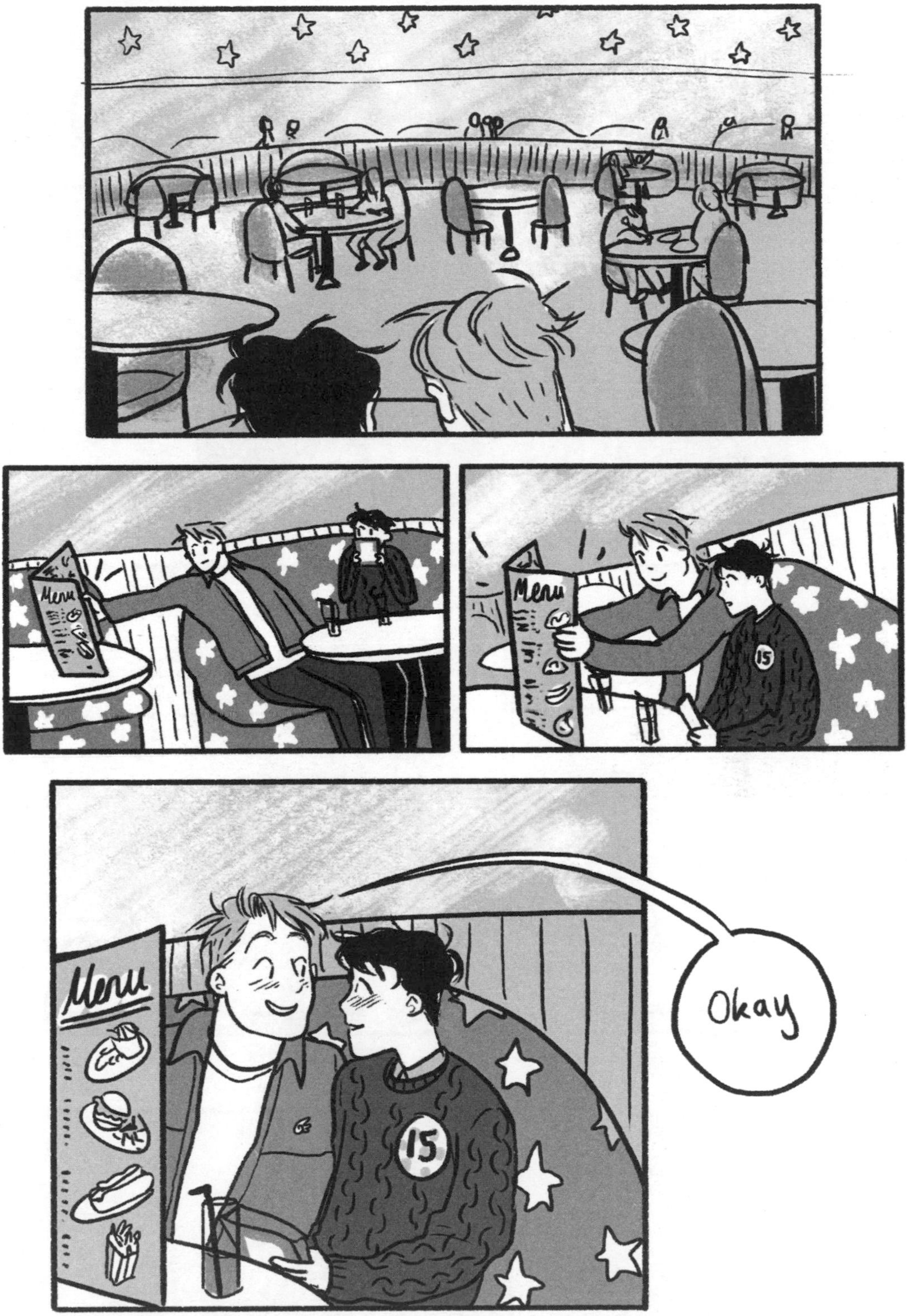
Menu
Menu
Menu
Okay

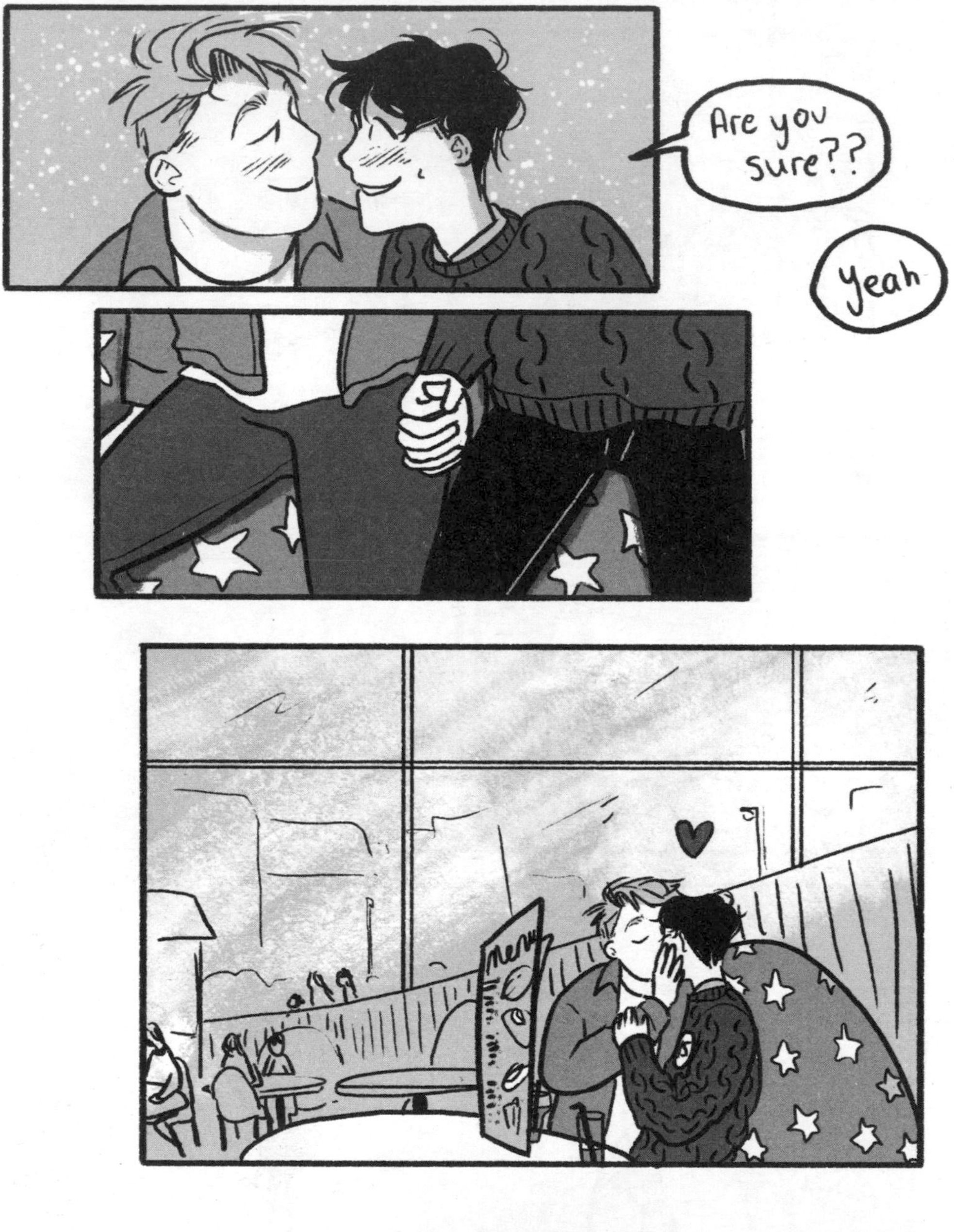
Are you sure??
Yeah
Ha ha

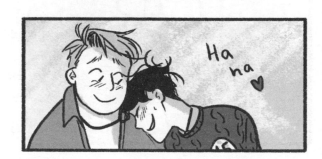

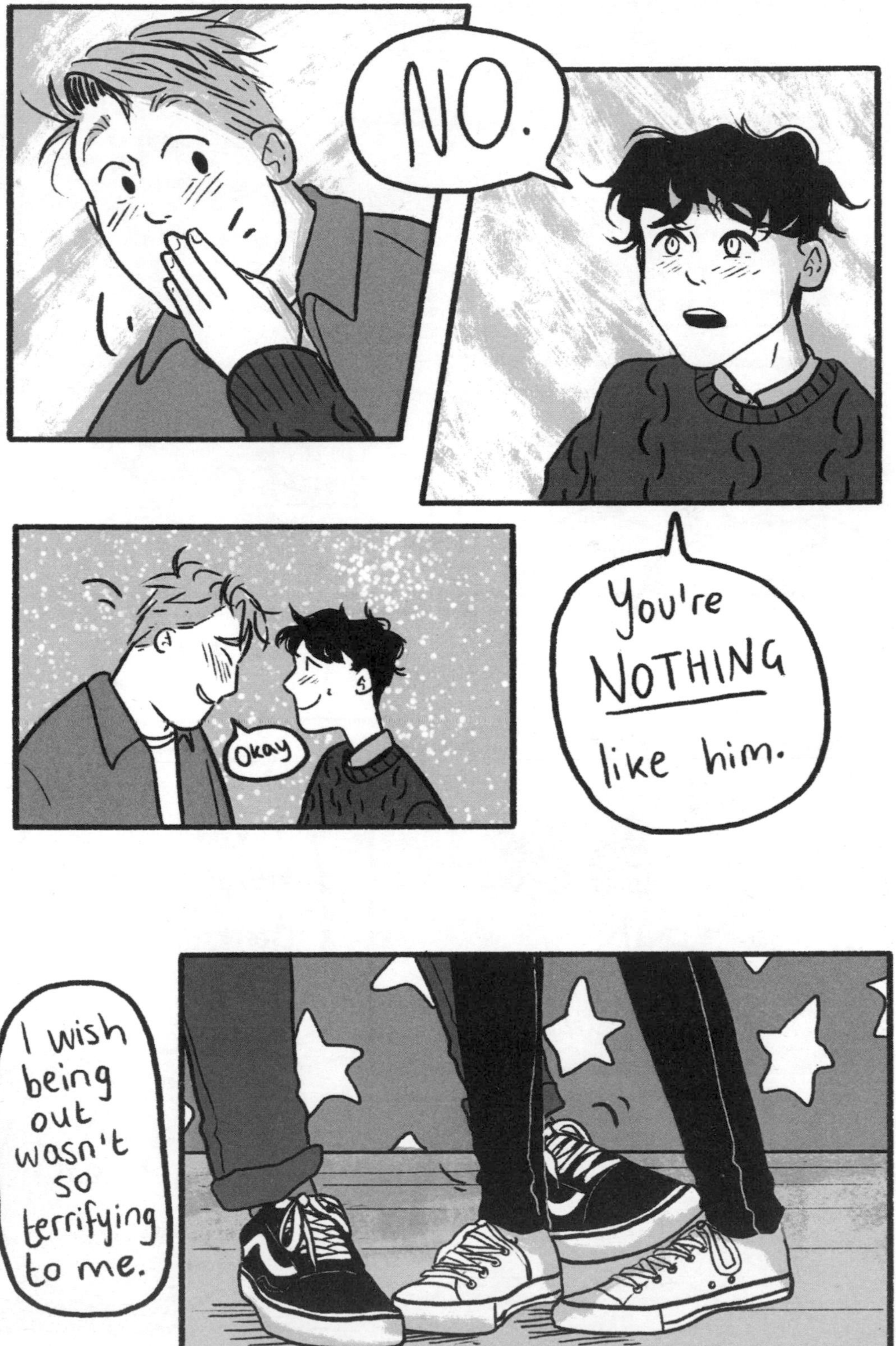
NO.
You're NOTHING like him.
Okay
I wish being out wasn't so terrifying to me.

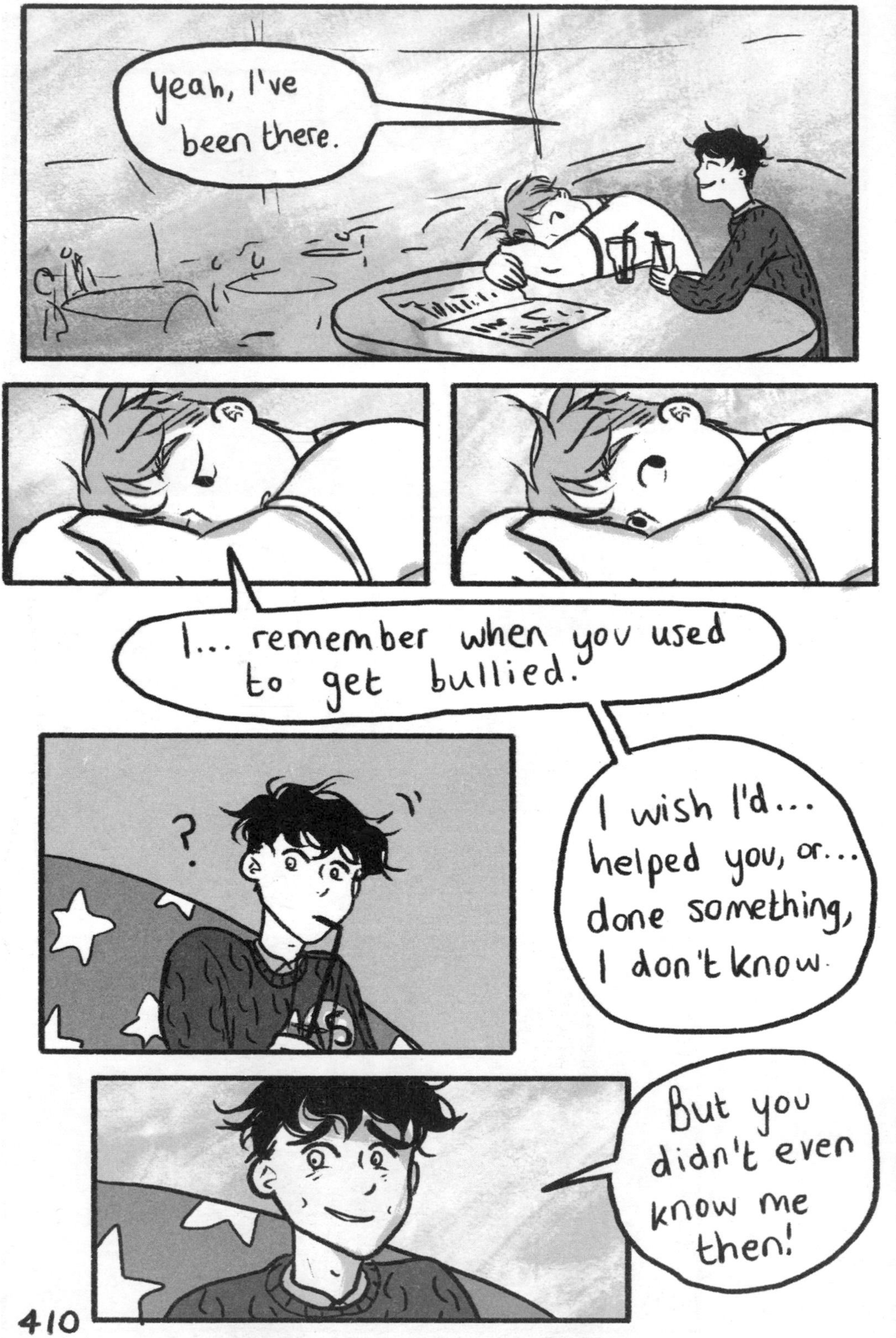
yeah, I've been there.
I... remember when you used to get bullied.
I wish I'd... helped you, or... done something, I don't know.
But you didn't even know me then!

414

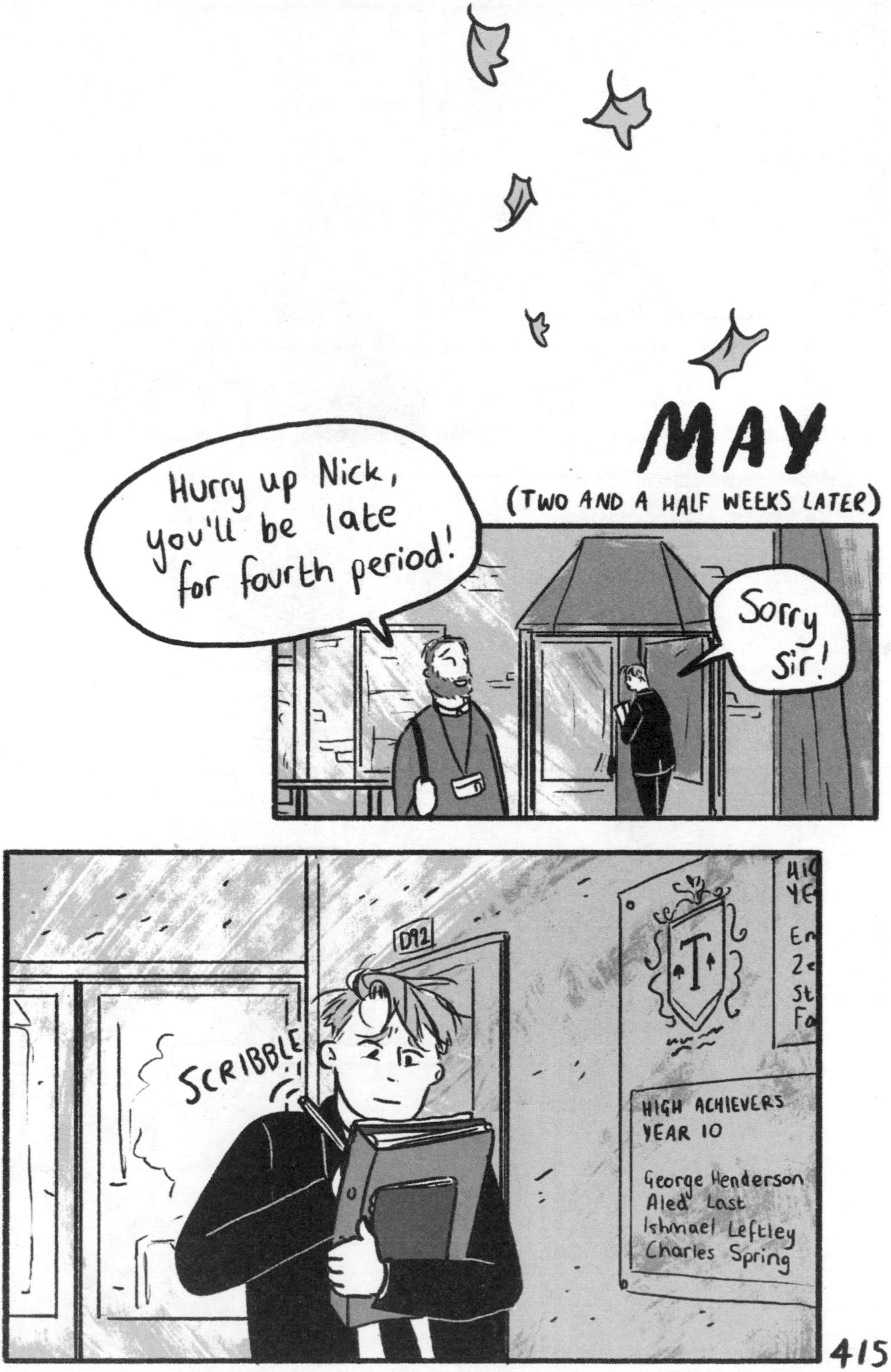
MAY
(TWO AND A HALF WEEKS LATER)
Hurry up Nick, you'll be late for fourth period!
Sorry sir!
D92
SCRIBBLE
HIGH ACHIEVERS
YEAR 10
George Henderson
Aled Last
Ishmael Leftley
Charles Spring

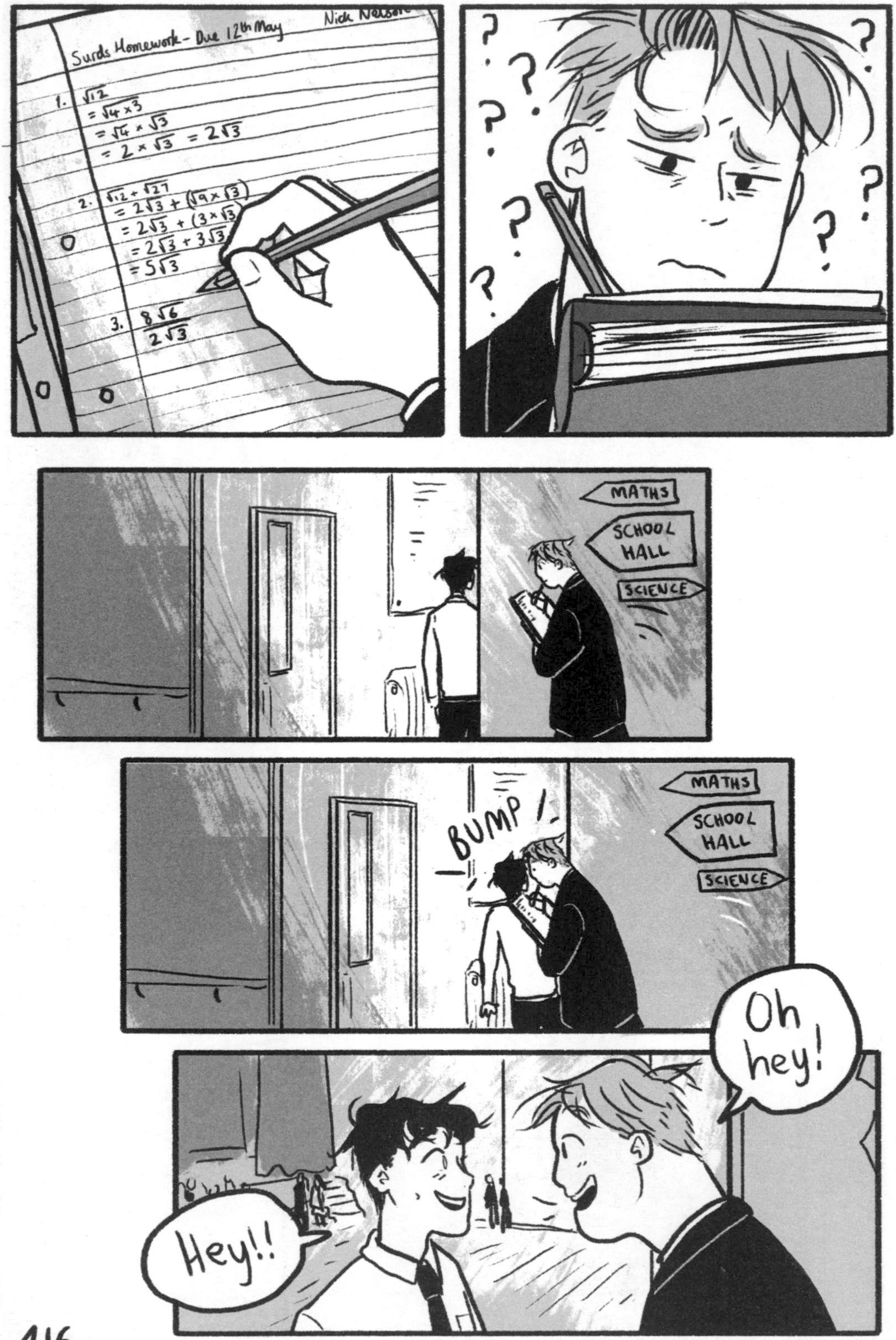
Nick Nelson
Surds Homework - Due 12th May
1. $\sqrt{12}$
$= \sqrt{4 \times 3}$
$= \sqrt{4} \times \sqrt{3}$
$= 2 \times \sqrt{3} = 2\sqrt{3}$
2. $\sqrt{12} + \sqrt{27}$
$= 2\sqrt{3} + (\sqrt{9 \times \sqrt{3}})$
$= 2\sqrt{3} + (3 \times \sqrt{3})$
$= 2\sqrt{3} + 3\sqrt{3}$
$= 5\sqrt{3}$
3. $\frac{8\sqrt{6}}{2\sqrt{3}}$
MATHS
SCHOOL HALL
SCIENCE
BUMP!
MATHS
SCHOOL HALL
SCIENCE
Oh hey!
Hey!!

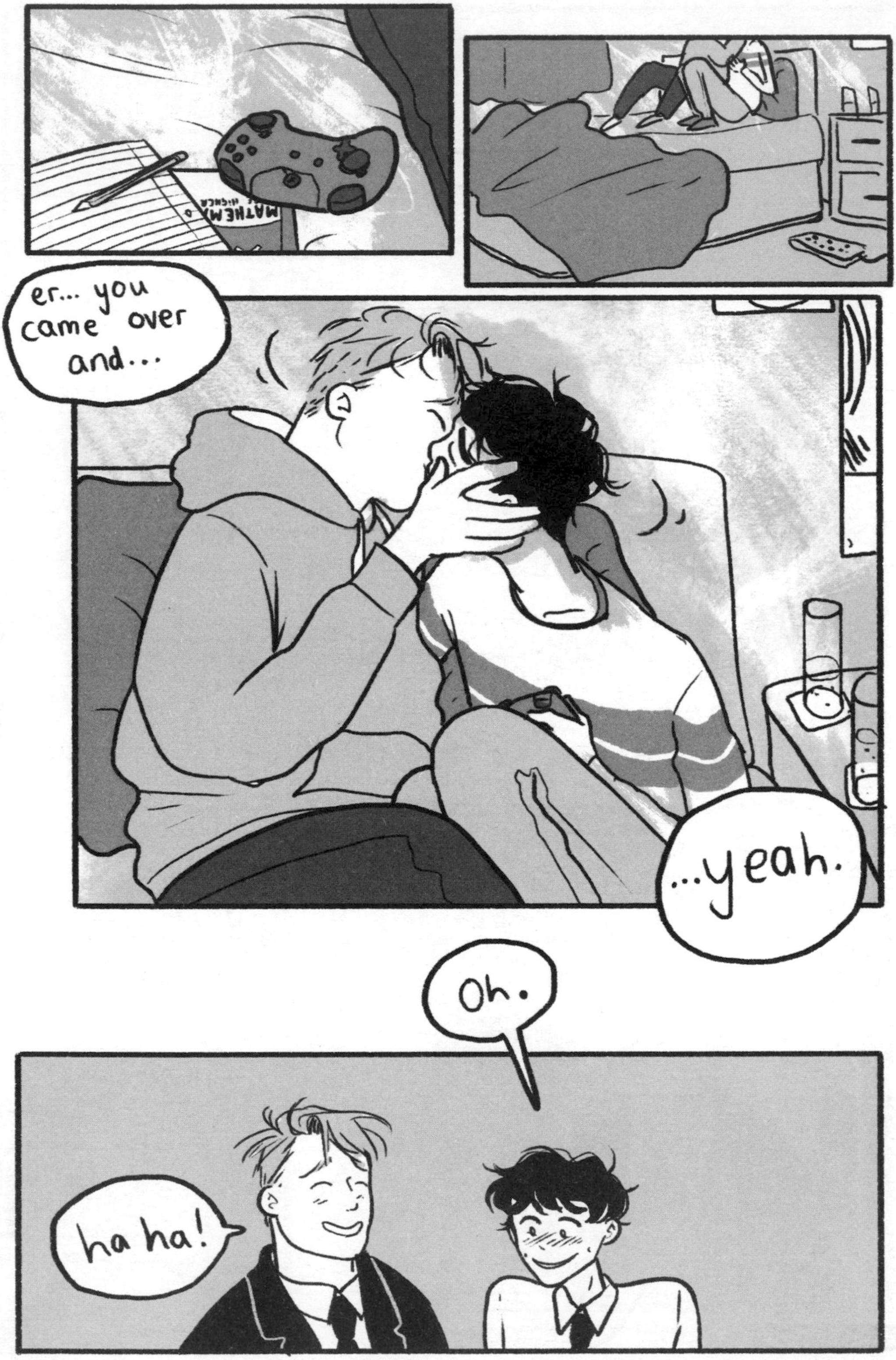
er... you came over and...
...yeah.
Oh.
ha ha!

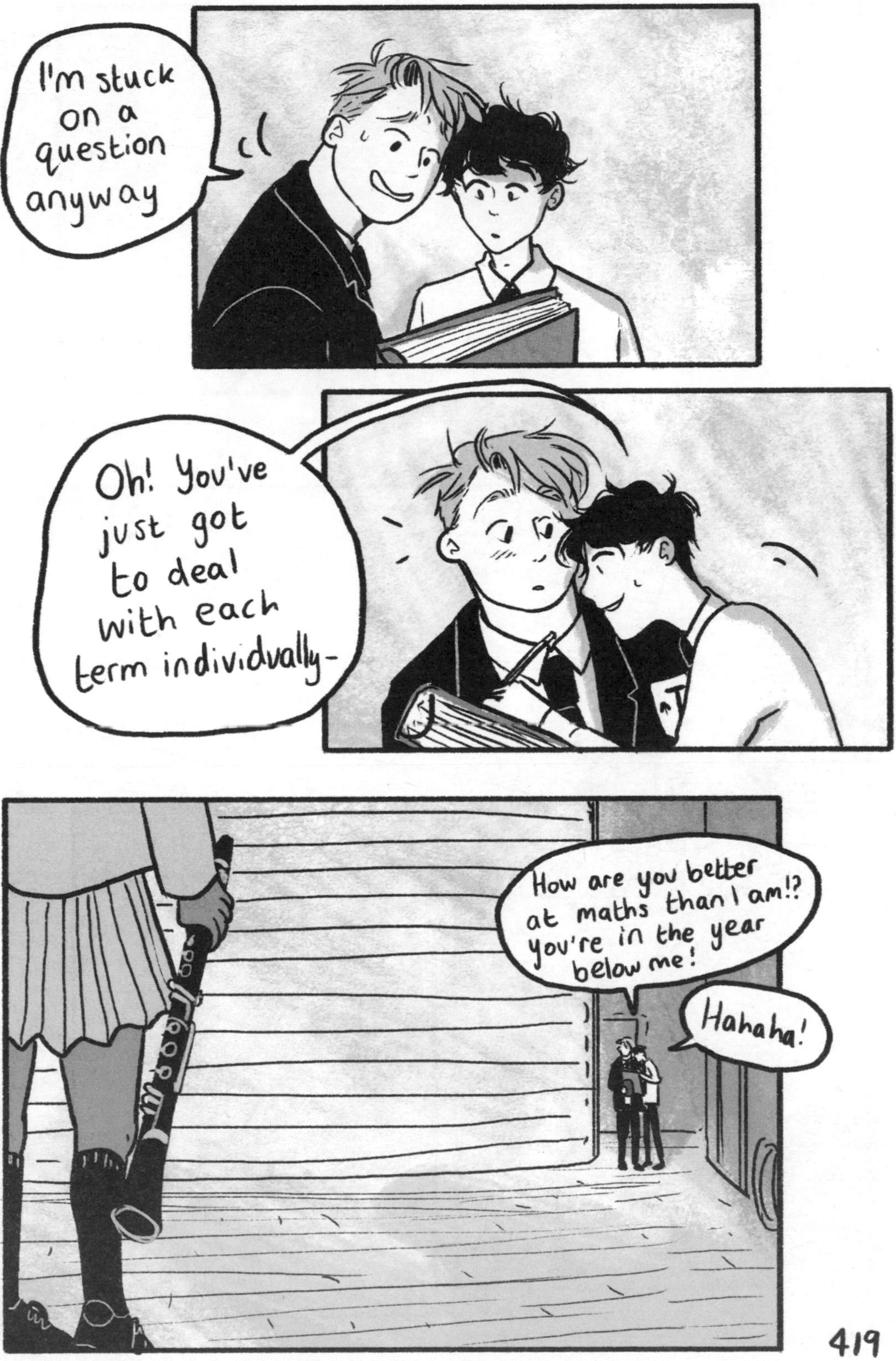
I'm stuck on a question anyway
Oh! You've just got to deal with each term individually-
How are you better at maths than I am!? You're in the year below me!
Hahaha!

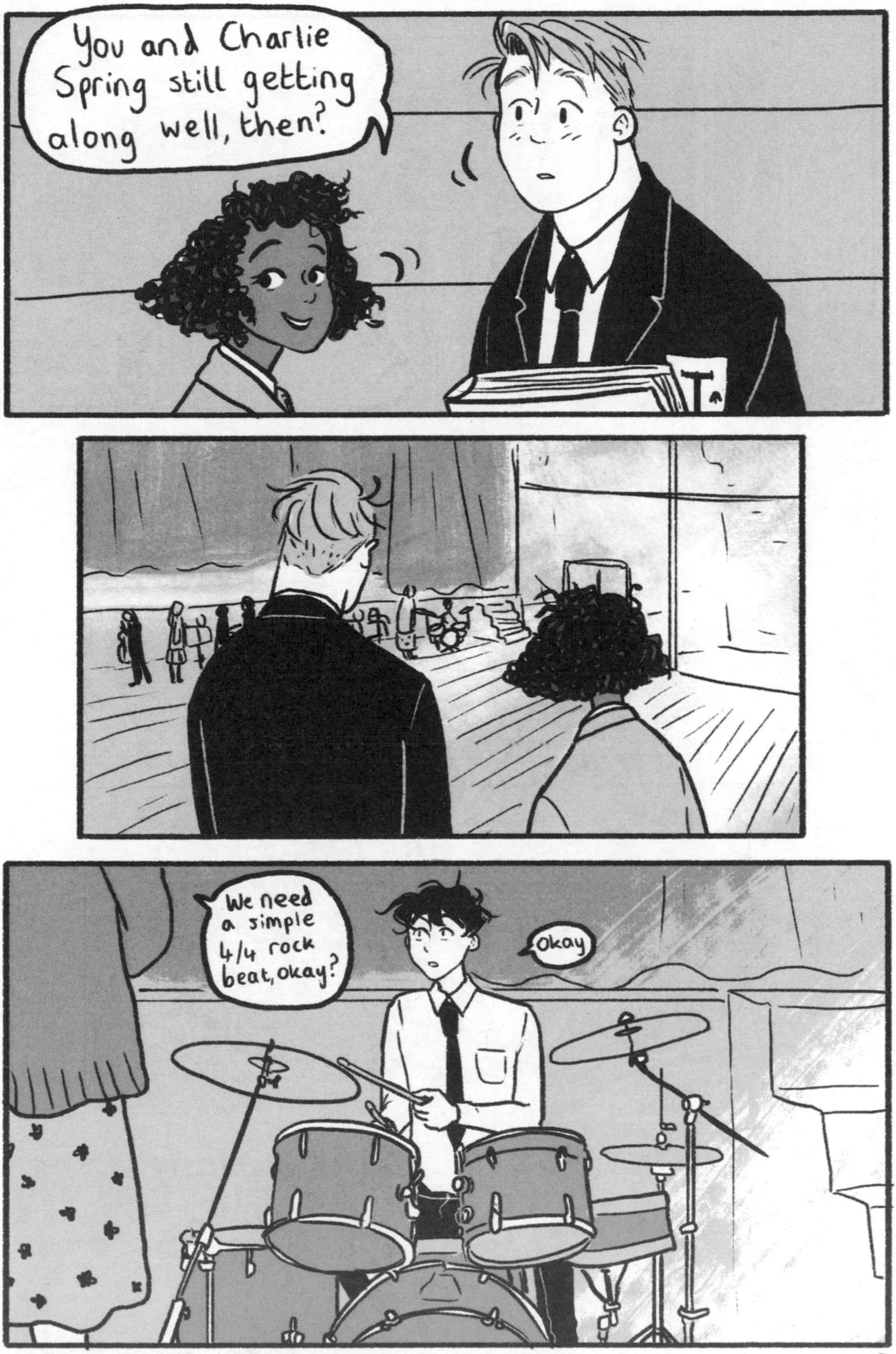

You and Charlie Spring still getting along well, then?
We need a simple 4/4 rock beat, okay?
Okay

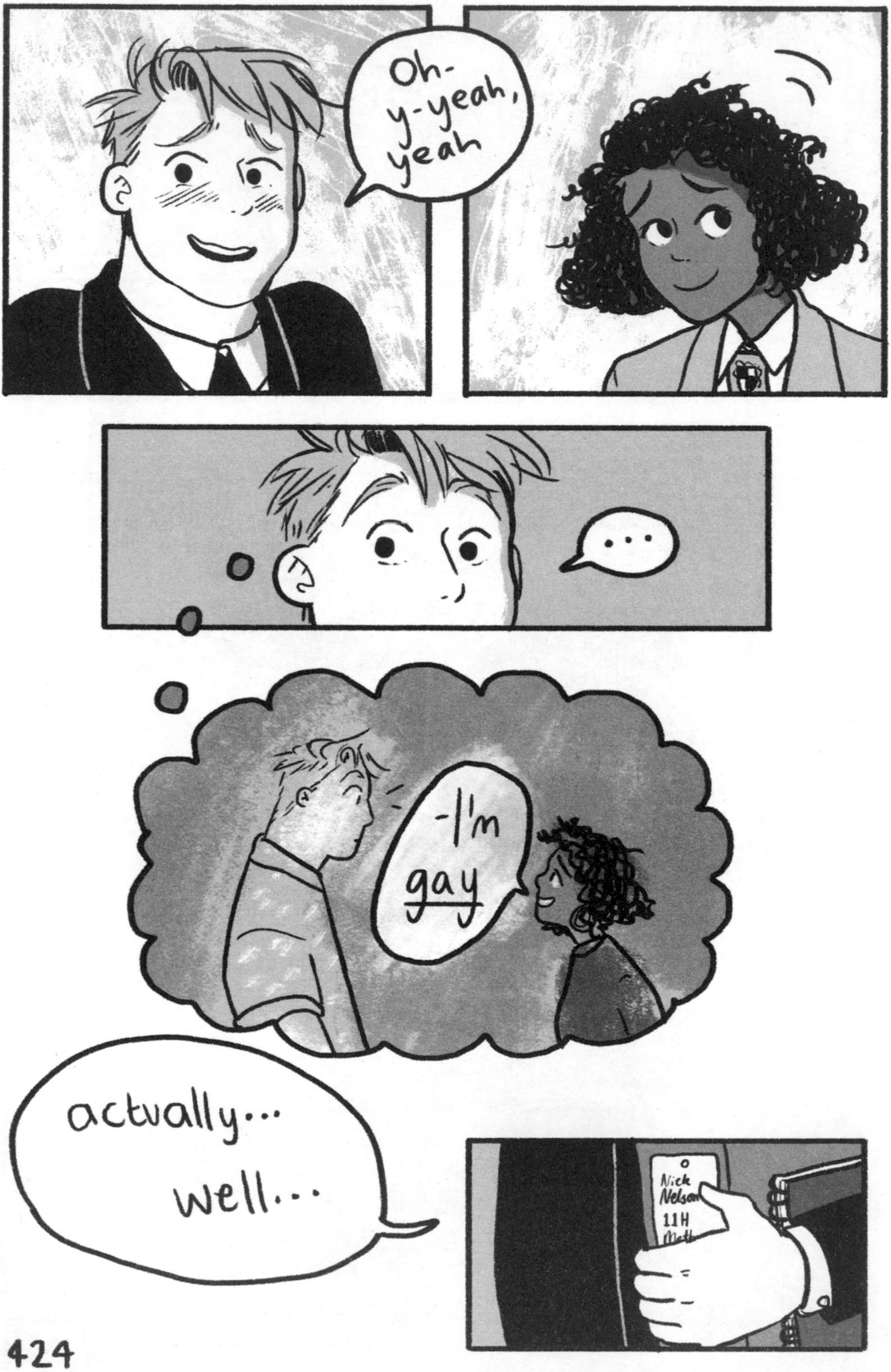
Oh- y-yeah, yeah
...
-I'm gay
actually... well...

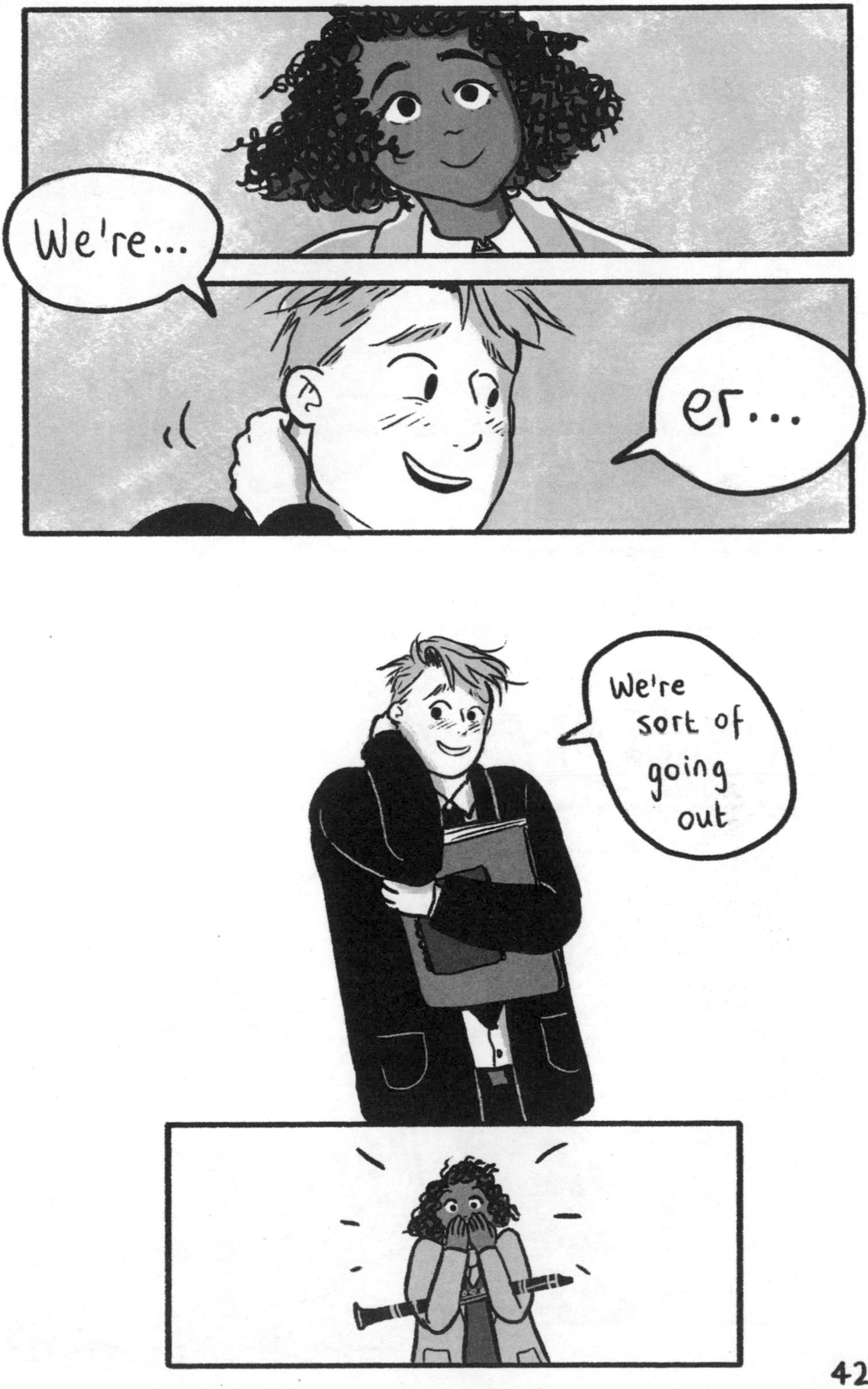
We're...
er...
We're sort of going out

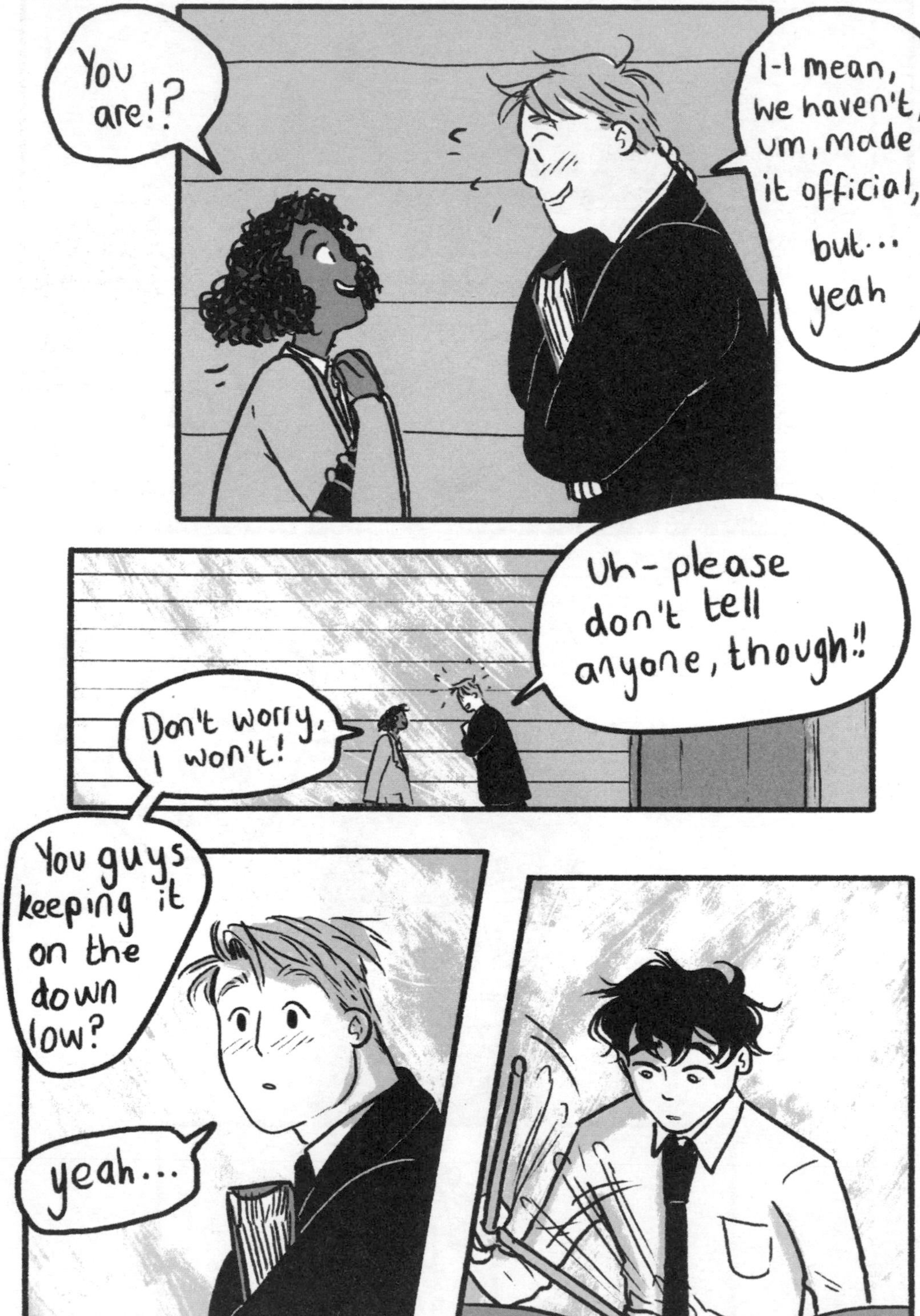
You are!?
I-I mean, we haven't, um, made it official, but... yeah
Uh-please don't tell anyone, though!!
Don't worry, I won't!
You guys keeping it on the down low?
yeah...

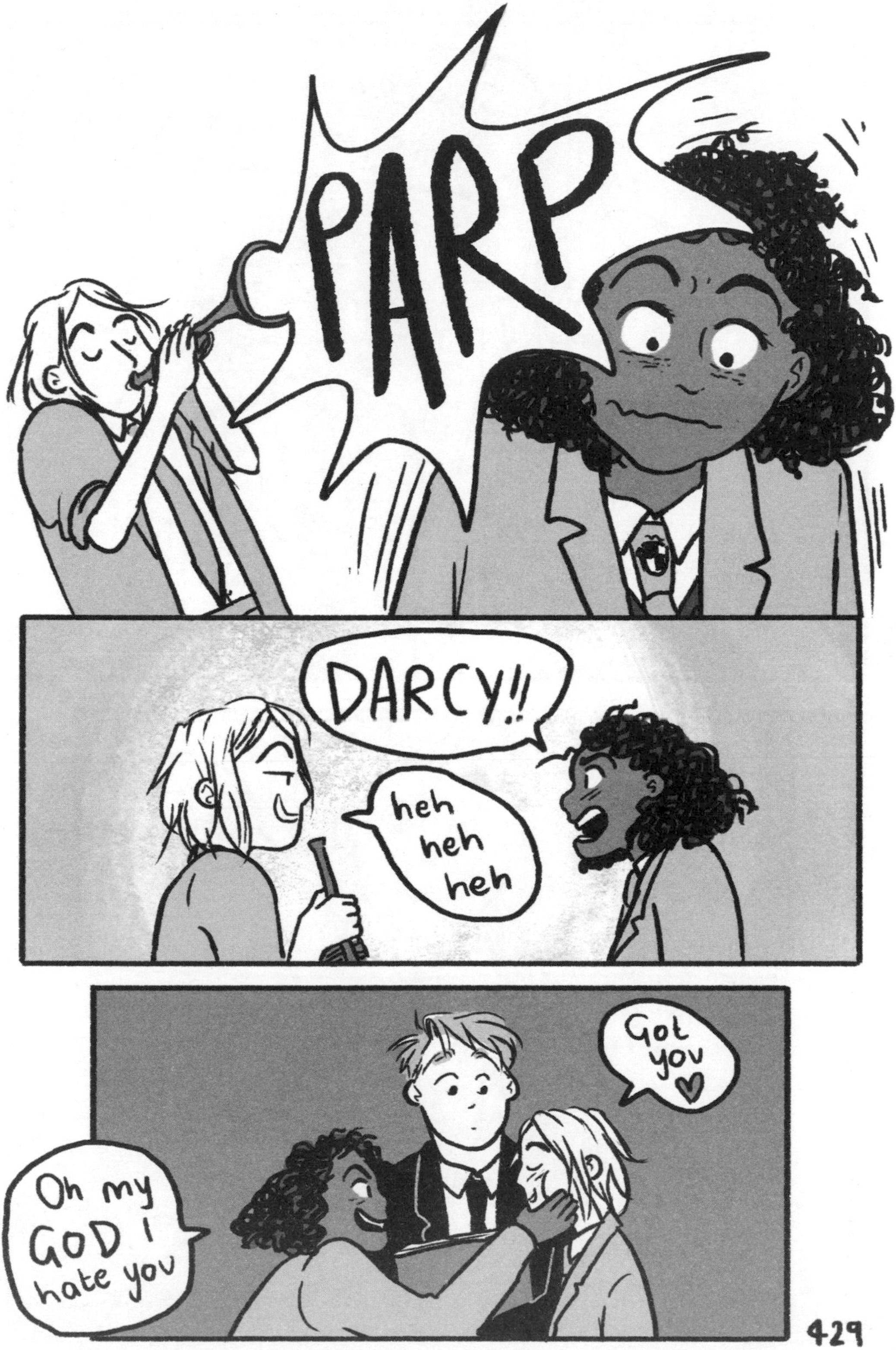
PARP
DARCY!!
heh heh heh
Oh my GOD I hate you
Got you ♥

431

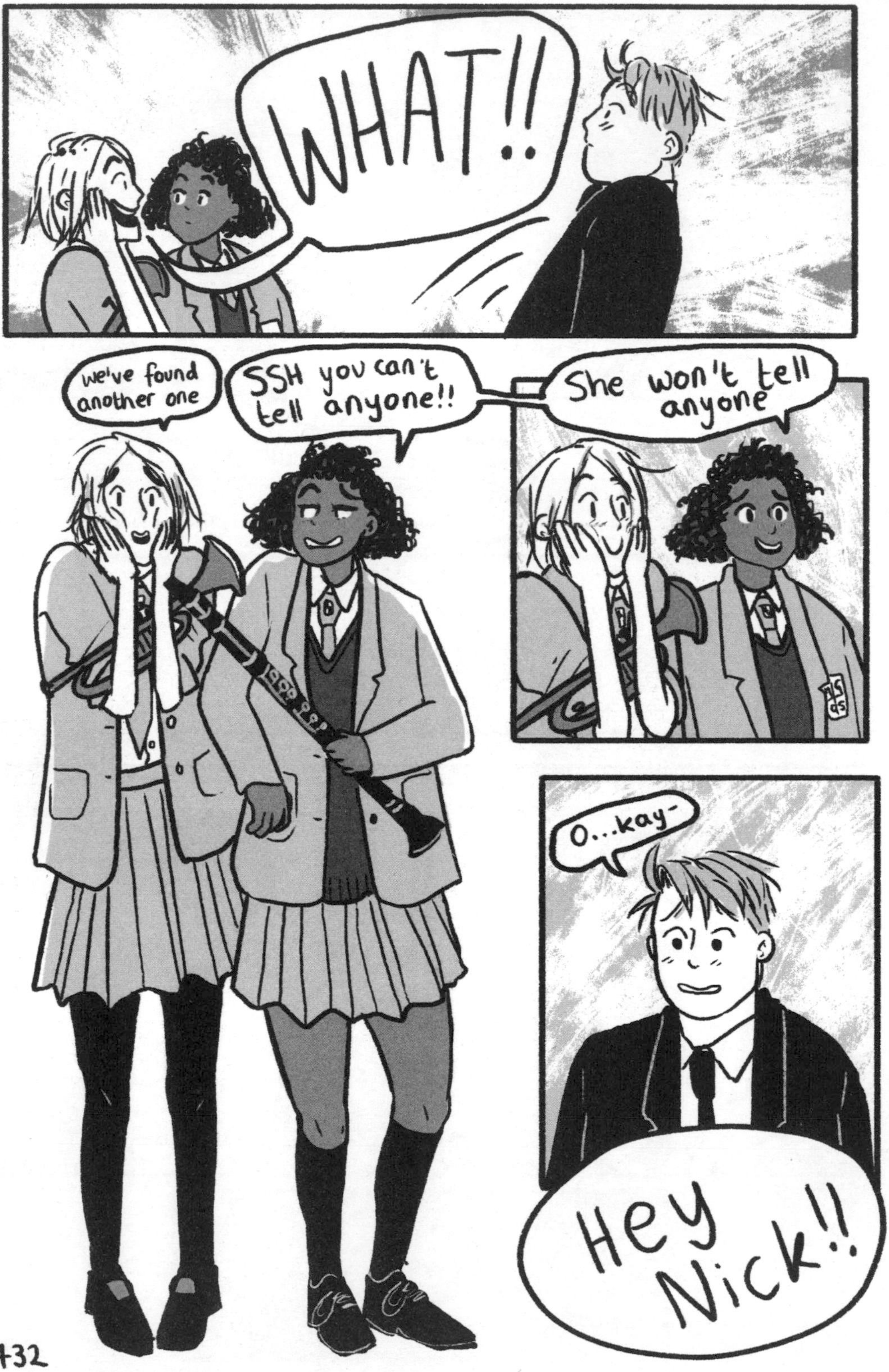

WHAT!!
we've found another one
SSH you can't tell anyone!!
She won't tell anyone
O...kay-
Hey Nick!!

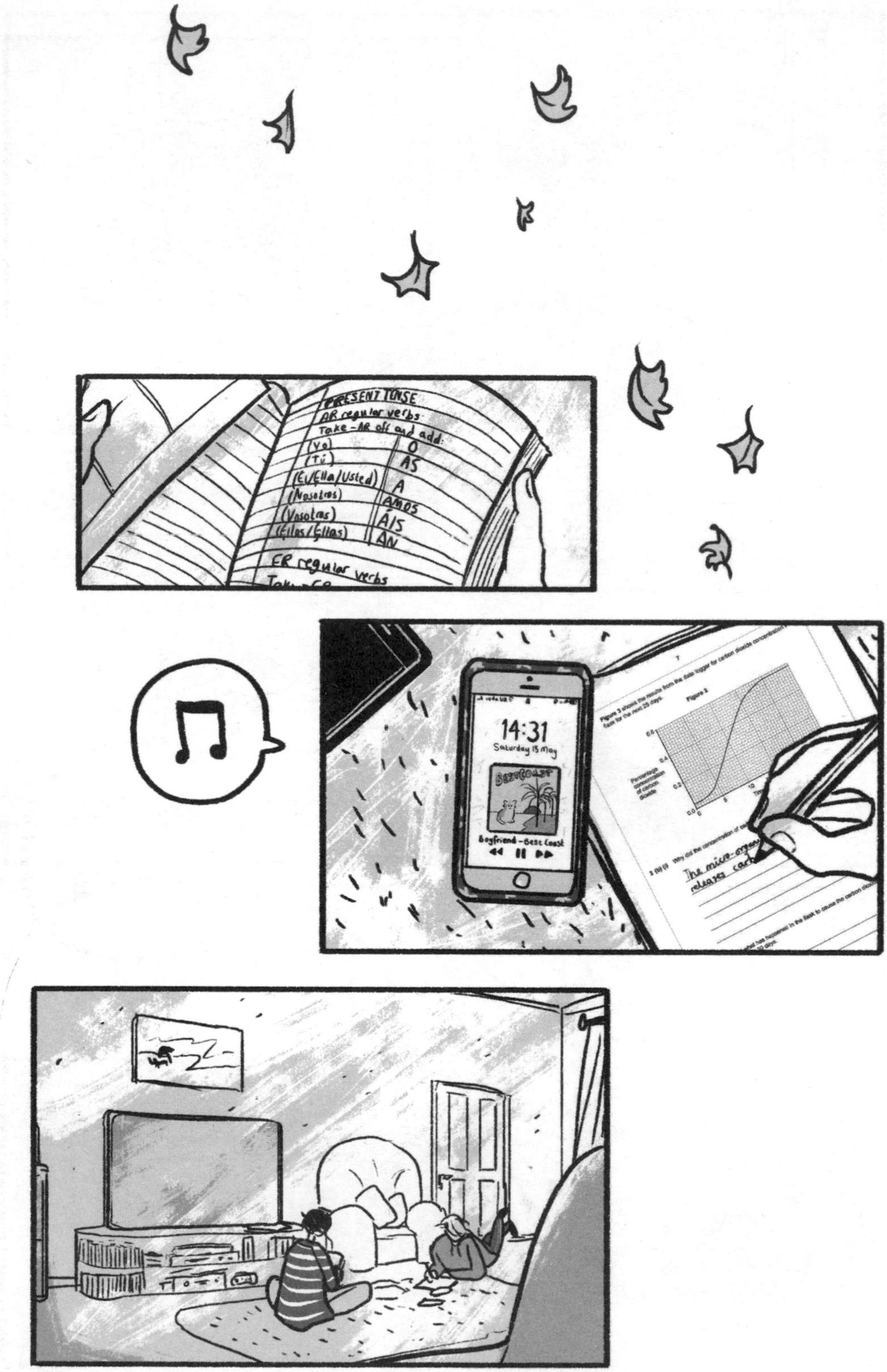
PRESENT TENSE
AR regular verbs
Take -AR off and add:
(Yo) O
(Tú) AS
(Él/Ella/Usted) A
(Nosotros) AMOS
(Vosotros) ÁIS
(Ellos/Ellas) AN
ER regular verbs
14:31
Saturday 15 May
Boyfriend - Best Coast

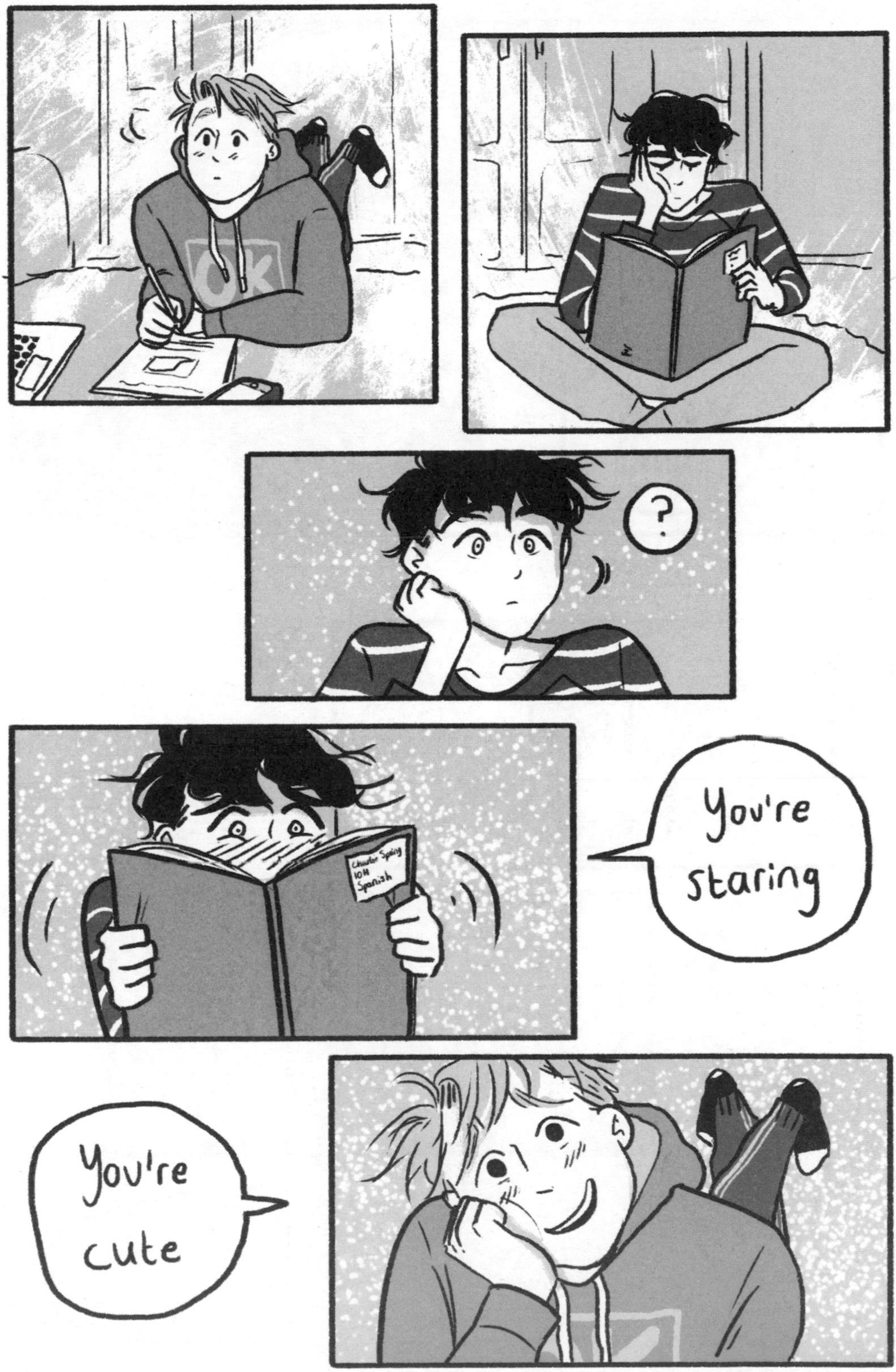
OK
?
You're staring
You're cute

441

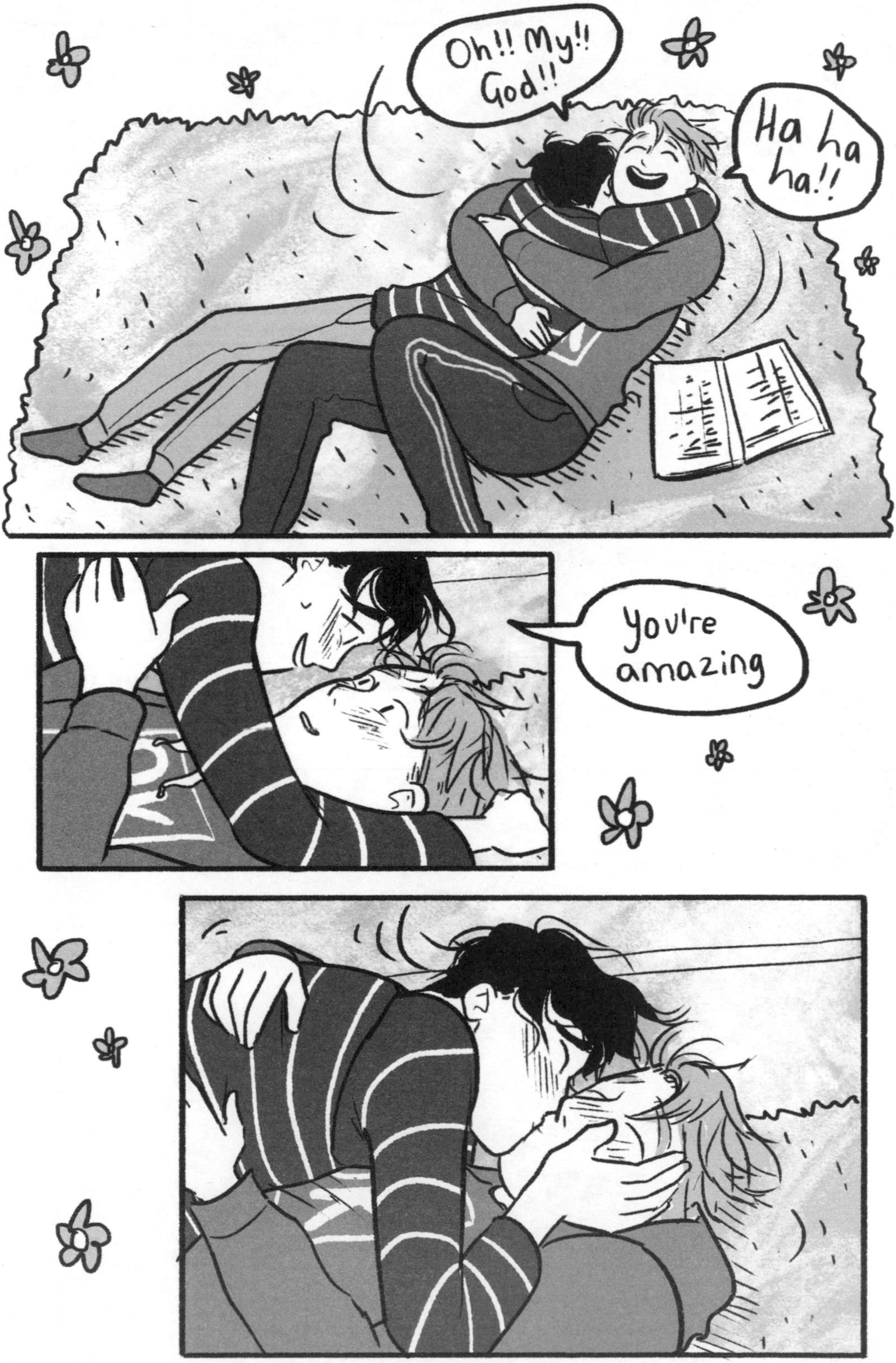
Oh!! My!! God!!
Ha ha ha!!
You're amazing

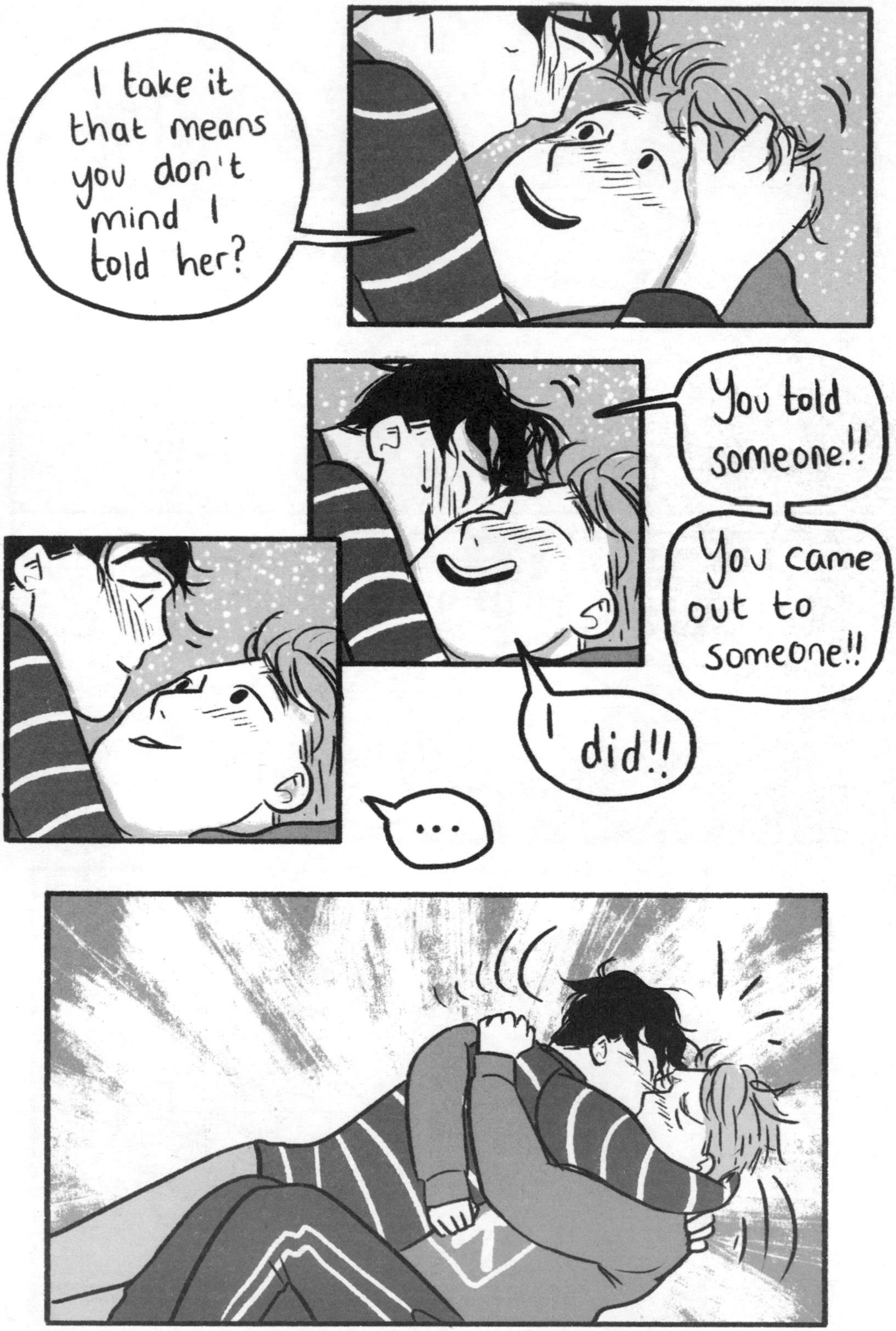
I take it that means you don't mind I told her?
You told someone!!
You came out to someone!!
I did!!
...

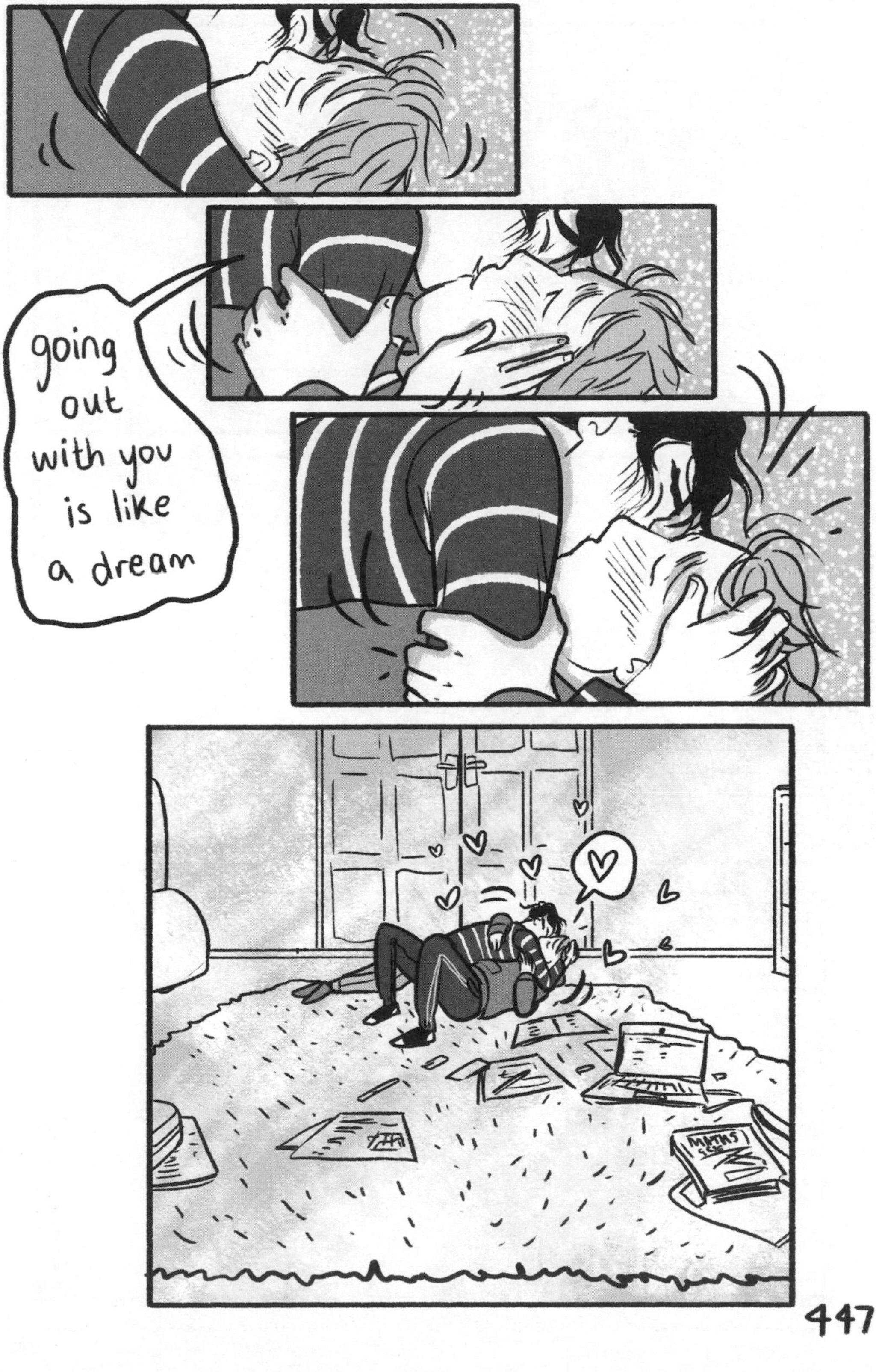
going out with you is like a dream
MATHS GCSE

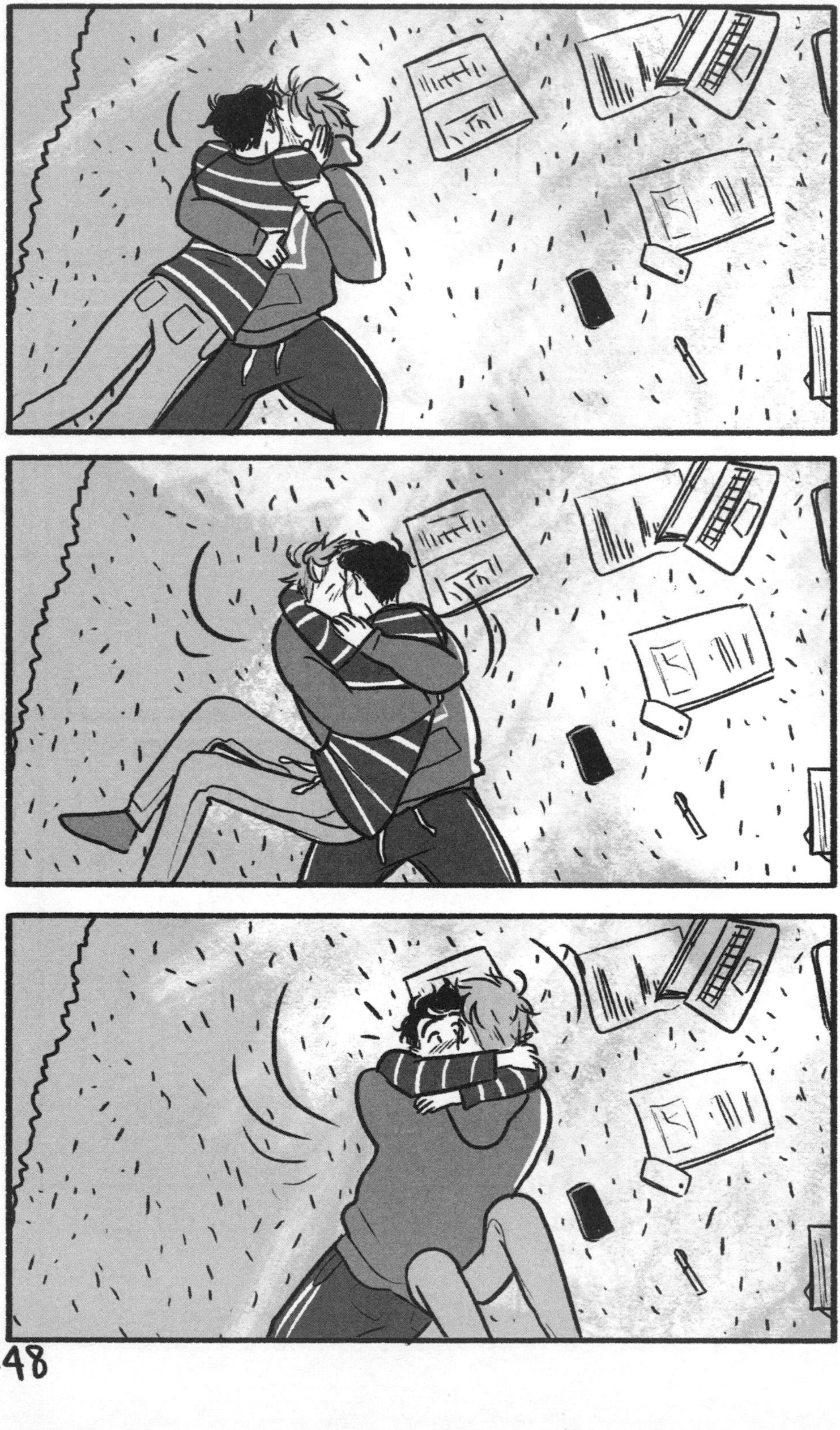

449

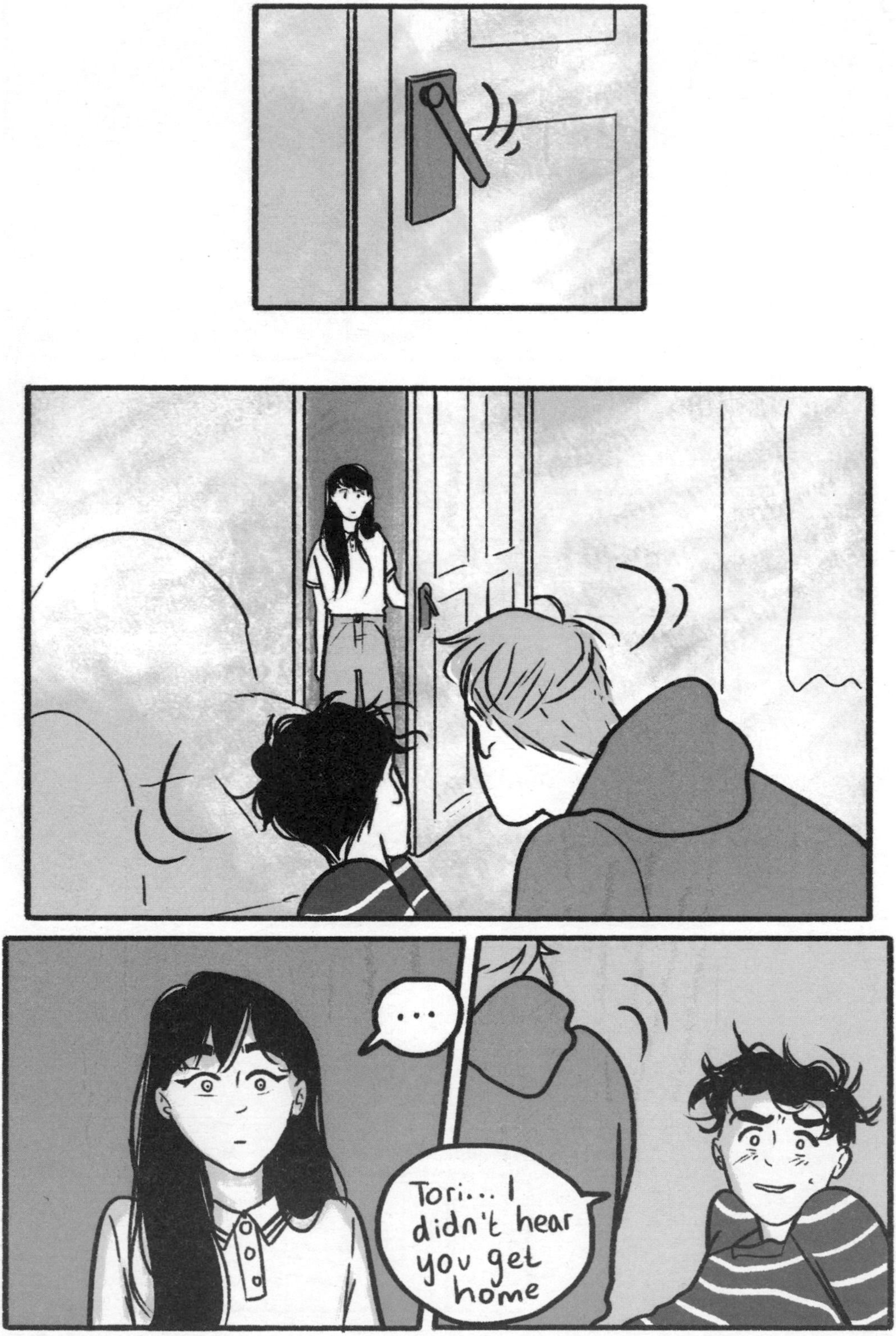
...
Tori... I didn't hear you get home

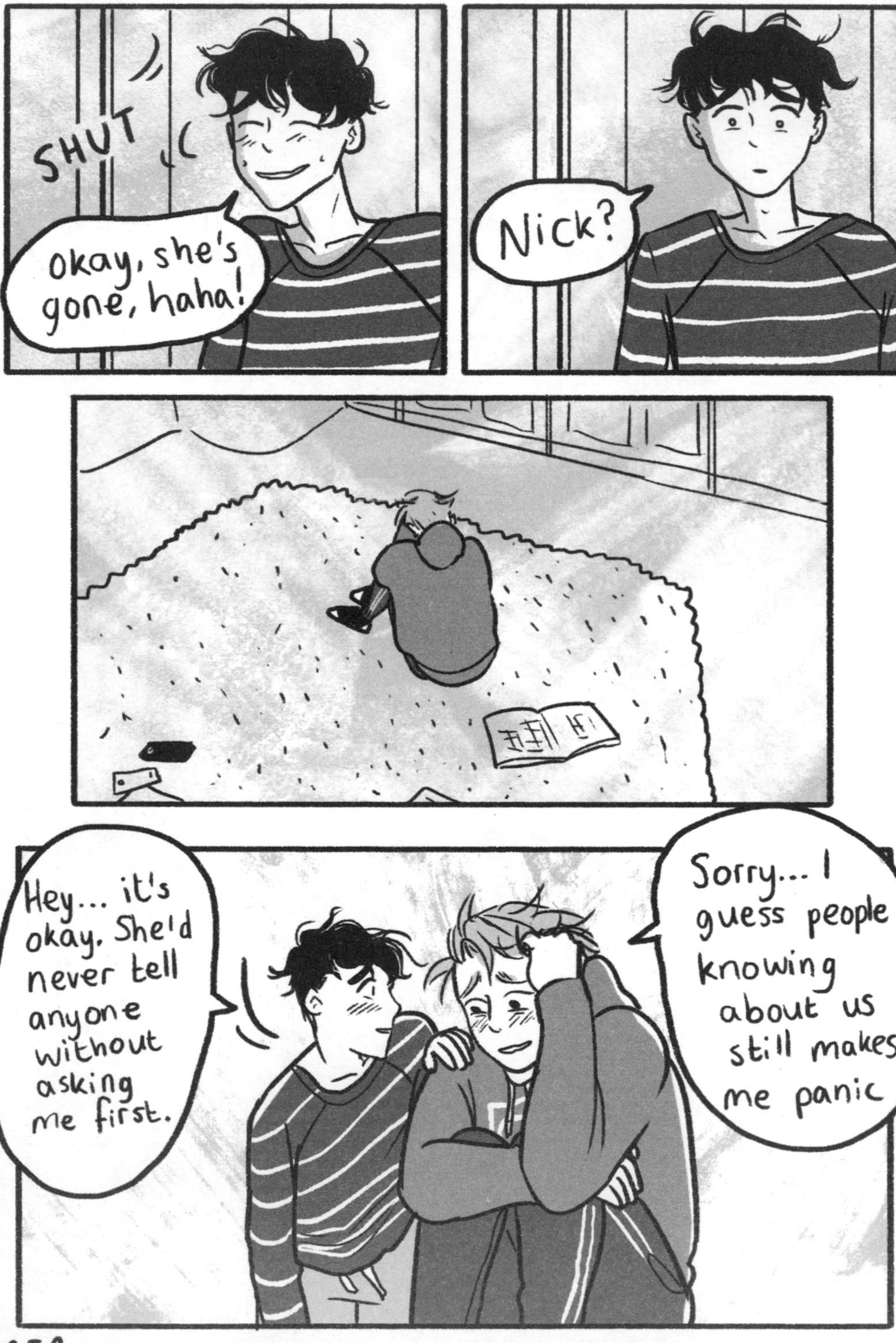
SHUT
okay, she's gone, haha!
Nick?
Hey... it's okay. She'd never tell anyone without asking me first.
Sorry... I guess people knowing about us still makes me panic

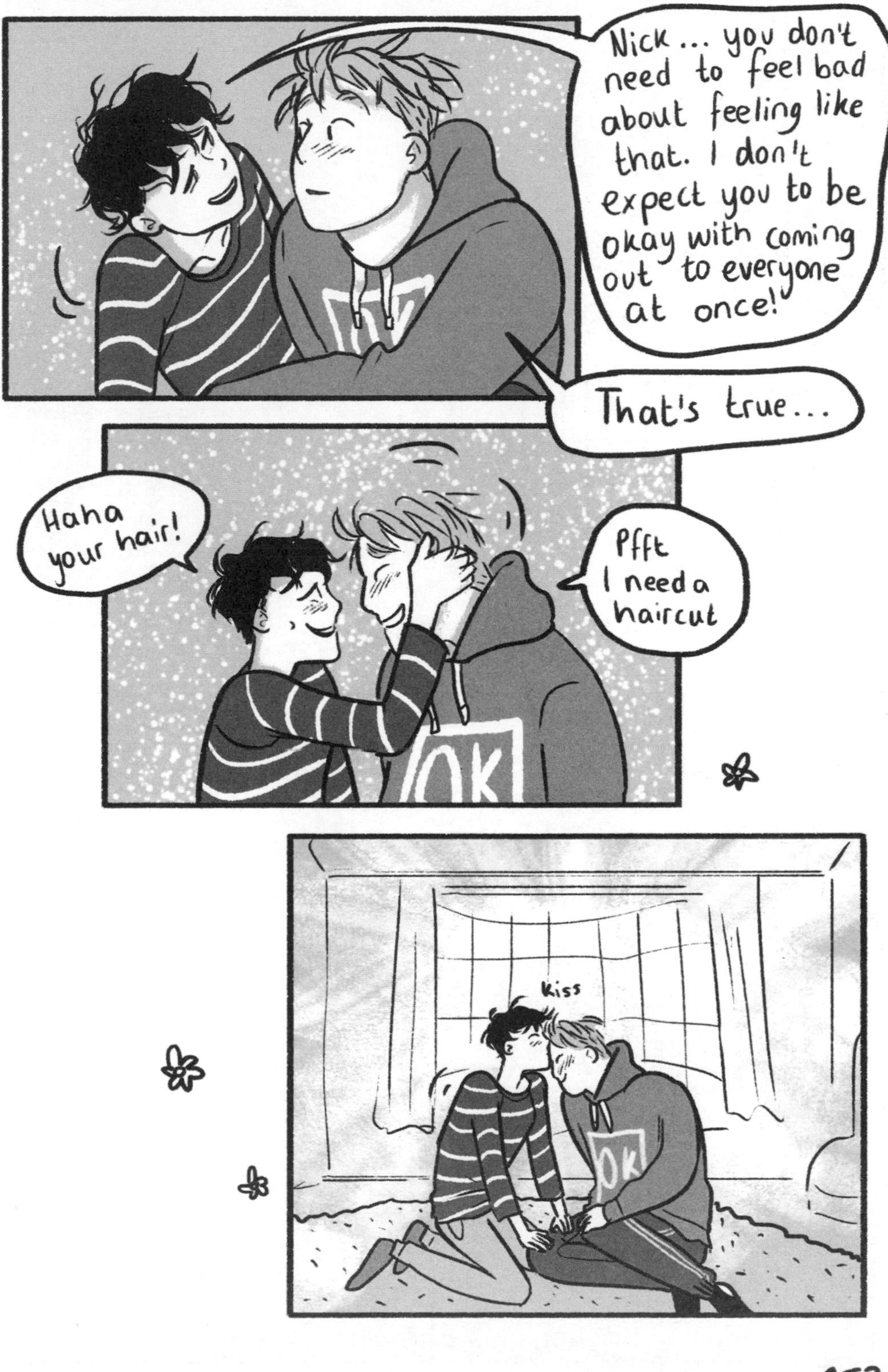
Nick... you don't need to feel bad about feeling like that. I don't expect you to be okay with coming out to everyone at once!
That's true...
Haha your hair!
Pfft I need a haircut
kiss

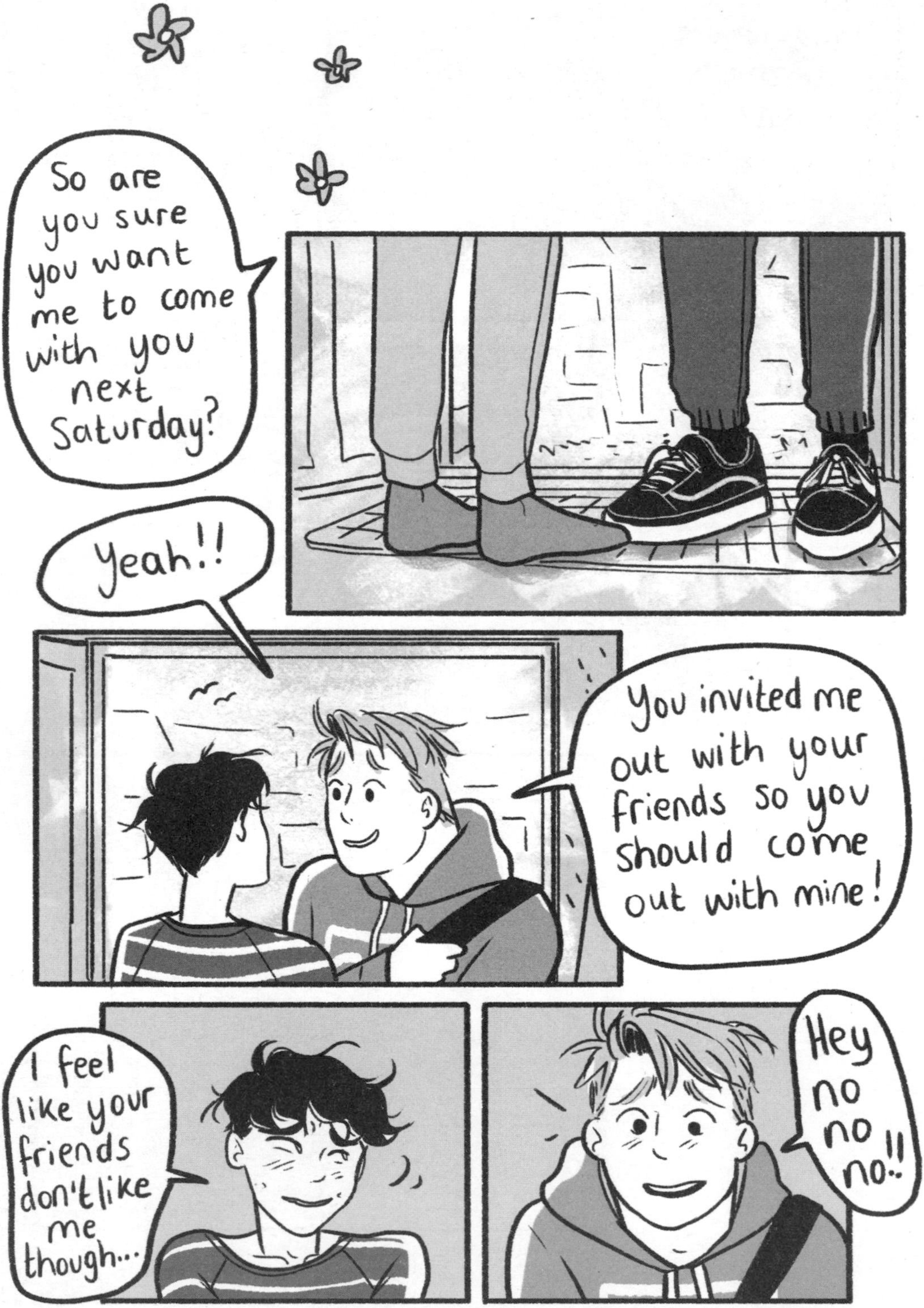
So are you sure you want me to come with you next Saturday?
Yeah!!
You invited me out with your friends so you should come out with mine!
I feel like your friends don't like me though...
Hey no no no!!

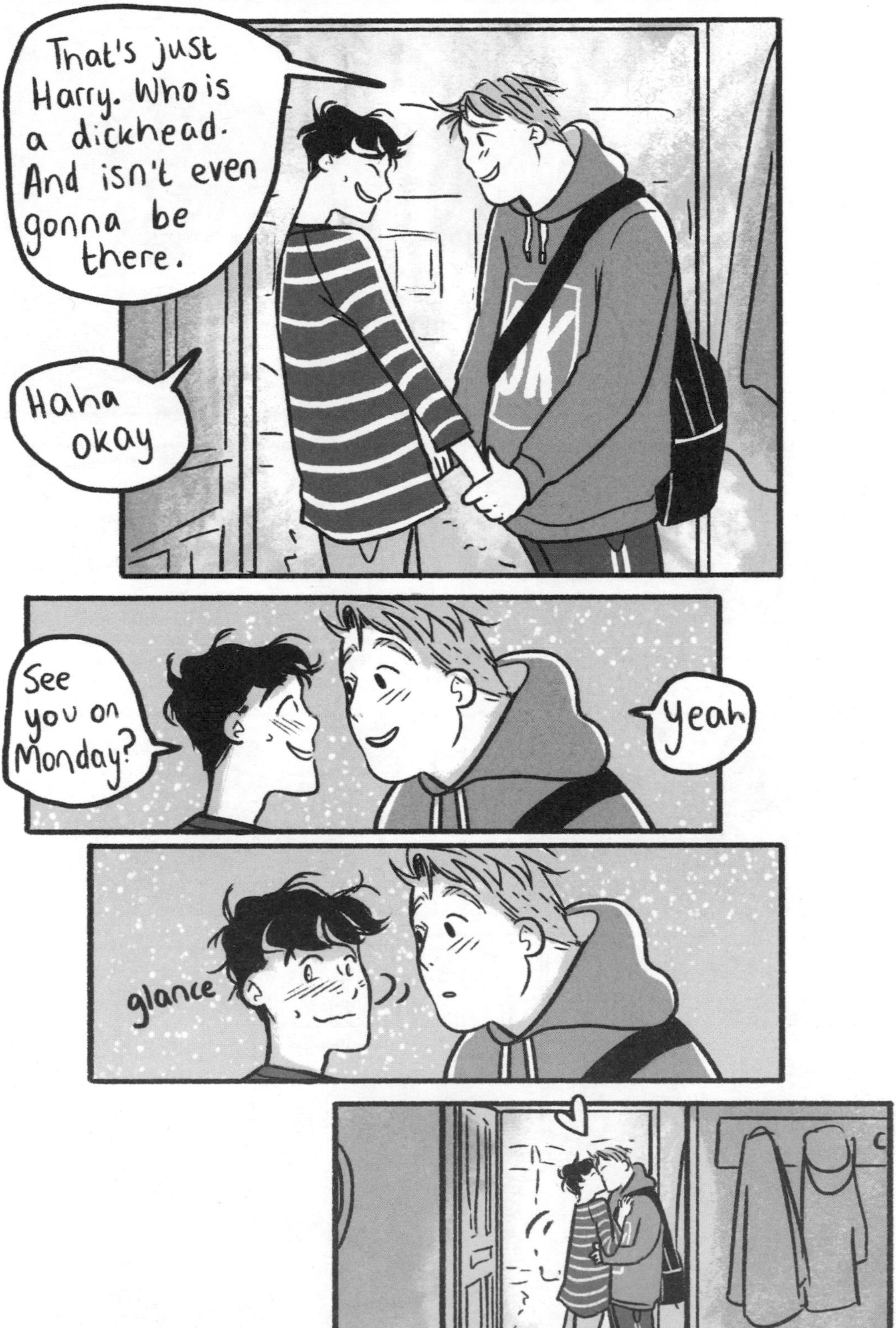
That's just Harry. Who is a dickhead. And isn't even gonna be there.
Haha okay
See you on Monday?
Yeah
glance

457

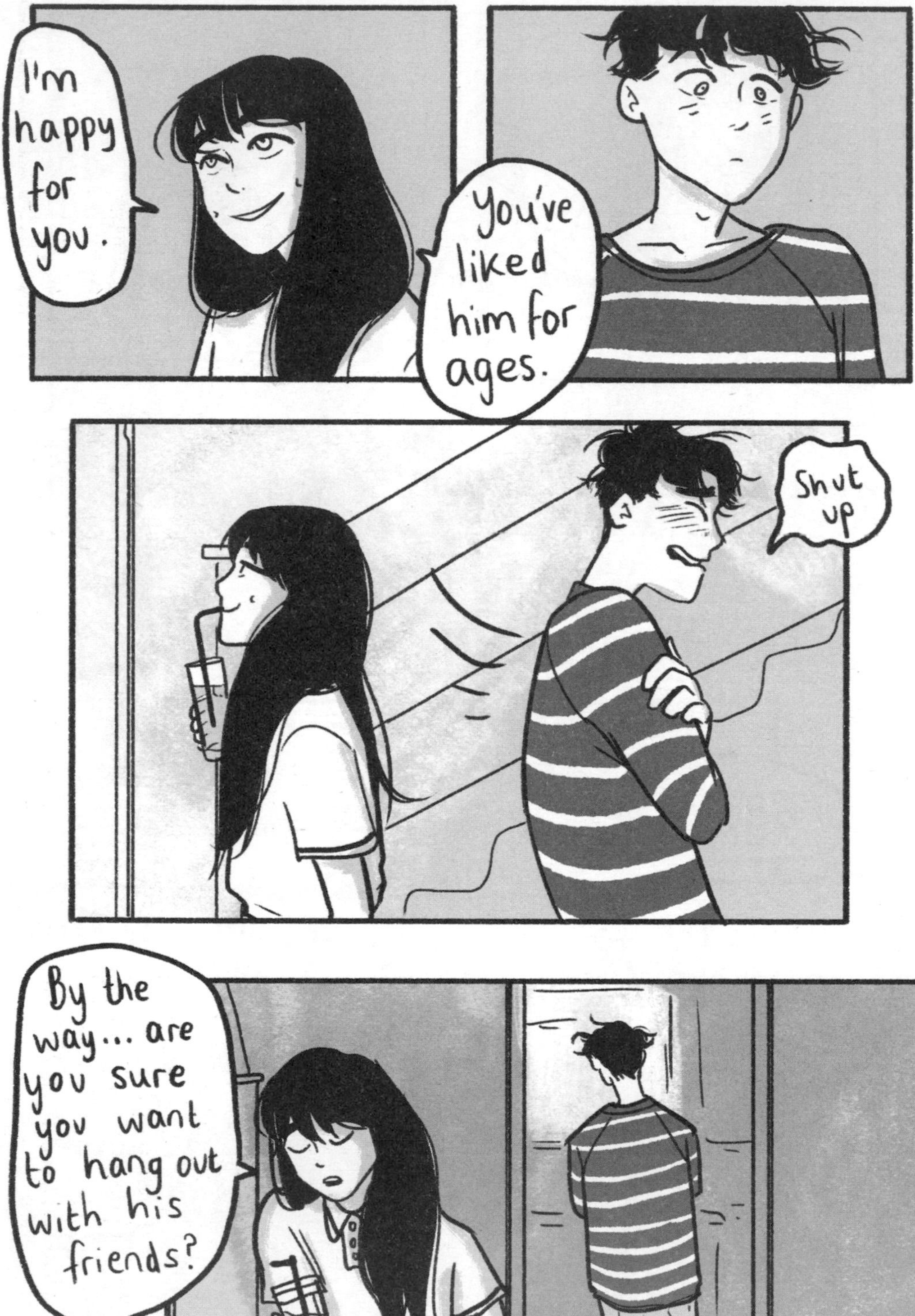
I'm happy for you.
You've liked him for ages.
Shut up
By the way... are you sure you want to hang out with his friends?

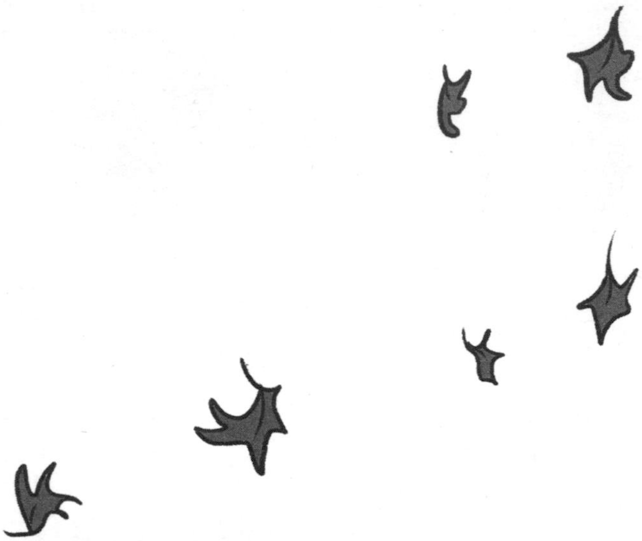

THE NEXT SATURDAY...

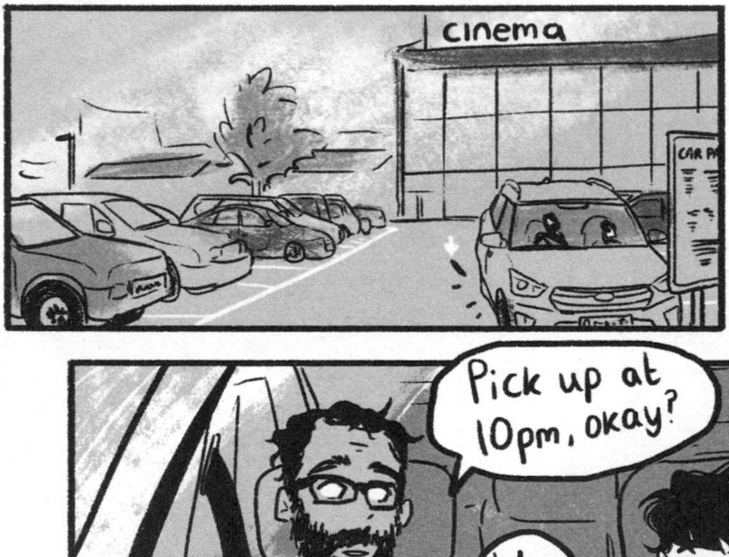
cinema

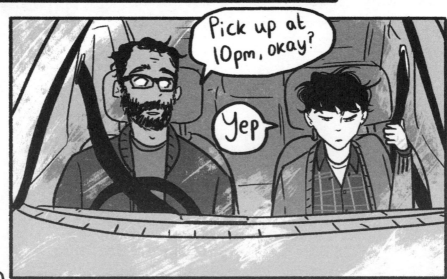

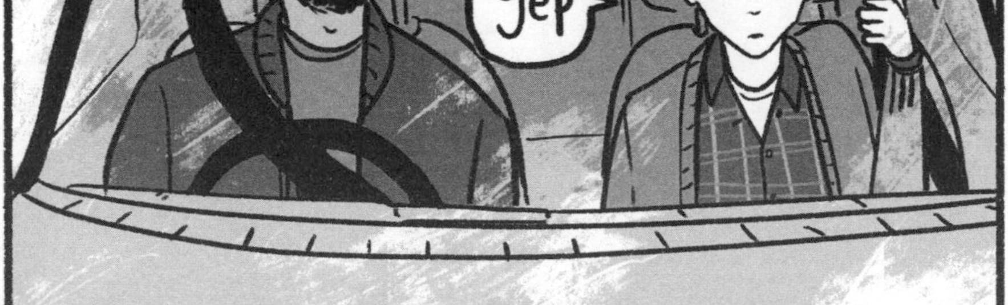
Pick up at 10pm, okay?
Yep

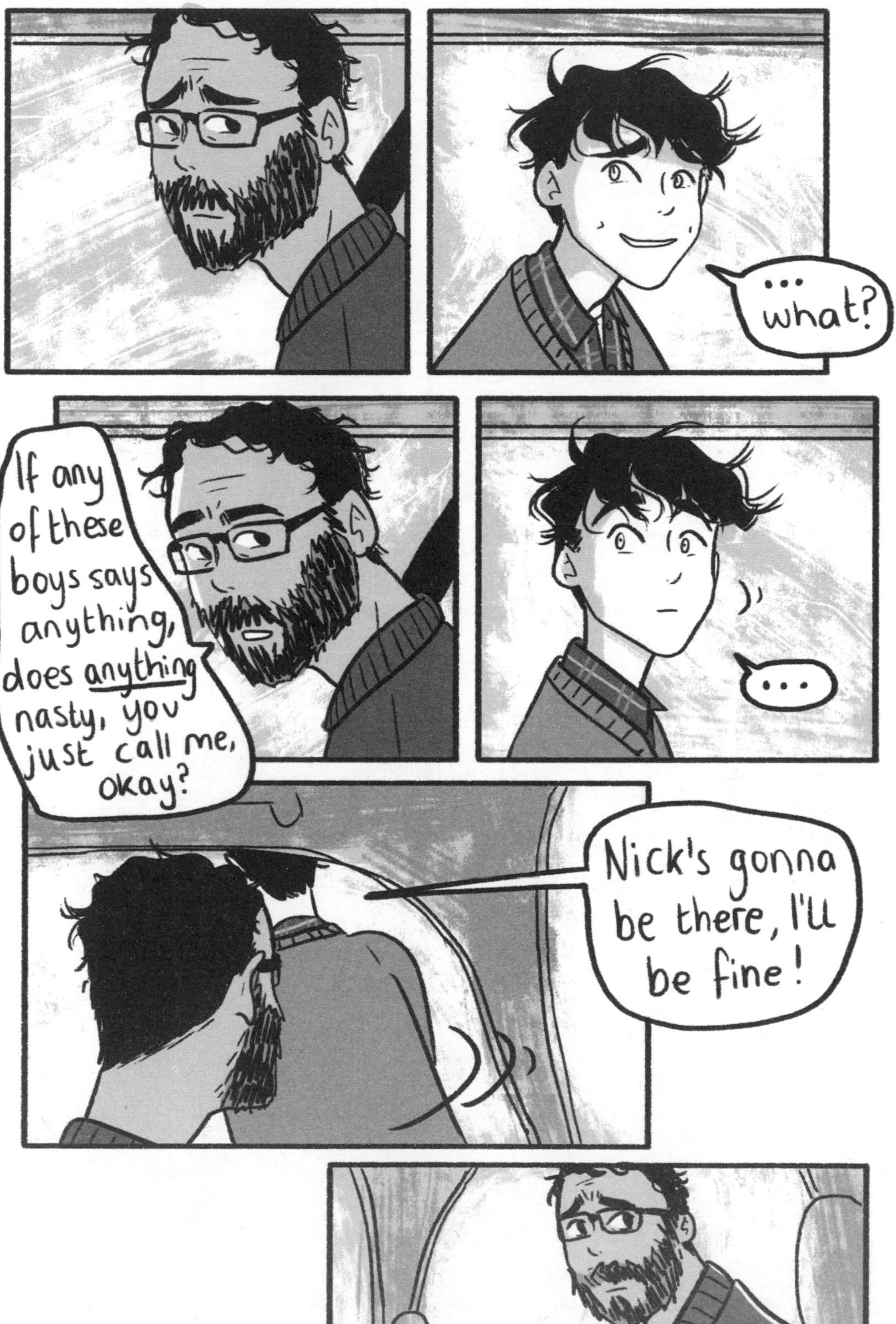

... what?
If any of these boys says anything, does anything nasty, you just call me, okay?
...
Nick's gonna be there, I'll be fine!

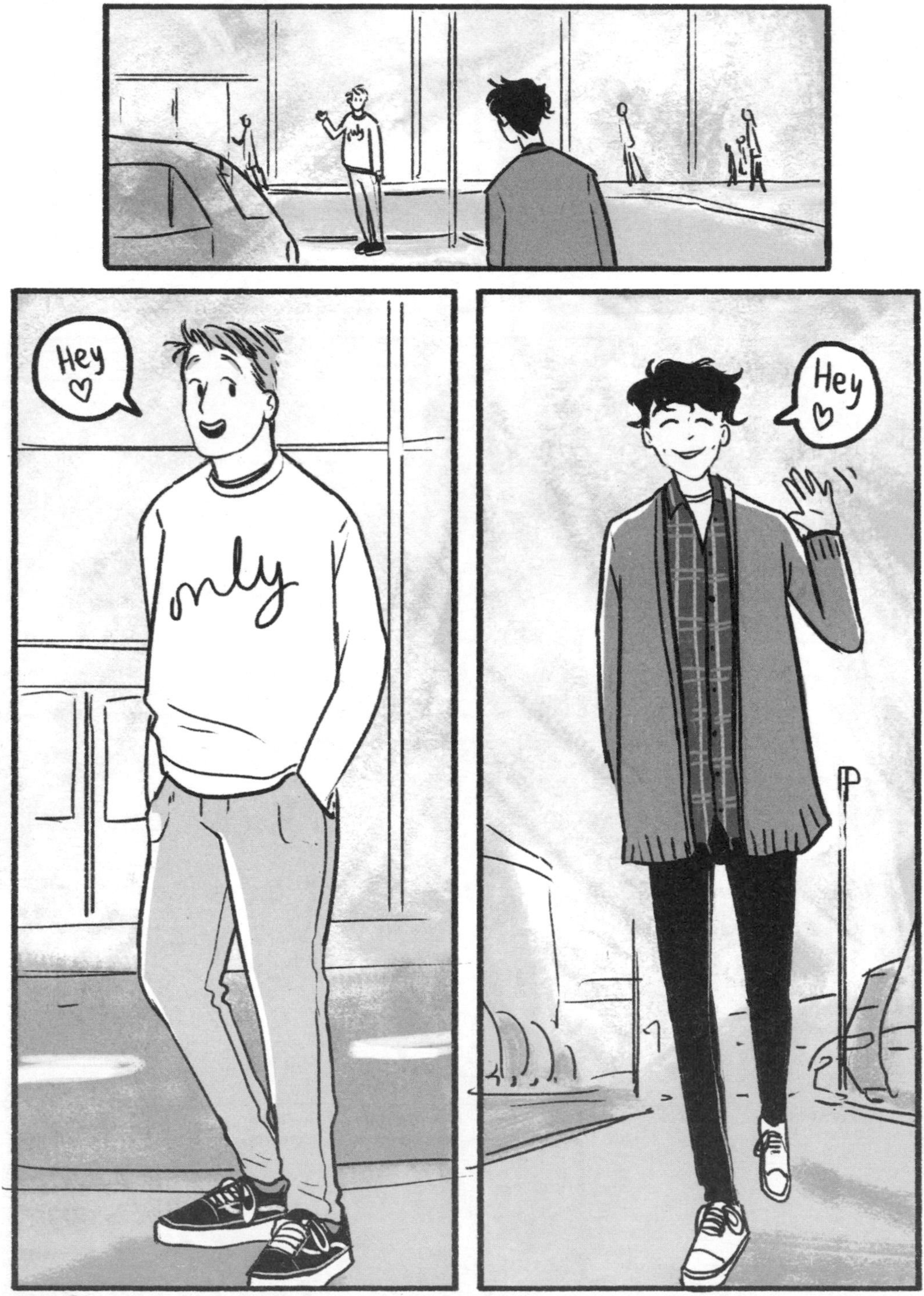
only
Hey ♡
only
Hey ♡

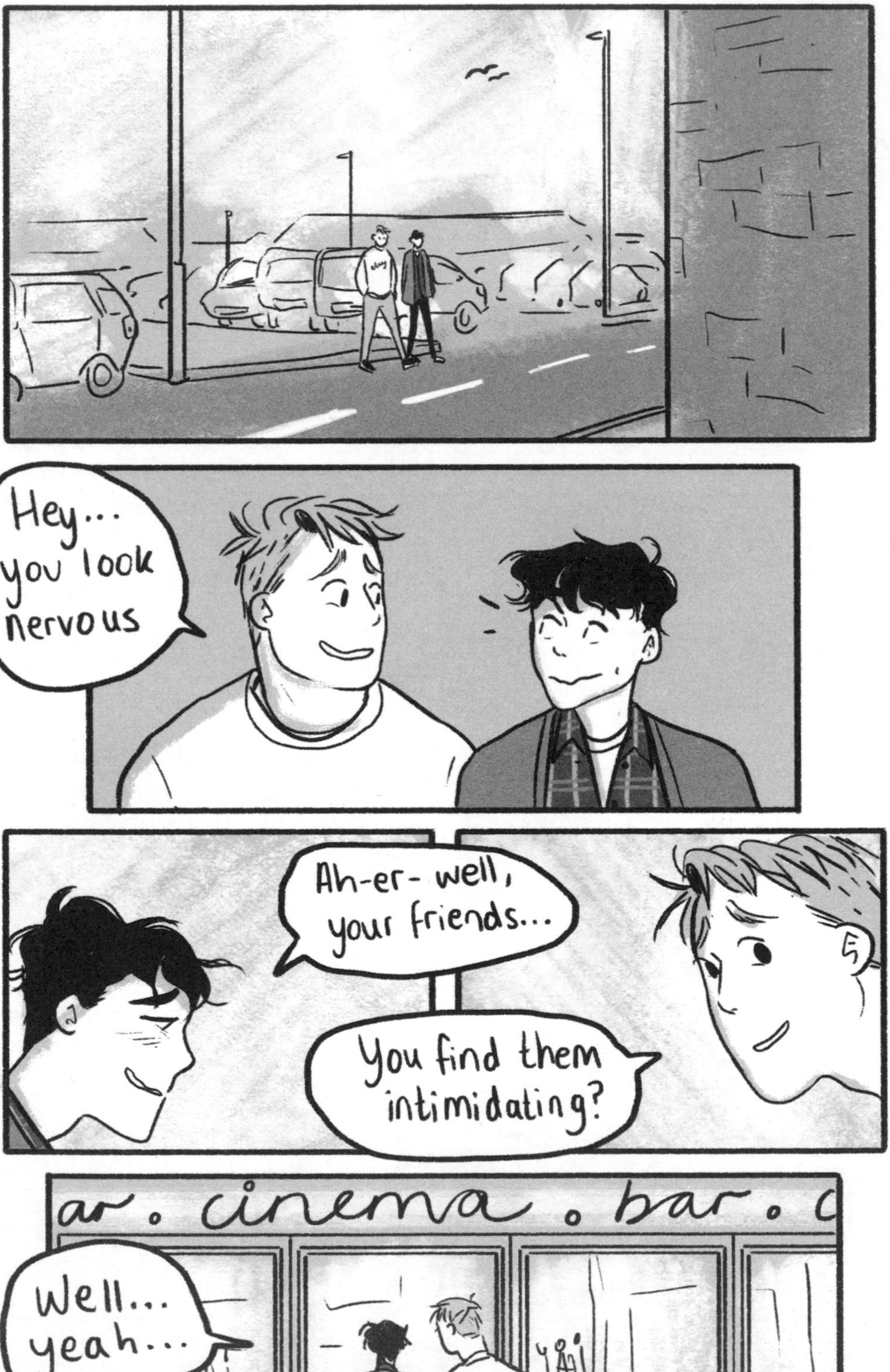
Hey... you look nervous
Ah-er- well, your friends...
You find them intimidating?
ar . cinema . bar . c
Well... yeah...

I don't know... They probably all just think I'm this... gay nerd...

Well, you are kind of a gay nerd

Shut up, rugby lad!!

Ha ha ha!

Don't worry, I'll look after you!

Okay ♥

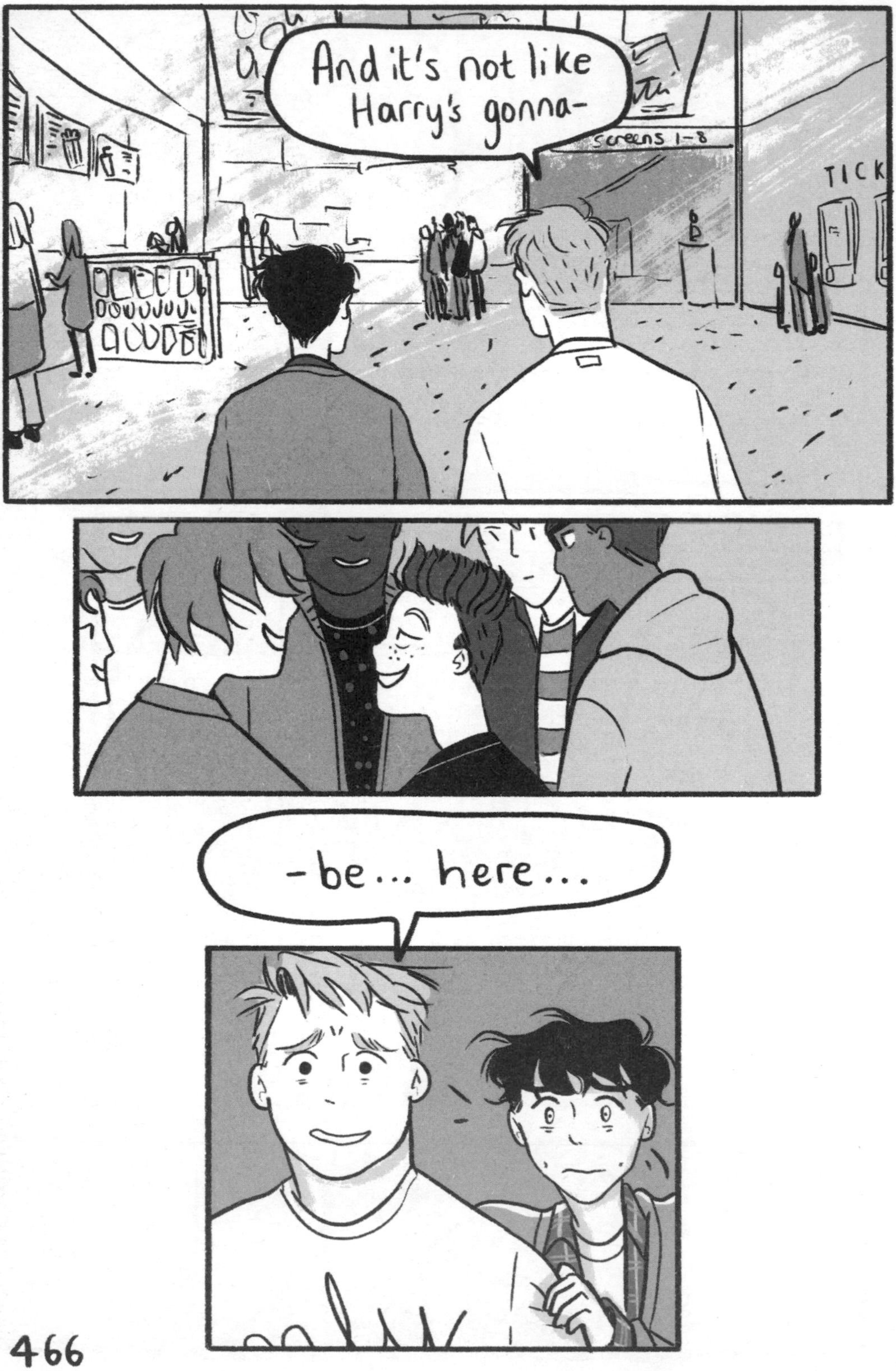
And it's not like Harry's gonna-
Screens 1-8
TICK
-be... here...

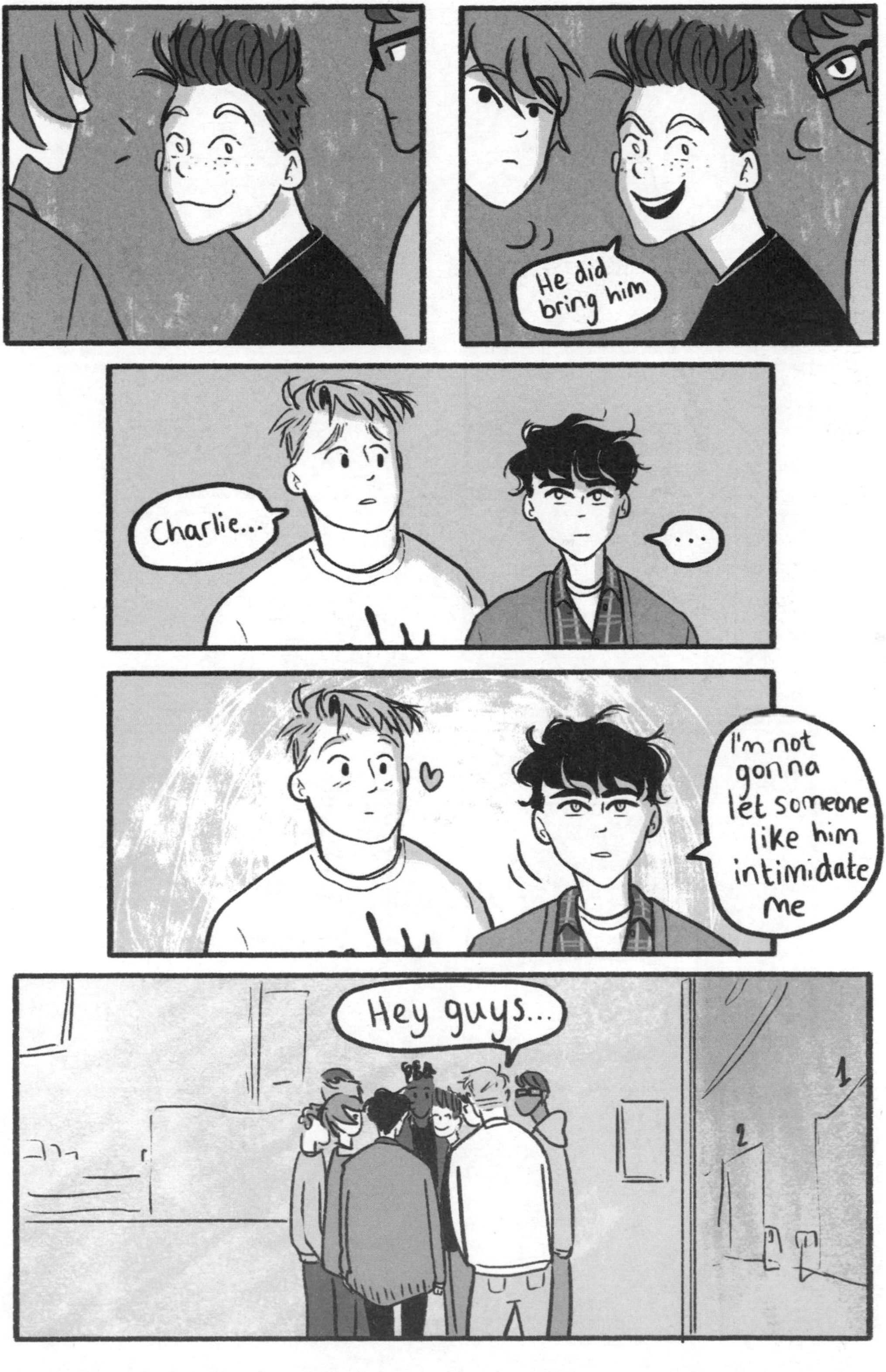
He did bring him
Charlie...
...
I'm not gonna let someone like him intimidate me
Hey guys...
1
2

469

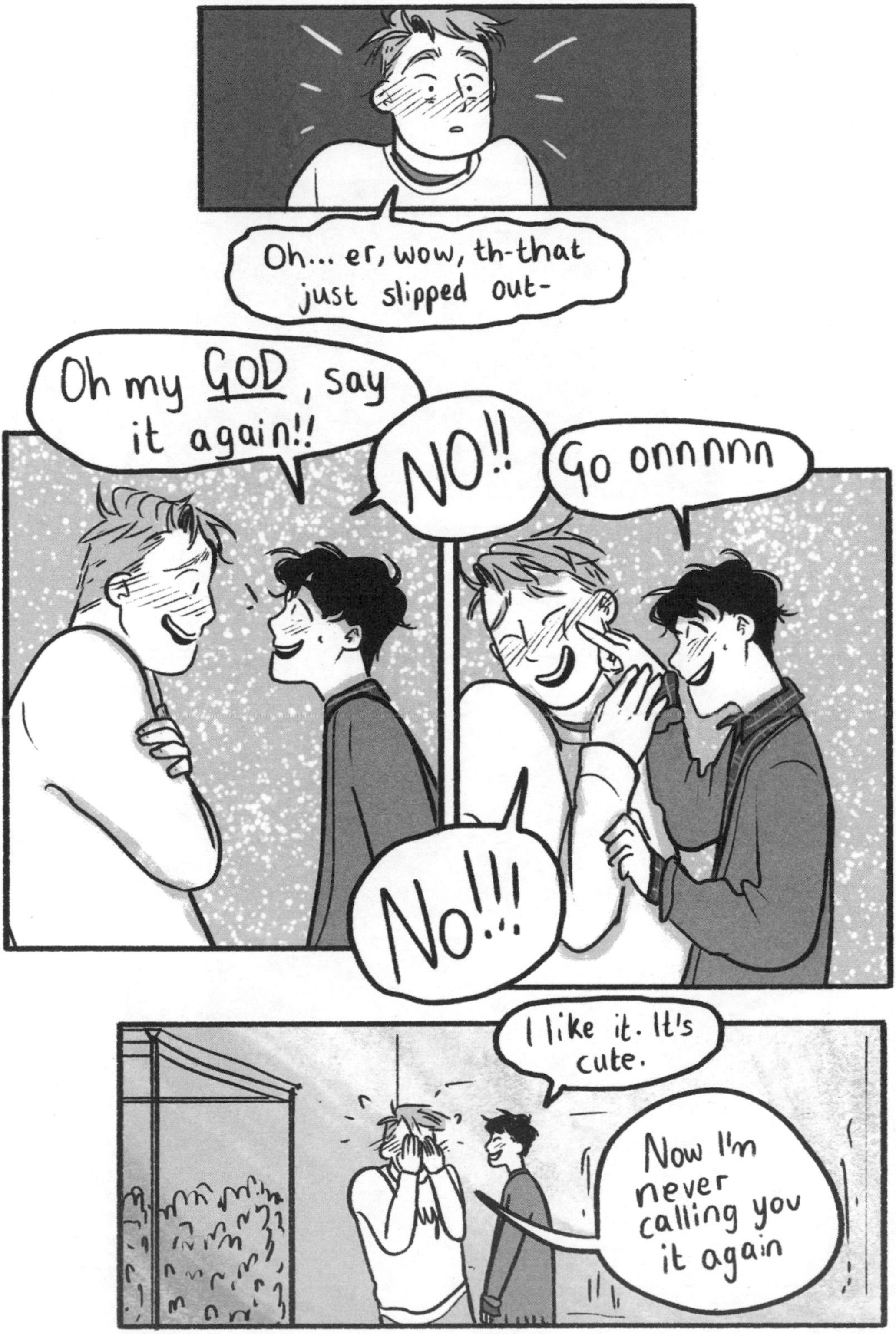
Oh... er, wow, th-that just slipped out-
Oh my GOD, say it again!!
NO!!
Go onnnnn
No!!!
I like it. It's cute.
Now I'm never calling you it again

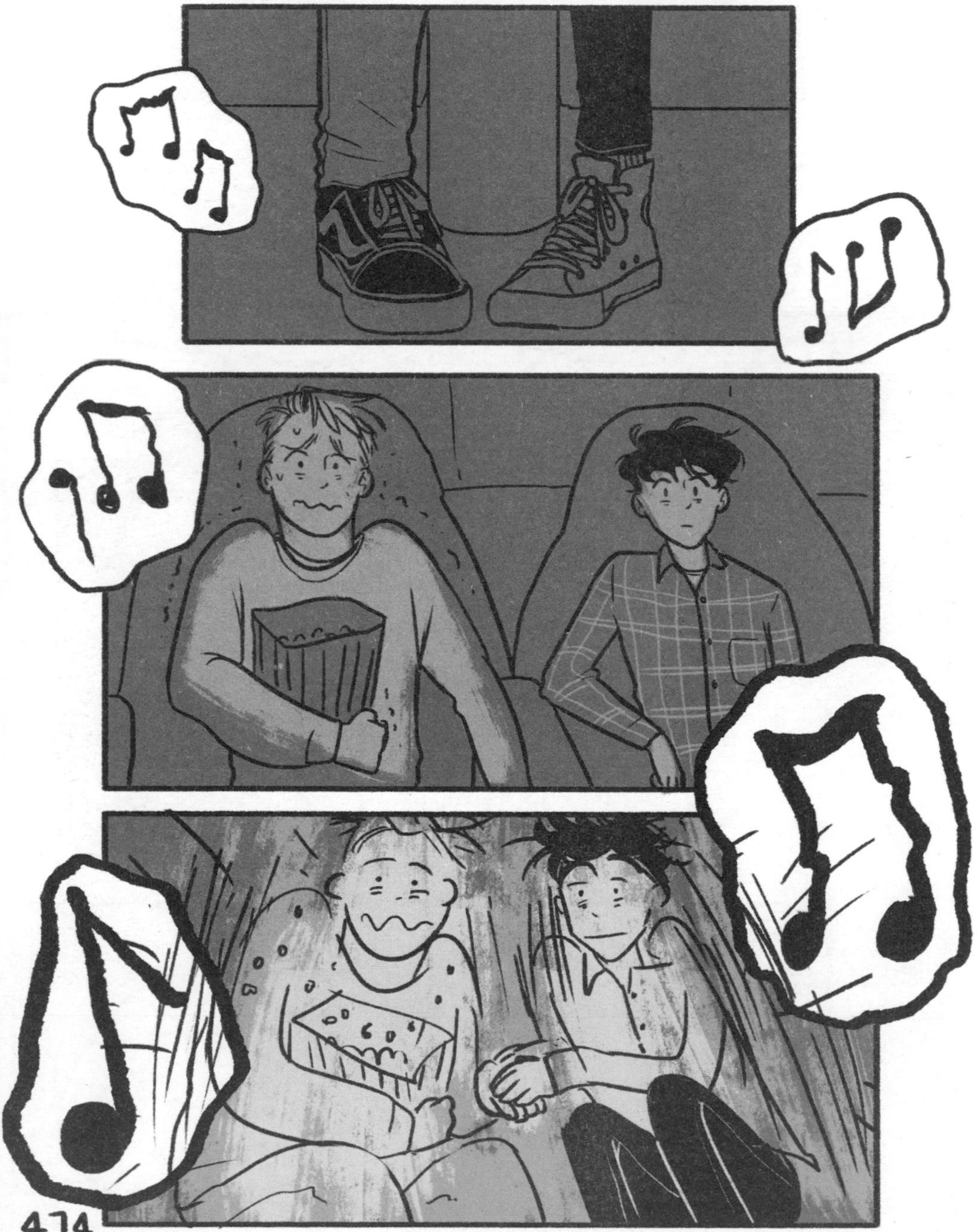

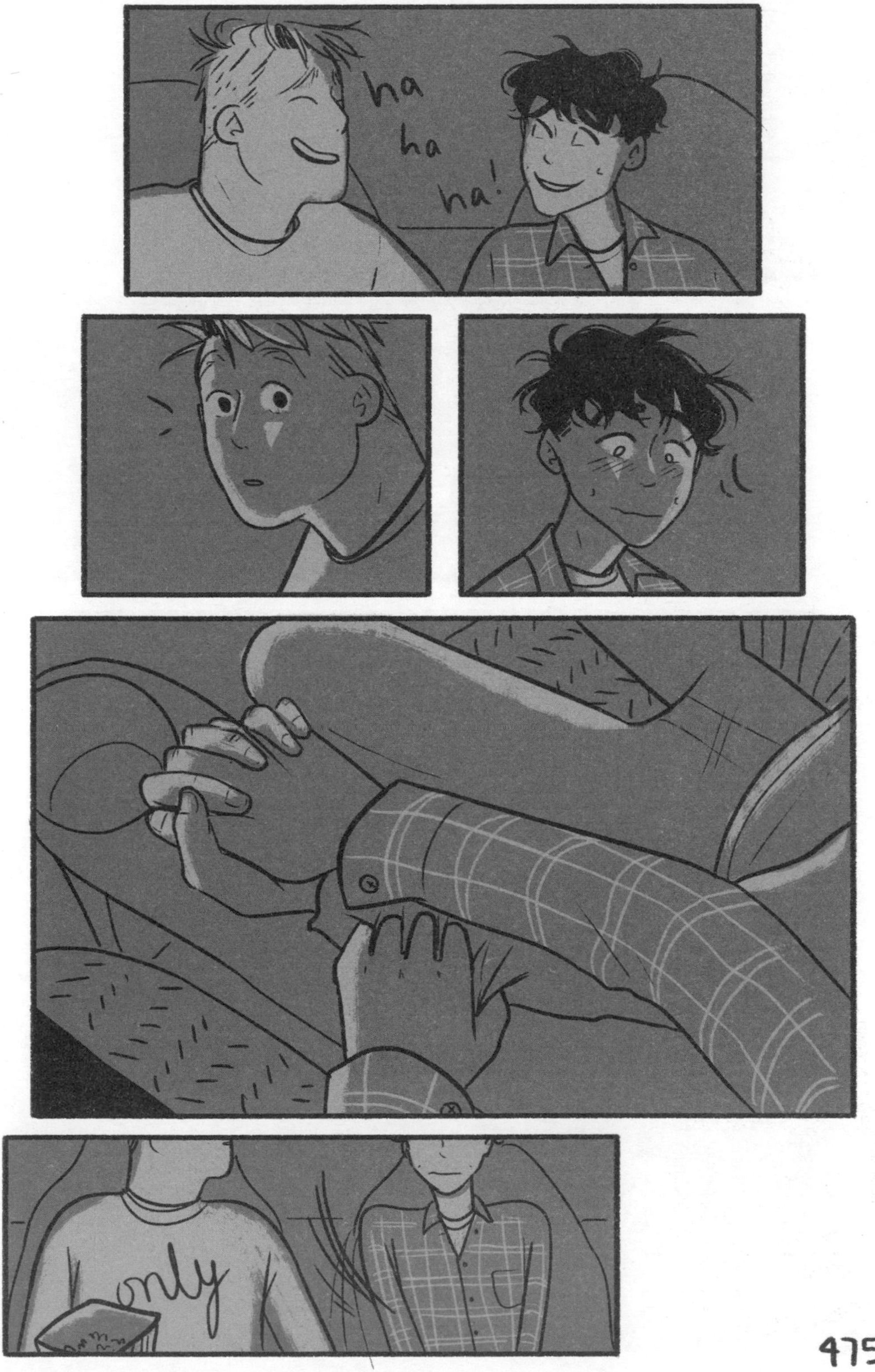
ha
ha
ha!
only

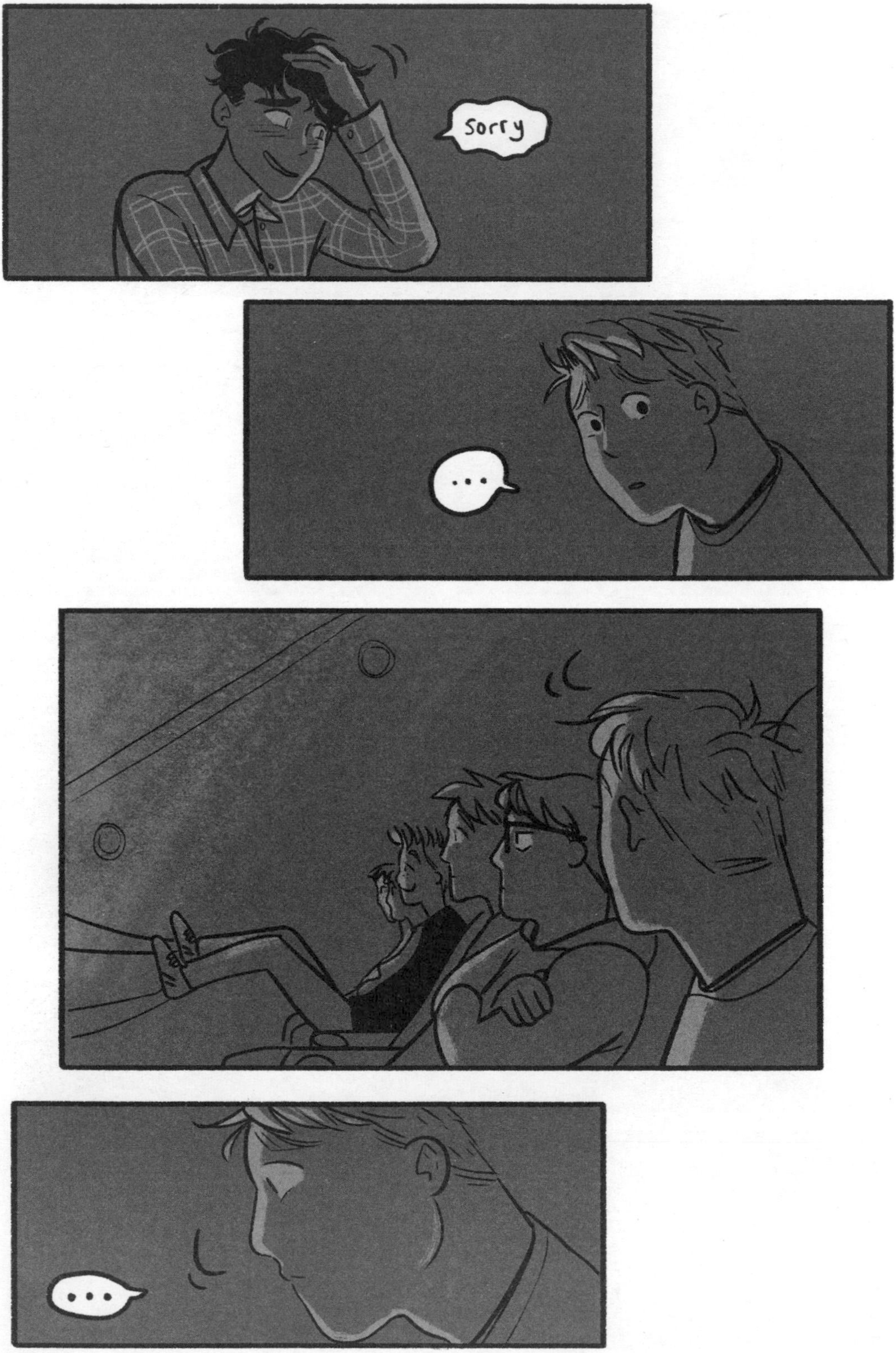
Sorry
...
...

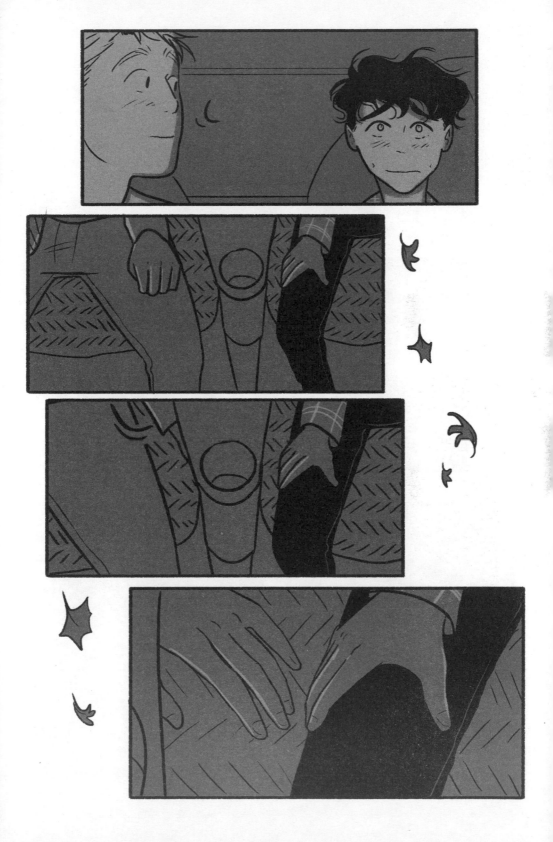

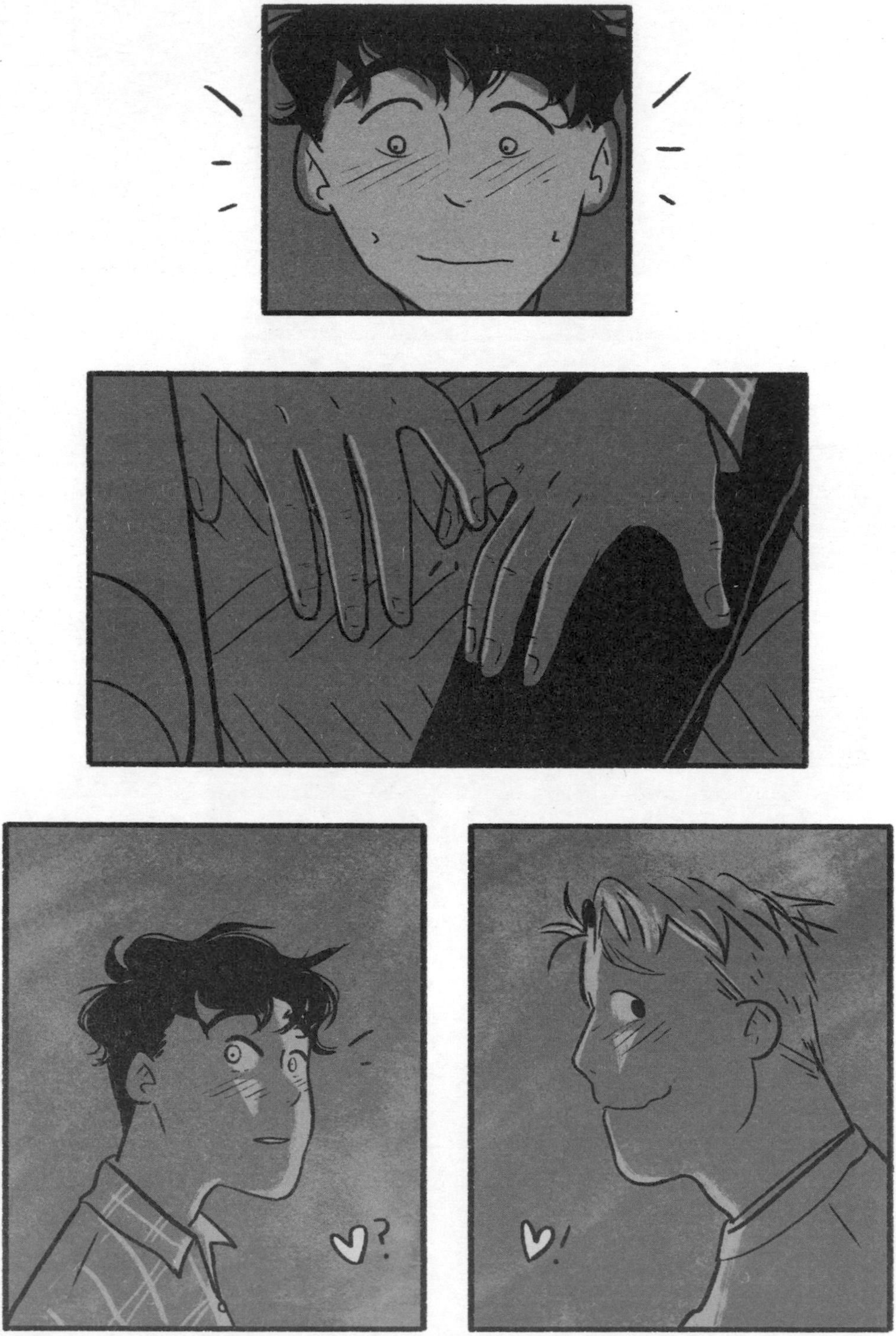
?
!

481

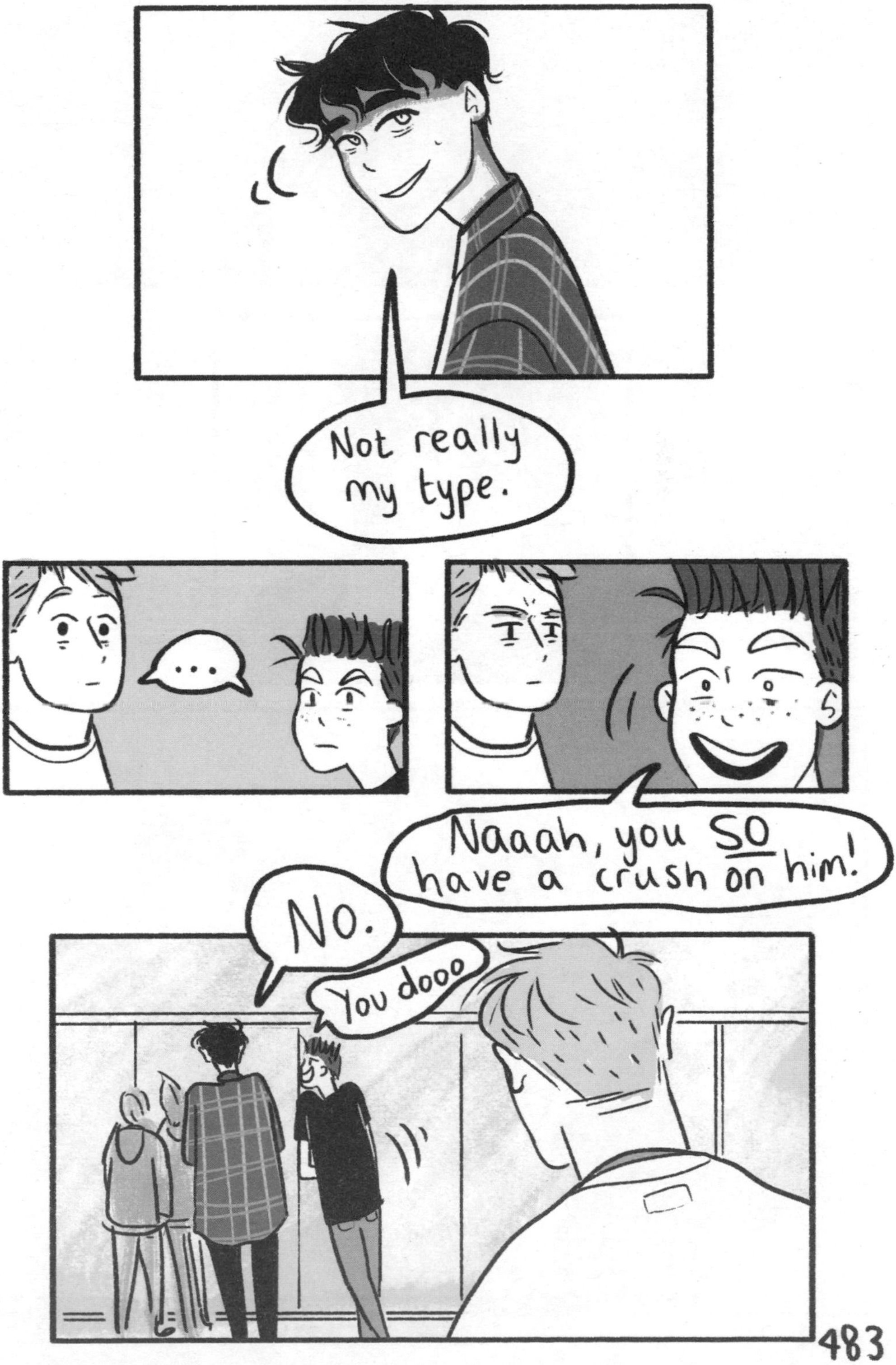
Not really my type.
...
Naaah, you SO have a crush on him!
No.
You dooo

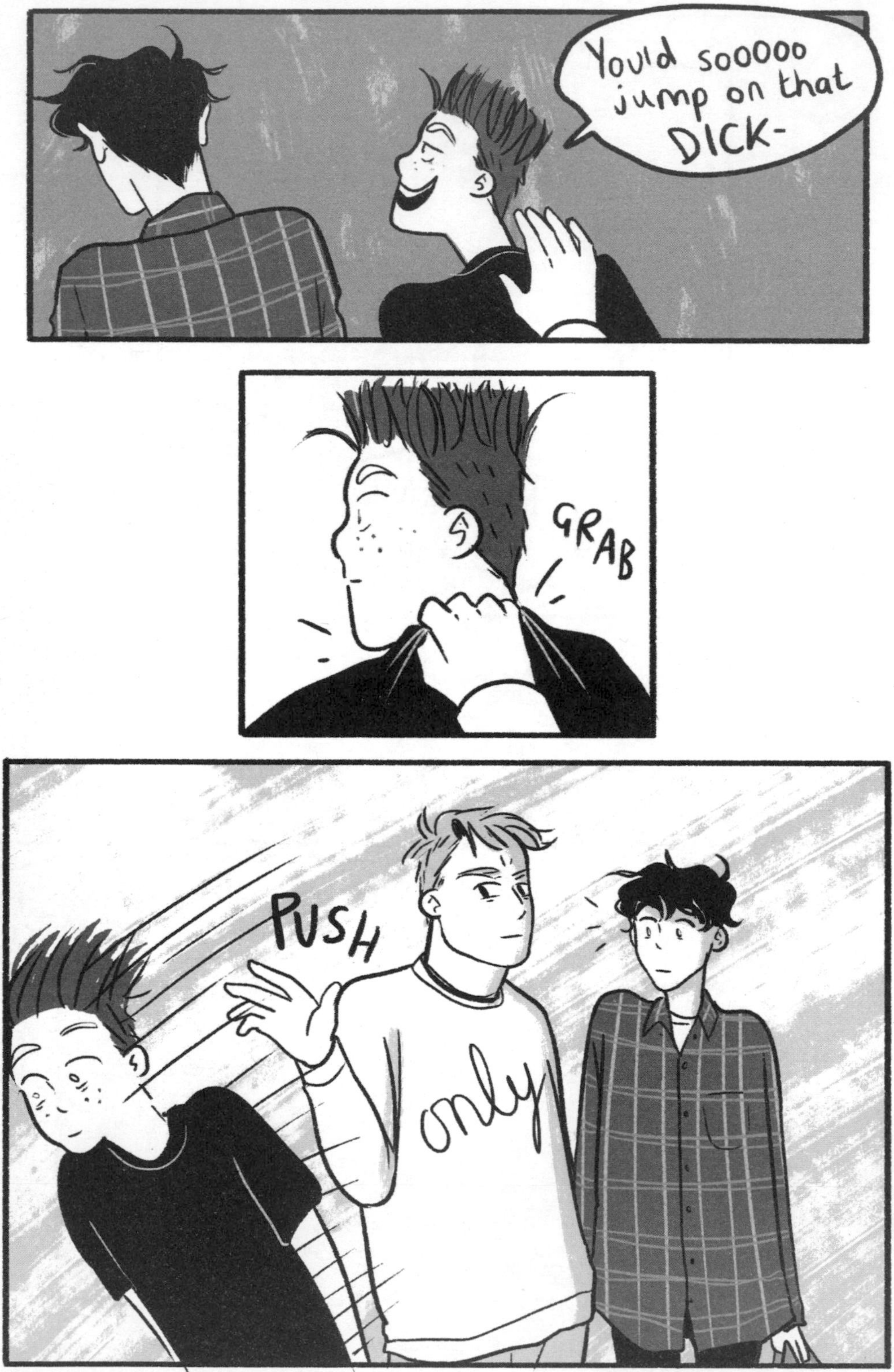
You'd sooooo jump on that DICK-
GRAB
PUSH
only

487

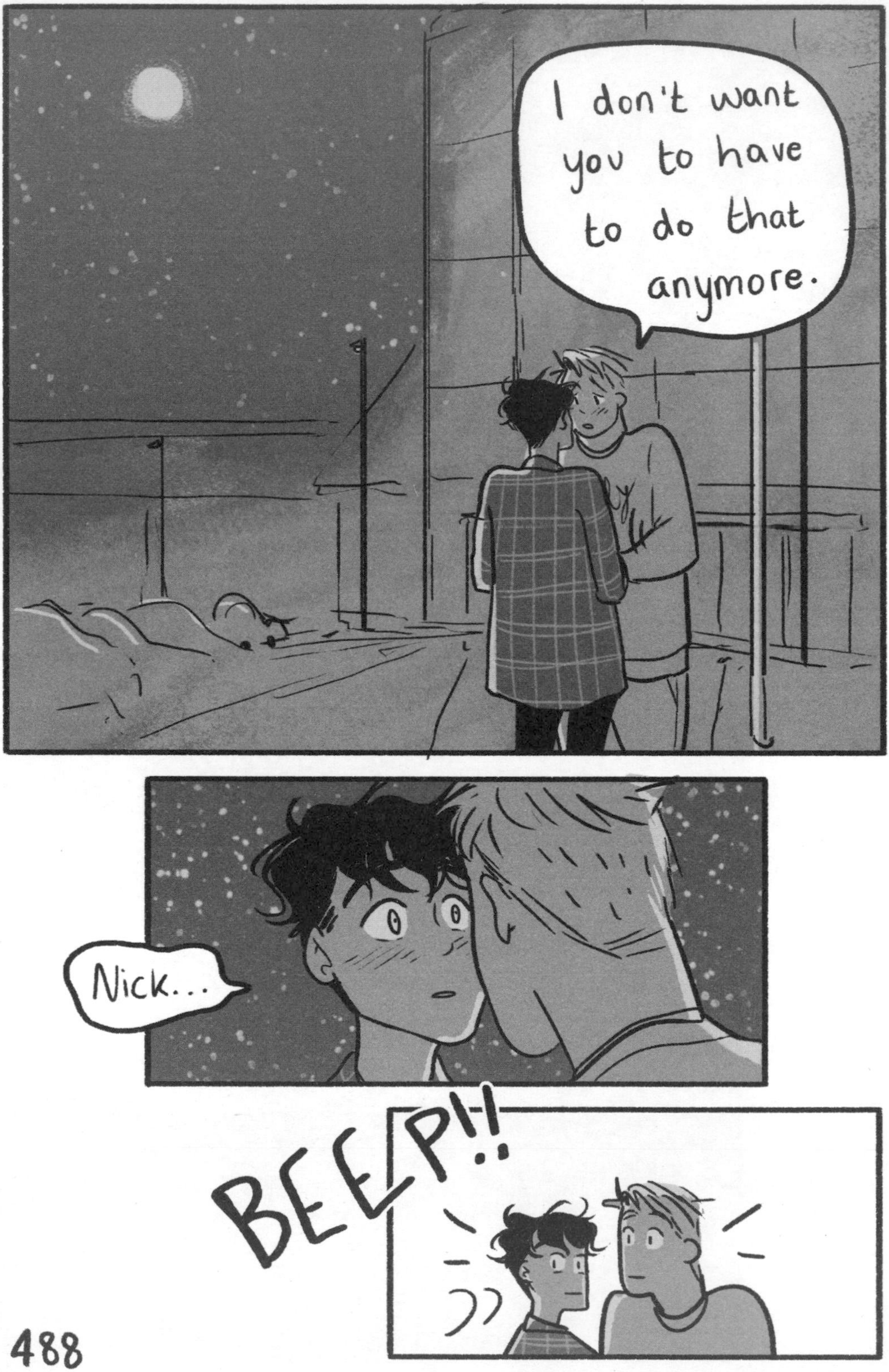
I don't want you to have to do that anymore.
Nick...
BEEP!!

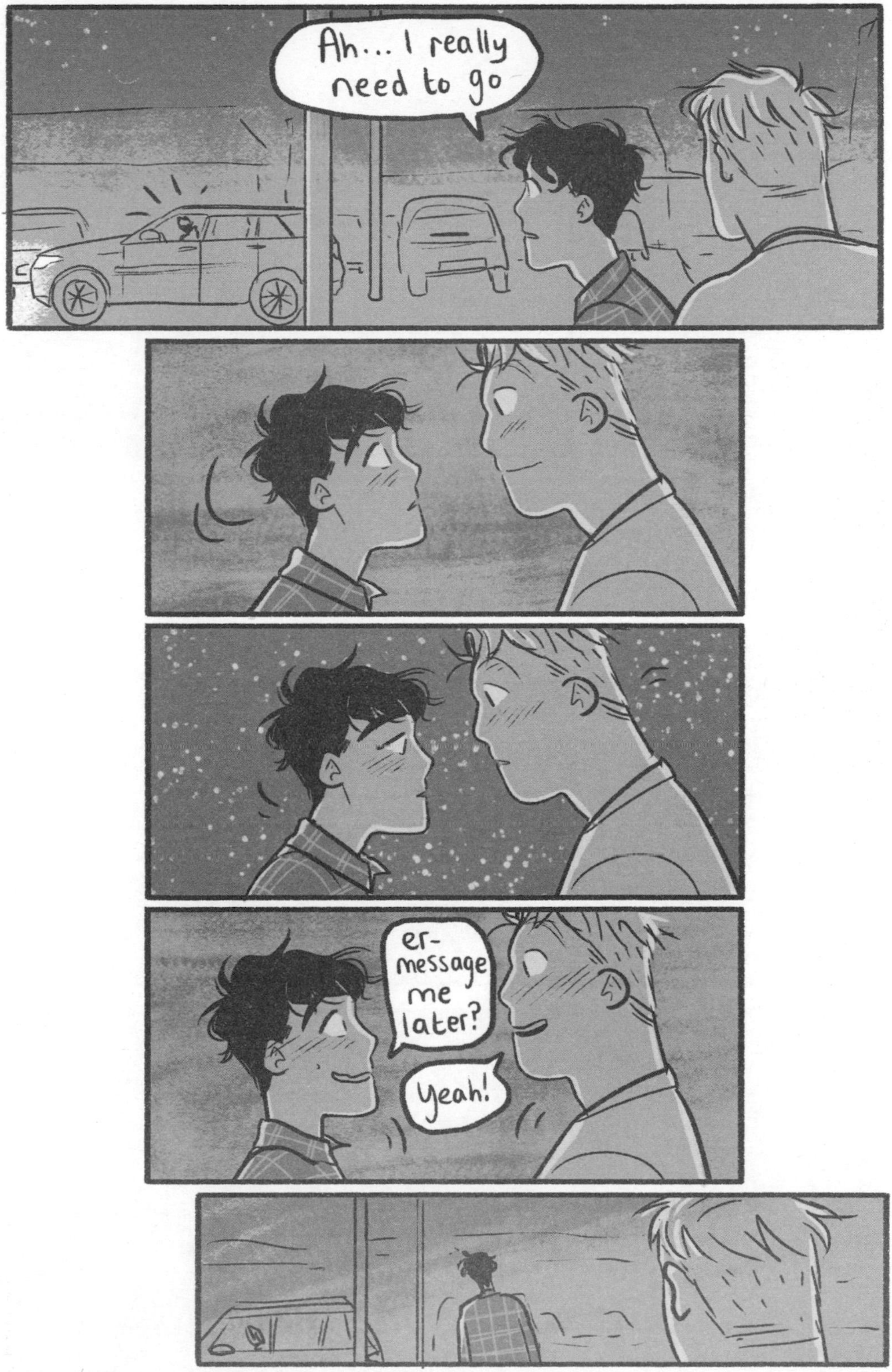
Ah... I really need to go
er- message me later?
Yeah!

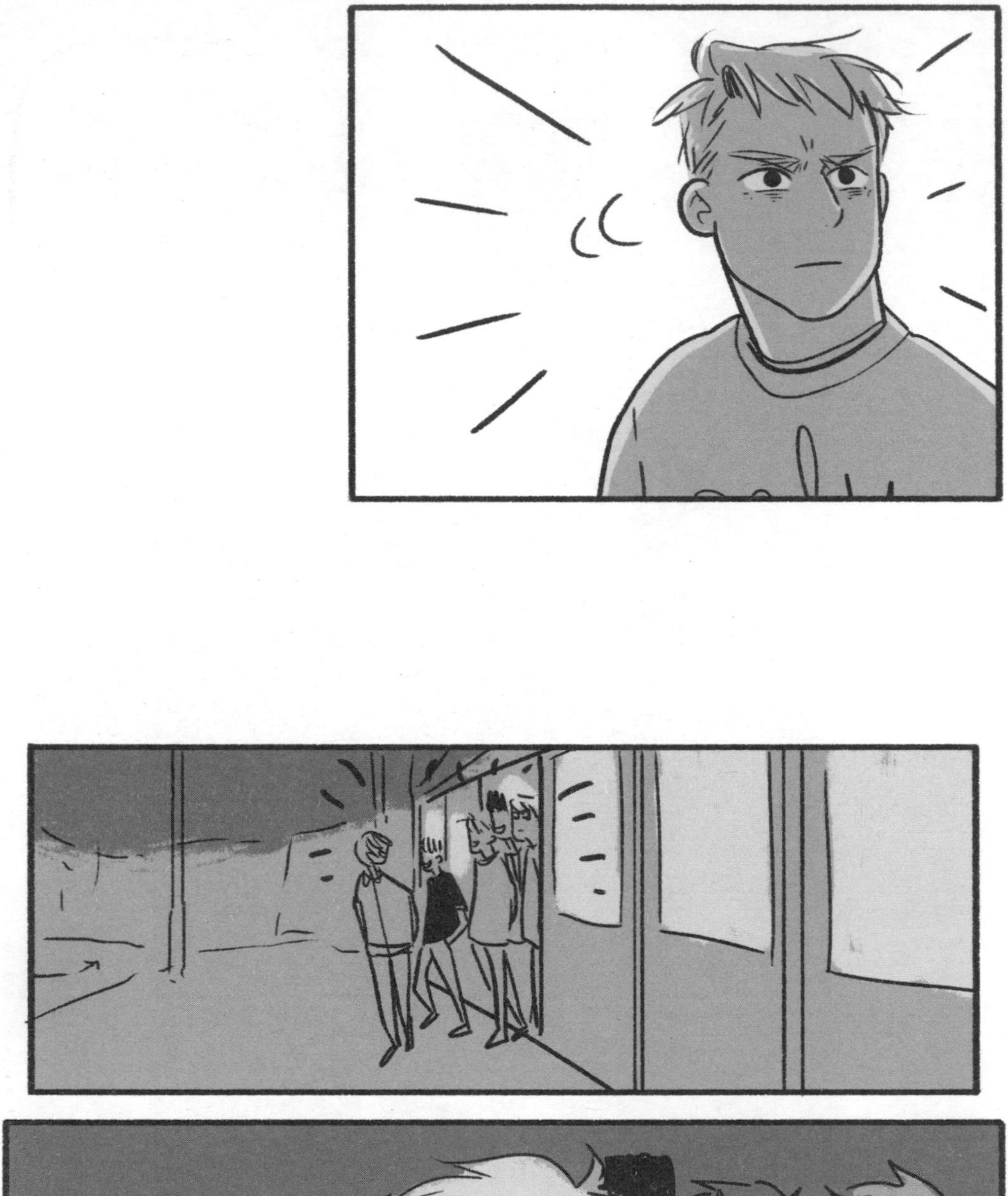

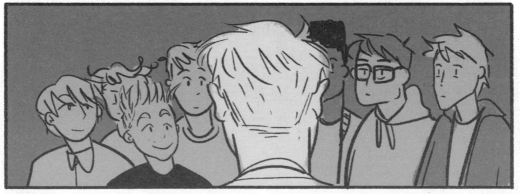

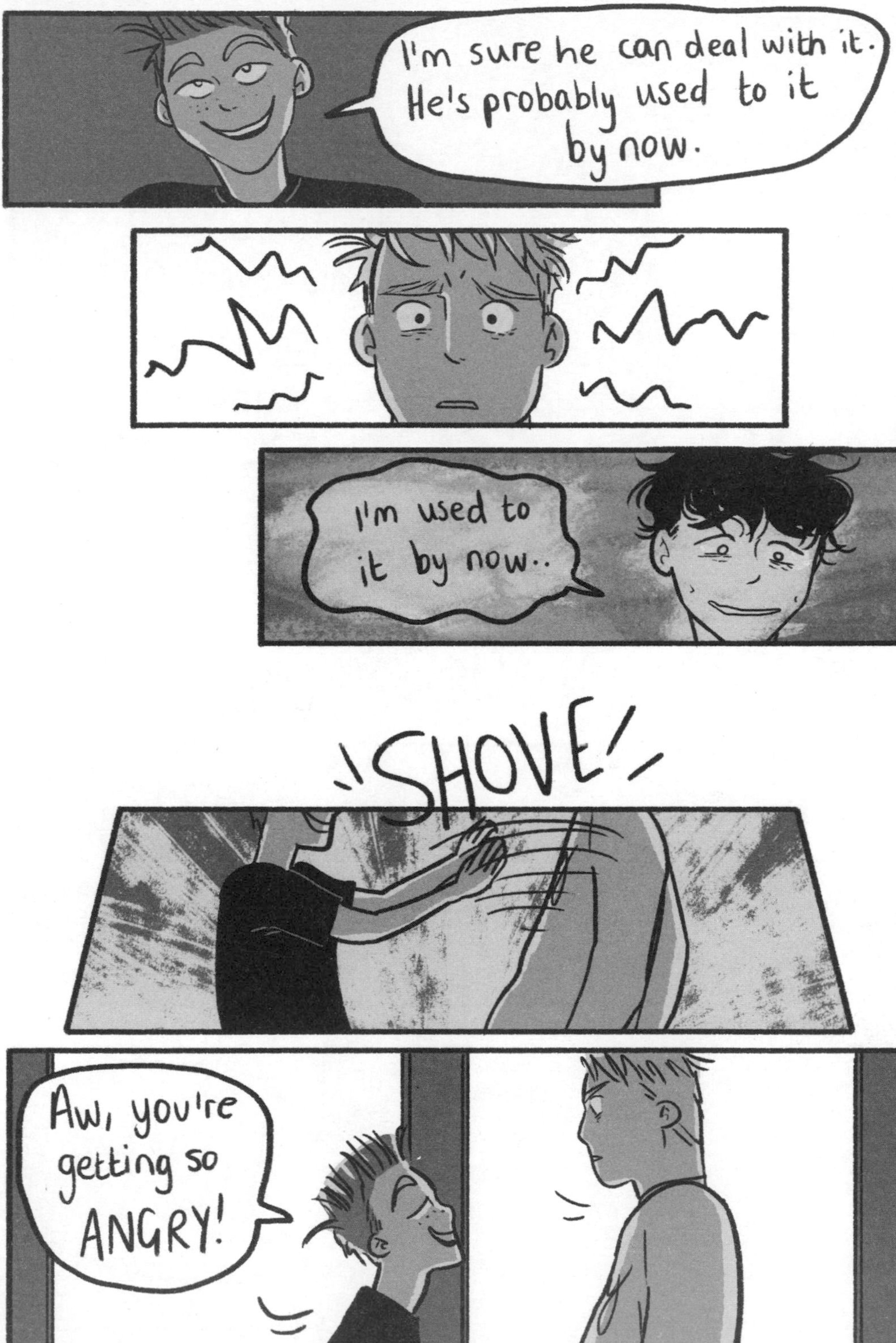
I'm sure he can deal with it. He's probably used to it by now.
I'm used to it by now..
SHOVE
Aw, you're getting so ANGRY!

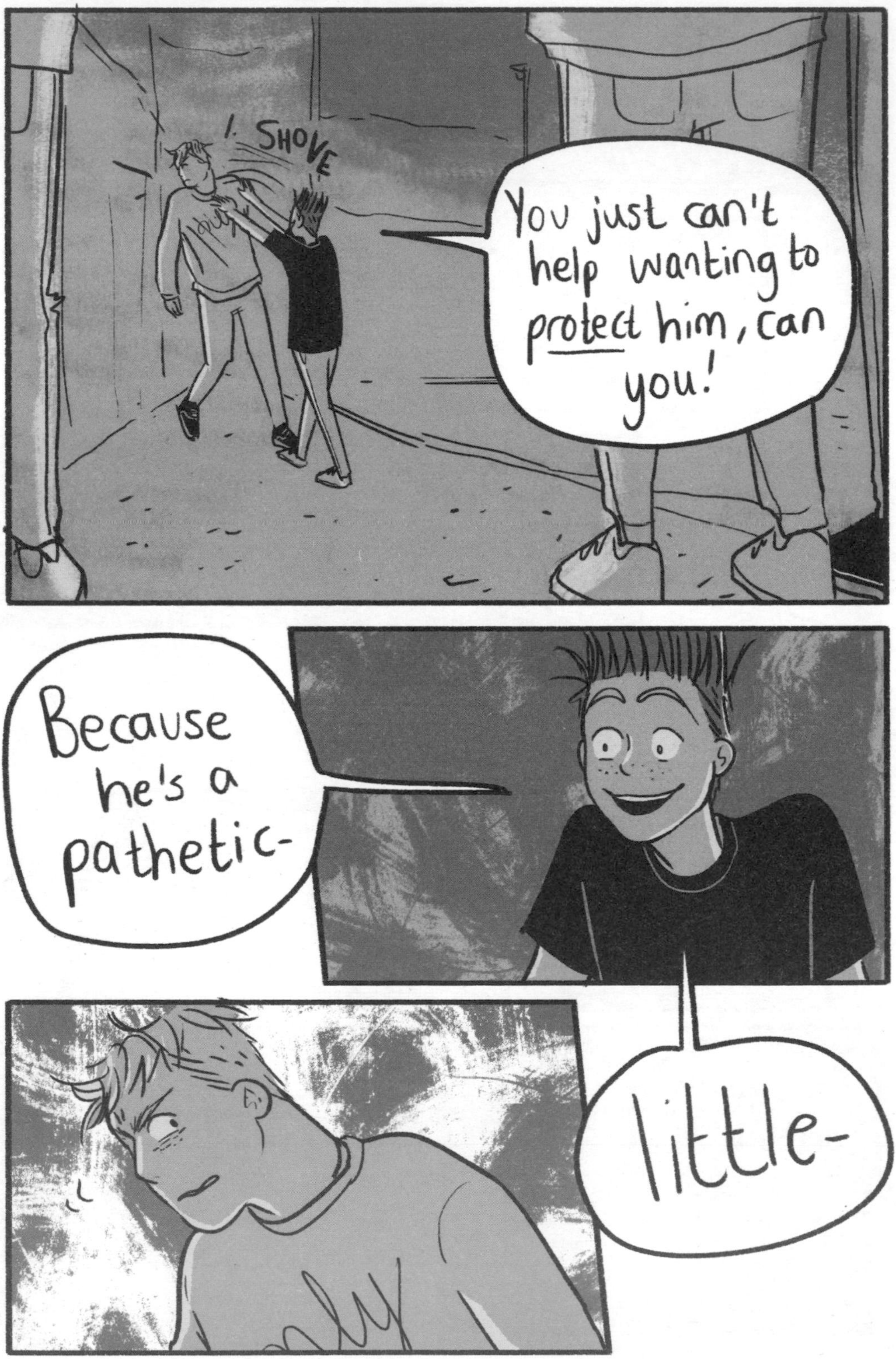
SHOVE
You just can't help wanting to protect him, can you!
Because he's a pathetic-
little-

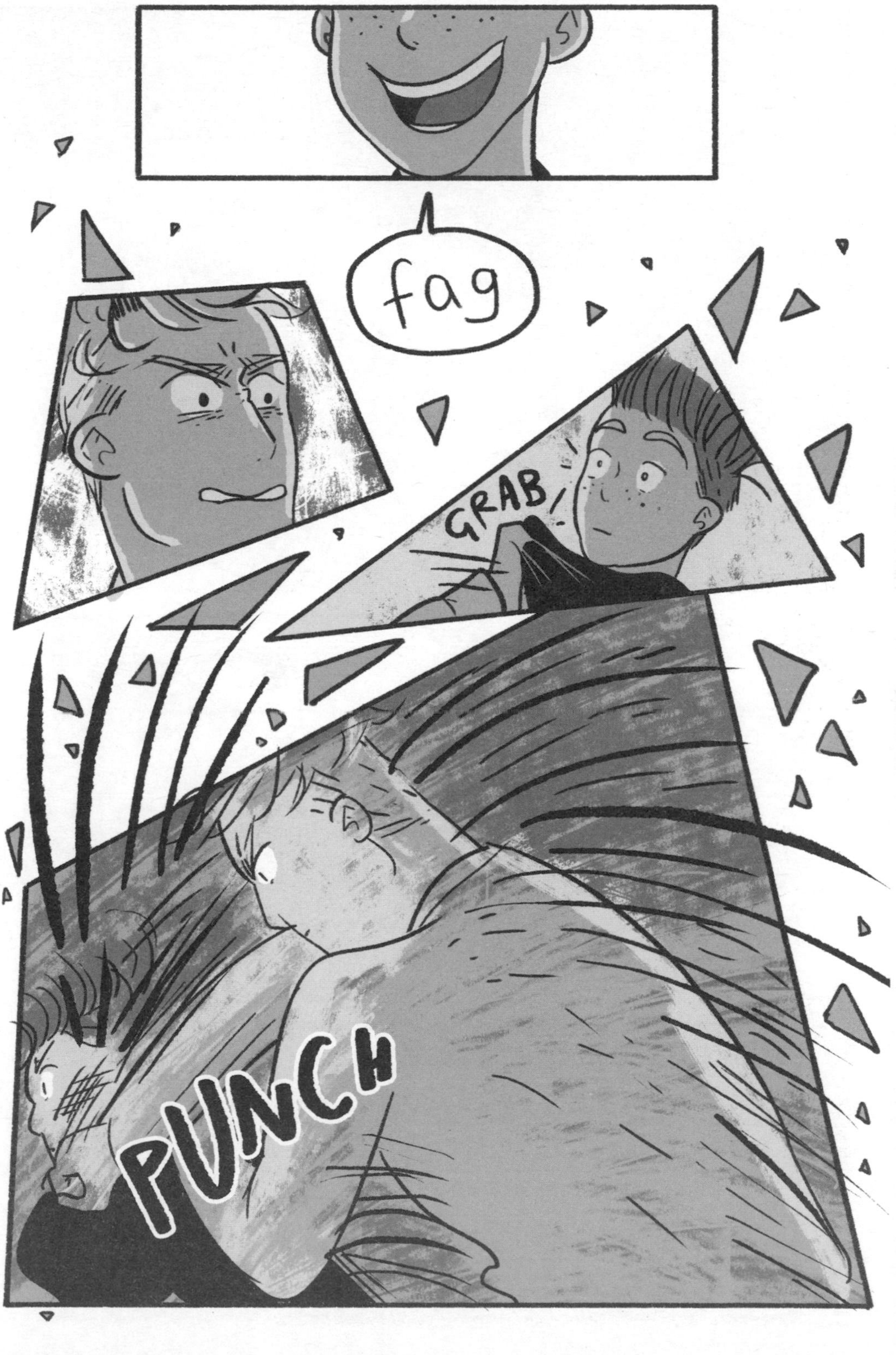
fag
GRAB
PUNCH

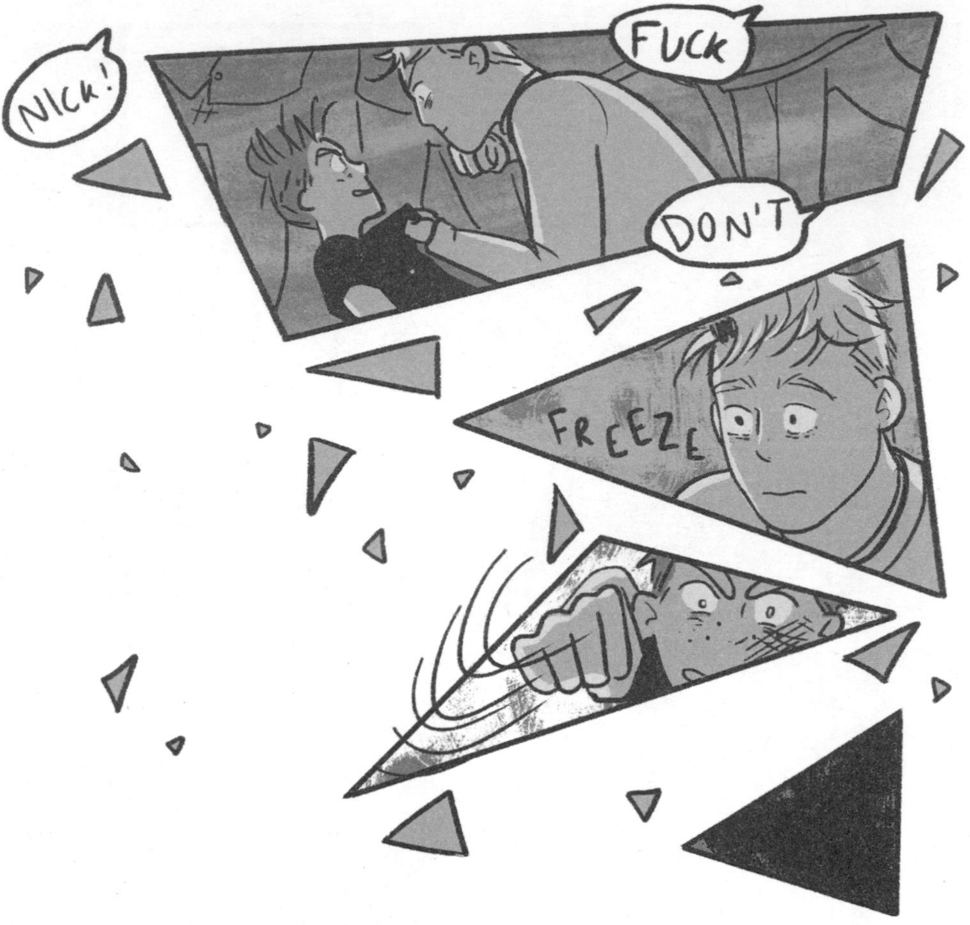
NICK!
FUCK
DON'T
FREEZE

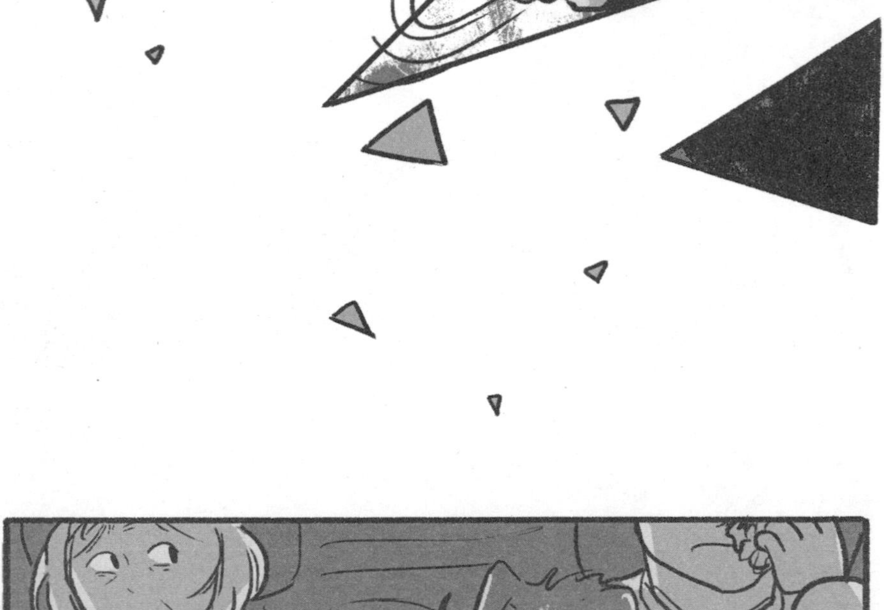

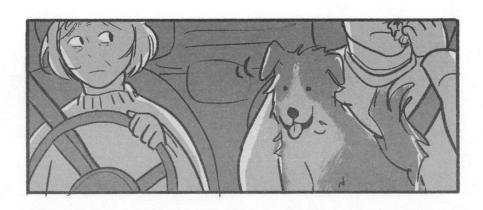

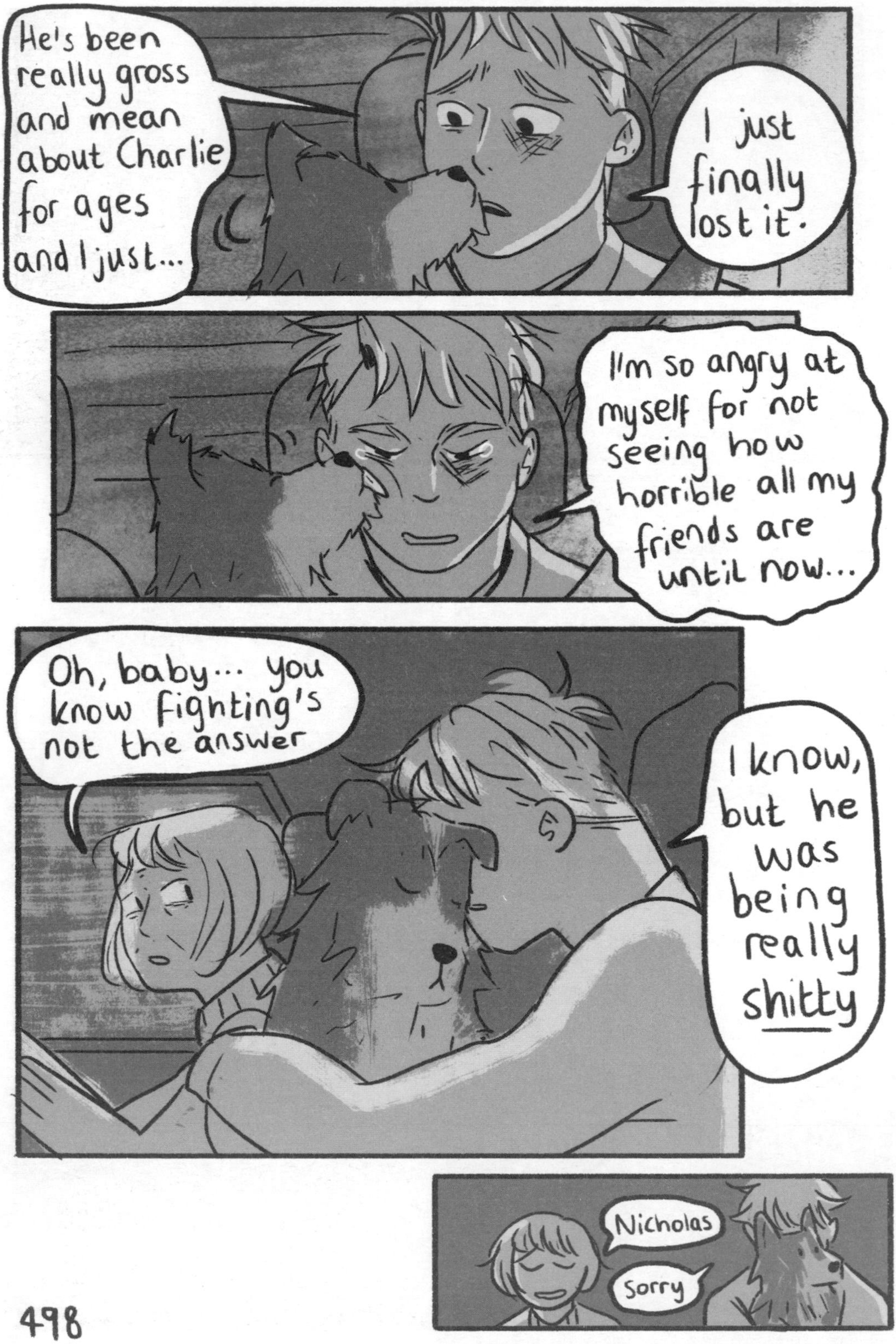
He's been really gross and mean about Charlie for ages and I just...
I just finally lost it.
I'm so angry at myself for not seeing how horrible all my friends are until now...
Oh, baby... you know fighting's not the answer
I know, but he was being really shitty
Nicholas
Sorry

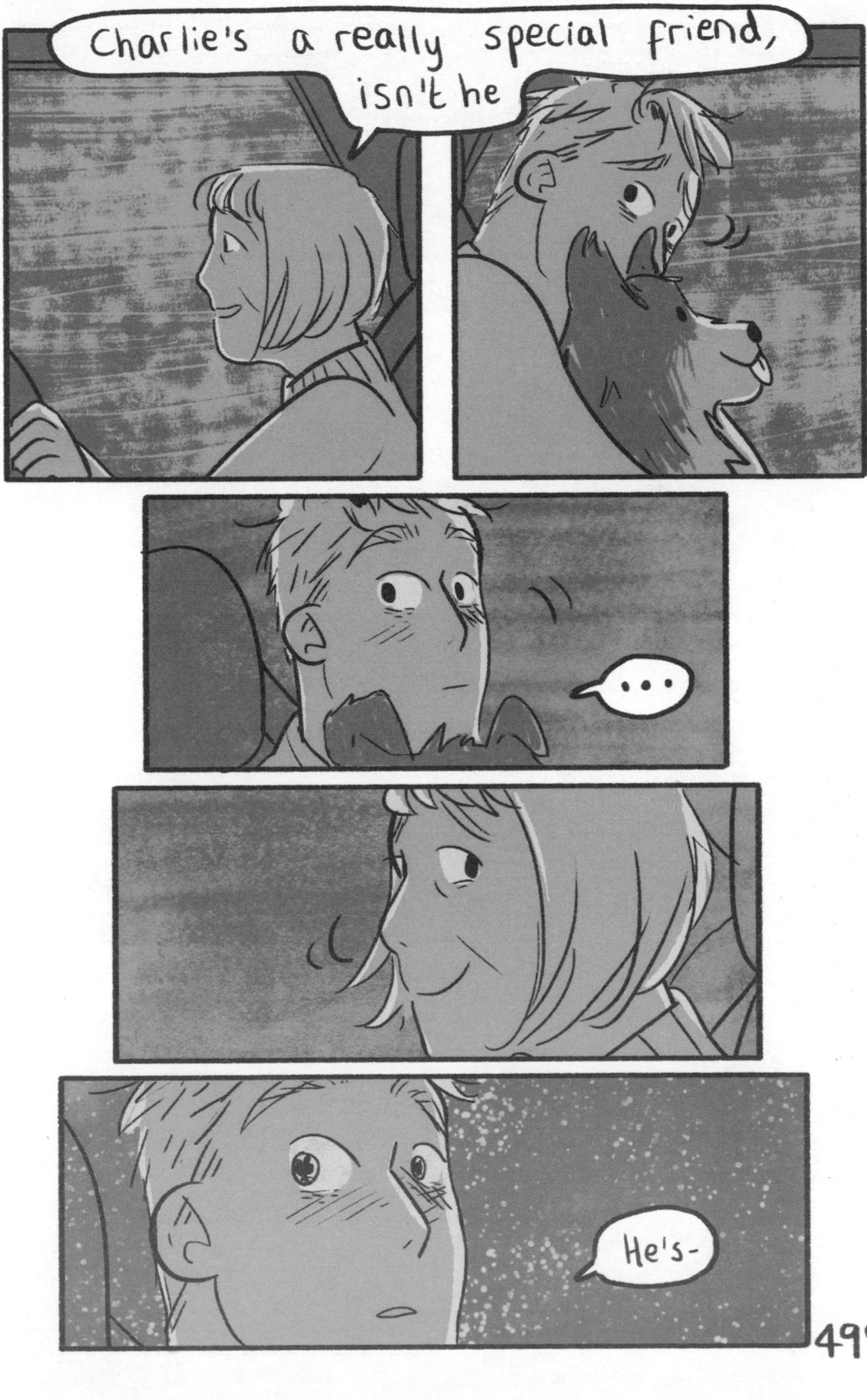
Charlie's a really special friend, isn't he
...
He's-

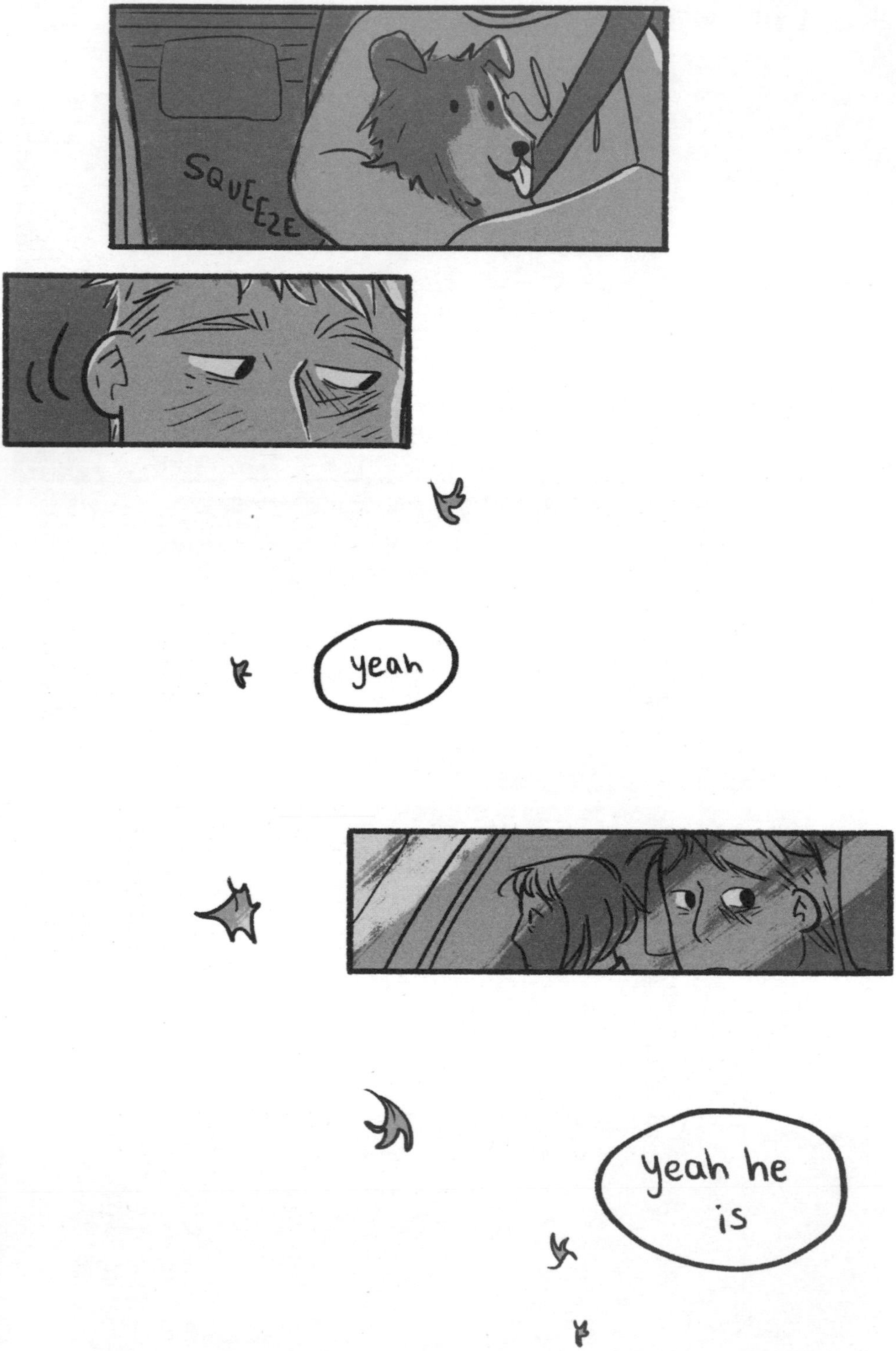
SQUEEEZE
yeah
yeah he is

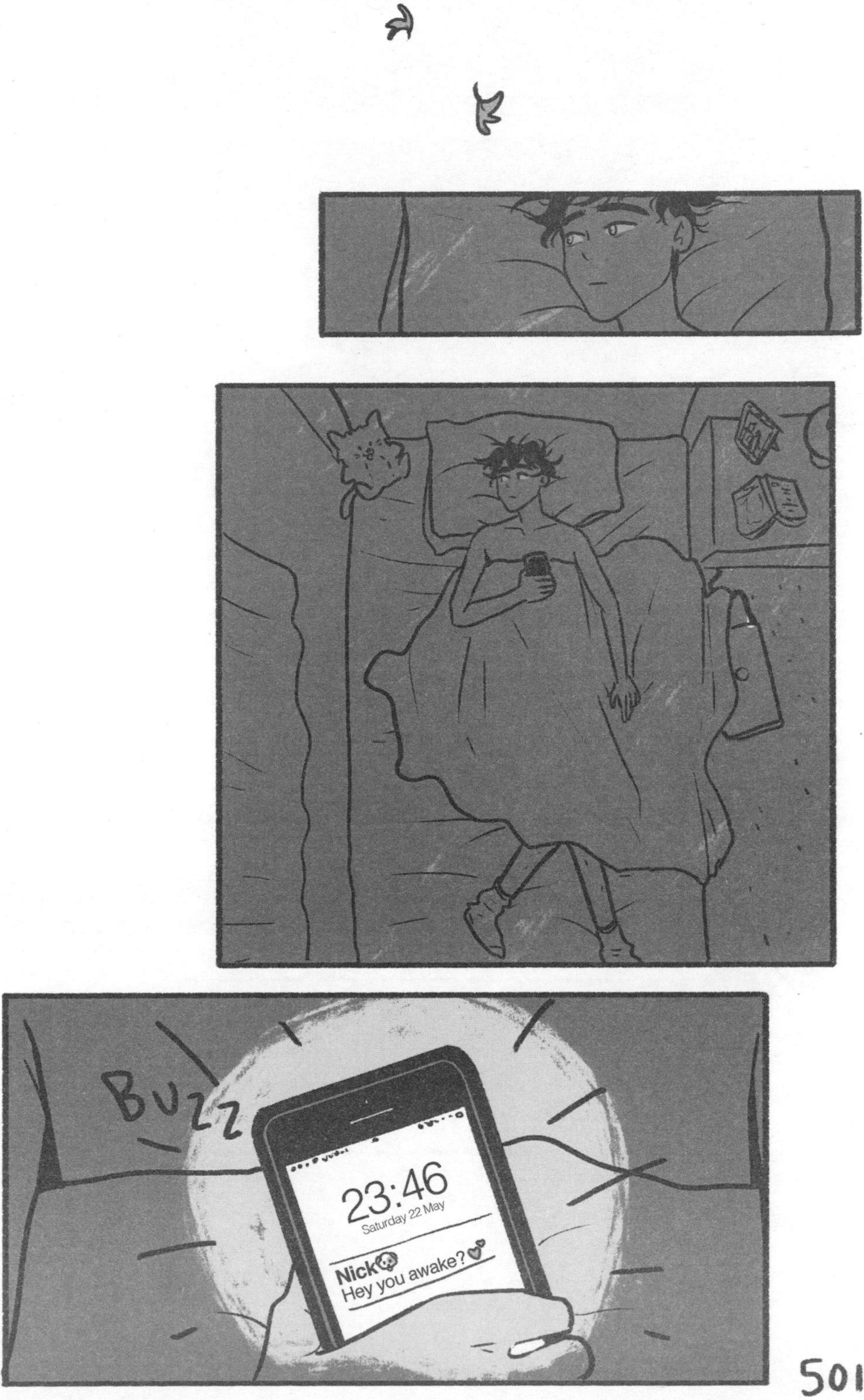
BUZZ
23:46
Saturday 22 May
Nick
Hey you awake?

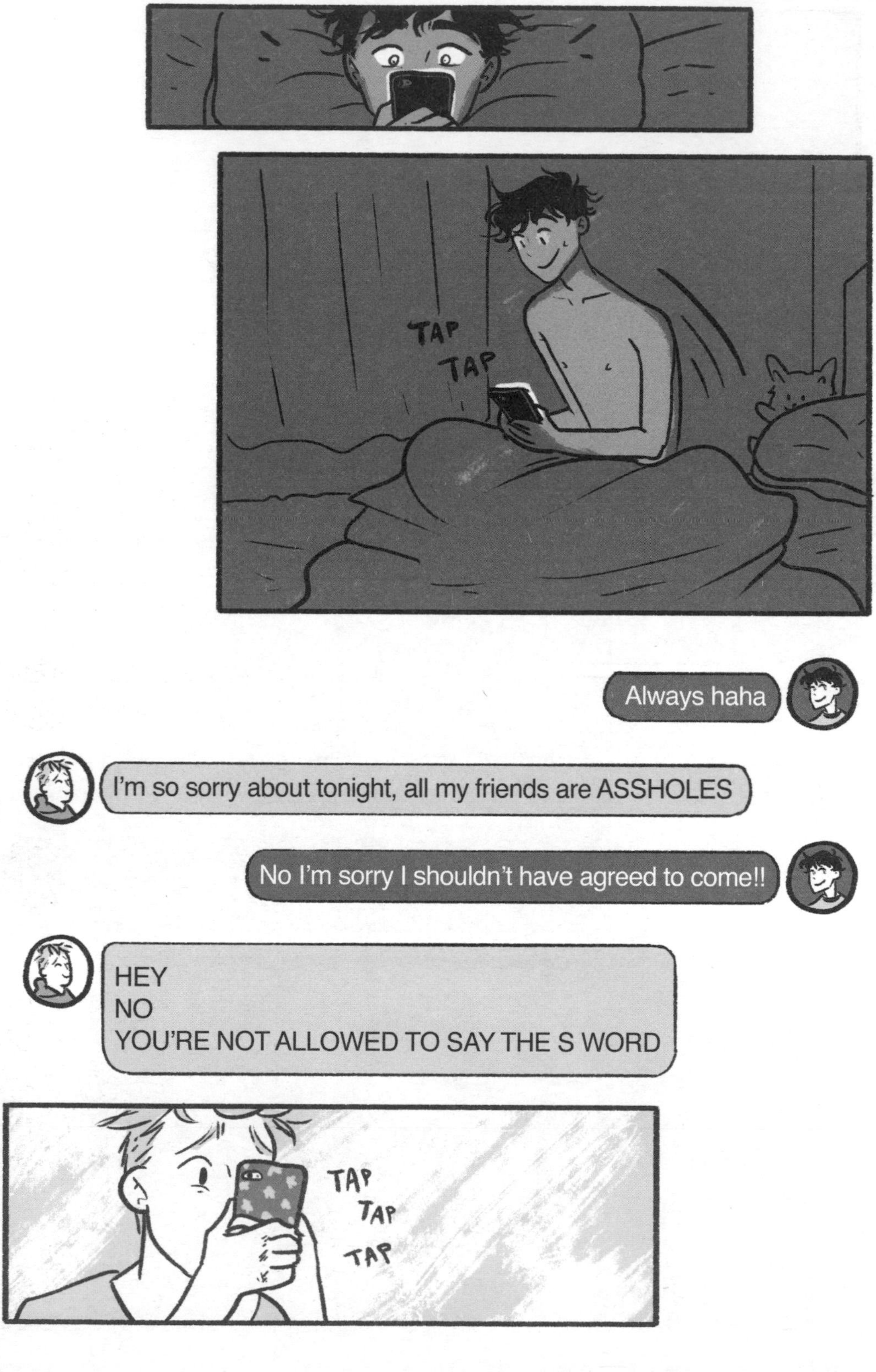
TAP
TAP
Always haha
I'm so sorry about tonight, all my friends are ASSHOLES
No I'm sorry I shouldn't have agreed to come!!
HEY
NO
YOU'RE NOT ALLOWED TO SAY THE S WORD
TAP
TAP
TAP

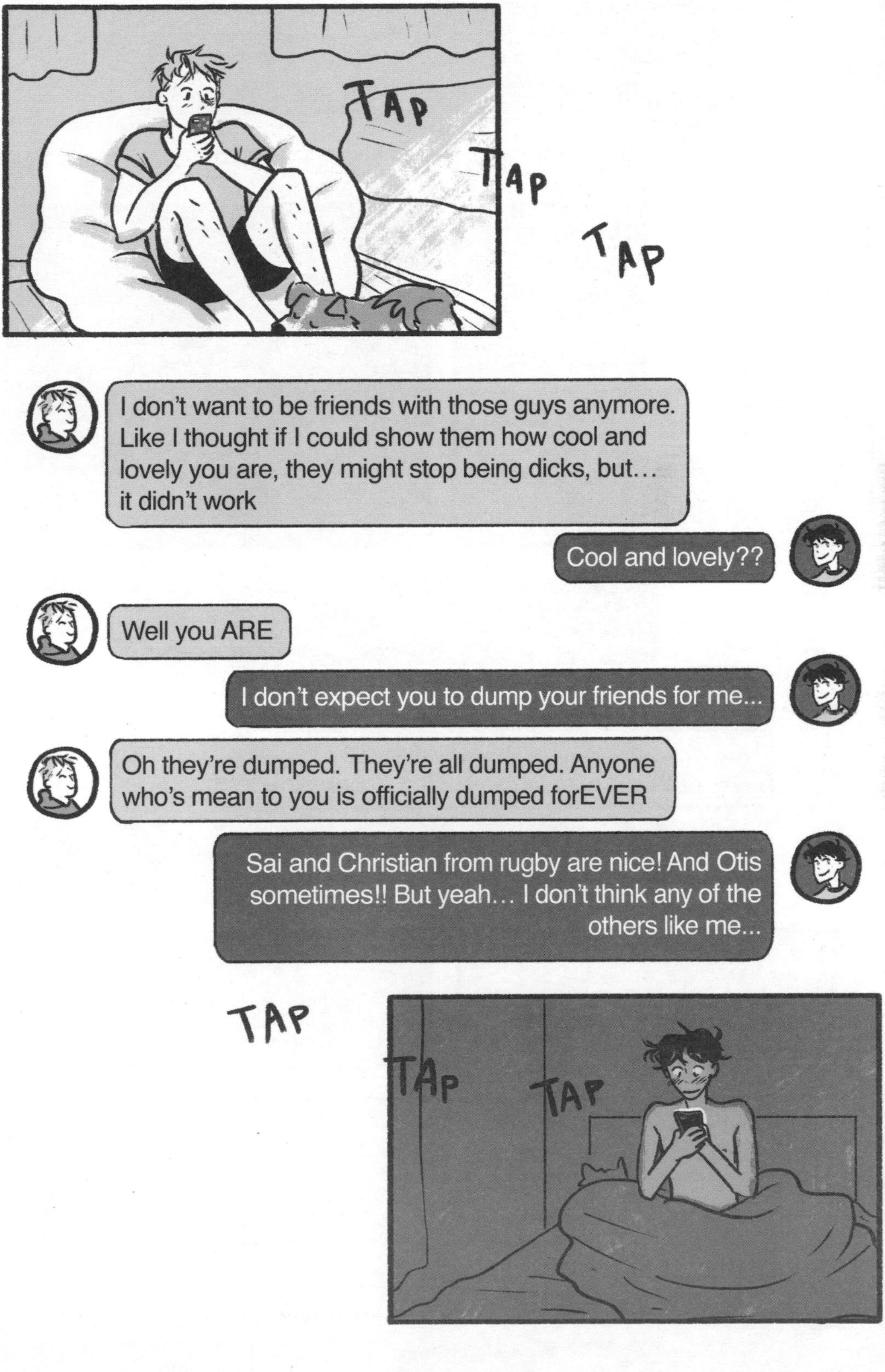
TAP
TAP
TAP
I don't want to be friends with those guys anymore. Like I thought if I could show them how cool and lovely you are, they might stop being dicks, but… it didn't work
Cool and lovely??
Well you ARE
I don't expect you to dump your friends for me...
Oh they're dumped. They're all dumped. Anyone who's mean to you is officially dumped forEVER
Sai and Christian from rugby are nice! And Otis sometimes!! But yeah… I don't think any of the others like me...
TAP
TAP
TAP

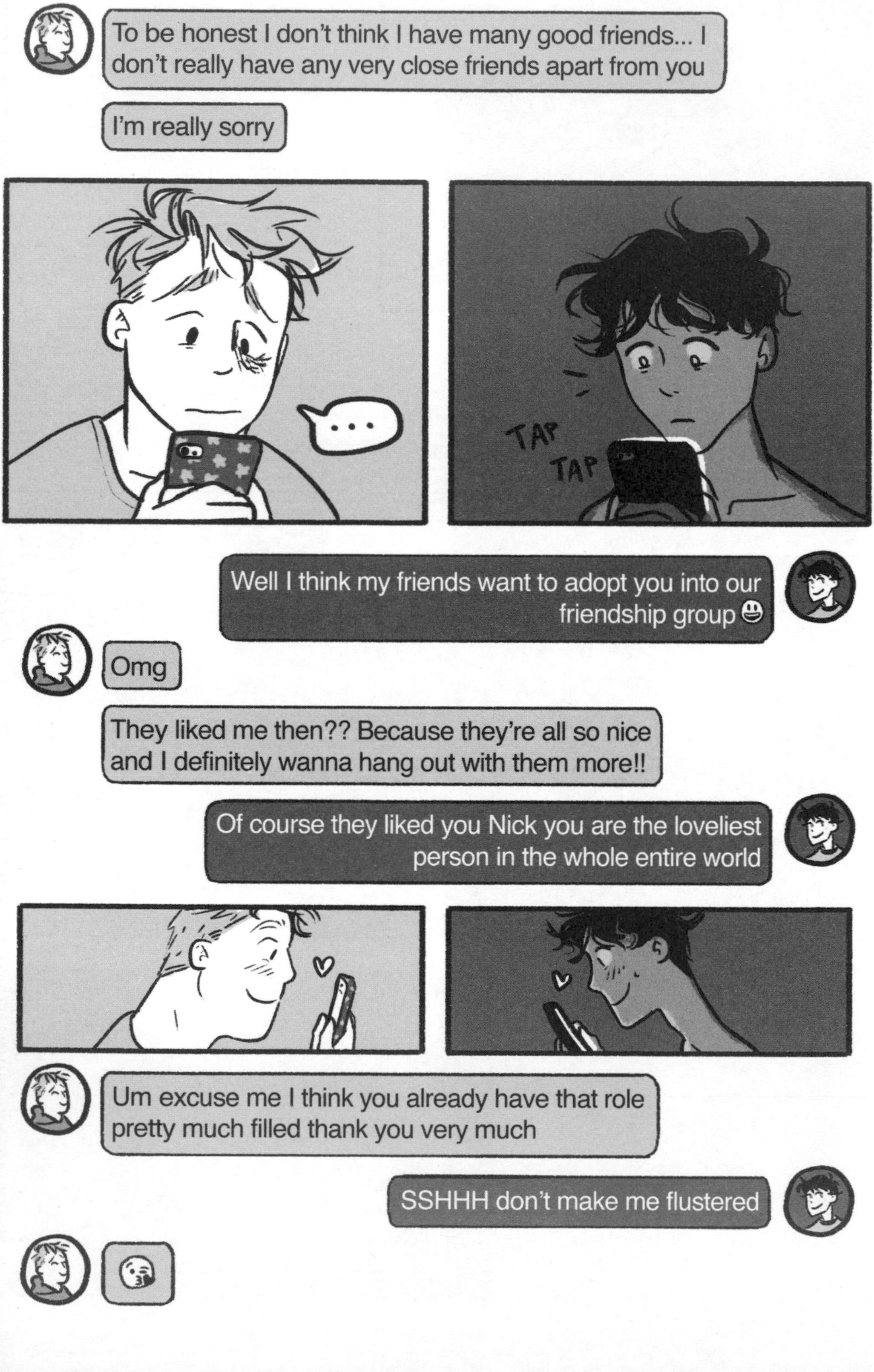
To be honest I don't think I have many good friends... I don't really have any very close friends apart from you
I'm really sorry
...
TAP
TAP
Well I think my friends want to adopt you into our friendship group 😃
Omg
They liked me then?? Because they're all so nice and I definitely wanna hang out with them more!!
Of course they liked you Nick you are the loveliest person in the whole entire world
Um excuse me I think you already have that role pretty much filled thank you very much
SSHHH don't make me flustered
😘

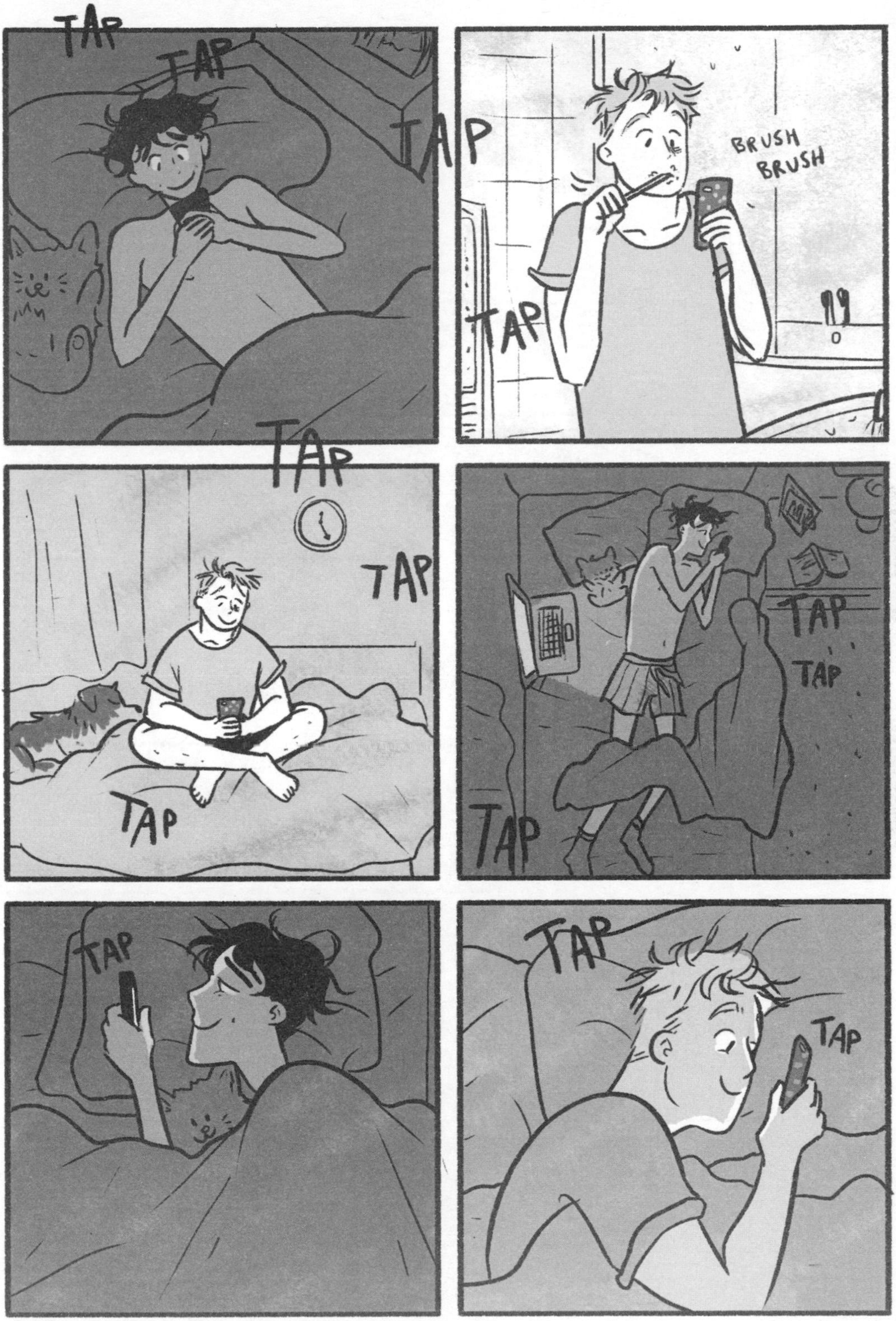
TAP
TAP
TAP
BRUSH
BRUSH
TAP
TAP
TAP
TAP
TAP
TAP
TAP
TAP
TAP
TAP

 You still ok to come over tomorrow?? 😃

Because I sorta have an idea

Do you wanna go on a proper date?

Omg... Formally asking me out…. This sounds slightly more sophisticated than just making out in our bedrooms

but yes of cOURSE

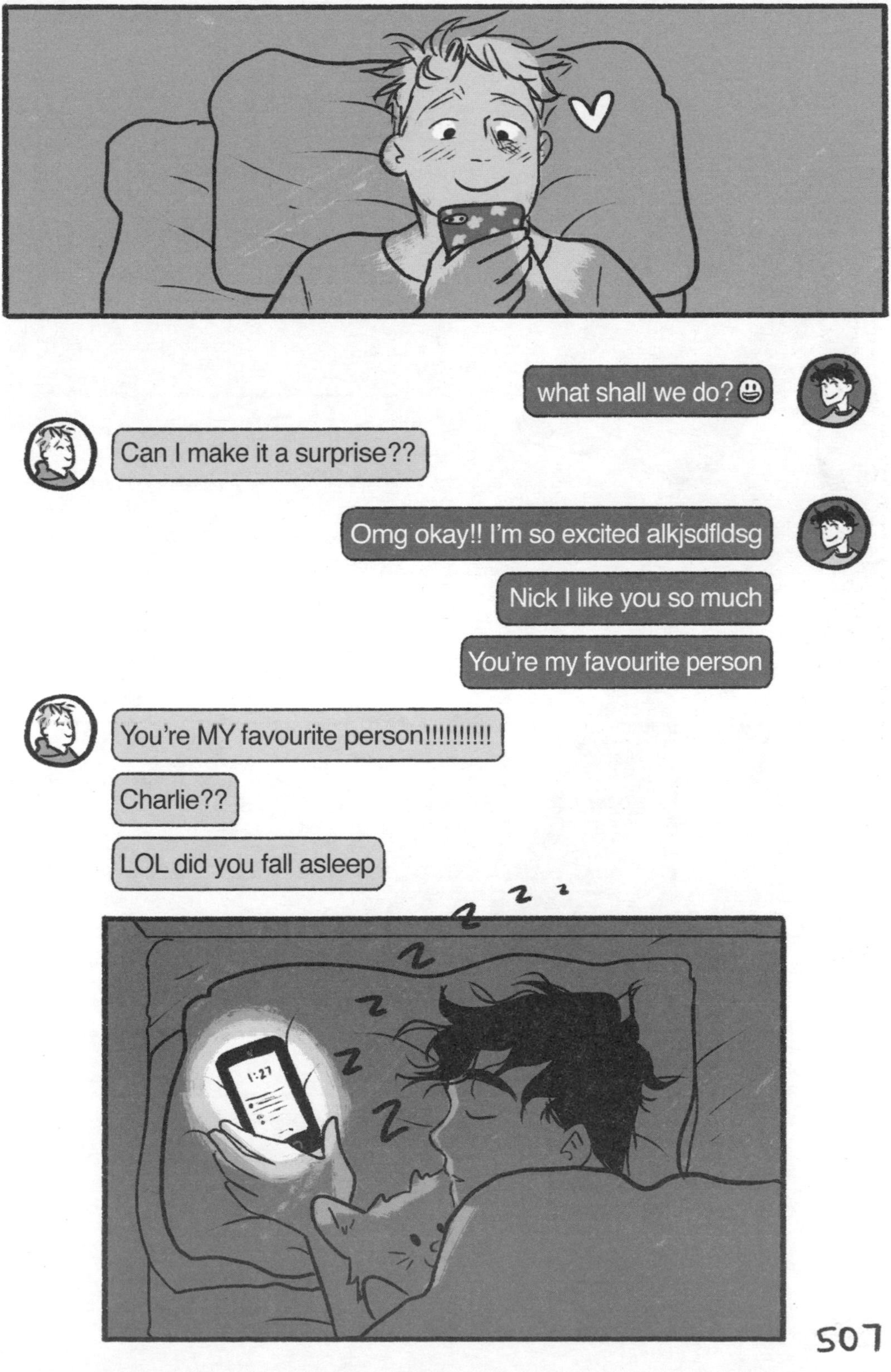
what shall we do? 😃
Can I make it a surprise??
Omg okay!! I'm so excited alkjsdfldsg
Nick I like you so much
You're my favourite person
You're MY favourite person!!!!!!!!!!
Charlie??
LOL did you fall asleep

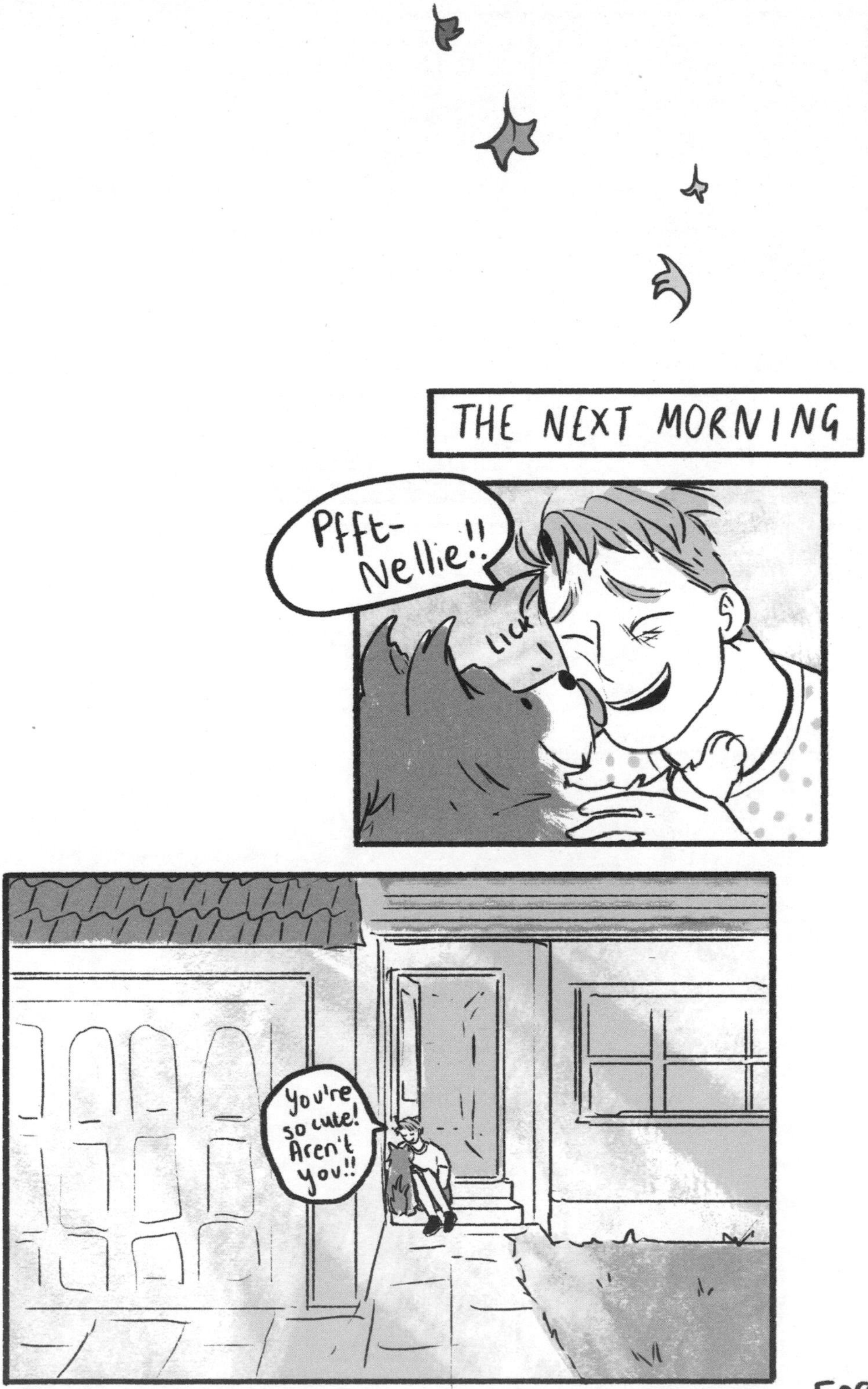
THE NEXT MORNING
Pffft- Nellie!!
LICK
You're so cute! Aren't you!!

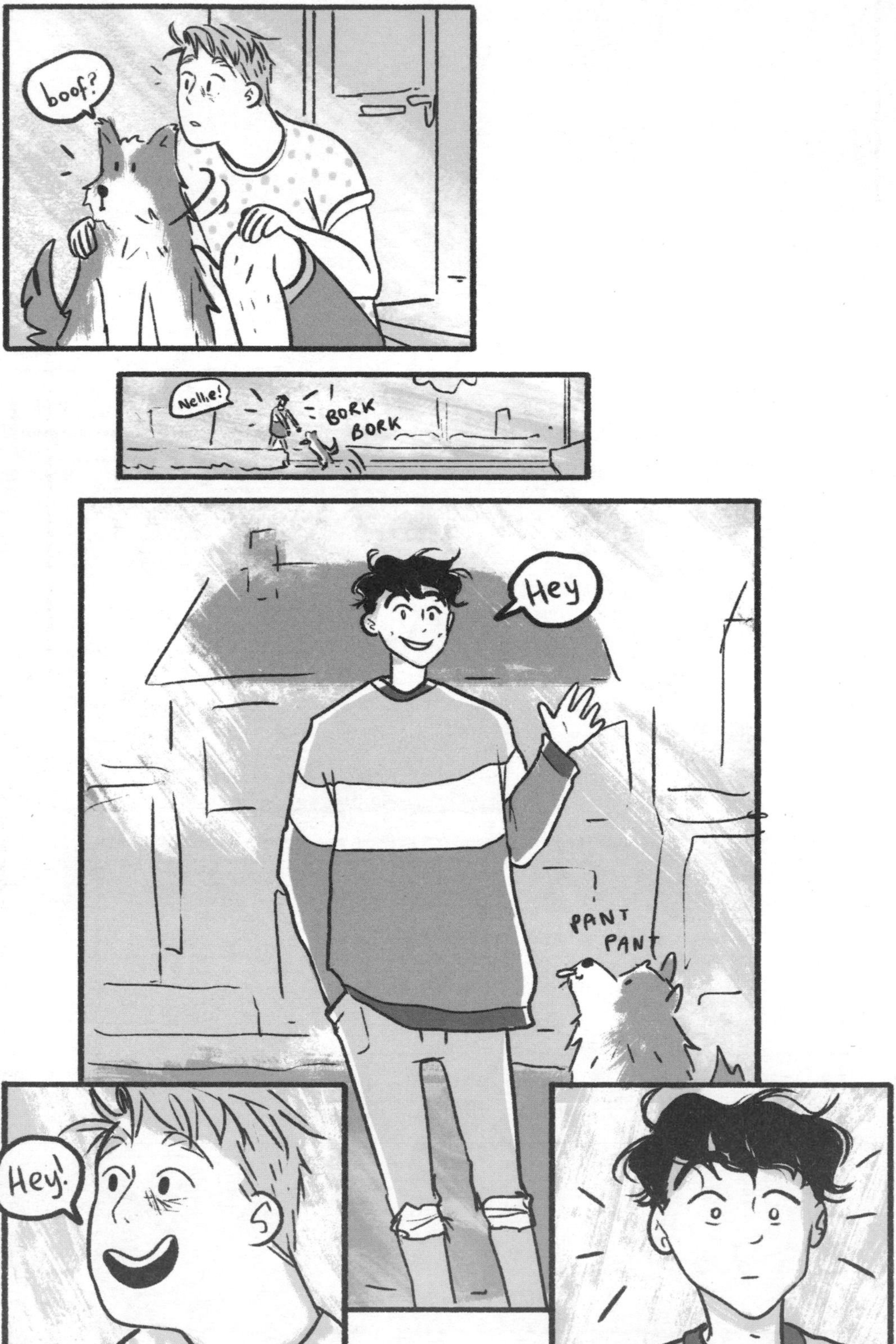
boof?
Nellie!
BORK
BORK
Hey
PANT
PANT
Hey!

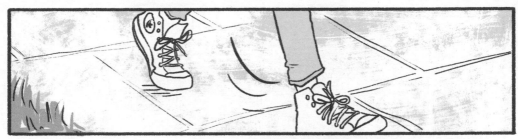

What happened?

Oh... yeah... erm...

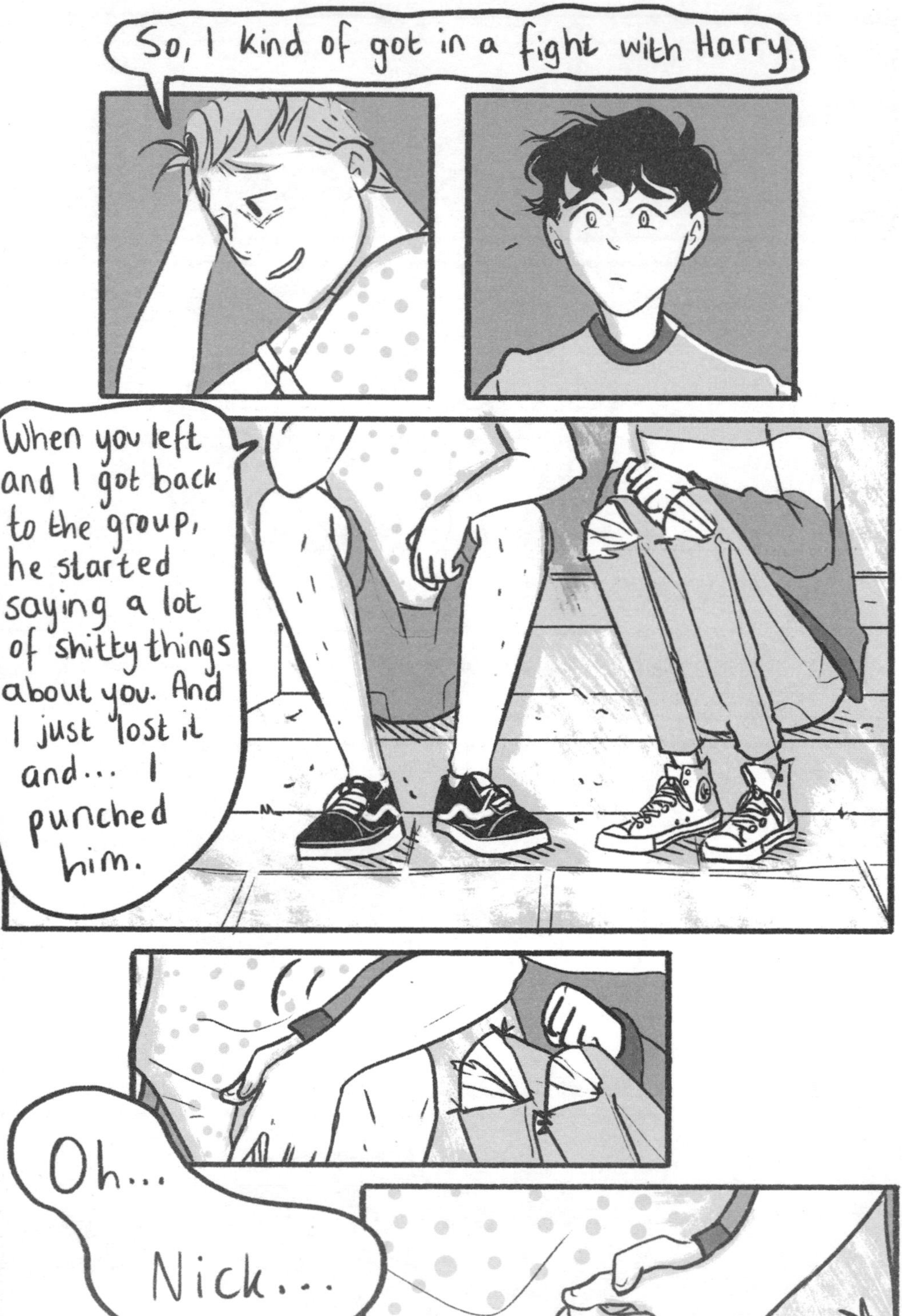
So, I kind of got in a fight with Harry.
When you left and I got back to the group, he started saying a lot of shitty things about you. And I just lost it and... I punched him.
Oh...
Nick...

515

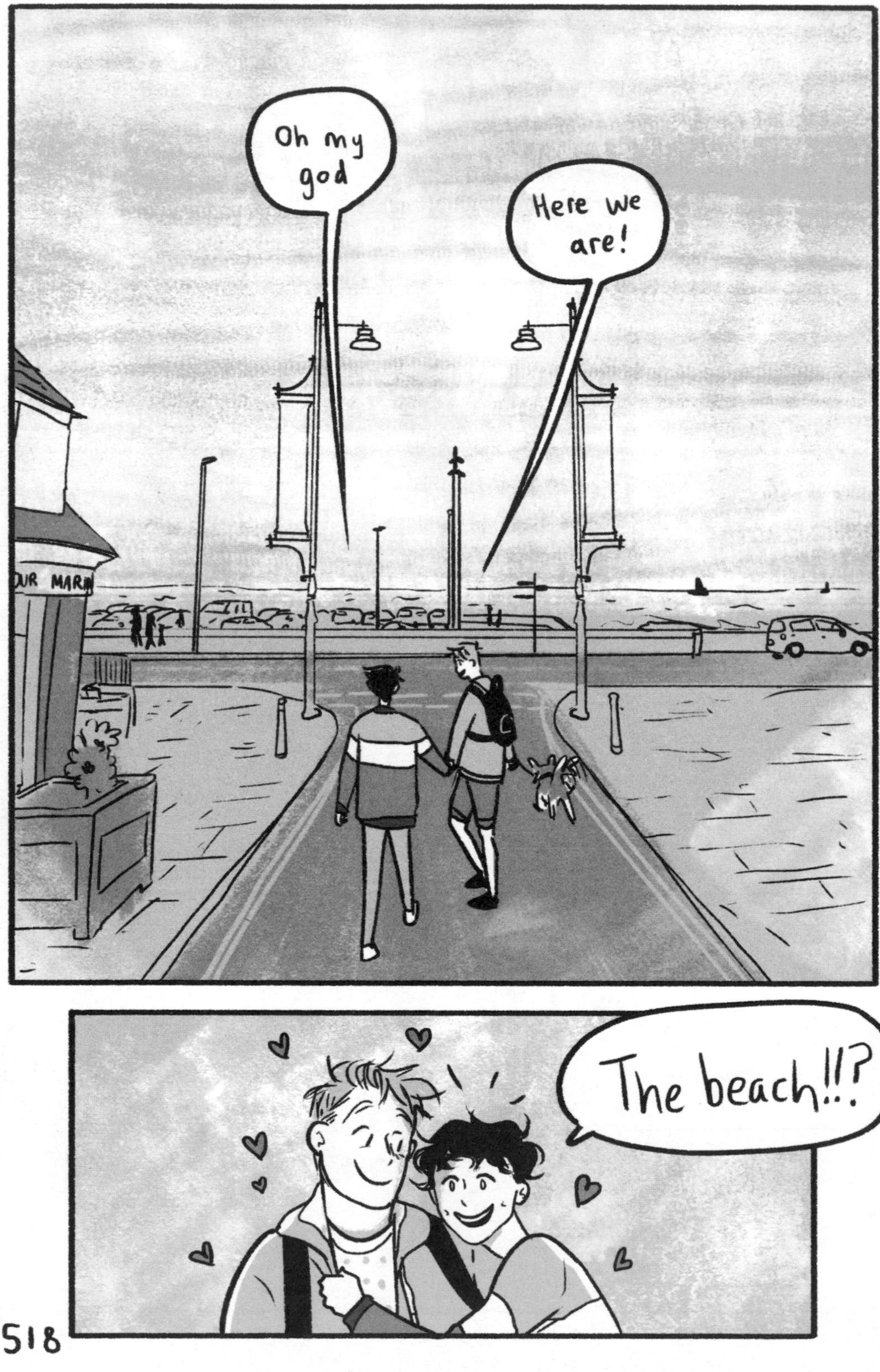
Oh my god
Here we are!
OUR MAR
The beach!!?

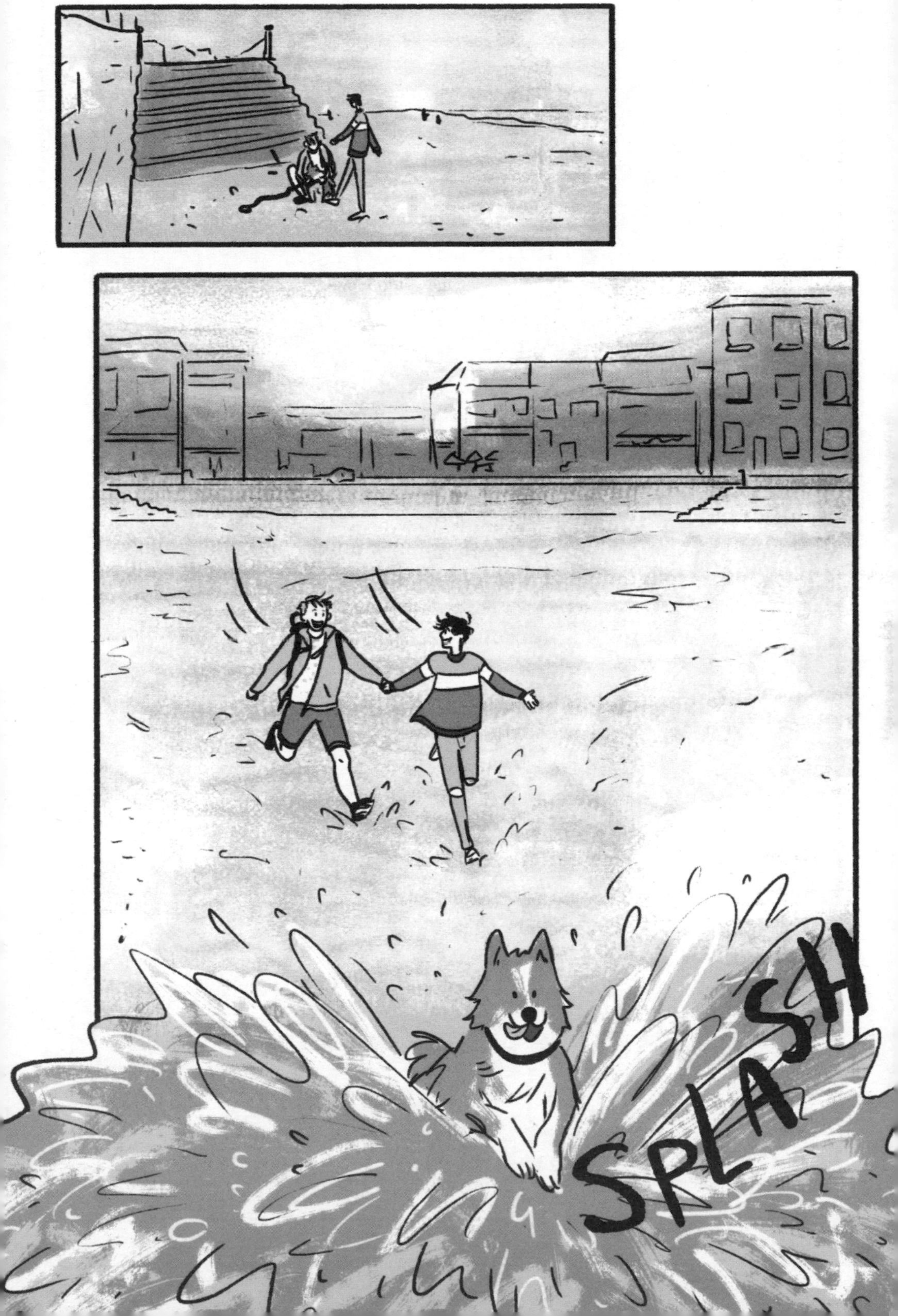
SPLASH

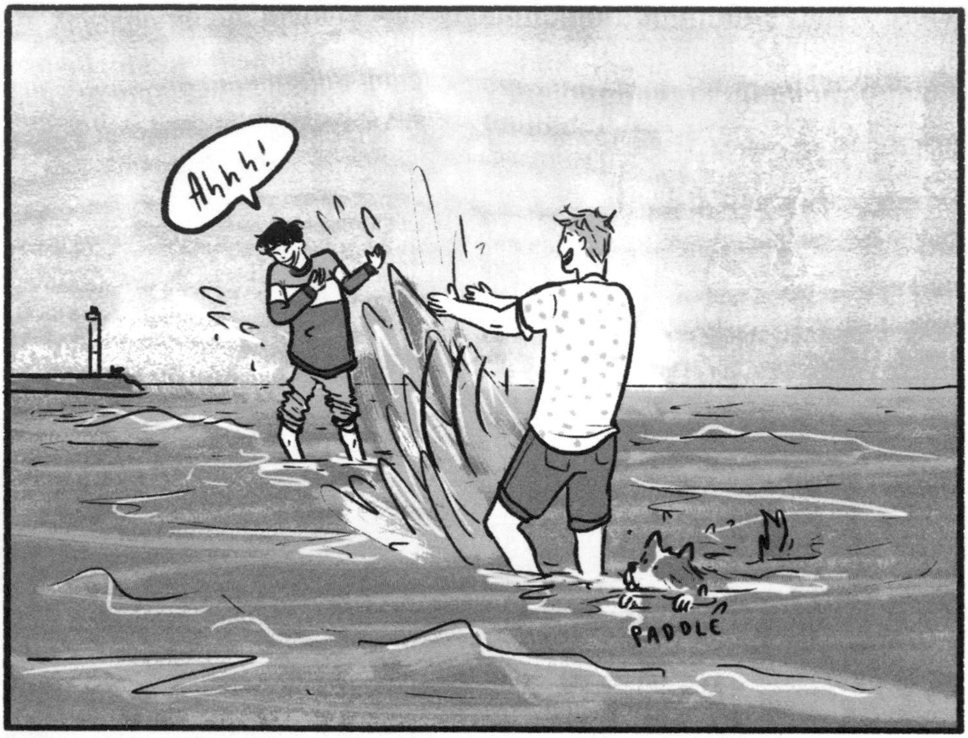
Ahhh!
PADDLE

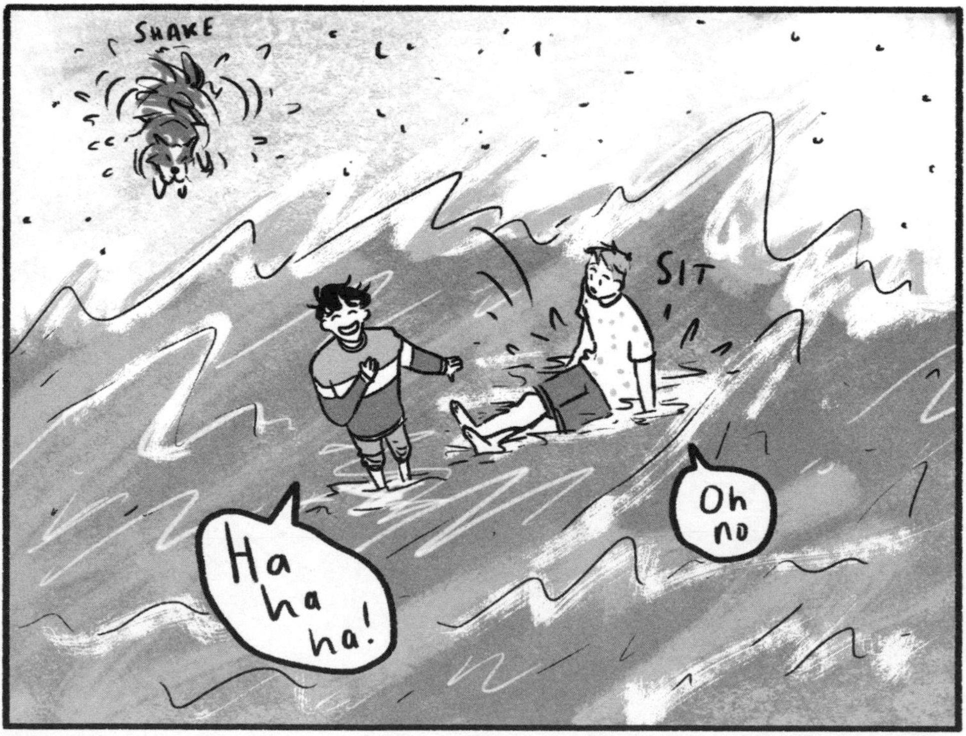
SHAKE
SIT
Oh no
Ha ha ha!

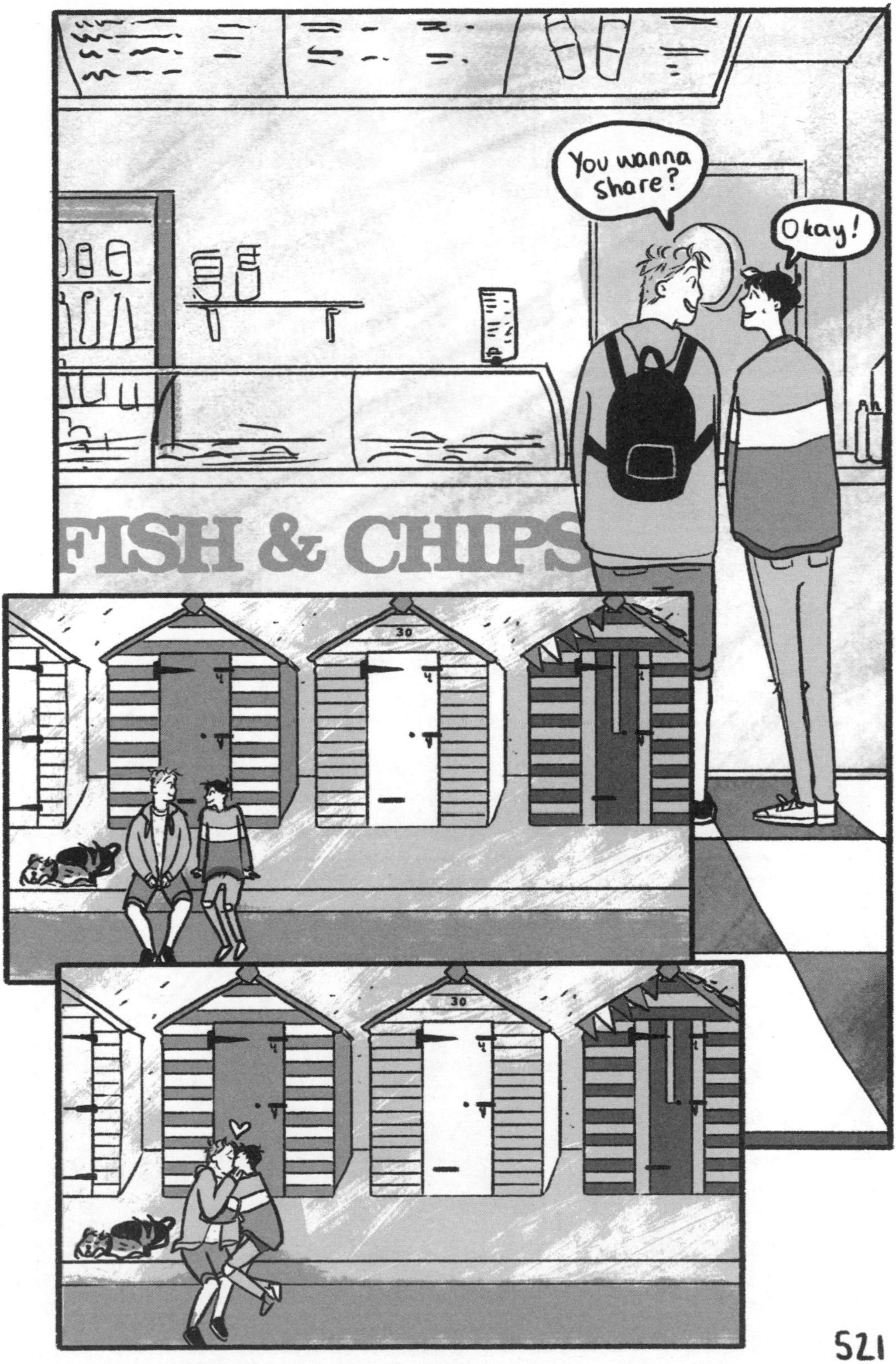
FISH & CHIPS
You wanna share?
Okay!
30
30

524

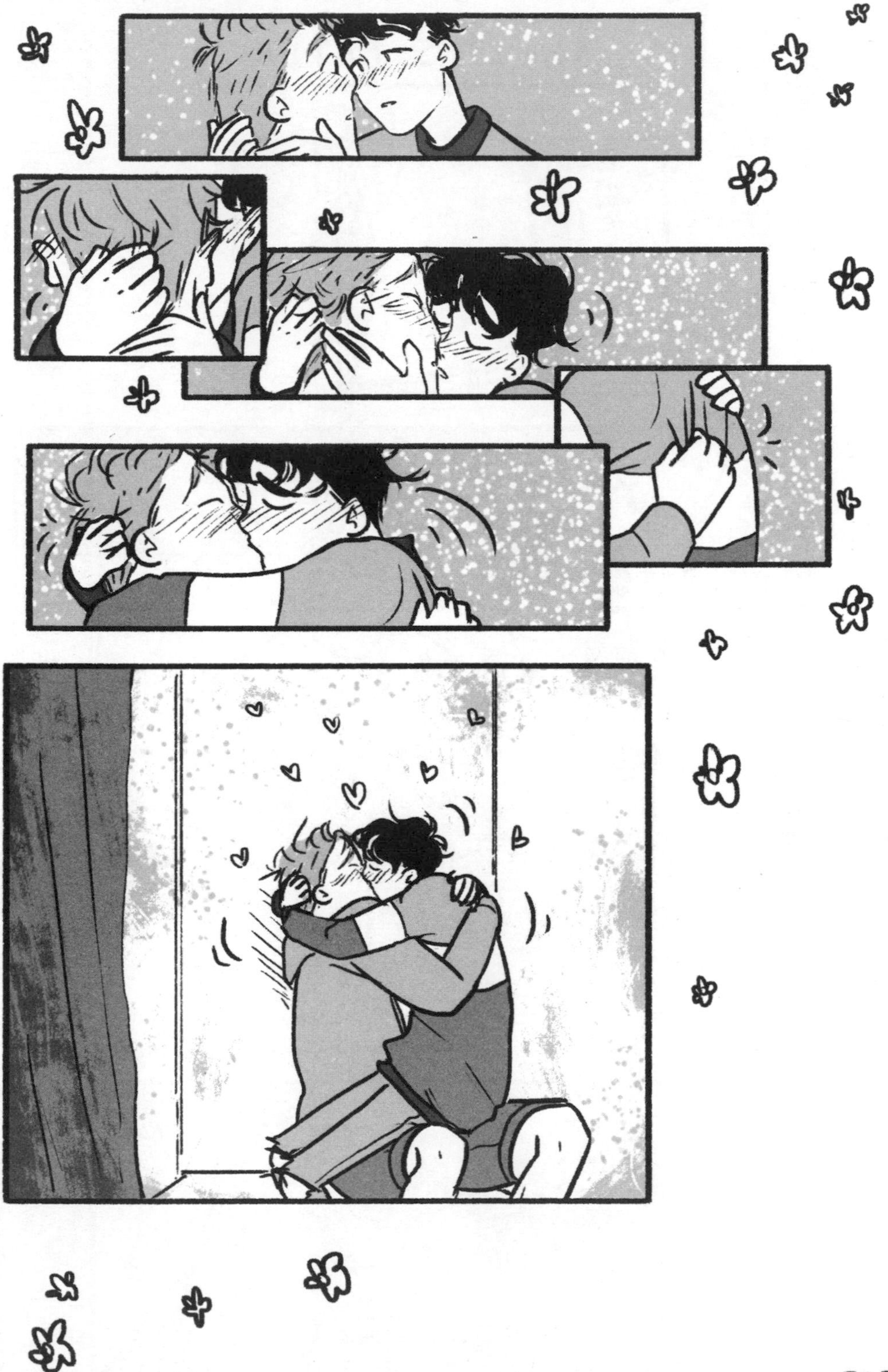

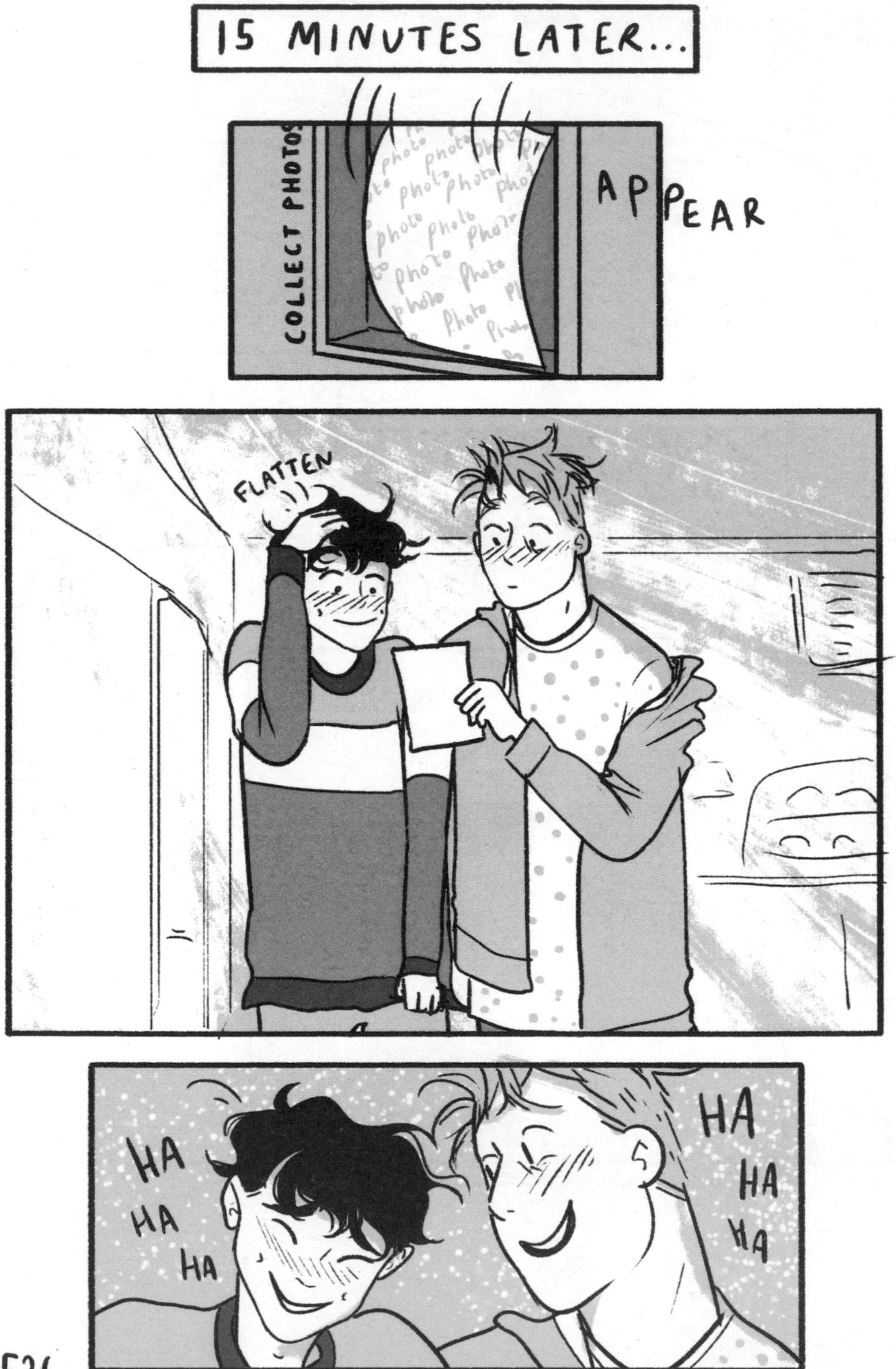
15 MINUTES LATER...
COLLECT PHOTOS
APPEAR
FLATTEN
HA
HA
HA
HA
HA
HA

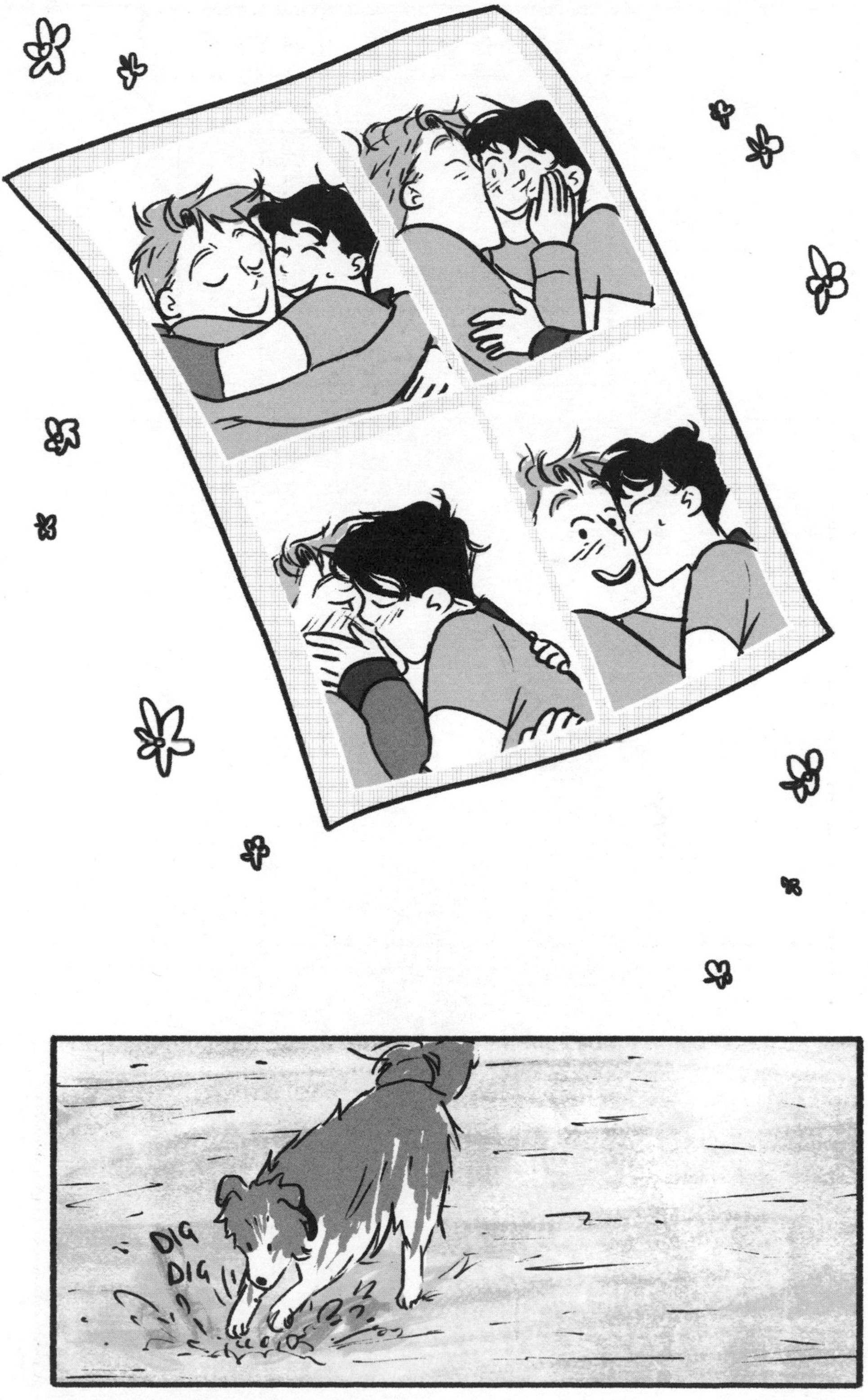
DIG
DIG

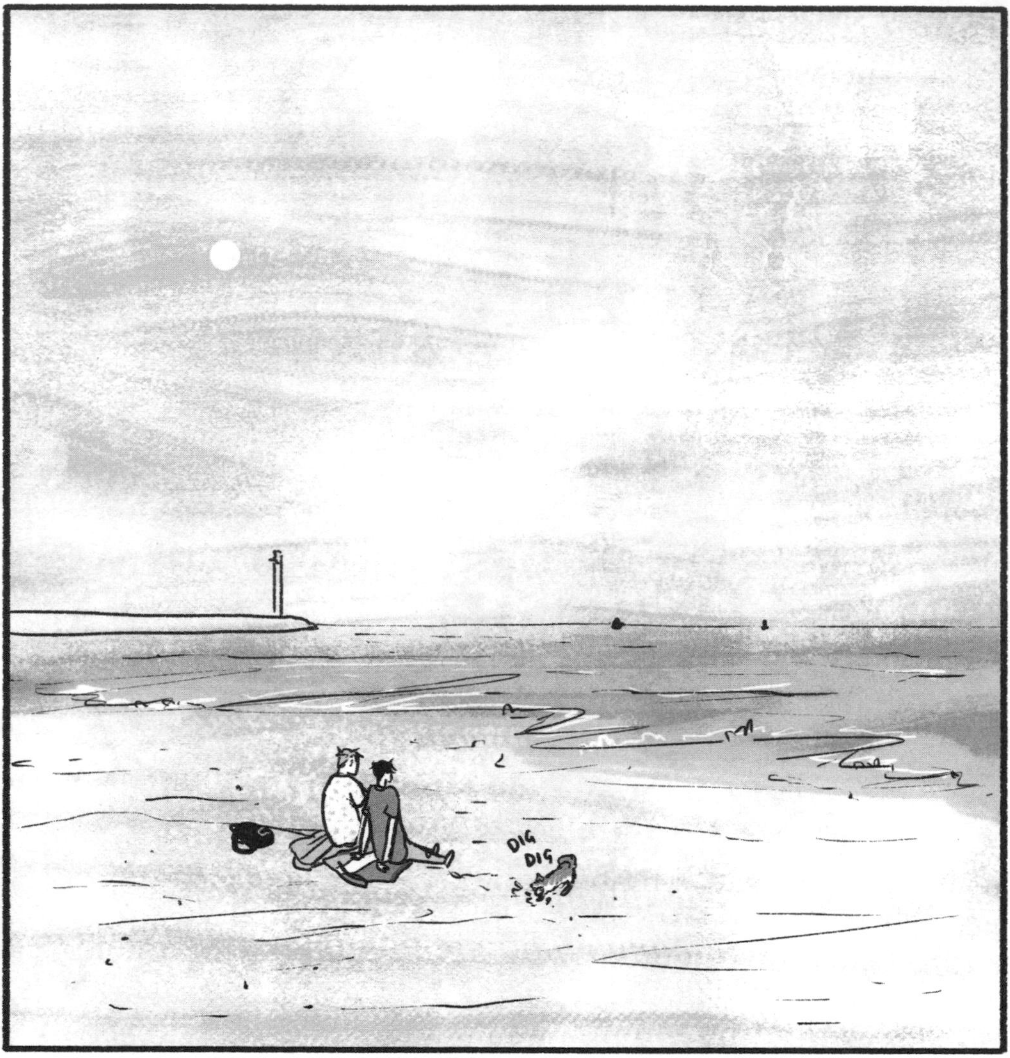
DIG
DIG

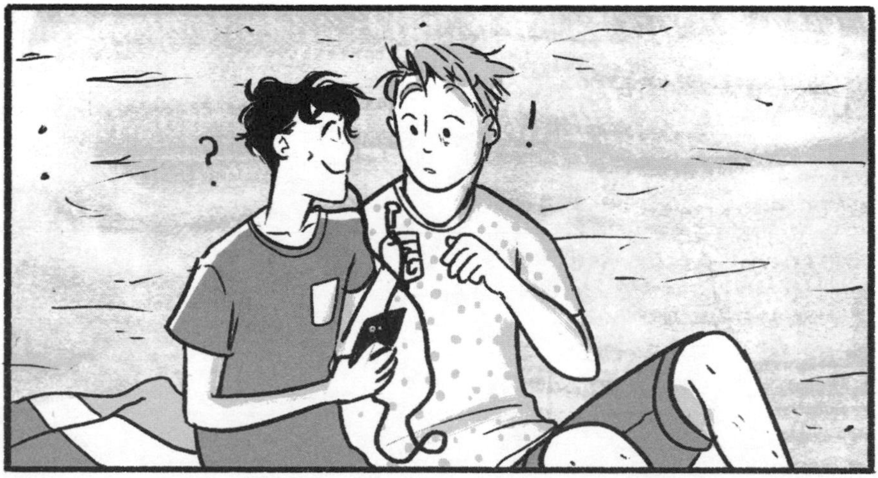
?
!

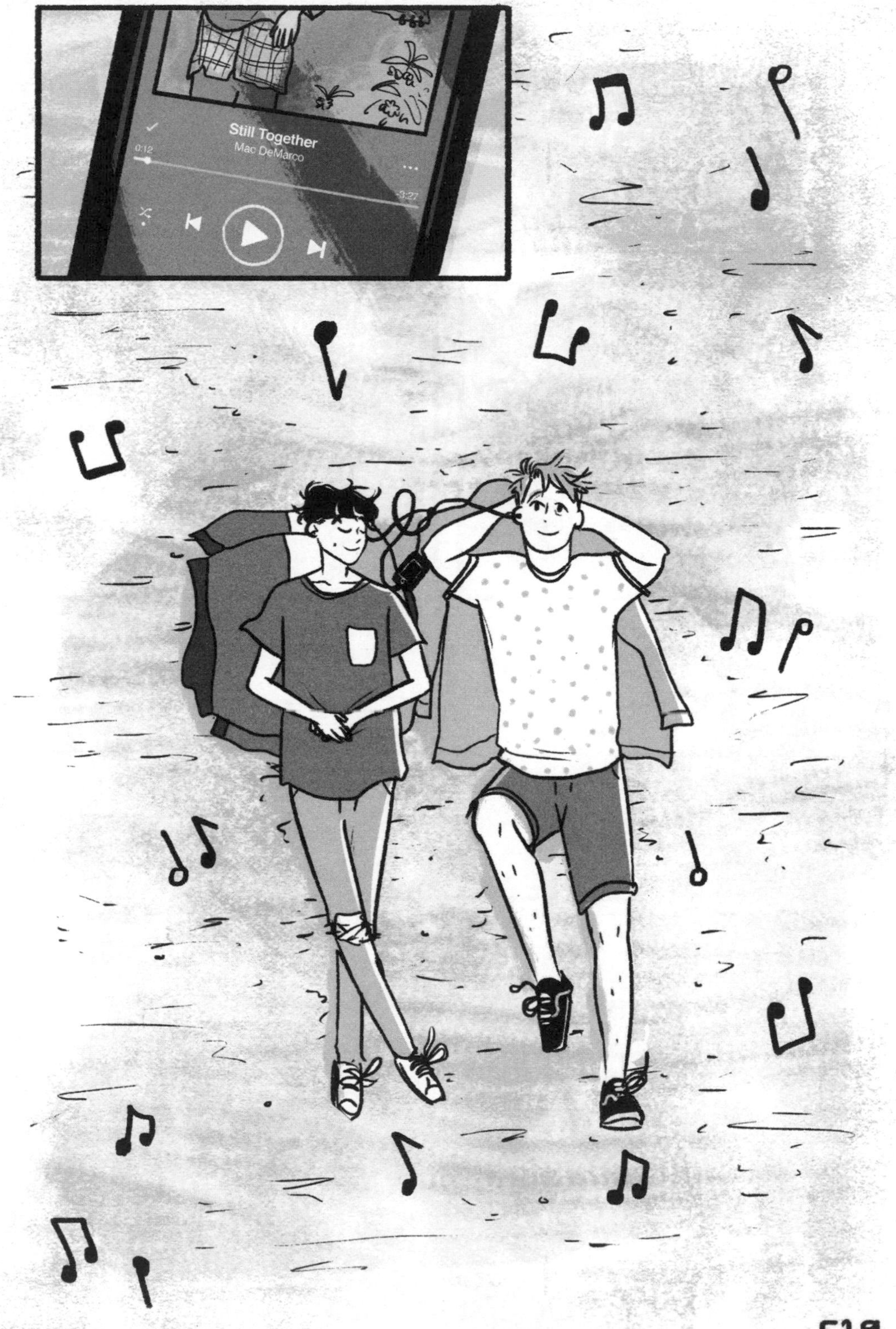
Still Together
Mac DeMarco
0:12
-3:27

Yesterday...

you said you didn't want me to cover for you anymore...

530

Does that mean you want to come out?

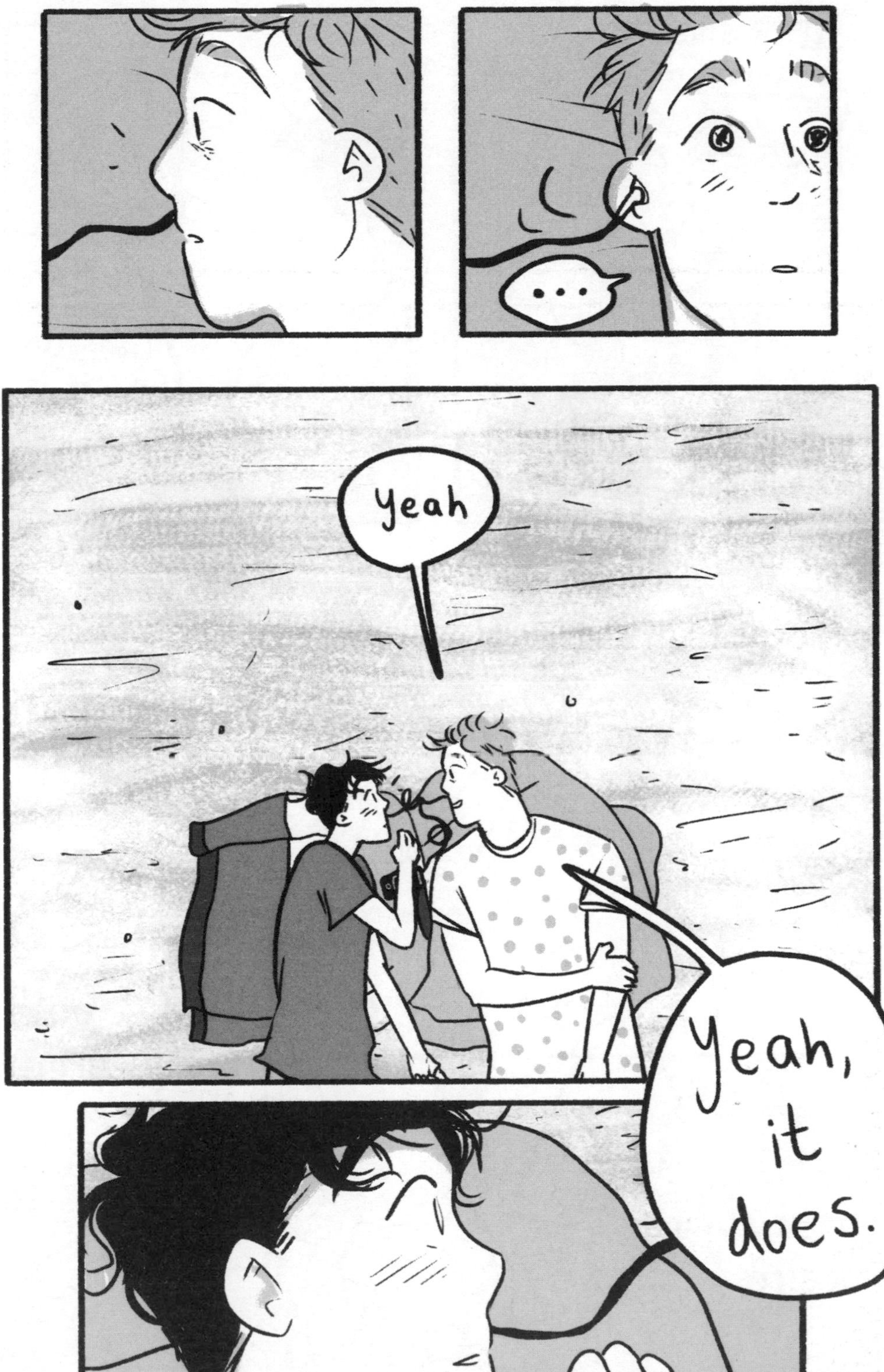
...
Yeah
Yeah, it does.

532

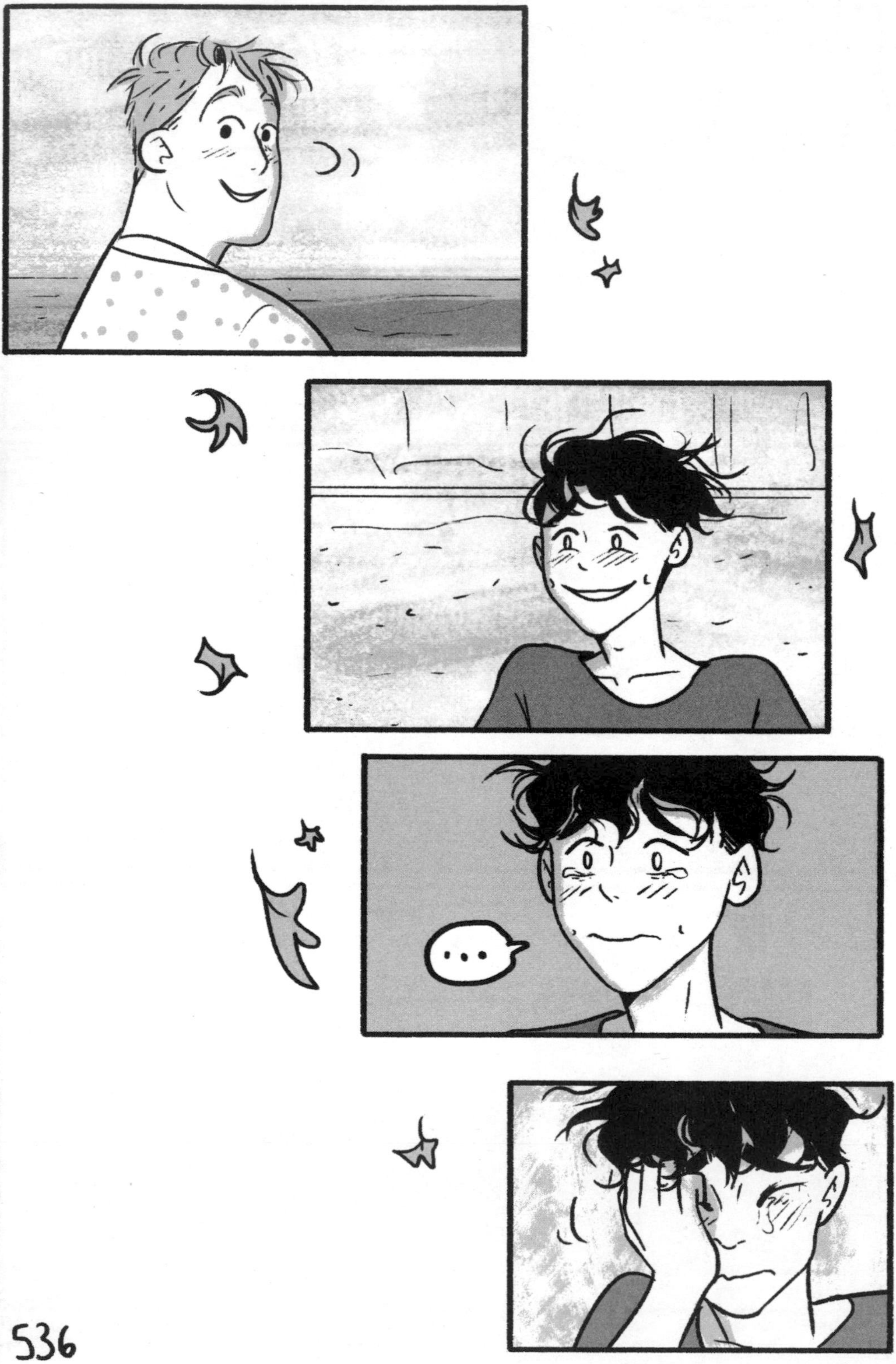
...

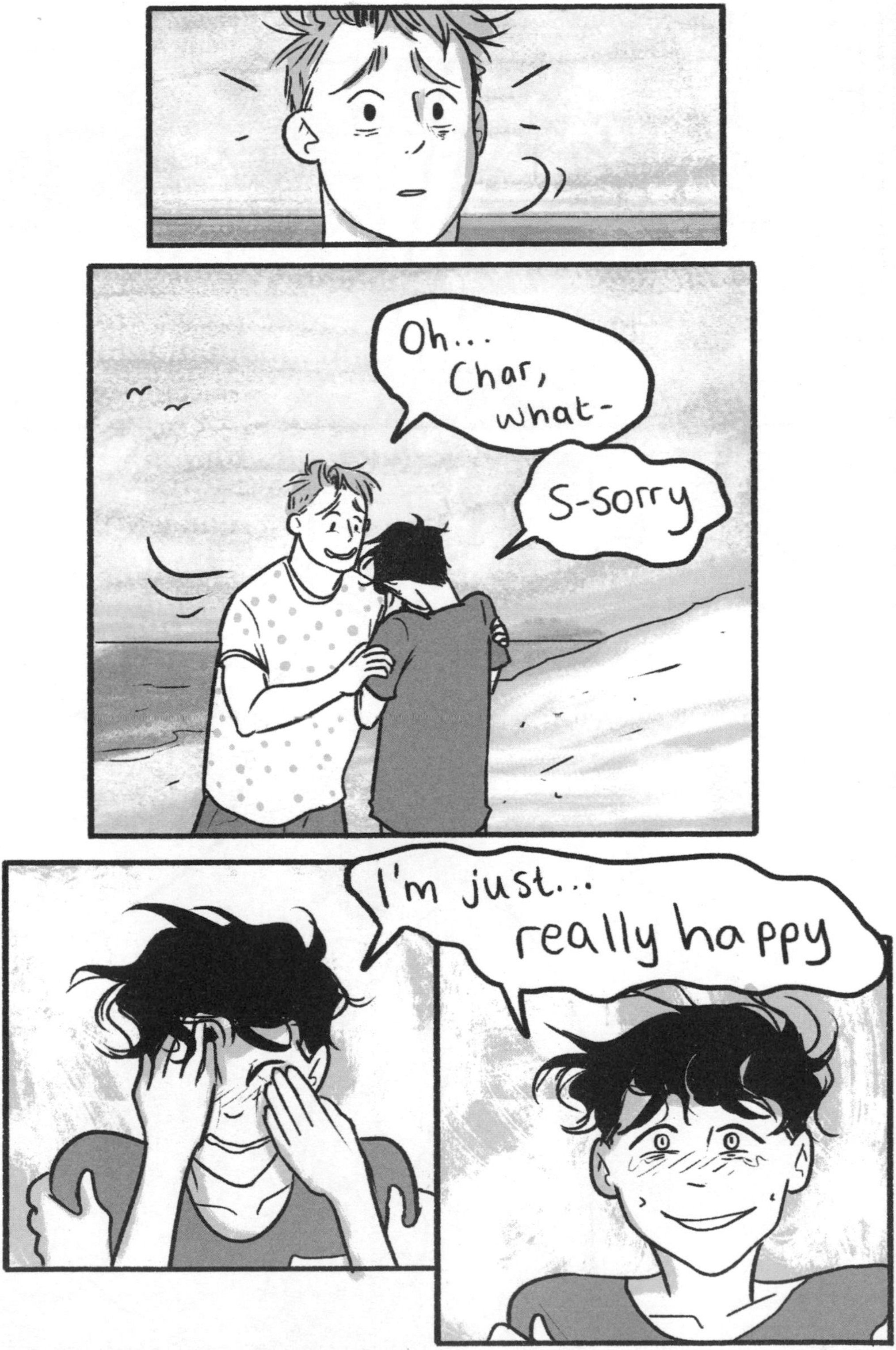
Oh... Char, what-
S-sorry
I'm just... really happy

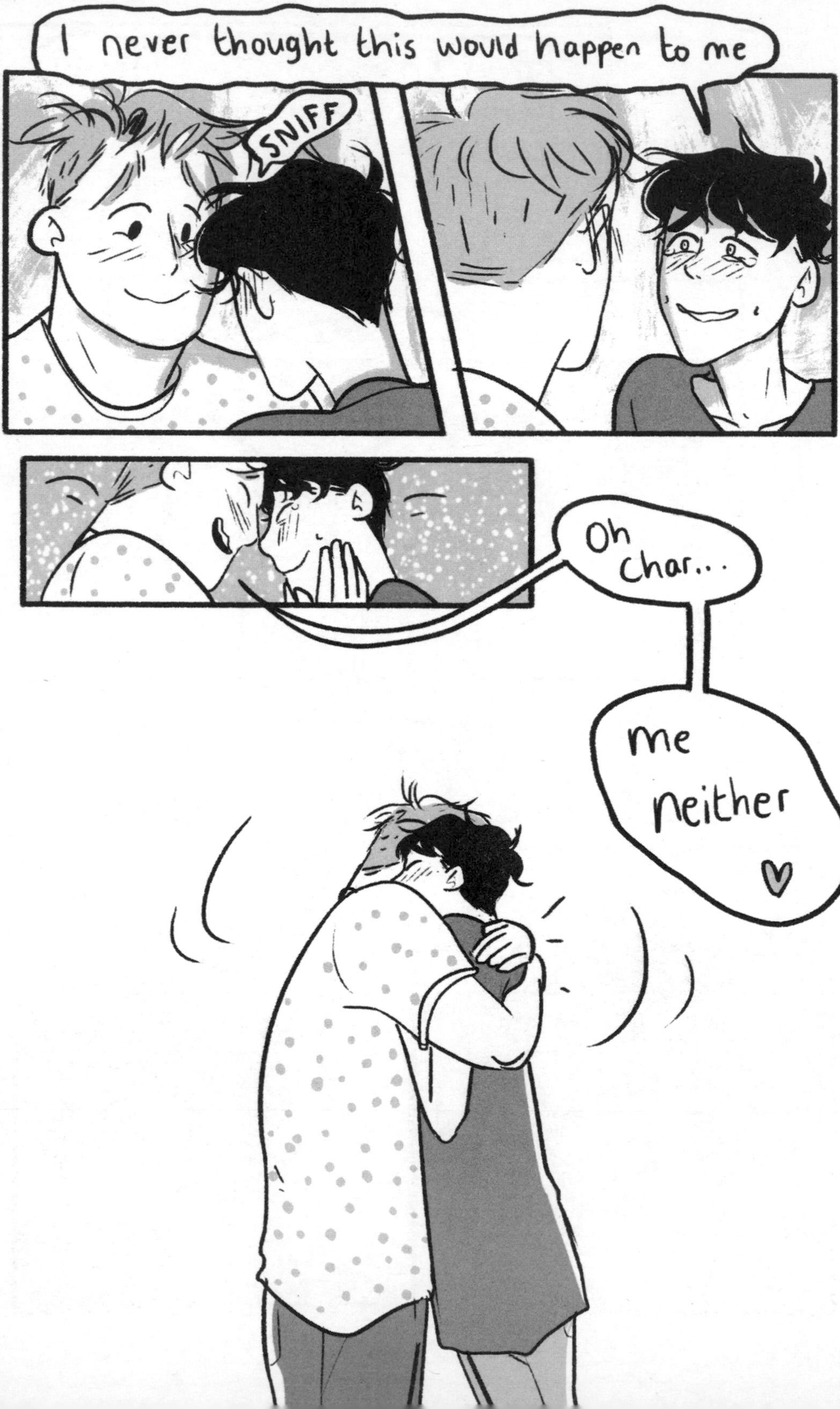
I never thought this would happen to me
SNIFF
Oh char...
me neither ♥

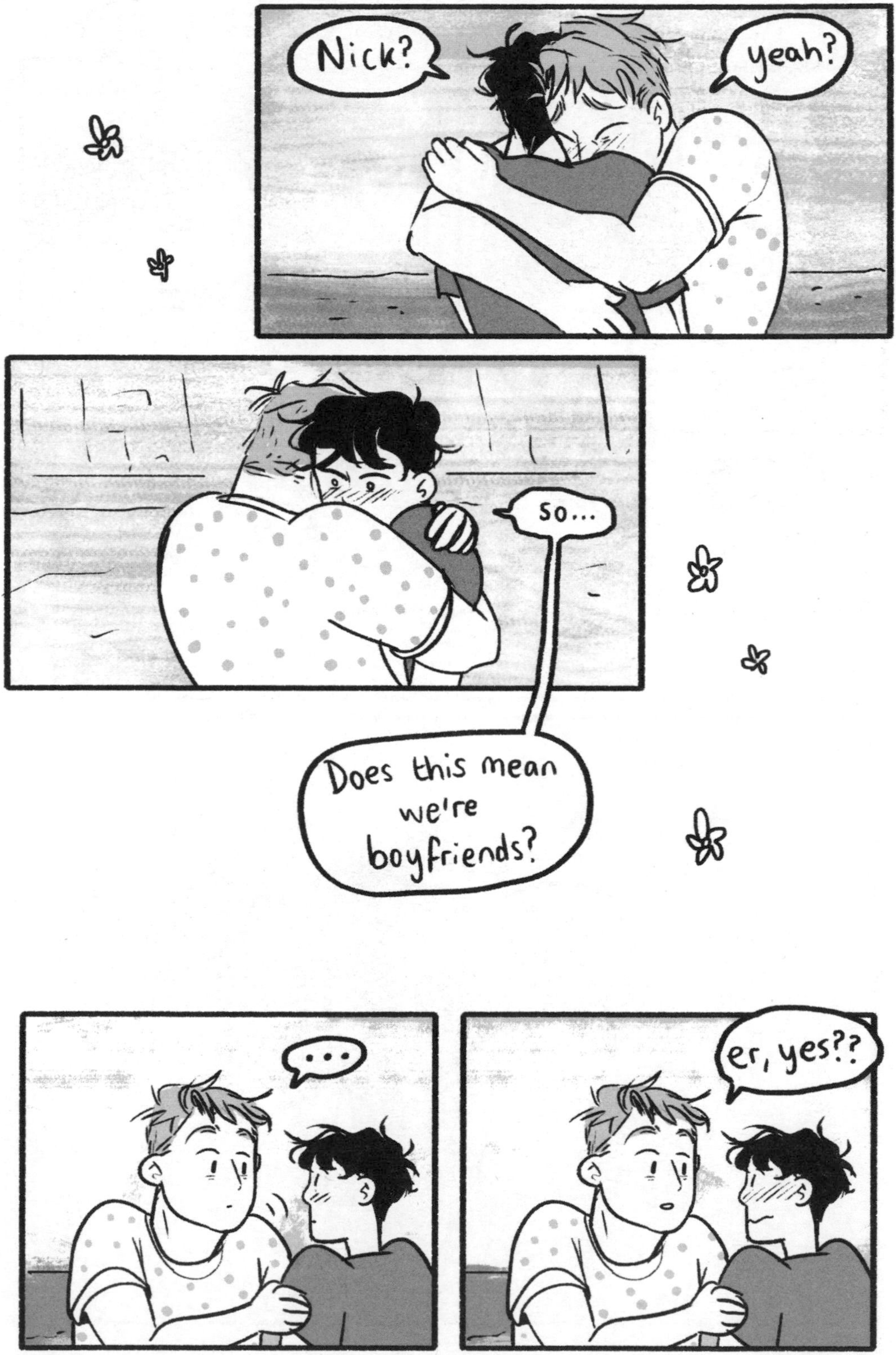
Nick?
yeah?
so...
Does this mean we're boyfriends?
...
er, yes??

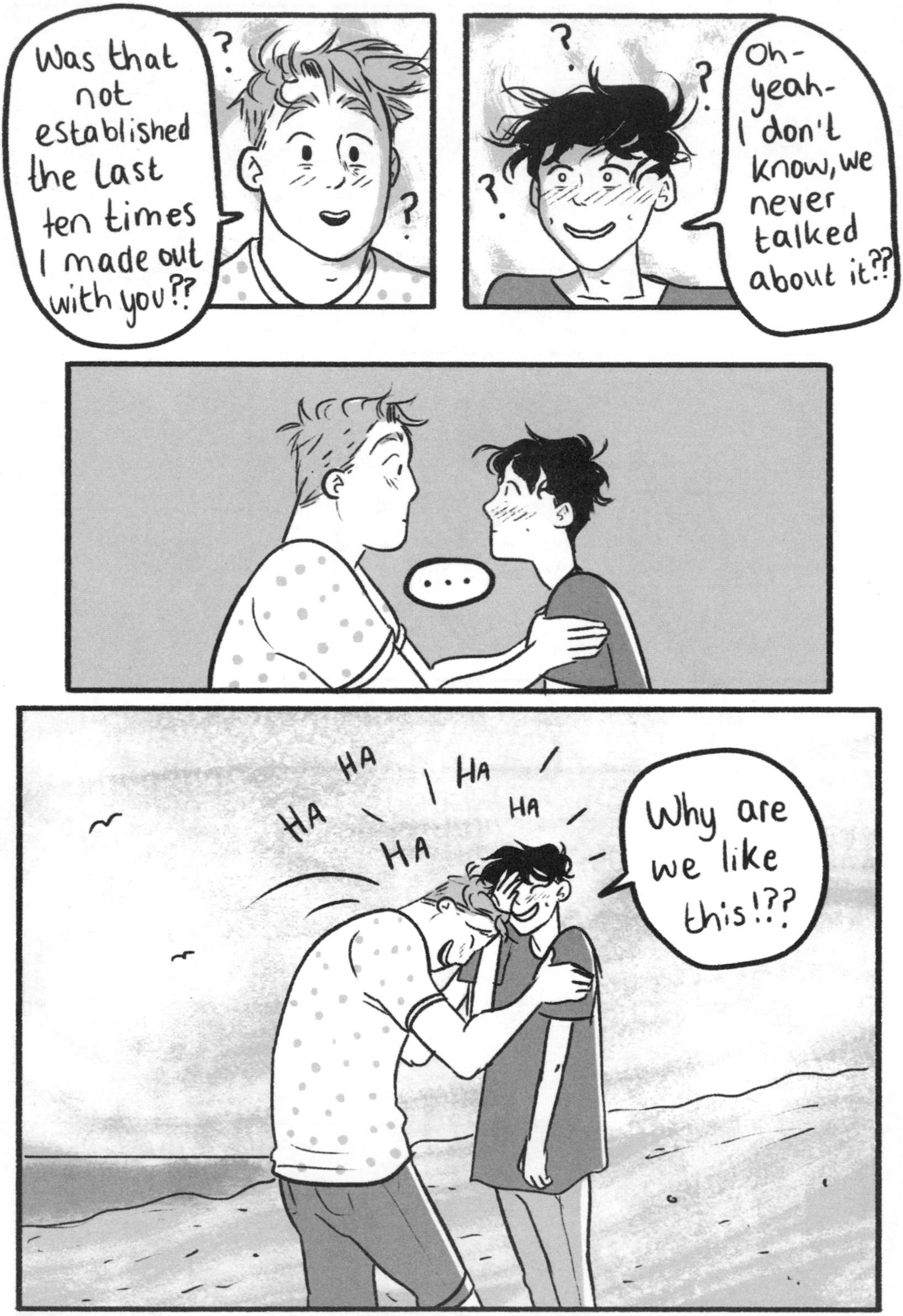
Was that not established the last ten times I made out with you??
Oh- yeah- I don't know, we never talked about it??
...
HA HA HA HA HA
Why are we like this!??

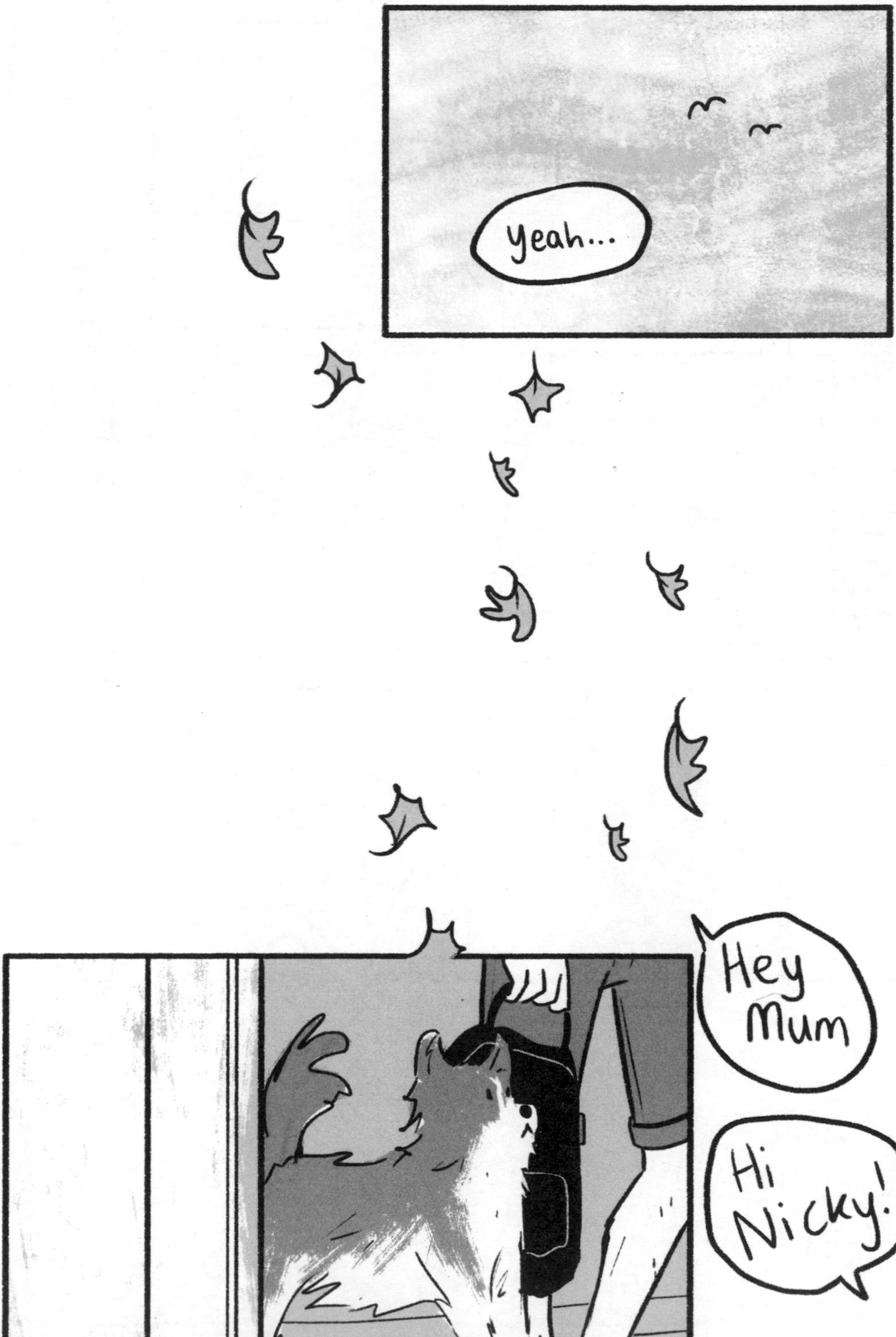
Yeah...
Hey Mum
Hi Nicky!

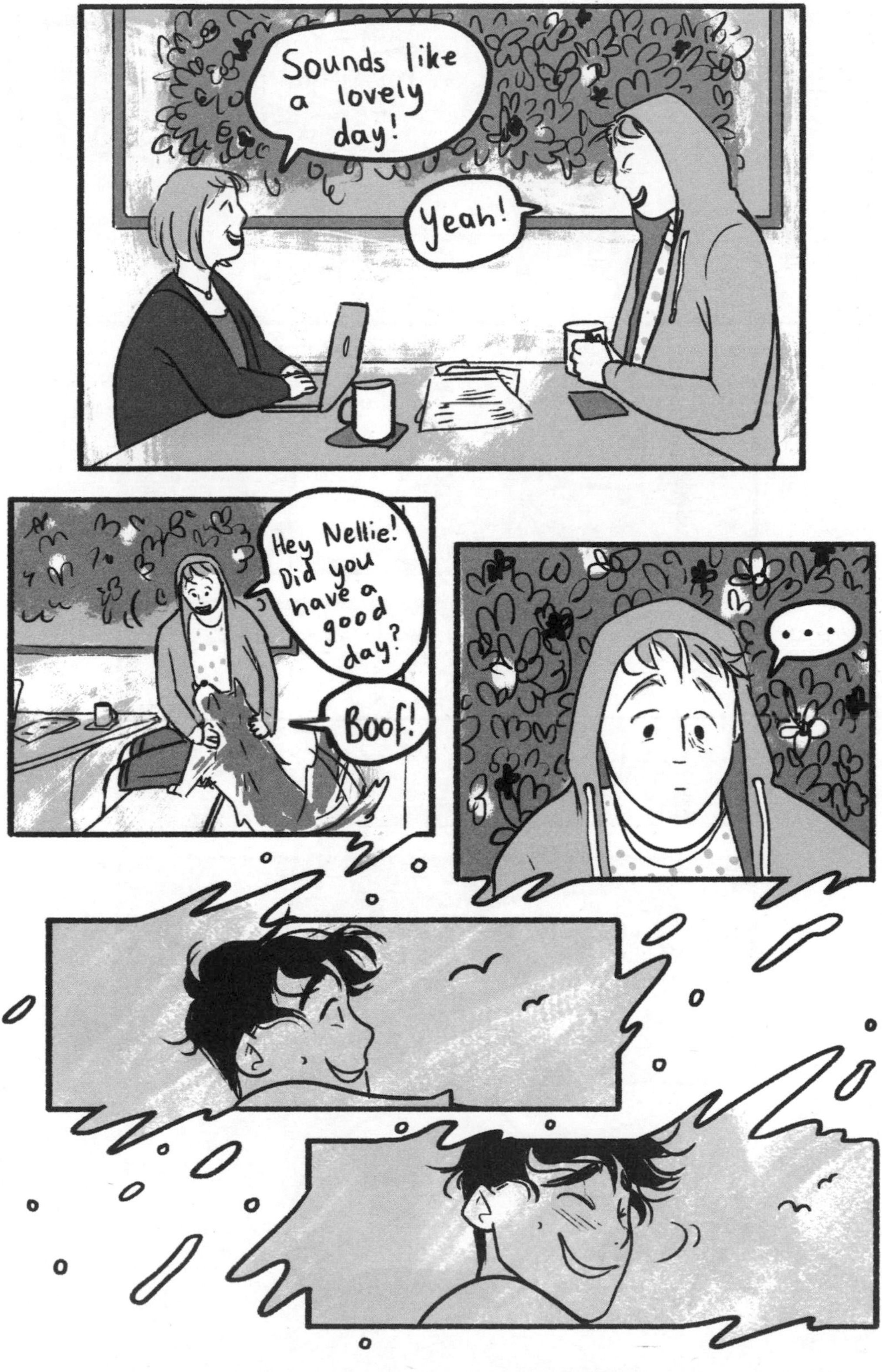
Sounds like a lovely day!
Yeah!
Hey Nellie! Did you have a good day?
Boof!
...

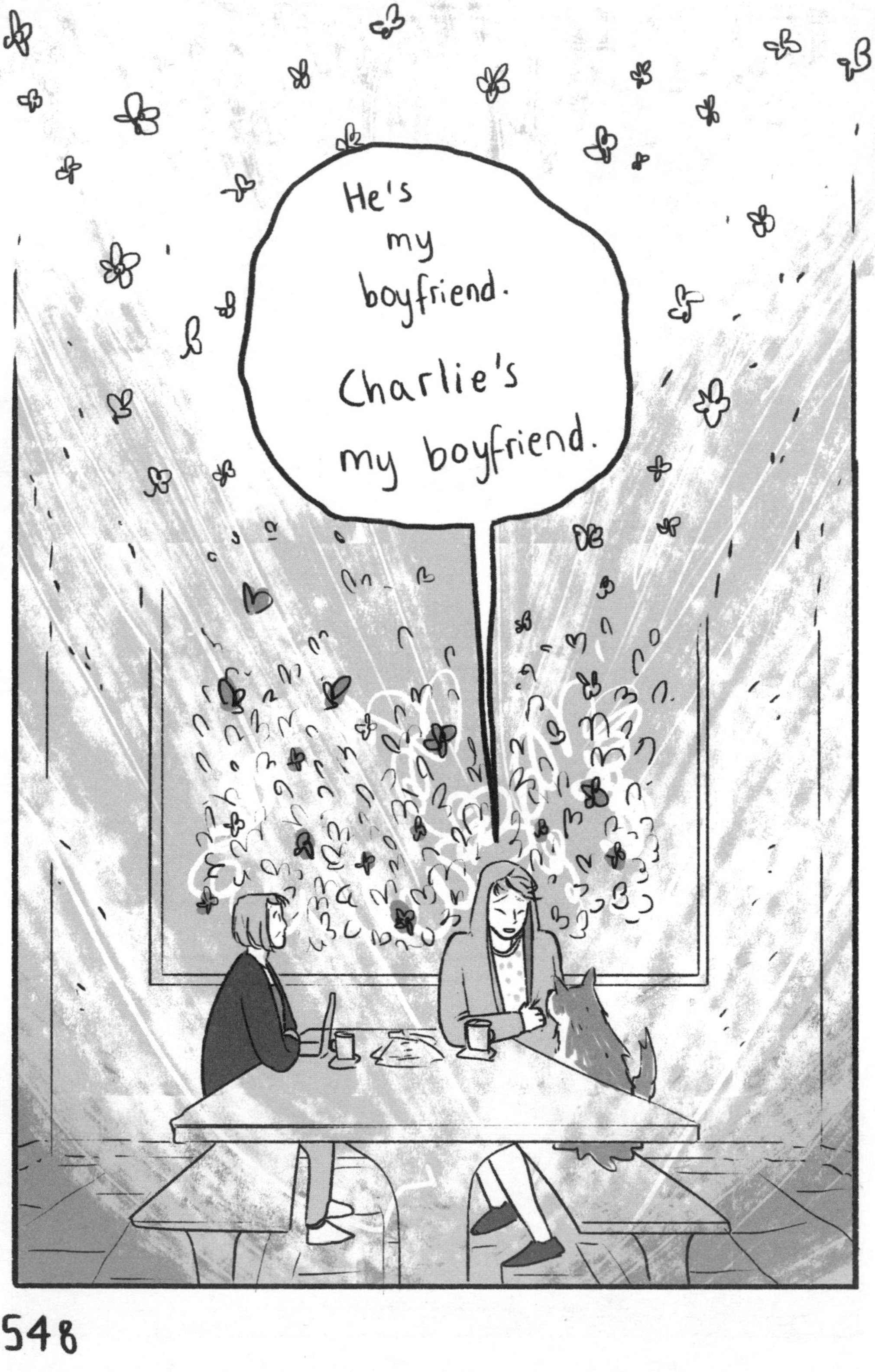
He's my boyfriend.
Charlie's my boyfriend.

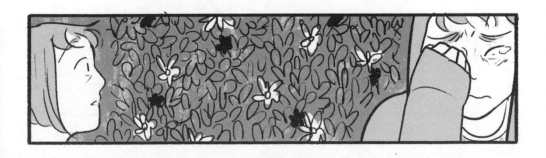

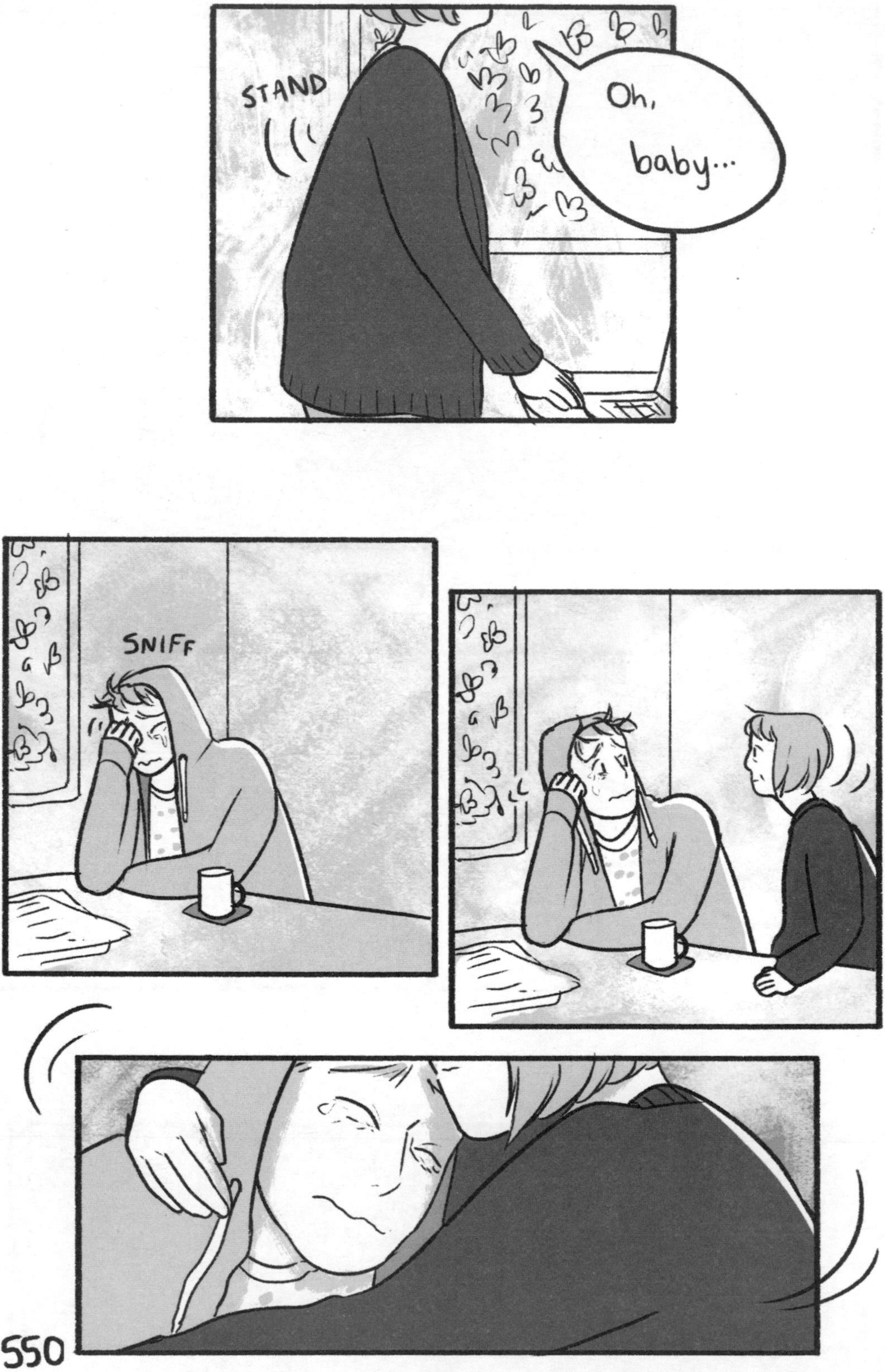
STAND
Oh, baby...
SNIFF

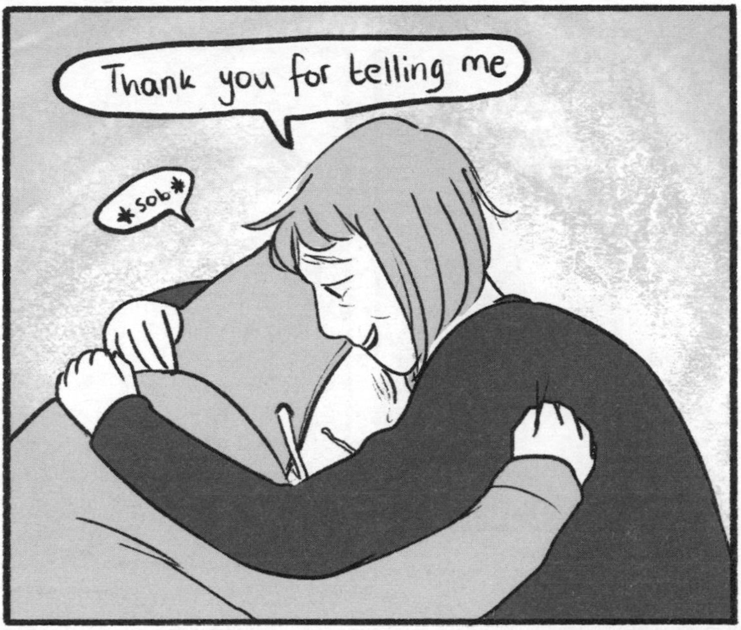
Thank you for telling me
sob

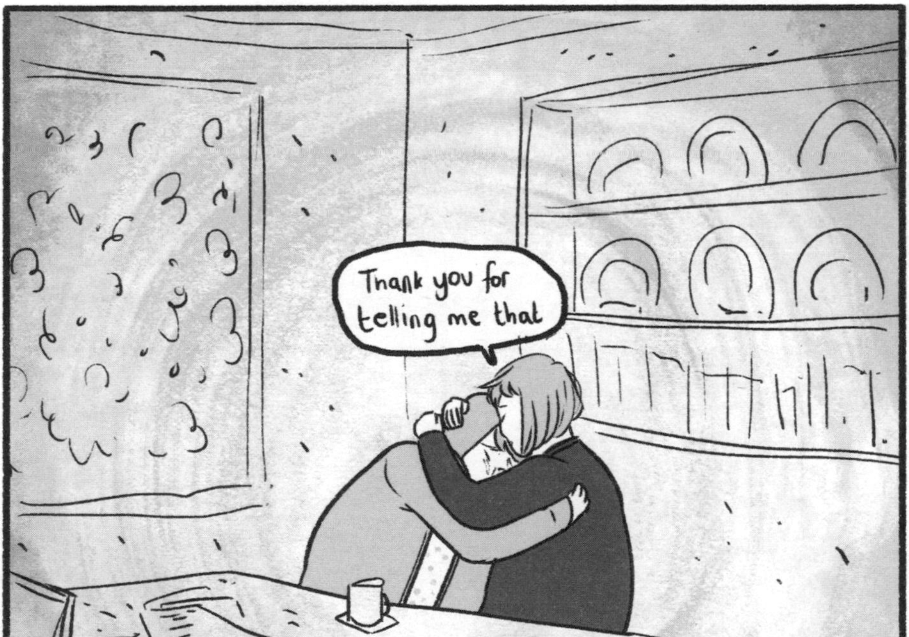
Thank you for telling me that

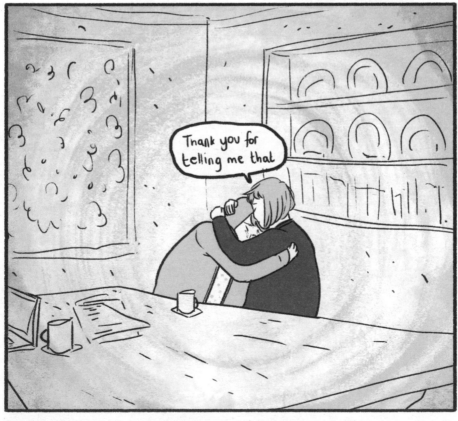

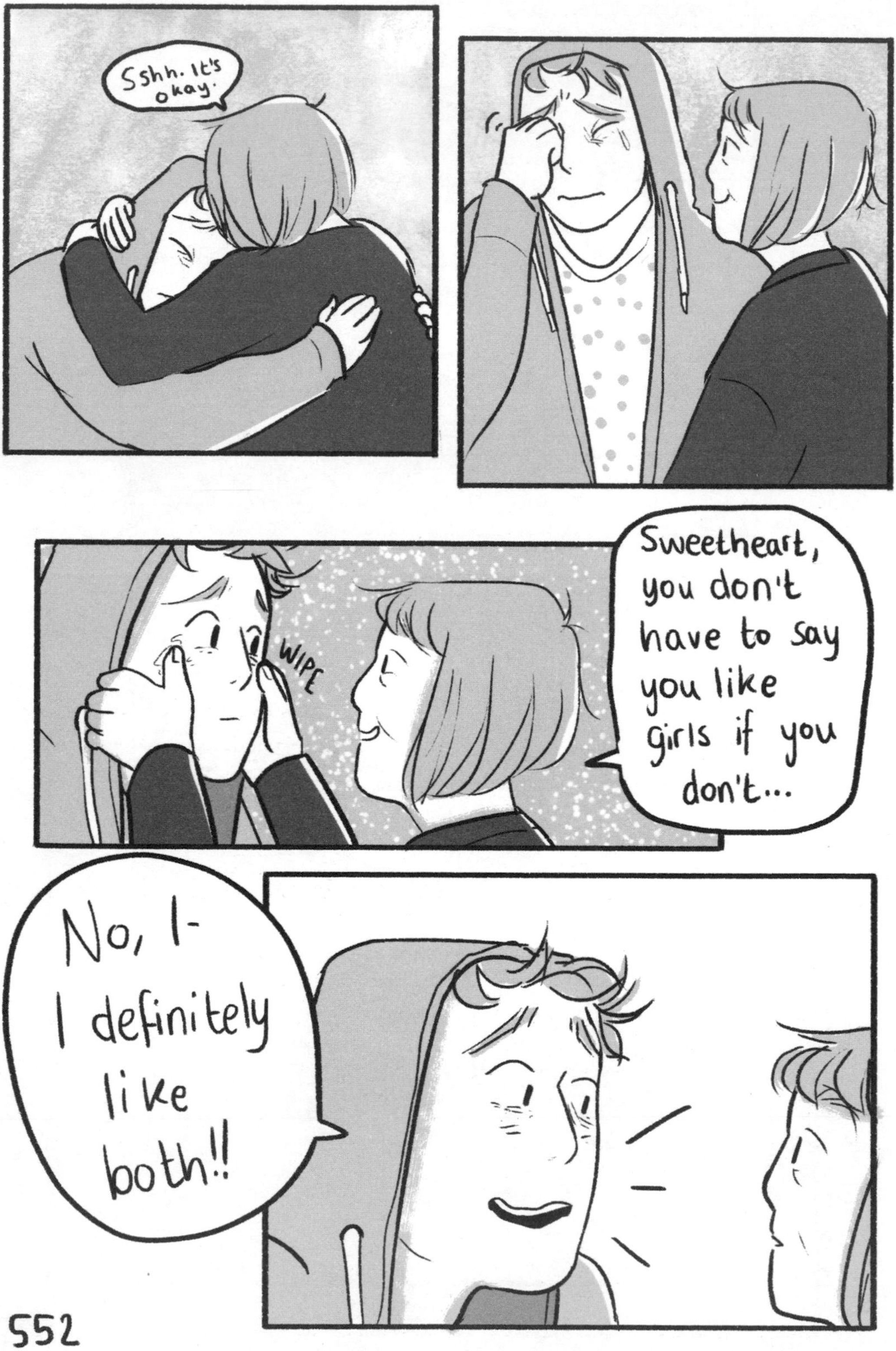
Sshh. It's okay.
Sweetheart, you don't have to say you like girls if you don't...
WIPE
No, I- I definitely like both!!

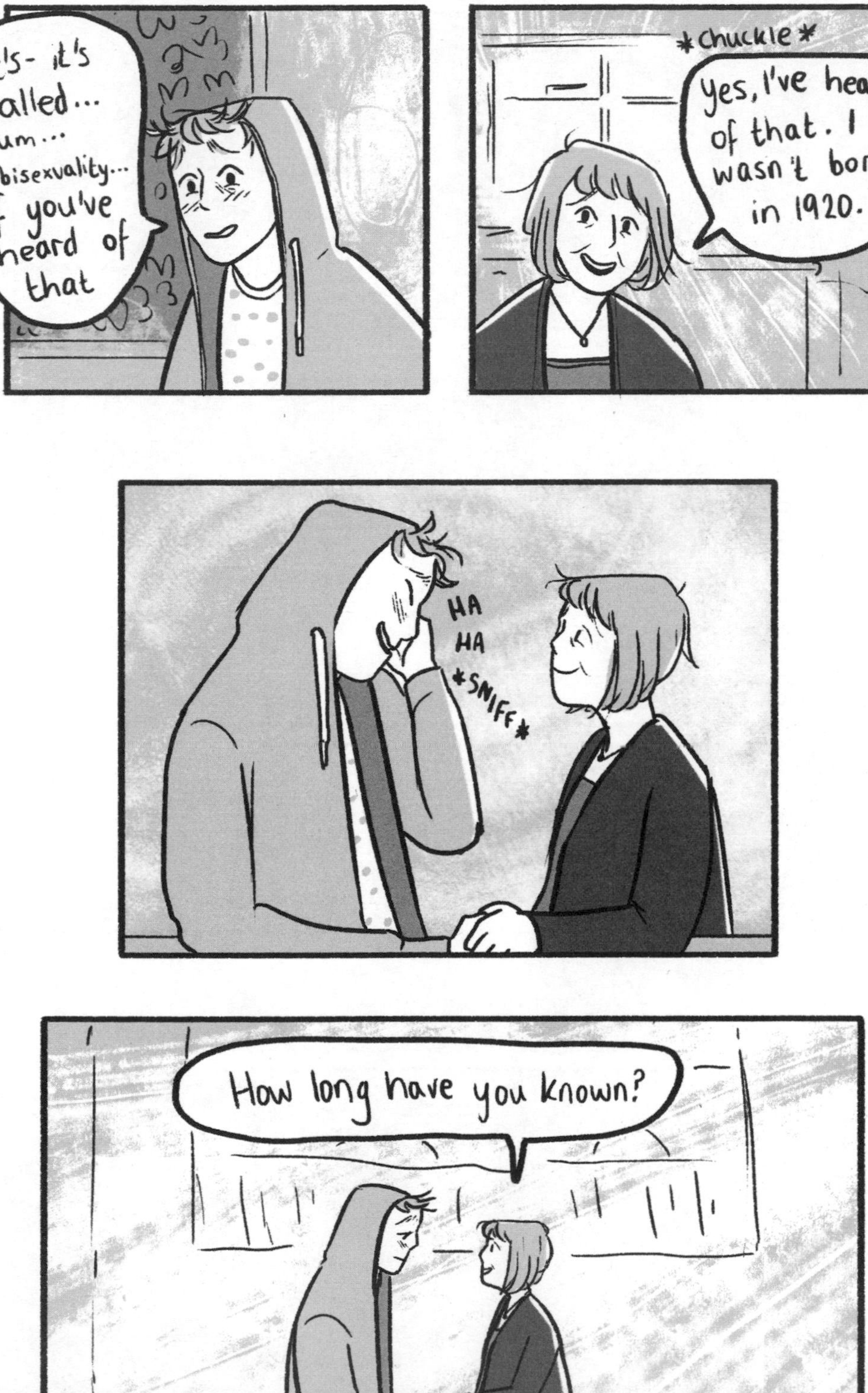
It's- it's called... um... bisexuality... if you've heard of that
chuckle
Yes, I've heard of that. I wasn't born in 1920.
HA HA *SNIFF*
How long have you known?

554

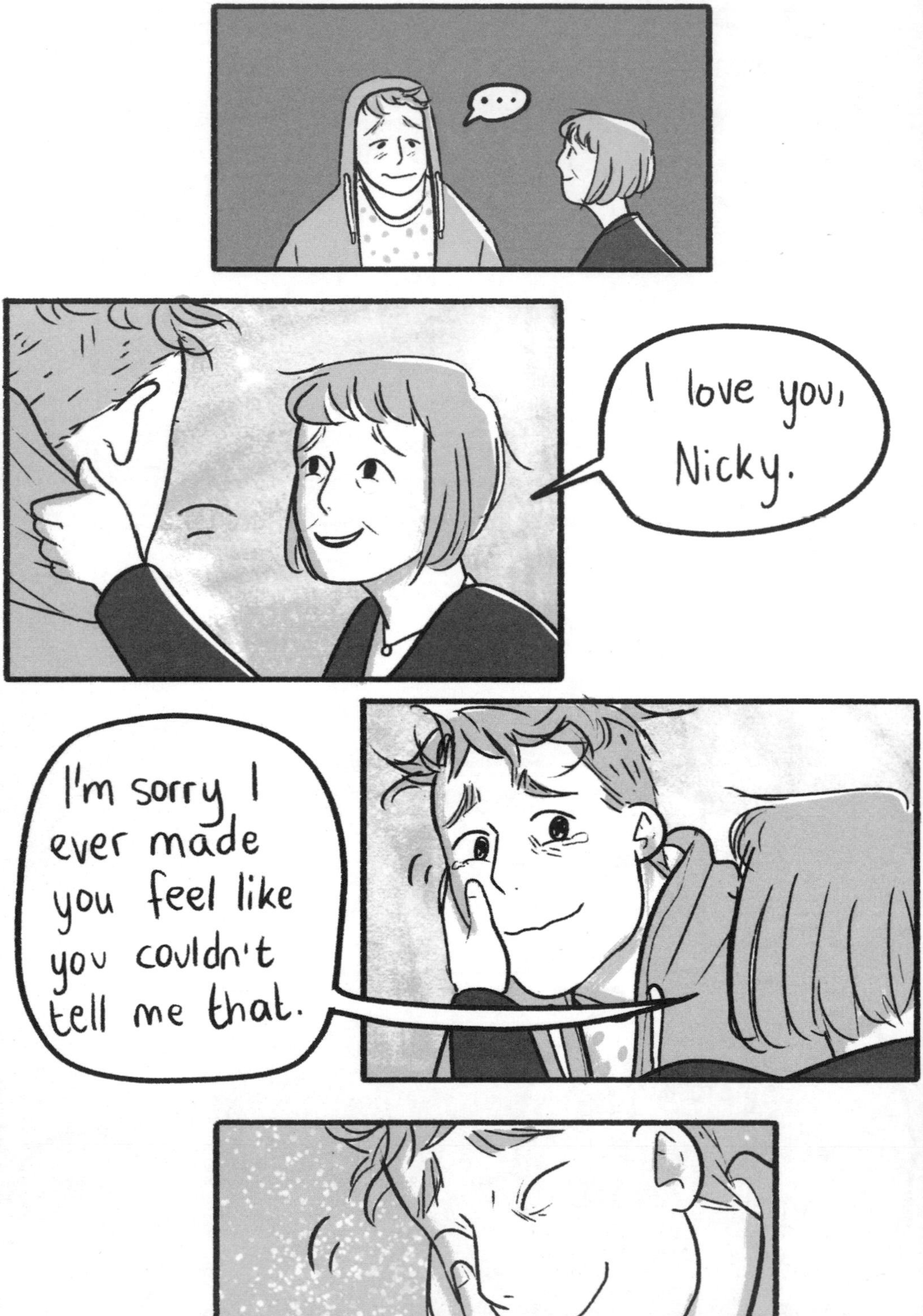
...
I love you, Nicky.
I'm sorry I ever made you feel like you couldn't tell me that.

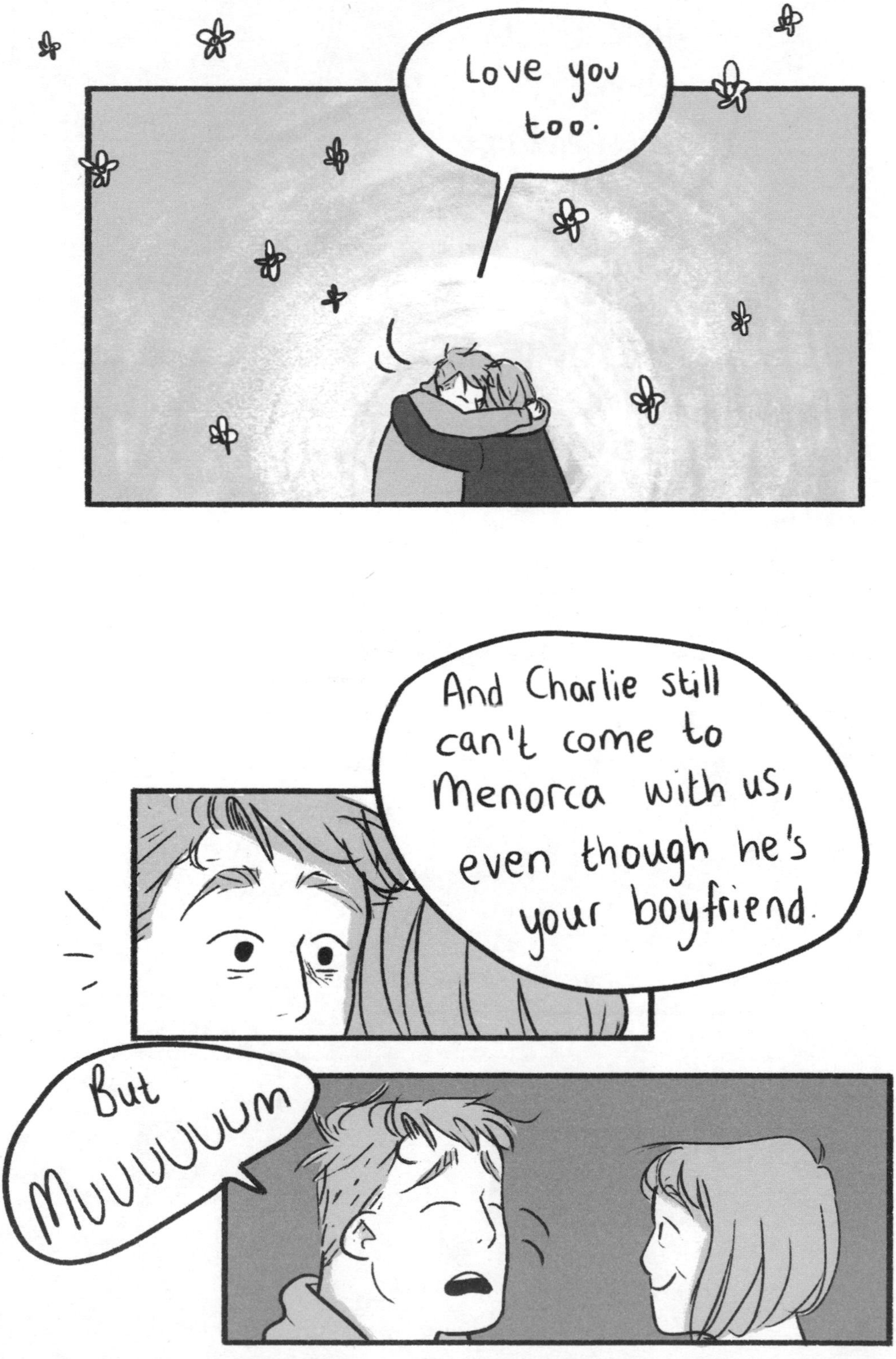
Love you too.
And Charlie still can't come to Menorca with us, even though he's your boyfriend.
But MUUUUUUM

Heartstopper will continue in

Volume 3!

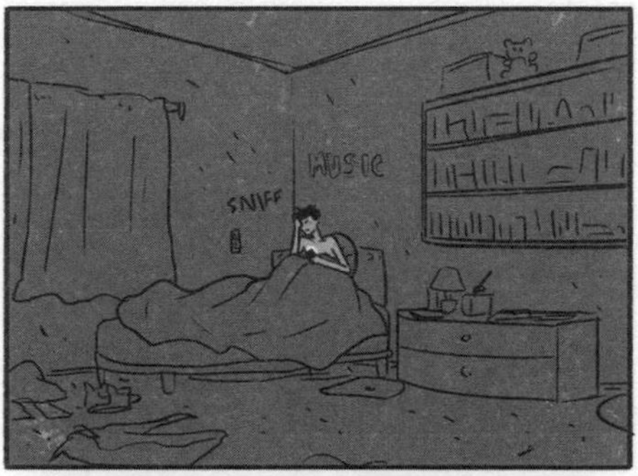
MUSIC
SNIFF

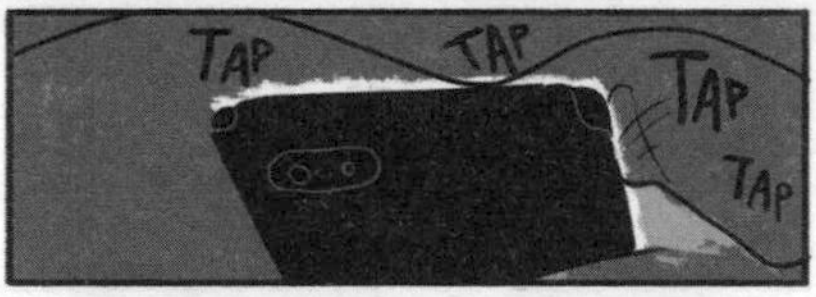
TAP
TAP
TAP
TAP

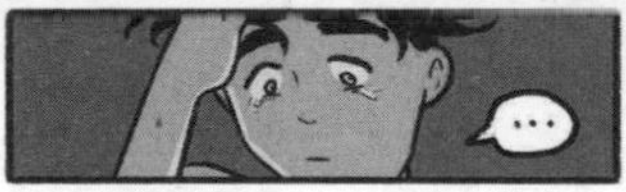
...

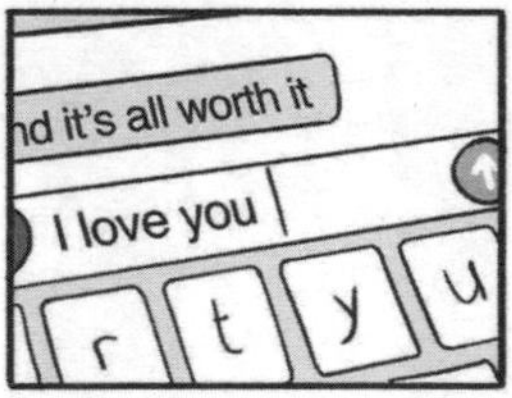
nd it's all worth it
I love you
r t y u

Read more of the comic online:

heartstoppercomic.tumblr.com
tapas.io/series/heartstopper

CASUAL CLOTHES

SMART CLOTHES

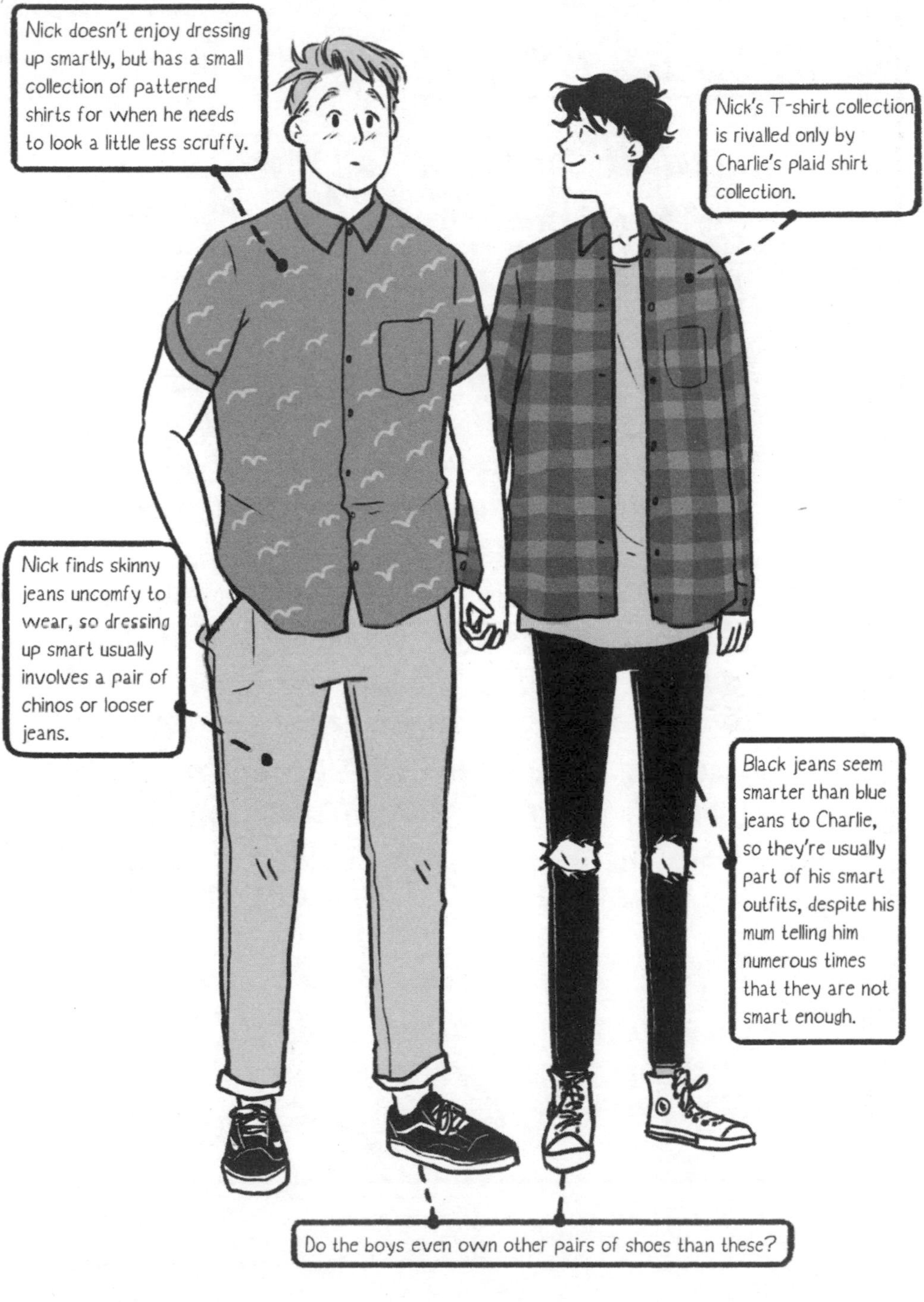
Nick doesn't enjoy dressing up smartly, but has a small collection of patterned shirts for when he needs to look a little less scruffy.
Nick's T-shirt collection is rivalled only by Charlie's plaid shirt collection.
Nick finds skinny jeans uncomfy to wear, so dressing up smart usually involves a pair of chinos or looser jeans.
Black jeans seem smarter than blue jeans to Charlie, so they're usually part of his smart outfits, despite his mum telling him numerous times that they are not smart enough.
Do the boys even own other pairs of shoes than these?

Sunday 18th April ♥

I realised something last night.
I really really really REALLY like Charlie.
So today I went to his house and we
kissed AGAIN. MULTIPLE TIMES.

I kinda meant to talk to him about last
night first but he just started saying sorry
over and over again because he thought I
rejected him - my own fault for running
off like a nervous idiot!! Add that to the
fact that he looked extremely adorable
in his pyjamas and socks and his hair
was all fluffy because he'd just woken
up...and his dimples...his eyes are so
fucking blue....uh..YEAH anyway, he kept
looking at me like he really wanted to
kiss me, so I just DID IT. And he
kissed me back!!!! HE LIKES ME BACK!!!

I think I gave him a bit of a shock, tbh.
Like, he didn't realise I liked him until
that moment. Gonna have to kiss him
MANY more times, just to get my
                              point across. ☺

18/4

So...please ignore everything from yesterday's entry. lol. I don't even know where to START. I thought last night was the end of it — I kissed him and he literally ran away.

But then this morning the doorbell rang and I answered it (in my PJs for god's sake!!!! With bed hair!!!!) and

NICK WAS THERE.

We went up to my room and I started apologising for last night but then... he kissed me. Like a proper SERIOUS kiss. God... I thought last night was out of my dreams but this was like heaven on Earth. Firstly he looked like an _angel_ — he was all damp from the rain and wearing those annoyingly hot skinny joggers and he just looked all out of breath and tall and big and ~~little~~ _GOD!!_ And when he kissed me... ~~so~~ I swear I couldn't BREATHE.

Yeah I think he might not be straight.

NAME: CHARLES "CHARLIE" SPRING
WHO ARE YOU: NICK'S BOYFRIEND
SCHOOL YEAR: YEAR 10   **AGE:** 15
BIRTHDAY: APRIL 27TH
GENDER: MALE   **SEXUALITY:** GAY
MBTI: ISTP   **HOGWARTS:** SLYTHERIN

NAME: Nicholas "Nick" Nelson
WHO ARE YOU: Charlie's boyfriend
SCHOOL YEAR: Year 11   **AGE:** 16
BIRTHDAY: September 4th
GENDER: Male   **SEXUALITY:** Bisexual
MBTI: ESFJ   **HOGWARTS:** Gryffindor

NAME: Tao Xu
WHO ARE YOU: Charlie's friend
SCHOOL YEAR: Year 10   **AGE:** 15
BIRTHDAY: September 23rd
GENDER: Male   **SEXUALITY:** Straight
MBTI: ENFP   **HOGWARTS:** Ravenclaw

NAME: Victoria "Tori" Spring
WHO ARE YOU: Charlie's sister
SCHOOL YEAR: Year 11   **AGE:** 16
BIRTHDAY: April 5th
GENDER: Female   **SEXUALITY:** ?
MBTI: INFJ   **HOGWARTS:** Hufflepuff

NAME: Tara Jones

WHO ARE YOU: Nick's friend

SCHOOL YEAR: Year 11   **AGE:** 15

BIRTHDAY: July 3rd

GENDER: Female **SEXUALITY:** Lesbian

MBTI: INFP   **HOGWARTS:** Gryffindor

NAME: HARRY GREENE

WHO ARE YOU: NICK'S CLASSMATE

SCHOOL YEAR: YEAR 11   **AGE:** 16

BIRTHDAY: APRIL 17TH

GENDER: MALE   **SEXUALITY:** STRAIGHT

MBTI: ESTJ   **HOGWARTS:** GRYFFINDOR

NAME: Elle Argent

WHO ARE YOU: Charlie's friend

NAME: Aled Last

WHO ARE YOU: Charlie's friend

NAME: Darcy Olsson

WHO ARE YOU: Tara's girlfriend

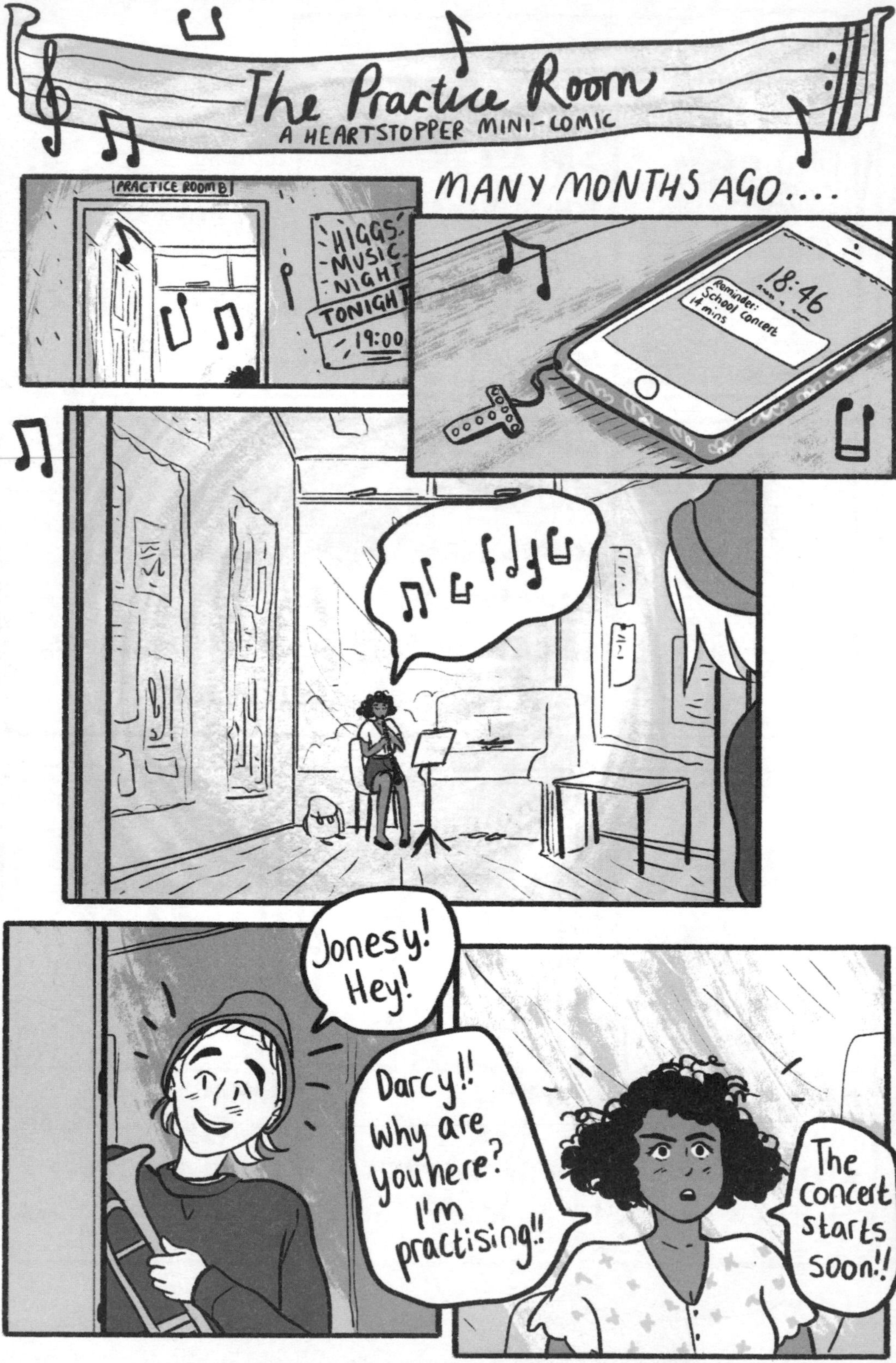
The Practice Room
A HEARTSTOPPER MINI-COMIC
MANY MONTHS AGO....
PRACTICE ROOM B
HIGGS MUSIC NIGHT
TONIGHT
19:00
18:46
Reminder: School concert
14 mins
Jonesy! Hey!
Darcy!! Why are you here? I'm practising!!
The concert starts soon!!

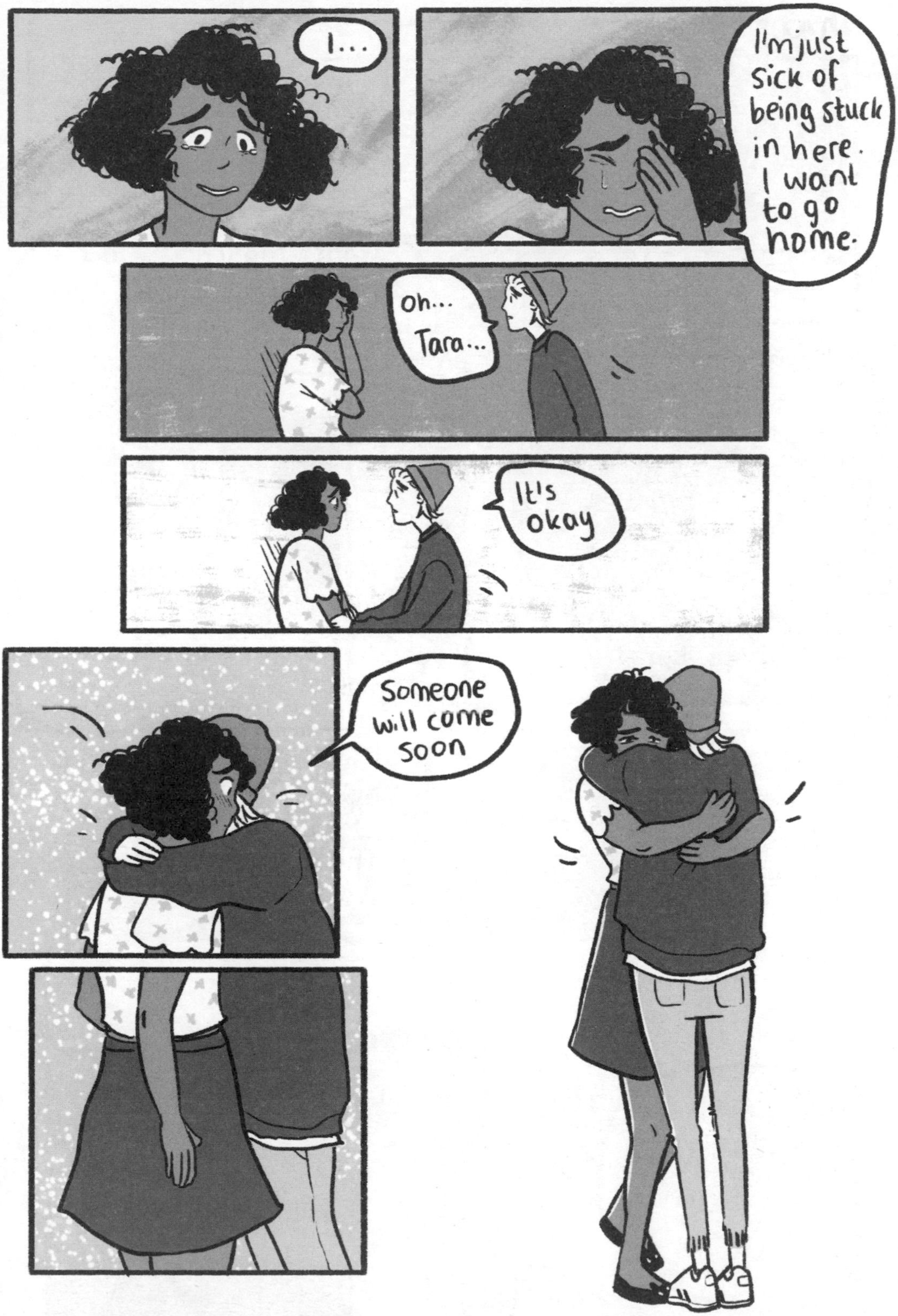
I...
I'm just sick of being stuck in here. I want to go home.
Oh... Tara...
It's okay
Someone will come soon

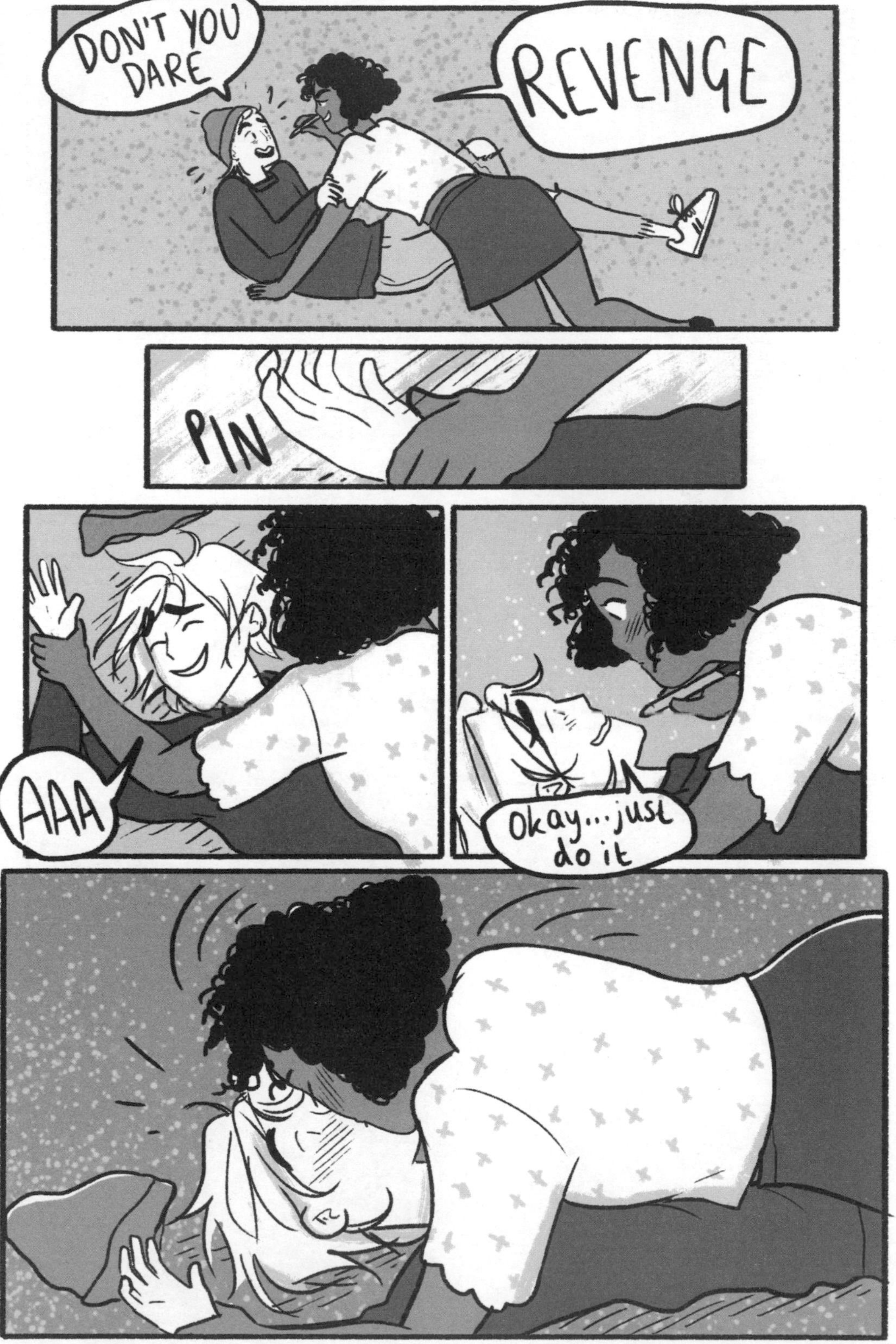
DON'T YOU DARE
REVENGE
PIN
AAA
Okay... just do it

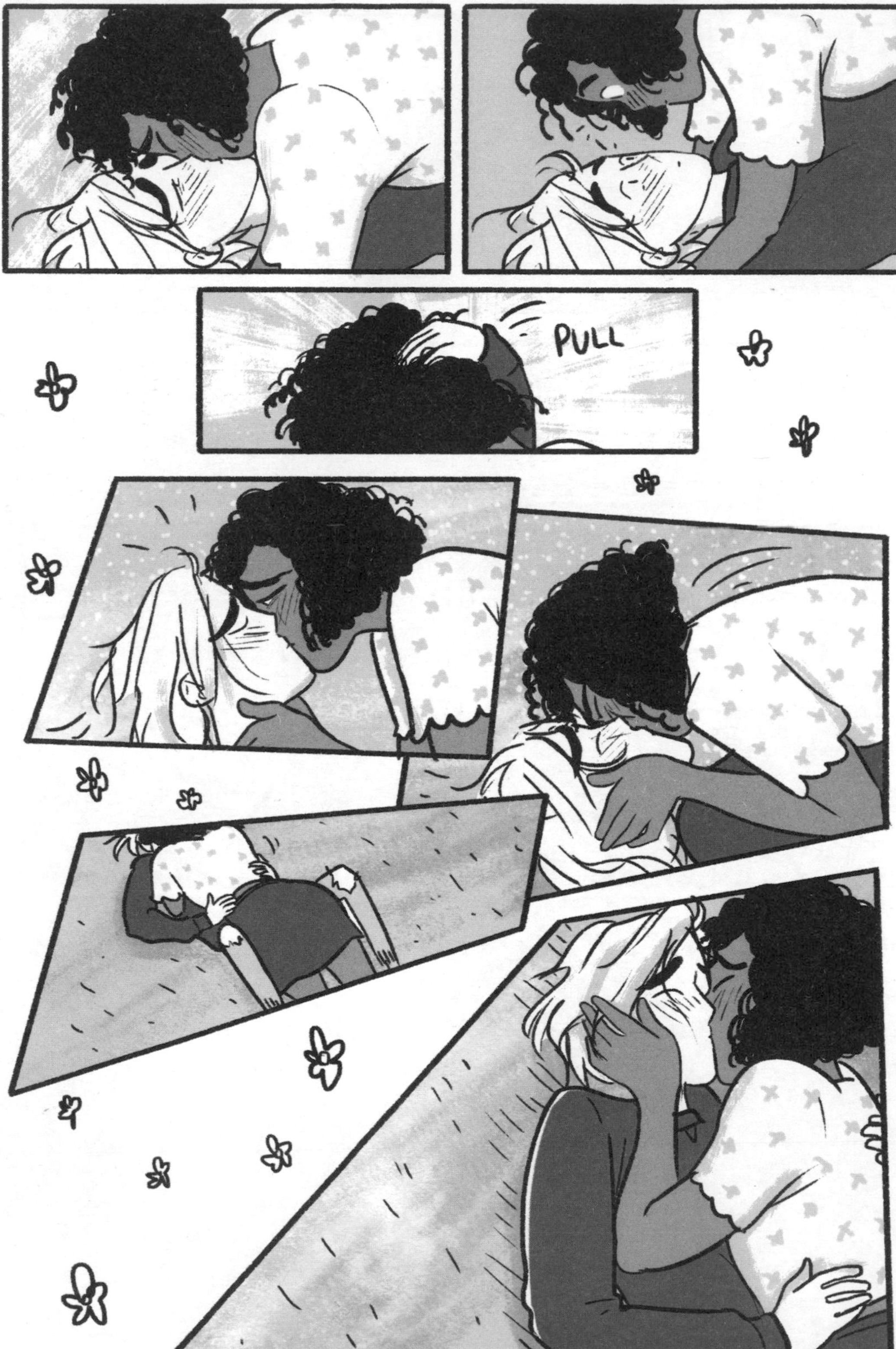
PULL

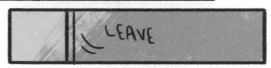

The end...?

Author's note

I'm amazed, overjoyed, and so grateful that there are now two whole volumes of Heartstopper. How on Earth have I managed to fill up that many pieces of paper? I'm so happy and excited to be telling this story and I very much hope you've been enjoying it so far.

Heartstopper focussed largely on Nick and his coming-out journey in this volume. I aimed to write the sort of story I would have loved to see when I was a teenager. Everyone deserves the time, space, and support to figure out their feelings and their identity. But even if you don't have a supportive partner, like Charlie, or a loving parent, like Nick's mum, or even just an adorable dog like Nellie to cuddle when things get tough, I promise that one day you will find someone who loves you just the way you are.

My biggest thanks is to all the online readers of Heartstopper, my Patreon patrons, and the Kickstarter supporters. Your support for the comic is the reason you're holding this book in your hands!

To Rachel Wade and the whole team at Hachette: I'm so thankful for the love you've shown my little comic and I feel so lucky to have found such a passionate group of people.

Thanks to my incredible agent, Claire Wilson, without whom I would probably be a mess.

And thank you, dear reader, for tuning in to Nick and Charlie's story once again.

I can't wait to tell you more in the next volume.

Alice

x

ALSO BY ALICE OSEMAN:

'The Catcher in the Rye for the digital age' – The Times
This is not a love story.
Solitaire
Alice Oseman

SOLITAIRE

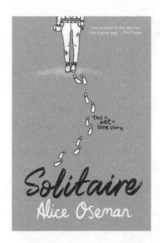

Read the novel Nick and Charlie first appeared in!

A pessimistic sixteen-year-old girl, a teenage speed skater with a penchant for solving mysteries, and a series of anonymous pranks at school by an online group who call themselves 'Solitaire'.

Alice's debut novel tells the story of Tori Spring.

Praise for debut novel Solitaire: 'The Catcher in the Rye for the digital age' – The Times
Radio Silence
Alice Oseman

RADIO SILENCE

Everyone thinks seventeen-year-old Frances is destined for a top university - including herself. But, in secret, Frances spends all her free time drawing fan art for a sci-fi podcast, 'Universe City'. And when she discovers that the creator of the podcast lives opposite her, Frances begins to question everything she knew about herself and what she wants from life.

What if everything you set yourself up to be was wrong?

Praise for debut novel Solitaire: 'The Catcher in the Rye for the digital age' – The Times
I Was Born for This
Alice Oseman

I WAS BORN FOR THIS

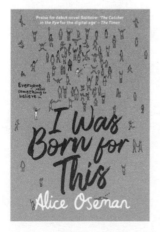

Angel, a massive fangirl of boyband The Ark, is headed to London to see The Ark live for the first time. Jimmy, frontman of The Ark, is struggling to deal with how famous he and his bandmates are becoming.

Over one week in August, Angel and Jimmy's lives begin to intertwine in mysterious ways, and when Angel and Jimmy are unexpectedly thrust together, they will discover just how strange and surprising facing up to reality can be.